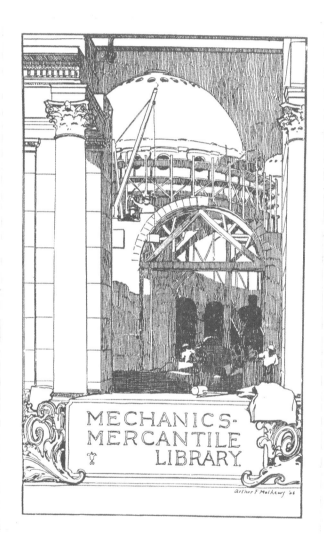

ZIG ZAG

a novel

rayo *An Imprint of* HarperCollins*Publishers*

José Carlos Somoza

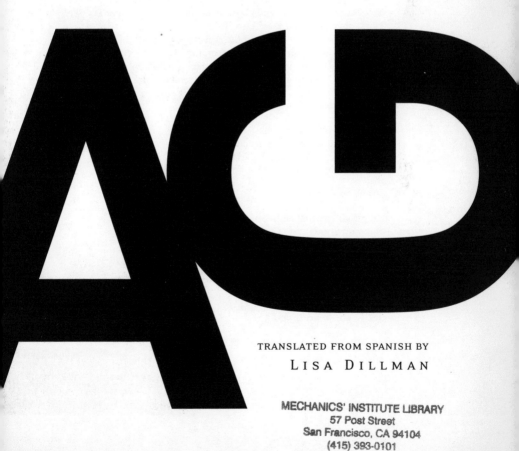

TRANSLATED FROM SPANISH BY
LISA DILLMAN

HarperCollins books may be purchased for educational,
business, or sales promotional use. For information, please
write: Special Markets Department, HarperCollins Publishers, 10 East 53rd Street, New York, NY 10022.

FIRST EDITION

Originally published in Spanish as *ZigZag* by Plaza Janés in
Spain in 2006.

Book design by Shubhani Sarkar

Library of Congress Cataloging-in-Publication Data has been
applied for.

ISBN: 978-0-06-119371-2

07 08 09 10 11 ❖/RRD 10 9 8 7 6 5 4 3 2 1

For my sons, JOSÉ and LÁZARO

The sea I sail has never yet been passed.

DANTE, *PARADISO*, CANTO II

PROLOGUE

The Outskirts of Olleros
Andalusia, Spain
July 12, 1992
10:50 P.M.

IT was neither foggy nor dark. The bright sun shone high in the sky. The world was green and filled with the scent of pines and flowers, with the sounds of cicadas and bees, and the gentle gurgling of a nearby stream. Nothing could disturb the idyllic scene, so bright, so vibrant, he thought. Though without knowing why, the *thought* itself disturbed him. Maybe he knew that any connection to perfection, thought or otherwise, could easily be destroyed; that there were thousands of ways a twist of fate (or something more sinister) could crush even the highest of spirits. It's not that he was a pessimist, but he'd reached a certain age, and the experiences he'd accumulated made him suspicious of anything that seemed so much like paradise.

He walked along the stream. From time to time, he stopped and looked around, as if he were soaking up his surroundings, deliberating even, only to then keep going. Finally, he reached a spot he liked. A few trees provided just enough shade, and there seemed to be less dust in the air. The air itself was cool. A little farther on, the path hugged the rocky banks of the river and came to an end at a stony hill. Here, he thought, he could count on solitude. It was almost as if he'd found a sort of refuge, or a shelter. He planned to sit on a large, flat rock and cast his line, taking pleasure in the wait, the quiet, the sparkling water. Nothing could be more relaxing. He crouched down, dropping his fishing rod and small tub of bait onto the ground.

He heard the voices when he stood back up.

At first he was startled, given the calm silence that preceded them. They were coming from some place on the hill he couldn't quite see, and judging by their high pitch the voices sounded like they belonged to children. They were shouting, probably playing some game. He assumed they lived in one of the nearby mountain houses. Although the presence of other people irritated him slightly, he tried to convince himself that children playing in the distance provided the ideal counterpoint to a perfect day. He took off his baseball cap and wiped the sweat from his face, smiling. Then, he froze.

It was no game. Something was wrong.

One of the kids was screaming, very strangely. The words were unintelligible, all blurred together in the still air. It was clear that whoever was shouting was not happy. A child screaming like that was in serious trouble.

Suddenly everything—even the birds and insects—went quiet, as if the world had stopped to take a breath, a pause at the start of some extraordinary event.

A moment later there came a very different kind of scream. A shriek that pierced the clean air, and seemed to shatter the china-blue sky.

As he stood beside the stream, he realized that this summer Sunday morning in 1992 was not going to turn out how he'd imagined. Even if only slightly, he knew that everything had forever changed.

IT was almost unreal, the way that scream kept reverberating for the long minute after it had stopped. Like embers of sound in Mrs. Portinari's ears, the scream had shattered her domestic silence. After a very brief pause, she heard it again, and only then was Mrs. Portinari able to react. She took off her reading glasses, which were attached to a tiny pearl chain, and let them hang from her chest.

"What on earth?" she said aloud. Despite the fact that given the time (9:05 according to the digital clock on the bookshelf, which had been a gift from the bank where she deposited her pension checks), the Ecuadorian cleaning girl had not yet arrived and, thus, she was alone. Ever since her husband died, four years ago, she talked to herself all the time. "Good God in Heaven, what the …?"

There it came again, louder.

Mrs. Portinari was reminded of a fire in her old apartment building in downtown Milan, fifteen years ago. She and her husband had almost lost their lives in it. After he died, she decided to move to an apartment on Via Giardelli, close to the university. It was smaller, but quieter, more fitting for a woman her age. She liked living there. Nothing bad ever happened in that little neighborhood.

Until that moment.

She ran to the door as fast as her swollen, arthritic joints would let her.

"Blessed Virgin!" she whispered, clutching the object in her hands. Later, she realized it was the pen she'd used to write out her weekly grocery list. But for the moment, she held onto it as if it were a crucifix.

Several residents of the building were out on the landing. All were looking up.

"It's coming from Marini's place," yelled Mr. Genovese, the man from across the hall. He was a young graphic designer whom Mrs. Portinari would have been quite fond of were it not for his very flamboyant manner.

"The professor!" she heard someone else shout.

The professor, she thought. What could have happened to that poor man? And who was shrieking so horrifically? It was definitely a woman. But, whoever it was, Mrs. Portinari was sure she'd never heard cries like that before. Not even during that terrible fire.

Then came the pounding footsteps of someone rushing down the stairs. Fast. Neither she nor Mr. Genovese immediately reacted. Dumbfounded, they stood staring at the landing. United in their fear and pallor, they suddenly seemed the same age. With her heart in her mouth, Mrs. Portinari steeled herself for whatever she might find: criminal or victim. Instinctively, she knew that nothing could be worse than standing there listening to that tortured soul howl. Hearing those echoes spiral through the air without being able to see who was making them shook her deeply.

But when she finally saw the face of the person screaming, she realized, with absolute certainty, that she'd been very wrong.

There indeed was something far worse than the sound of those horrible screams.

ONE

The Phone Call

Dangers are no more light, if they once seem light ...

SIR FRANCIS BACON

01

Madrid
March 11, 2015
11:12 A.M.

EXACTLY six minutes and thirteen seconds before her life took a drastic, horrifying turn, Elisa Robledo was working at something quite ordinary. She was teaching an elective on modern theories of physics to fifteen second-year engineering students. She in no way intuited what was about to happen. Unlike many students, and even a fair few professors for whom the setting proved formidable, Elisa felt more at ease in the classroom than she did in her own home. That was the way it had been at her old-fashioned high school and in the bare-walled classrooms of her university, too. Now she worked in the bright, modern facilities of the School of Engineering at Madrid's Alighieri University, a luxurious private institution whose classrooms boasted views from the enormous windows overlooking campus, perfect sound from their superb acoustics, and the rich aroma of fine wood. Elisa could have lived there. She unconsciously assumed that nothing bad could happen to her in a place like that.

She couldn't have been more wrong, and in just over six minutes she would realize that.

Elisa was a brilliant professor who had a certain aura about her. At universities, certain professors (and the occasional student) are the stuff of legend: the enigmatic Elisa Robledo had given rise to a mystery everyone wanted to solve.

In a way, the birth of *the Elisa Mystery* was inevitable. She was young and a loner; she had long, wavy black hair and the face and body of a model. She was sharp and analytical, and she had a prodigious talent for abstraction and calculation—characteristics that were key in the cold world of theoretical physics, where the principles of science rule all. Theoretical physicists were not only respected, they were revered—from Einstein to Stephen Hawking. They fit people's image of what physics was all about. Though most people found the field abstruse (if not wholly unintelligible), its champions always made a big splash and were seen as stereotypical, socially awkward geniuses.

Elisa Robledo was not cold at all. She was passionate about her teaching, and she captivated her students. What's more, she was an excellent academic, and a kind, supportive colleague, always willing to help out in a crisis. On the surface, there was nothing strange about her.

And that was what was so strange.

People thought she was too perfect. Too intelligent and too worthy to be working in a mediocre physics department at a business-oriented university like Alighieri, where no one truly cared about physics. Her colleagues were sure that she could have had her pick of careers: a post at the Spanish National Research Council, a tenured professorship at a public university, or some important role at a prestigious center abroad. Elisa was wasted at Alighieri. Then, too, no theory (and physicists love theories) adequately explained why, at thirty-two, almost thirty-three (her birthday was in April, just a month away), Elisa was unattached, had no close friends, and yet seemed perfectly happy. She appeared to have all she wanted in life. No one knew of any boyfriends (or girlfriends), and her friendships were limited to colleagues with whom she rarely if ever spent free time. She wasn't conceited or even arrogant despite her obvious good looks. And although she accentuated her attractiveness by wearing a whole range of perfectly tailored designer clothes that often made her look downright provocative, she never seemed to be trying to hard to attract the attention of men (who often turned to gawk when she passed) with the clothes she wore. Elisa spoke only about her profession, was courteous, and always smiled. The Elisa Mystery was unfathomable.

Occasionally, she seemed unsettled. It was nothing concrete: maybe a look, or a momentary dullness in her brown eyes, or just a feeling she gave people after a quick conversation. As though she was hiding something. Those who thought they knew her—Noriega, the department chair, among others—thought it was probably best that she never reveal her secret. For whatever reason, some people, regardless of how insignificant their role in others' lives, or how few close moments they've shared, are unforgettable. Elisa Robledo was one of them, and people wanted it to stay that way.

Professor Víctor Lopera, one of Elisa's only real friends, was a notable exception. Sometimes he was overwhelmed by an urgent need to unravel her mystery. Víctor had experienced the temptation on several occasions, the most recent being last year, in April 2014, when the department decided to throw Elisa a surprise birthday party.

Noriega's secretary, Teresa, had come up with the idea, and everyone had jumped at it, including some students. They spent a month enthusiastically preparing, as if they thought it would be the ideal way to infiltrate Elisa's magic circle and touch her ephemeral surface. They bought a cake, balloons, a giant teddy bear, and candles shaped into the number thirty-two; the chair even went in for a few bottles of champagne. They shut themselves into the seminar room, decorated it quickly, drew the curtains, and turned off the lights. When Elisa arrived that morning, one of the custodians told her they had called an "urgent faculty meeting." Everyone waited in the dark. The door opened and Elisa's hesitant silhouette was framed by the doorway, outlining her cropped cardigan, tight pants, and long hair. Suddenly, laughter and applause erupted, the lights were turned on, and Rafa, one of her best students, was there recording the young professor's disconcerted expression on one of those state-of-the-art video cameras that was no bigger than a pair of eyes.

The party was brief and made no inroads at all into the Elisa Mystery. Noriega said a few emotional words, people sang the same old songs, and Teresa stood before the camera, waving a funny banner with caricatures of Isaac Newton, Albert Einstein, Stephen Hawking, and Elisa Robledo sharing a cake (Teresa's brother, a graphic designer, had made it). Everyone was jovial and affectionate and tried to show Elisa that they gladly accepted her without asking anything in return, except that she continue to enliven them with her mystery, to which they'd grown accustomed. As always, Elisa was perfect, her face an ideal picture of surprise and happiness. She even seemed a little moved: her eyes looked like they'd welled up. Judging from the video, and seeing her perfect body outlined by her sweater and pants, she could have passed for a student, or maybe the presenter at some spectacular event or (as Rafa later told his friends on campus) a porn star winning her first award. "Einstein and Marilyn Monroe, all rolled into one," he said.

But an attentive observer would have noted something that didn't quite fit. When the lights had flipped back on, Elisa's face had changed.

No one really noticed because, after all, no one spends their time scrutinizing other people's birthday party videos. But Víctor Lopera had caught the fleeting yet significant change. When the room lit up, Elisa's features reflected not the emotion of someone caught off guard but something deeper, more disturbed. Of course, it had lasted only tenths of a second. As instantly as she has flashed that pure reaction, she had then smiled and gone back to being perfect. The Mystery. But for that brief moment her beauty had been transformed into something else. Aside from Víctor, everyone watching the video laughed at her "surprise." But Lopera saw something else. What was it? He wasn't sure. Maybe just displeasure at something she really didn't think was funny, or intense shyness, or something else.

Maybe fear.

Víctor, intelligent and observant, was the only one who wondered what it was that Elisa might have thought she was going to find in that dark room. What kind of "surprise" had distant, beautiful Professor Robledo thought awaited her in that darkened seminar room, before the lights went on and she heard the laughter and the clapping? He'd have given anything to find out.

What was going to happen to Elisa in a serene classroom that morning, in just over six minutes, would have given Víctor Lopera some clues, but, unfortunately for him, he wasn't there.

ELISA always tried to give examples that would appeal to the insipid minds of the rich kids who sat in her classes. None of them would ever major in physics, and she knew it. They just wanted to breeze through abstract concepts superficially, pass their classes, and get out of there as quickly as possible, degree in hand, so they could stroll into privileged, hotshot positions in business or technology. They couldn't care less about the whys and wherefores that had comprised the basic enigmas of science; what they wanted were the solutions, the effects, the concrete answers they had to come up with in order to get their grades. Elisa tried to change all that, teaching them to think about causes and the unknowns.

At that moment, she was trying to get her students to visualize the extraordinary phenomenon of our reality having more than three dimensions, possibly many more than the easily observable length-width-height trio. Einstein's theory of relativity had proven that time was the fourth dimension, and the complex string theory that was challenging contemporary physics hypothesized that there were at least nine further spatial dimensions—something almost inconceivable to the human mind.

Sometimes, Elisa wondered whether people even had a clue

about all the varied and important discoveries that had been made in physics. Here we were well into the twenty-first century—the Age of Aquarius—and the general public still couldn't get enough of so-called supernatural and paranormal phenomena, as if we'd already solved all the mysteries of the natural and the normal. It didn't take flying saucers or ghosts to see that we live in a very disturbing world. As far as Elisa was concerned, there was far too much to take in right here in this world, even for the wildest imagination. And she planned to prove it, at least to the fifteen students sitting in her small class.

She started with a fun, easy example. First, she put a transparency up on the overhead projector. On it, she'd drawn a human stick figure and a square.

"This man," she explained, pointing to him, "lives in a world with only two dimensions: length and width. He's worked hard all his life and earned a fortune: one euro." She heard a few snickers and knew she'd grabbed the attention of several sets of glazed-over eyes. "So that no one can steal this euro from him, he decides to keep it in the safest bank in his world: a box. This box has only one opening, on one side, which our man uses to deposit his fortune, and which no one else can open."

Elisa quickly extracted the euro coin she'd had with her from her jeans, and placed it in the square on the transparency.

"Our friend feels safe with his euro in that bank. Nobody, absolutely no one, can penetrate any of the box's sides. Or, at least, no one from his world. But I can steal it easily, from the third dimension—height—which is invisible to the inhabitants of his flat universe." As she spoke, Elisa took the coin back and replaced the transparency with another one that had on it a different drawing. "You can imagine how the poor man feels when

he opens his box and finds that all his savings have disappeared. How could anyone have robbed him if the box was never opened?"

"Guess he's pretty pissed off," whispered a boy in the front row with brightly colored glasses and a crew cut. Laughter. Elisa didn't mind that they were laughing, nor did she care about their apparent lack of concentration. She knew it had been a simplistic example, rudimentary for top-notch students, but that was exactly what she wanted. She wanted to open the door as wide as possible on their way in, because she knew only a few would be able to find their way out. So she stifled their laughter, speaking now in a different, much quieter, tone.

"Just as that man can't even conceive of how he was robbed, *we* can't conceive of more than three dimensions around us. Now then," she said, stressing each word carefully, "this example proves that dimensions can affect us, even lead to events we wouldn't hesitate to call 'supernatural' ..." Suddenly, they were all murmuring, talking over her. She knew they would. *They think I'm exaggerating, veering into science fiction. They're physics students, they know I'm talking about reality, but they can't accept it.* From the little forest of hands that had shot up, she chose one. "Yes, Yolanda?"

Blonde-haired and wide-eyed, she was one of the few women in a class full of young men. Elisa was pleased that she'd been the first to take things seriously.

"Your example is unfair," Yolanda said. "The coin is three-dimensional. Even though it's not very tall, it does possess height. If it had been drawn inside the box, like it should have been, you couldn't have stolen it."

Intense whispering. Elisa, who was ready for this, feigned surprise so as not to dishearten her clever student.

"Good point, Yolanda. And you're right. Good science is based on that kind of observation: apparently simple, yet vital. However, even if the coin had been drawn onto the paper, like the man and the square, I still could have erased it." Laughter erupted, keeping her from continuing for a few seconds. Five, to be exact.

Though she didn't know it, she had twelve seconds left before her entire life would blow up around her.

The big clock on the wall at the back of the class showed the time. Elisa glanced at it quickly, never suspecting that the long hand sweeping across the clock's face had begun a countdown to what would destroy her present and her future.

Forever. Irreversibly.

"What I want you to see," she continued, patting the air to indicate that they should simmer down, oblivious to everything but the wavelength that she and her students were on, "is that different dimensions can affect each other, in one way or another. Let me give you another example."

When she was planning class, she'd initially intended to draw this example on the board. But now she saw the newspaper folded on the lectern. On days when she had class, she always bought the paper at the kiosk on the way into campus and then read it in the cafeteria afterward. Now it occurred to her that her students might understand this next example better (it was far more complicated) if she used an object instead.

She opened the paper to a page at random and spread it out.

"Imagine that this piece of newspaper is a spatial plane ..."

She glanced down to extract the page without messing up the rest of the paper.

And saw it.

Horror is quick. We can be horrified before we're even aware of it. Before we realize why, our hands tremble, the blood drains from our face, something falls to the pit of our stomach. Elisa had glanced momentarily at one of the headlines on the upper-right-hand side of the page, and, even before understanding what it meant, she felt a rush of adrenaline and froze.

She took in the basic information in a matter of seconds. But those seconds were eternal. While they lasted, she was barely aware of her students' existence, of the fact that they'd all fallen silent and were waiting for her to continue. That they'd begun to realize that something was not right, to nudge one another, clear their throats, turn around to glance questioningly at each other.

A new Elisa looked up and confronted the silent expectancy she'd given rise to.

"Uh, so ... Imagine that I fold the plane here," she continued unfalteringly, in the monotonous voice of an automaton.

Without knowing how, she carried on. She wrote equations on the board, solved them effortlessly, asked questions, and gave additional examples. It was a heroic, superhuman feat that no one seemed to pick up on. Or did they? She wondered if Yolanda, ever attentive in the front row, had noted the panic coursing through her.

"Let's leave it here for today," she said, when there were five minutes of class left. "I warn you that from here on out, everything is going to get much more complicated," she added, trembling at the irony of her words.

HER office was at the end of the hall. Luckily, her colleagues were all busy and she didn't bump into anyone on her way back. She walked in, closed the door, locked it, sat down at her desk, opened the newspaper, and almost tore the page, inspecting it as carefully as someone poring over a list of dead, praying not to find a loved one's name but knowing, inevitably, that it will jump out as if in another color.

The news offered almost no details, just the probable date of the incident: it hadn't been discovered until the following day, but it seemed likely it had taken place Monday, some time during the night of March 9, 2015.

The day before yesterday.

She couldn't breathe.

Just then, a shadow filled the frosted glass of her office door.

Though she knew it had to be something run of the mill (a cleaner, a colleague), Elisa stood up, unable to utter a word.

You're next.

The shadow stood motionless before her door. She heard the sound of the lock.

Elisa was not a coward; she was tremendously brave, in fact. But at that moment a child's laughter could have sent shivers down her spine. She felt something cold on her back and realized that she'd unconsciously backed so far up that she was pressed against the wall. Long, damp hair half-covered her sweaty face.

Finally, the door opened.

Sometimes terror is almost like death, a dry run that momentarily strips away your voice, your sight, your vital functions, and for as long as it lasts, you can't breathe, can't think, your heart stops beating. At that horrific moment, that was what happened to Elisa. When the man saw her, he started. It was Pedro, one of the custodians. He held a ring of keys and a stack of mail.

"Oh. Sorry. I didn't realize you were in here. I just thought … since you never come straight back after class … OK if I come in? I was just going to leave you your mail."

Elisa murmured something. Pedro smiled, walked in, and dropped the stack of envelopes on her desk. Then he left, though not without first glancing down at the paper and at Elisa's face. She didn't care. Actually, his sudden interruption had helped her shake off the feeling of absolute terror that had overcome her.

She suddenly realized exactly what she had to do.

She folded up the paper, stuck it in her bag, flicked through the mail (internal memos and correspondence from other universities, nothing she had to deal with immediately), and walked out.

Above all, she had to save her life.

02

VÍCTOR Lopera's office was right across from hers. Víctor, who had just arrived, was taking moderate pleasure in photocopying the rebus from the morning paper. He was a huge fan of rebuses, riddles, word games, and puzzles, and had whole albums full of things he'd taken from the Internet, newspapers, and magazines. As the sheet of paper slid into its tray, he heard the knock on his door.

"Yep?"

The change in his mild expression when he saw Elisa was barely even perceptible. His dark, bushy eyebrows raised slightly, and beneath his glasses and smooth-shaven cheeks the corners of his mouth lengthened just slightly, in what might (on Víctor's understated scale of conduct) be interpreted as a smile.

Elisa was used to his character. She was very fond of Víctor, despite his shyness. He was one of the people she most trusted. But right then, there was only one way he could help her.

"How's the puzzle looking today?" She smiled, tucking her hair back. It was a routine question. Víctor liked the fact that she showed an interest in his hobby and often told her about the most interesting rebuses. There weren't many people he could talk to about that sort of thing.

"Pretty easy." He showed her the photocopy, which bore the caption "Where to look for encouragement," and showed a picture of a pointed instrument that resembled an ice pick, suspended above what looked like a large flounder, or some kind of flat fish. "All over the place. Get it? *Awl* over the *plaice?*"

"Not bad," said Elisa, laughing. *Try to look nonchalant.* She wanted to scream, to run away, but she knew she had to keep her cool. No one was going to help her, at least not yet. She was alone. "Hey, Víctor, would you tell Teresa I'm not going to be able to make it to the quantum seminar this afternoon? She's not in her office and I really need to take off."

"Sure." Another almost imperceptible eyebrow movement. "Anything wrong?"

"I have a headache, and I think I may have a fever, too. Might be the flu."

"Oh, dear."

"Yeah, I know."

That "oh, dear" was as close as Víctor would come to showing his affection, and Elisa knew it. They looked at each other for a second, and then Víctor said, "No problem. I'll tell her."

She thanked him. As she was walking out, she heard a faint "Feel better."

Víctor stood, photocopy in hand, staring after her, for quite some time. Beneath his large, old-fashioned wire-rimmed glasses, his face showed only a slightly disconcerted look. But deep down, he was worried.

THERE'S *no one to help you.*

She headed to her car in the university lot. The sky was almost white on that cold, March morning, and she shivered. She knew that she didn't have the flu, but she thought that given the circumstances, one little white lie was more than forgivable.

Every few seconds, she turned to glance around her.

No one. You're alone. And you haven't even gotten the call. Right?

She took her cell phone out of her purse to check her messages. Nothing. And no new e-mails on her computer watch.

Alone.

Thousands of questions raced through her mind, an incessant stream of concerns and possibilities. She realized how nervous she was when she fumbled and almost dropped her remote-control door opener. Once in the car, she maneuvered carefully, gripping the steering wheel with both hands and thinking through every movement of the clutch and the accelerator as if this were her first driving test. She decided not to hook up the car's computer, preferring to drive with no assistance. It would help her keep calm.

She pulled out of the faculty lot and took the Colmenar road, heading back toward Madrid. Nothing unusual in her rearview mirror: cars passing each other, no one following her as far as she could tell. When she came to the northern edge of town, she took the road heading down toward her neighborhood.

Then, as she was crossing Hortaleza, her cell phone rang. She glanced over at the passenger seat. The phone was inside her purse, and she hadn't connected it to the car's speakers. She slowed down and slid one hand into her purse, rummaging frantically for it. *This is it, this is the call.* The sound and vibration seemed to be coming from underground. She felt around like a blind person: change purse, charger, the shape of the phone. *Answer it, answer it now.*

Finally, she managed to pull it out of her bag, but as she did, it slipped from her sweaty fingers, falling onto the car seat and then bouncing from there to the floor. She had to retrieve it.

Suddenly, a shape came out of nowhere and filled her windshield. She didn't even have time to scream. She instinctively jammed on the brakes. The force of the sudden stop slammed her hard against the seat belt. The guy, a young man, jumped back and then angrily pounded the hood of the car with his fist. Elisa realized she was in a crosswalk. She hadn't been paying attention. She raised her hand in apology and could easily hear the man's insults through the window's glass. Other pedestrians glowered at her disapprovingly. *Calm down. You can't do anything in this state. Calm down and get yourself home.*

Her phone had stopped ringing. Still sitting there in the crosswalk, Elisa ignored the other cars' honking and bent down, grabbed the phone, and glanced at the screen. Blank. No phone number showing where the call had come from. *Don't worry; if that was it, they'll call again.*

She placed her cell carefully on the passenger seat and continued on her way. Ten minutes later, she pulled into her building's parking garage on Silvano. Ruling out the elevator, she rushed up the three flights of stairs to her apartment.

Though she knew it would do no good, she locked each of the four security locks and the magnetic chain on her reinforced door (she'd had it installed three years ago, and it had cost a fortune). Then she set the alarm. Next, she made her way through the apartment, systematically closing all of her electronic blinds (even the ones on the kitchen door that led to the laundry room) and turning on all the lights. Before closing the dining-room blinds, she peeked out to look down at the street.

Cars drove by, people strolled along, their sounds muffled as if they were in an aquarium; she saw almond trees and graffiti on walls. Life went on. Nothing seemed out of the ordinary. Elisa closed the last blind.

Next, she turned on lights in the bathroom, the kitchen, and her little exercise room, which had no windows. Then she switched on the night-table lamps flanking her unmade bed, magazines and math and physics notes scattered across it.

A wad of black silk lay bunched up at the foot of the bed. Last night she'd been playing Mr. White Eyes and still hadn't picked up the underwear strewn across the floor. She bent down and grabbed it now, shuddering (thinking about her "game" now made it seem even creepier), and stuffing it untidily into a dresser drawer. Before leaving the room, she stopped for a moment in front of her huge framed picture of the moon (the first thing she saw when she awoke every morning) and flicked the switch on its frame. The celestial body took on a white, phosphorescent glow. Back in the dining room, she turned on the remaining lights (floor lamps, undershelf lighting) from a central control panel. Finally, she did the same with two battery-charged lamps.

Her answering machine flashed the number "2." She listened to her messages, holding her breath. One was from the publisher of a scientific journal she subscribed to, and the other from her cleaning woman. Elisa only had her come when she could be home; she didn't want anyone invading her privacy in her absence. The cleaning woman wanted to know if she could change days next week so she could go to the doctor. Elisa didn't call back. She just erased the message.

Then she turned on her forty-inch digital TV. On several news channels, she found the weather, sports, and financial reports. She opened a dialogue box, typed in a few keywords, and the television did an automatic search for the news she wanted. No results. She left CNN on in English and muted it.

After thinking for a minute, she ran to the kitchen and opened an electronic drawer below the thermostat. Elisa found what she was looking for at the back of it. She'd bought it a year ago for this very purpose, despite the fact that she knew it would do no good.

She stared for a moment at her own terrified eyes, reflected on the blade of the sixteen-inch butcher knife.

ELISA waited.

She'd gone back to the dining room and, after picking up the phone to make sure it was still working, and double-checking the battery on her cell, dropped into an armchair in front of the TV, the knife in her lap.

Waiting.

The enormous teddy bear her colleagues had given her for her birthday last year sat in a corner of the sofa across from her. It wore a bib that had "Happy Birthday" stitched in red, with the Alighieri University logo (Dante's aquiline profile) underneath. On its stomach, in gold, was the university motto: *The sea I sail has never yet been passed.* The bear's plastic eyes seemed to spy on Elisa, and its heart-shaped mouth looked like it was speaking to her.

Go ahead, do whatever you want. Protect yourself, fool yourself into thinking you're safe now. But you know you're dead.

She glanced back at the screen, which was broadcasting the launch of a new European space probe.

Dead, Elisa. Just like the rest of them.

The shrieking of the telephone made her jump. But then a surprising thing happened: she reached out calmly and picked up the receiver in something resembling absolute composure. Now that she'd finally received the call, she felt unbelievably serene. There was no hint of trembling in her voice.

"Hello?"

"Elisa? It's Víctor ..."

The overwhelming disappointment left her dazed. It was as if she'd tensed up for a punch and suddenly the fight had been called off. She took a breath, as an irrational wave of hatred for her friend suddenly flowed through her. It wasn't Víctor's fault, but right then she couldn't have wanted to speak to anyone less. *Leave me alone. Hang up and leave me alone.*

"I just wanted to see how you were doing. You seemed a little ... Well, just not yourself. You know ..."

"I'm fine, don't worry. Just a headache ... I don't even think it's the flu."

"Oh, good." He cleared his throat. And paused. Though she was used to Víctor speaking at a snail's pace, right now it was thoroughly exasperating. "Don't worry about the seminar. Noriega says no problem. If you can't come in this week ... just ... let Teresa know in advance ..."

"I will. Thanks a lot, Víctor." She wondered what he'd think if he could see her now: sweaty, trembling, curled up in an armchair with a sixteen-inch stainless-steel butcher knife in her right hand.

"I ... I was also calling to tell you ... something else," he added. "There's been some news." Elisa stiffened. "Are you watching TV?"

Frantically, she snatched up the remote to switch to the channel Víctor said it was on. A man stood in front of an apartment building with a mike in his hand.

" ... at home in Milan's leafy residential neighborhood near the university has rocked Italy to its core ..."

"You knew him, didn't you?"

"Yeah," said Elisa calmly. "What a shame."

Act indifferent. Don't you dare give anything away over the phone.

Víctor's voice began the struggle to commence another sentence. Elisa decided it was time to cut him off.

"Sorry, I've got to go ... I'll call you later ... Thanks, Víctor, really." She didn't even wait for his reply. She hated to be so brusque with Víctor, of all people, but there was nothing else she could do. She turned up the volume and hung on every word. The newscaster assured viewers that the police were not ruling anything out, though robbery seemed the most likely motive.

She clung to that idiotic hope as best she could. *Yes! Maybe that was it. A simple robbery. After all, I still haven't gotten the call ...*

The newscaster held an umbrella. The sky was gray in Milan. Elisa felt like she was watching the apocalypse.

THE lights at the Medical Institute at the University of Milan were blazing, despite the fact that almost all the employees had gone home. A light but unrelenting rain fell on the city that night, and the Italian flag drooped from its pole at the entrance of the somber building, a steady stream of water coursing off of it. There, on Via Mangiagalli, a dark car pulled to a stop beneath the flag. The shadow of an umbrella could be seen, and a man waiting in the doorway greeted the two individuals who emerged from the backseat. No one spoke: they all knew who they were and why they were there. The umbrella closed. The silhouettes disappeared.

Their footsteps rang out through the institute's hallways. They all wore dark suits, though the new arrivals also wore overcoats. The man leading their way was the one who'd been waiting in the doorway; he was young, pale, and so nervous that he gave little leaps with each step. He waved his hands around constantly as he spoke. Though his English was good, he had a strong Italian accent.

"They're making a detailed study ... Still nothing definite. The discovery was made yesterday morning, and it took until today to round up the specialists."

He stopped to open the door to the Dental and Anthropological Forensics Laboratory. Inaugurated in 1995 and remodeled in 2012, it boasted state-of-the-art technology; Europe's top-notch forensic scientists worked here.

The new arrivals hardly noticed the photos and sculptures lining the hallway. They sped past plaster models of three human heads.

"How many witnesses?" asked the older one. His hair was white, thinning on top, though he disguised that by wearing it slightly long. His English was unidentifiable, a blend of several accents.

"Just the woman who cleaned his flat every morning. She was the one who found him. The neighbors hardly saw a thing."

"'Hardly?' What does 'hardly' mean?"

"They heard the cleaning lady scream and questioned her, but no one entered the apartment. They called the police right away."

They'd stopped by a painstakingly detailed anatomical drawing of a woman, no skin, a fetus inside her open uterus. The young man opened a metal door.

"What about the woman?" inquired the white-haired man.

"In the hospital. Sedated. And under protective custody."

"She *must not* be released until we've spoken to her."

"I've taken care of all that."

The white-haired man spoke with apparent indifference: his face expressionless, hands in pockets. The young man responded in the urgent tones of a lackey. And the third man seemed lost in his own thoughts. He was burly, and his suit and overcoat looked like they were two sizes too small for him. He looked younger than the older man, and older than the young one. He had a crew cut, clear, green eyes, a neck as thick as a Gothic column, and a grayish five-o'clock shadow. It was patently obvious that he was the only one not used to executive attire. He moved determinedly, swinging his arms, and had a military air about him.

They crossed another hallway and entered another room. The young man closed the door behind them.

It was cold in there. The walls and floor were a soft, reflective apple green, like cut glass. Several individuals wearing surgical gear stood in a row, surrounded by tables covered with scientific instruments. They were looking at the door the three men had just come through, as if their mission was none other than to form a sort of welcome committee. One of them, his silvery hair parted down the side, a suit and tie rather incongruously peeking out from beneath his green scrubs, stepped forward. The young man made the introductions.

"Mr. Harrison, Mr. Carter. Dr. Fontana." The doctor nodded his greeting; the white-haired man and the burly one followed suit. "You can speak to them freely, Doctor."

No one said a word. The trace of a smile, or perhaps a grimace, played on the doctor's pale, shiny face; he looked waxen. His right eye was twitching. When he finally spoke, he resembled a ventriloquist's dummy, controlled from a distance.

"I have never seen anything like this . . . in all my time in forensics."

The other doctors stood aside, inviting the visitors to step forward. An examination table lay behind them. Overhead lights shone down on a sheet-covered shape. One of the physicians peeled it back.

Aside from the white-haired man and the burly one, no one looked at what lay beneath the sheet. They were watching the visitors' reactions, as if *they* were the ones who needed to be carefully examined.

The white-haired man opened his mouth, but then closed it again and looked away.

For a moment, the burly man looked at what lay on the table.

He stood there, frowning, his body rigid, as though forcing his eyes to stare at what no one else could keep looking at was the only thing keeping him from fainting.

NIGHT had fallen. Elisa's apartment was an island of light. The apartments around hers were growing dark. She was still sitting in the same position, in front of a television that was no longer on, cradling the enormous knife in her lap. She hadn't eaten all day, nor had she stopped to rest. More than anything, she wanted to do some exercise and then take a long, relaxing shower, but she didn't dare move.

She waited.

She'd wait as long as necessary, though she had no idea how long that might be.

They've abandoned you. They lied. You're all alone. And that's not the worst of it. You know what's worse?

The teddy bear's arms were outstretched, his heart-shaped mouth smiling. His black-button eyes reflected a tiny, pale Elisa.

The worst is what's to come. What hasn't happened yet. What's going to happen to you.

Her cell phone suddenly came to life. Like so many things we yearn for (or fear), the arrival of the long-awaited (or feared) event began a new stage for her, a new way of thinking. Even before she picked up, her brain had already begun to formulate and discard hypotheses, to take what had not yet occurred as a given.

She answered on the second ring, sure that it wouldn't be Víctor.

It wasn't. It was the call she'd been waiting for.

The message took no more than two seconds. But it was enough to make her burst into tears when she hung up.

Now you know. Finally. Now you know.

She cried for a long time, balled up, still clutching the receiver. Once she got it out of her system, she stood and looked at the clock. She had some time before the meeting. She'd exercise, have a shower, grab a bite to eat ... And then she'd decide whether to go it alone or try to find help. She'd thought about trying to ask for help, someone unconnected, someone who knew nothing about any of it and who she could explain it to in a logical fashion, some-one unbiased. But who?

Víctor, possibly. Yes, maybe Víctor.

But that was risky. And there was an additional problem: how was she going to let him know she needed his help urgently? She had to find a way to get him the message.

First, she had to calm down and think it through. Intelligence had always been her best weapon. She was well aware that human intelligence was far more dangerous than the knife she held.

She thought that if nothing else, at least she'd finally received the call she'd been waiting for since that morning, the one that would decide her fate from that moment on.

The voice had been so unsteady and quavering she almost hadn't recognized it, as if the speaker were as terrified as she was. But there was no doubt that it was *the call.* The only thing the man had said was exactly what she'd been expecting.

"Zig Zag."

03

AT that moment, Víctor Lopera was wondering, somewhat transcendentally, whether he could consider his aeroponic aralias *natural* or not. On first glance it seemed clear that they indeed formed part of nature, since they were living things, *Dizygotheca elegantissima,* that breathed and absorbed light and nutrients. But then, nature could never have reproduced them with such exactitude. They were clearly man-made, the product of technology. Víctor kept them in clear plastic so he could see the astonishing fractals of their roots, and he controlled their temperature, pH, and growth with electronic instruments. To keep them from growing to their standard five-foot height, he used specific fertilizers. So really, those four dainty aralias, no more than six inches tall, with their bronze, almost silvery leaves, were largely his creations. Without him, and without modern science, they would never have existed. He felt his question rather reasonable.

He concluded that they were natural, after all. Maybe not unconditionally, but they were definitely natural. For Víctor, the issue did not merely apply to plant life. Answering that question was a declaration of faith (or skepticism) in progress and technology. And he was committed to science. He firmly believed that science was another form of nature, and, like Teilhard de Chardin, even a new way to conceive of religion. His optimistic outlook on life had begun when he was a child and saw that his father, who had been a surgeon, could modify life and correct mistakes.

Even though he admired his father tremendously, he had not opted for a "biological" career like his brother, who was also a surgeon, or his sister, a vet. He had chosen to go into physics. He thought his siblings' jobs were too hectic; he liked peace and quiet. At one point, he'd even considered a career as a professional chess player, since his math and logic skills were remarkable, but he'd soon learned that competition was stressful, too. It wasn't that he was idle, far from it; he just liked peace to reign on the outside so he could psychologically battle enigmas, ask questions like the one about his aralias, and solve complicated riddles and puzzles.

He filled one of the sprinklers with a new fertilizer he was going to try exclusively on Aralia A. He'd put them each into their own little stalls so he could experiment on each one individually. At first, he'd toyed with the idea of giving them more original names, but he ended up opting for the first four letters of the alphabet.

"Come on, now, why are you making that face?" he whispered affectionately as he snapped the sprinkler head shut. "Don't you trust me? You should learn from C, who always adapts so well to change. You've got to learn to adapt, little one. You and I could both take some lessons from C."

He stood there for a minute, wondering why he'd just said that. Lately, he seemed more melancholy than usual, as if he, too, needed some new fertilizer. But, good heavens, that was just pop psychology. He thought of himself as a happy man. He liked teaching, and he had plenty of free time to read, take care of his plants, and work on his puzzles. He had the best family in the world, and his parents, though they were retired and now getting old, were still in good health. He was an exemplary uncle to his nieces and nephews, his brother's kids, who adored him. Who else had that much love, peace, and quiet in their lives?

It was true he was alone. But that was his choice. He was master of his own destiny. Why ruin everything by rushing into some relationship with a woman who could never make him happy? At thirty-four, he still felt young and hadn't given up hope. Life was a waiting game: an aralia didn't bloom in two minutes, and nor did love. One of these days, he'd meet someone, or someone he knew would give him a call …

"And then, bam! I'll blossom like C," he said aloud, and laughed.

Just then the phone rang.

As he walked over to a bookcase in his small dining room to answer it, he speculated on who it could be. Given the hour, it was probably his brother, who had been pestering him for a few months to go over the accounts at the private surgical clinic he ran. "You're the math genius; how hard would it be to give me a hand?" Luis Lopera—or Luis'll Opera, as he jokingly pronounced it (*operar* was Spanish for "operate," so "Louis'll *Operate*" had been a long-standing pun among the family surgeons)—didn't trust computers and wanted Víctor to go through the files himself to make sure all was in order. Víctor had grown tired of telling him that mathematicians specialized, just like surgeons. A brain surgeon couldn't, just like that, perform heart transplants. Likewise, he worked on elementary particles, not on tallying up a grocery bill. If anything, his brother needed his stubborn brain operated on.

He fished the receiver out from a sea of framed photos (nieces and nephews, sister, parents, Teilhard de Chardin, the monk and scientist Georges Lemaître, Einstein). Stifling a yawn, he said, "Hello?"

"Víctor? It's Elisa."

His sense of tedium shattered like a pane of glass. It was like suddenly waking from a dream.

"Hi." Víctor's mind was racing. "How're you feeling?"

"Better, thanks … At first I thought it was allergies, but now I'm pretty sure it's just a cold …"

"Good! Glad to hear it. Did you see the report?"

"What report?"

"On the news ... about Marini's death."

"Oh, yeah. Poor guy." That was the extent of the sorrow she expressed.

"You were in Zurich with him, weren't you?" Víctor began. But Elisa spoke over him, rushing to get to the heart of the matter.

"Yeah. Listen, Víctor. I was calling ..." She stopped, then she giggled. "You're going to think this is idiotic, I'm sure ... But it's really important to me. OK?"

"OK."

He frowned and tensed up. Elisa's voice was carefree and bubbly. And that was exactly what worried him, because he thought he knew her pretty well, and carefree and bubbly were two things she was not.

"Well, it's my neighbor, you see ... She's got a teenage son, a really nice kid ... Anyway, she just found out that he really loves those word puzzles ... you know, those rebuses you do from the paper? Turns out he's got all kinds of books and magazines. So, I told her I'm friends with the number one rebus puzzler. And it turns out that he's been trying to solve one, and he can't do it. He's really worked up about it, and his mother's worried that he'll give up on this wholesome hobby and take up something more questionable instead. And when she told me about the specific puzzle in question, I realized that I knew that one because you'd told me about it, but I can't remember the answer. So I thought, 'I need *help*. And Víctor's the only one who can *help me*. Do you understand?"

"Of course. Which one is it?" Víctor had picked up on Elisa's strange intonation and felt shivers descend, like unexpected visitors from another planet. Was he imagining it, or was she trying to tell him something else, something he could only pick up on by reading between the lines?

"It's the one with the steak and the atom, remember?" She burst out laughing. "You do remember that one, don't you?"

"Sure, that one was ..."

"Listen," she cut him off. "I don't *need you* to tell me the answer.

Just do what it says, *tonight*. It's urgent. Do it as soon as you pos-sibly can. I'm relying on you." Suddenly she cackled again. "The kid's mother is relying on you, too. Thanks, Víctor. Bye."

There was a click, and then the dial tone.

The hair on Víctor's neck stood up as if the phone had given him an electric shock.

RARELY in his life had he had this feeling.

His sweaty hands slid down the steering wheel, his heart was pounding harder and harder, his chest hurt, and he felt like no matter how deeply he inhaled, he couldn't get enough air into his lungs. For Víctor, this had only ever meant the possibility of sex.

The few times he had gone out with girls who he knew, or suspected, he could end up in bed with, he'd felt the same sort of torment. Unfortunately, or fortunately, none of them ever made passes at him, and his dates had always ended with a quick peck and the promise of a phone call.

But what about this? What kind of bed could he end up in to-night? This date was with none other than Elisa Robledo.

Whoa!

He'd been to her house before, sure (they were friends, after all, or he liked to think they were), but always with other colleagues and never so late at night; the other times being for some sort of celebration (Christmas, the end of the semester) or to work on or-ganizing a seminar together. He'd fantasized about this ever since they met, ten years ago, at an unforgettable party on the Alighieri campus. But he'd never imagined it might come about in such a strange way.

Besides, he would have sworn sex wasn't exactly what Elisa was at home waiting for.

Thinking about it, he laughed, and it did him good, put him slightly more at ease. He pictured Elisa in her underwear, giv-ing him a hug when he arrived, kissing him and whispering provocatively, "Hello, Víctor. Glad you got the message. Come on in." His laughter swelled like a balloon in his stomach, until finally it popped and his customary serious nature returned. He ran through all the things he'd thought, done, and fantasized about since the bizarre phone call an hour ago: doubts, nerves, the desire to call her back and ask for an explanation (but she'd told him not to), the rebus. Paradoxically, the word puzzle was, in this case, the easiest thing to understand. He remembered the answer perfectly, though he'd still rushed to pull out his photo album and find the clipping. It was a recent one, and showed what looked like a side of beef, an atom, an eye, and finally the word "how" repeated three times. The question was "Where's the party?" He'd solved it in less than five minutes the day it was published. The words "meat," "atom," "I," and the repeated "how" made the sentence "Meat + Atom + I + Hows"; said quickly, it was "Meet at my house."

That was the easy part. What he couldn't figure out was why, for example, Elisa couldn't just ask him to come to her place. Why not tell him straight out that she needed him to come over? What was the matter? Could there be someone with her (no, please, God), someone there threatening her?

Then there was another possibility. One that was even more unsettling. Elisa might be mentally ill.

The best possible explanation, the most likely, was one he didn't care for. He pictured it would go like this: he'd arrive, she'd open the door, and they'd have a ridiculous conversation. "Víctor, what are you doing here?" "You told me to come over." "Me?" "Yes, you said I should do what the rebus said." "Oh, no, you didn't think ...!" And then she'd burst out laughing. "I told you to *do the puzzle* tonight, to solve the riddle, not do what the *answer said!*" "But you told me not to call ..." "I just meant not to go to any trouble, I was going to call you later." And Víctor would stand there in the doorway feeling ridiculous as Elisa laughed at him.

No.

That was impossible. He was sure.

Something was wrong. Something terrible. In fact, he knew Elisa had been going through something terrible for years.

He'd always suspected it. Like all reserved people, Víctor had an uncanny ability to gauge things that interested him. And few things interested him more than Elisa Robledo Morandé. He watched her when she walked, talked, and moved, and he thought, "Something's wrong." Whenever she passed by, her past was like a magnet to him. He couldn't help but be attracted to her long black hair, her athletic body, and he never doubted it. "She's hiding something."

He even thought he knew when and where the secret began. Her time in Zurich.

He navigated a detour and turned down Silvano. Slowing down, he began to search for a parking place. No luck. He saw a man behind the wheel of a parked car, but the guy waved him on, signaling that he wasn't leaving.

Víctor passed Elisa's building and kept looking. Suddenly he saw a great spot, braked, and started to back up.

That's when it all happened.

A moment later, he wondered what made the human brain react the way it did in these extreme situations. Because the first thing that occurred to him when she appeared out of nowhere and knocked on the passenger window was not how petrified she looked, or that she was as white as a sheet; nor was it how odd it was that she'd practically leaped into the car the second he leaned over to open the door. She whipped her head around to look behind her as she shouted, "Go! Go! Drive!"

He did not stop to think about the irate honking that his maneuver had caused, or the headlights in his rearview mirror, or the screeching of tires behind him that brought to mind—oddly—the parked car he passed moments earlier, with its lights off, its driver behind the wheel. He *felt* all of those things, but none of them made it above his spinal cord.

There, in his brain, his intellect was entirely focused on one thing.

Her breasts.

Elisa was wearing a low-cut T-shirt under her leather jacket, something she'd clearly just thrown on at the last minute, too summery for the cold March night. And her magnificent, round breasts were in plain view. He couldn't tell if she was wearing a bra. When she leaned in the window before climbing into the car, he'd stared at them. Even now, as she sat beside him and he breathed in the smell of her soap and leather jacket, feeling dizzy, he couldn't stop himself from glancing sidelong to peek at her gorgeous chest.

He didn't think it was wrong. He knew it was the only way his brain could deal with the situation, set the world back in its place after having suffered the terrible experience of seeing his friend and colleague leap into the car, crouch down, and begin shouting desperate orders. Sometimes men have to clutch at straws in order to preserve their sanity. He'd clutched at Elisa's breasts. Correction: he used the image of her chest in his mind to help himself calm down.

"Are we ... are we being followed?" he stammered as they reached Campo de las Naciones.

She turned to look back and said, "I don't know."

"Where do you want me to go?"

"Take the Burgos highway."

And suddenly she crumpled, her shoulders shaking spasmodically.

Her howling was horrific. Seeing her like this, the image of her breasts vanished from Víctor's mind. He'd never seen an adult cry like that. Forgetting everything, including his own fear, he spoke with a determination that surprised even himself.

"Elisa, you've got to calm down. Listen to me. I'm here for you. I always have been. I'm going to help you. Whatever it is, I'm going to help you. I swear."

She recovered suddenly, but he had the feeling it wasn't his words that had that effect on her.

"I'm sorry to drag you into this, Víctor, but I had no choice. When I'm scared to death, I'm evil. A total bitch."

"No, Elisa, I ..."

"Anyway," she cut him off, "I don't want to waste time apologizing."

That was when he noticed the long, flat, plastic-wrapped object in her hand. It could have been anything, but the way she held it was intriguing: her right hand wrapped around one end of it, and the left one stroked it almost imperceptibly.

THE two men, having just arrived at Madrid's Barajas International Airport, were not asked to show any identification or go through security. They didn't take the same tunnel to the terminal as the rest of the passengers, either. Instead, they walked up an adjacent stairway. A van awaited them. The young man in the driver's seat was polite, courteous, and kind; he clearly wanted to practice his night-school English on them.

"In Madrid, there isn't so much cold, eh? I mean, now."

"You said it," replied the older man, good-naturedly. He was tall and thin, with snowy hair and a bald spot on top that he hid with a comb-over. "I love Madrid. Come whenever I get the chance."

"In Milan, I think it was cold," the driver continued. He knew where their plane had come in from.

"Too true. Though more than cold, rain." And then, linguistically reciprocating, the older man added, in second-rate Spanish, "Much pleasing to return to good Spanish climate."

They both laughed. The driver couldn't hear the other man laugh, the burly one. And, judging by his looks and the expression on his face when he'd climbed into the van, he decided he'd rather not hear him laugh, anyway.

If he even knew how to laugh.

Businessmen, the driver thought. *Or a businessman and his bodyguard.*

The van circled the terminal. Now it stopped and another dark-suited man opened the door and stood aside to let the two men out. The van drove off, and that was the last the driver saw of them.

The Mercedes had tinted windows. As they settled into the wide leather seats, the older man got a call on the cell phone he'd just turned on.

"Harrison," he said. "Yes. Yes. Wait, I need more information. When did it happen? Who is it?" He pulled a flexible computer screen, thin as a strip of fabric, from his coat pocket and unrolled it on his knees like a tablecloth, touching the interactive surface as he spoke. "Yeah. Yeah. No, no change of plans. Fine."

But after he hung up, nothing seemed "fine." He pursed his lips tightly as he watched the floppy, illuminated screen on his legs. The burly man glanced away from the window to look at it, too. On it shone some sort of blue map with moving red and green dots.

"We've got a problem," said the white-haired man.

"I don't know if we're being followed or not," she said, "but take this exit and drive through San Lorenzo for a while. The streets are narrow there; maybe we can throw them off."

Víctor silently followed her orders. He got off the freeway and took an access road to the labyrinthine subdivision. His car was an old Renault Scénic with no computer or GPS, so Víctor had no idea where he was going. He read out street names as if in a dream: Dominicos, Franciscanos ... Nerves made him feel there was some form of divine intervention responsible for all this. A memory suddenly popped into his anguished mind: he used to drive Elisa home in his old car, the first one he'd had, when they were both students in David Blanes's summer course at Alighieri University. Those were happier times. Now things were a little different. He had a bigger car, he taught at the university, Elisa had gone crazy and was armed with a huge knife, and they were both fleeing some unknown danger as fast as they possibly could. *This is real life,* he surmised. *Things change.*

He heard the crinkling of plastic and saw that she'd taken her knife partway out of its wrapper. The streetlights' reflection twinkled on the blade.

He felt as if his heart skipped a beat. No, worse. He felt as if it was melting, or being stretched out like a spit-covered piece of gum, auricles and ventricles forming one solid mass. *She's lost her mind,* his common sense told him. *And you let her get into your car and now she's forcing you to take her wherever she wants to go.* It was all coming clear. The following day, his car would be found abandoned in some ditch, his body inside it. What would she have done? Decapitate him, maybe, judging by the size of that knife. Slit his throat, though maybe she'd kiss him first. "I always loved you, Víctor, I just couldn't tell you." Then *zzzzzzzzzzzip.* He'd hear it before he felt it, the sound of her slashing his carotid artery, the blade slicing through him with the unexpected precision of a paper cut on a fingertip.

Still, even if she's insane, I have to try to help her.

He turned down another street. It was Dominicos again. They were just going around in circles, like his thoughts.

"What now?"

"Let's go back to the freeway," she said. "Head toward Burgos. It doesn't matter if they're still following us. I don't need much time." *To do what?* he wondered. *Kill me?* But then she added, "To explain all this to you." She paused and then asked, "Víctor, do you believe in evil?"

"Evil?"

"Yes. You're a theologian, right? So. Do you believe in evil?"

"I'm not a theologian," he murmured, slightly put off. "I read theology, that's all."

It was true that he'd once wanted to go to seminary school, study theology, but he'd eventually discarded the idea, deciding simply to study on his own instead. He read Barth, Bonhoeffer, and Küng. He'd told Elisa this, and under different circumstances he would have been flattered that she'd brought it up. But right then the only thing he could think was that things were stacking up in favor of his insanity hypothesis. Had Elisa lost it?

"Whatever," she said. "Do you think there exists some form of wickedness beyond what can be scientifically explained?"

Víctor pondered his answer.

"There's nothing that cannot be scientifically explained except faith. Are you talking about the Devil?"

Elisa didn't answer. Víctor stopped at an intersection and turned back toward the freeway, his mind racing faster than he was driving.

"I'm a Catholic, Elisa," he added. "I believe that there is an evil, supernatural force that science will never be able to explain."

He waited for some kind of reaction, wondering if he'd put his foot in his mouth. How could he possibly know what a mentally disturbed person wanted to hear? But her response left him ill at ease.

"I'm glad to hear you say that; it means you'll have less trouble believing what I'm about to tell you. I don't know if it's about the Devil, but it's definitely a force of evil. An inconceivable, mind-boggling, sickening evil that has no scientific explanation ..." For a second, he thought she was going to burst into tears again. "You have no idea, no idea, the degree of evil I'm talking about, Víctor. I've never told anyone; I swore I wouldn't. But I can't take it anymore. I have to tell someone, and you're the one I chose."

He would have liked to respond with the easy self-confidence of a Hollywood heartthrob and say something like "You're doing the right thing, babe!" Though he didn't like movies, he felt his life had suddenly turned into a horror flick. But he couldn't re-spond. He was trembling. It wasn't a figure of speech, an internal shiver, or any kind of tingling. He was literally trembling. Though he gripped the steering wheel tightly, his arms shook as if he were sleeveless in the Antarctic. Suddenly, Víctor doubted his theory about Elisa's insanity. She spoke with such assurance that it ter-rified him to listen to her. He realized it would be worse, much worse, if she wasn't crazy. It was scary to think she might have lost her mind, but if she hadn't, Víctor didn't know if he could face up to whatever she was going to say.

"I won't ask you to do anything besides listen to me," she con-tinued. "It's almost eleven. We've got an hour. After that, just put me in a taxi, if you ... if you decide not to come with me." He stared at her. "I have to be at a very important meeting at twelve thirty tonight. I can't miss it, no matter what. You can do whatever you want."

"I'll go with you."

"No ... Don't make that decision before you hear me out." She stopped and took a deep breath. "After that, feel free to kick me out. And forget everything that's happened. I swear I won't hold it against you if you do ..."

"I ...," Víctor whispered, and then coughed. "I won't do that. Go on. Tell me everything."

"It started ten years ago," Elisa said.

Out of the blue, Víctor suddenly became very sure of some-thing. *She's going to tell me the truth. She's not crazy. She's going to tell me the truth.*

"It was early summer, at that party in 2005, the party where you and I met, remember?"

"The orientation party for summer school at Alighieri?" *When she met me and Ric*, he thought. "Of course, I remember, but ... nothing happened at that party ..."

Elisa stared at him, her eyes wide. Her voice faltered. "That was where it *all* started, Víctor."

TWO

The Beginning

We're all ignorant,
but we're not all ignorant about the same things.

ALBERT EINSTEIN

04

Madrid
June 21, 2005
6:35 P.M.

IT had been an eventful afternoon. Elisa had almost missed the last bus to Soto del Real after an absurd argument (yes, another one) with her mother about her messy room. She got to the station right when the bus was pulling out, and as she made a run for it, one of her tattered sneakers had come off. She'd had to beg them to stop and wait for her. The passengers and conductor glared at her reproachfully as she boarded the bus. It occurred to her that their stares had less to do with the few seconds they'd been forced to wait than they did with her appearance. Elisa wore frayed, ripped jeans and a tank top with a grimy neckline. Her long hair hung down to her waist, accentuating how conspicuously greasy it was. But she was not entirely to blame for her unkempt look. For the past few months, she'd been under incredible pressure, the kind that only college students during finals week can relate to. She'd barely even thought about necessities like food or sleep, and looking presentable figured nowhere on her list of priorities. She'd never cared about her appearance or anyone else's. It seemed like such a stupid thing to worry about.

The bus stopped twenty-five miles outside Madrid, in a pretty spot near the Pedriza Mountains, and Elisa walked up a road lined with hedges and almond trees to Alighieri's summer school, having not the slightest idea that two years later, the same place would hire her as a professor. The sign on the entrance had a worn profile of Dante and, underneath it, one of his verses: *L'acquea ch'io prendo già mai non si corse.* Elisa had read the translation in one of the university brochures (she spoke perfect English, but that was as far as her language skills went). *The sea I sail has never yet been passed.* That was the school's motto, though she realized that it could apply to her as well, since there was no other course in the world like the one she was about to take.

She crossed the parking lot and walked over to the quad, which was surrounded by faculty buildings. A large group of people gathered there, listening to someone speak from a podium. She pushed her way through the crowd to the front, but couldn't see who she was looking for.

"... give a warm welcome to all those who are enrolled, and also ...," a bald man in a linen suit and blue shirt (no doubt the dean) was saying. He had the self-assured air of a man who knows that people have to listen to him.

Suddenly, someone beside her whispered, "Excuse me, are you Elisa Robledo?"

She turned and saw John Lennon. Or one of the thousands of Lennons always milling around universities the world over. This particular clone wore the de rigueur wire-rimmed spectacles and had a mop of curls. He stared at Elisa intensely. His face was so red that his head looked like his neck had produced one giant pimple. When she nodded, the boy seemed to relax slightly and his wide, fleshy lips made a shy attempt at a smile.

"Congratulations. You got the highest score of all the people accepted to Blanes's course." Elisa thanked him, despite the fact that—obviously—she already knew she'd come in first. "I was fifth. My name is Víctor Lopera. I just graduated from the Complutense. You went to the Autonomous University, right?"

"Yeah." Elisa was no longer surprised when strangers recognized her. Her name and picture were in college papers regularly. But she wasn't proud of her reputation as a studious intellectual.

In fact, it got on her nerves, especially because it seemed to be the only thing her mother liked about her. "Is Blanes here?" she asked.

"Looks like he couldn't make it."

Elisa frowned, irritated. The only reason she'd come to this stupid orientation was to catch a glimpse of the physicist she admired most in the world (well, along with Stephen Hawking). Now she'd have to wait until the next day, when Blanes himself began teaching. She debated whether to stay or not when Lennon-Lopera piped up again.

"I'm glad we'll be classmates." He sank back into silence. He seemed to think a long time before he got up the nerve to say anything. Elisa assumed he was shy, or worse. She knew that almost all good physics students were weird, herself included. She politely replied that she was glad, too, and waited.

After another pause, Lopera said, "See that guy in the purple shirt? That's Ricardo Valente Sharpe, but everyone calls him Ric. He came in second. We used to . . . We're friends."

"Mmm." Elisa remembered his name perfectly, because she'd seen it immediately after her own on the list of test scores, and because it was such a strange last name. "Valente Sharpe, Ricardo: 9.85." Elisa had scored 9.89 out of 10, which meant that this kid had come in only four one-hundredths of a point below her. That had caught her attention, too, of course. *"So that's Ricardo Valente Sharpe."*

He was skinny, with short, straw-colored hair and an aquiline profile. Just then, he seemed to be concentrating as hard as everyone else on the speaker's words, but there was no doubt that he had an air about him, something that made him seem different from everyone else. Elisa picked up on it instantly. He wore (in addition to the purple shirt) a vest and black trousers, which in and of itself was enough to make him stand out in a sea of jeans and T-shirts. And he certainly seemed to think he was special. *Welcome to the club, Ric Valente Sharpe,* she thought brazenly.

Right at that moment, he turned and looked at her. He had incredible blue-green eyes, but they were somehow cold and disconcerting. If he noticed Elisa in any way, he gave no sign of it.

"Are you staying for the party?" Lopera asked, when Elisa made as if to leave.

"I haven't decided yet."

"OK. Well … see you."

"Yeah, sure."

Actually, she was planning to get out of there as fast as possible, but a feeling of tedium made her dawdle when the brief applause died down after the speech. The music came on and the students began to make their way toward a makeshift bar where drinks were being served, below the dais. She told herself that after having made that much effort to get there, taking that awful bus ride, it might actually be a good idea to hang out for a little while, although she suspected it would be the average dull party with no atmosphere.

She had no idea that that particular evening would turn out to be the beginning of her living nightmare.

THERE were jokey signs taped to the bar, the kind that science students find so hilarious. The one for physics was a few sentences long and bore no graphics:

THEORY MEANS KNOWING WHY THINGS WORK
EVEN IF THEY DON'T WORK.
PRACTICE MEANS THINGS WORK
EVEN IF NOBODY KNOWS WHY.
IN THIS PHYSICS DEPARTMENT,
THEORY AND PRACTICE GO HAND IN HAND,
BECAUSE NOTHING WORKS AND NOBODY KNOWS WHY.

Elisa was amused. She ordered a Diet Coke and held the nap-kin-wrapped plastic cup, looking for a quiet place to have her drink and then leave. In the distance, she saw Víctor Lopera chat-ting with his friend, the ineffable Valente Sharpe, and some other oddballs. She didn't feel like joining the Round Table of Geniuses just then, so she decided to leave it for another time and instead walked down the embankment and found a spot to sit on the grass. She leaned back against the trunk of a pine tree.

She could see the sky starting to dim and caught sight of the moon rising on the horizon. She watched it as she sipped her soda. She'd loved the night sky ever since she was a little girl. At first she'd wanted to become an astronomer, but then she'd discovered that simple mathematics were infinitely more wonderful. Math was something nearby, something she could manipulate. Not so the moon. The only thing the moon could do was mesmerize her.

"The ancients used to think she was a goddess. Scientists are less flattering."

As she heard the voice, she thought, surprised, that this was the second time this evening that a stranger had decided to strike up a conversation with her. She turned to face the person speak-ing, her brain emitting a lightning-speed report on the most likely (most *desirable?*) possibility. She was wrong. It wasn't Four-One-Hundredths-Less Ric Valente Sharpe (how could she even have thought?), but another young man, tall and attractive, with dark hair and light eyes. He wore a T-shirt and khaki Bermuda shorts.

"The moon, I mean. You were staring at it very curiously." He had a backpack, which he dropped on the grass to hold out his hand. "I'm Javier Maldonado. That's the moon. And you must be Elisa Robledo. I saw your picture in the school paper, and here you are. Lucky me. Do you mind if I sit down?"

She did mind, especially because he'd already sat down, invad-ing her personal space and forcing her to scoot over in order to avoid his huge, flip-flopped feet touching hers. Elisa, however, told him to go ahead. She was intrigued. She watched the guy take some papers from his backpack. At least he had an original pick-up line.

"I snuck in through the back door," Maldonado confessed conspiratorially. "I'm not even a science major. I'm doing journalism at Alighieri, and for our final project we have to write a special report. I'm supposed to interview graduating physics majors. You know, talk to them, ask little questions about their lives, their studies, what they do in their free time, their favorite sexual position." Maybe he picked up on the calm seriousness with which Elisa was staring at him, because suddenly he stopped. "OK, I'm an asshole. But the interview is serious, I swear." He showed her his papers. "I chose you guys because you're famous."

"Us?"

"The students doing Blanes's course. I mean, my God, they say he's the biggest hotshot there is in physics. Would you mind answering a few questions for an aspiring journalist?"

"Actually, I was just getting ready to go."

All of a sudden, Maldonado leaped comically to his knees.

"I'm begging you ... I haven't gotten a single person to accept yet ... I have to finish this project or I'll never even get hired as a copywriter for *Soap Opera Digest*. Worse, they'll make me go interview a politician at parliament. Have mercy. It won't take much time, I promise ..."

Smiling, Elisa looked at her watch and got up.

"I'm sorry. The last bus back to Madrid leaves in ten minutes and I can't miss it."

Maldonado stood, too. A malicious expression danced on his face, and Elisa admitted to herself that she found it slightly alluring. She was amused. *Probably thinks he's gorgeous.*

"Well, look, I'll make you a deal. You answer a few questions, and I'll drive you home. All the way to your front door. Word of honor."

"Thanks, but ..."

"You don't want to. Of course. I understand. After all, we just met. OK, what about this? Today, I ask you a few questions, and only if you want to, we finish up another day. How's that? Five minutes. That way you'll make your bus."

Elisa was still smiling, both amused and intrigued. She was about to relent when Maldonado spoke again.

"You liked that one, right? OK, come on."

He gestured to the very spot they'd just stood up from. *I can listen to him ask questions for five minutes,* she thought.

ACTUALLY, she listened to him for longer than that and spoke for even longer. But she couldn't blame Maldonado, who, far from playing dirty, was friendly and attentive. He even went so far as to remind her, at just the right time, that her five minutes were up.

"Should we leave it here?" he asked.

Elisa stopped to consider the other alternative. She hated the idea of leaving this little Eden to get back on that awful bus. Besides, over the past few months she'd been living in her own world, and now that she was finally talking to someone (someone who respected her as a person and didn't just think she was a brilliant student or a cute girl), she realized that she actually needed the company. "I still have a little time," she said. A few minutes later, Maldonado interrupted once more to warn her that she was going to miss her bus. She appreciated his polite concern. And told him to continue. He didn't remind her again.

Elisa felt totally at ease chatting away with him. She answered questions about why she studied physics, what the department was like, whether it was a friendly atmosphere, and about her infinite passion for the natural world. Maldonado let her blather on, jotting down a few things here and there as she spoke. At one point, he said, "You know, you don't really fit my image of a scientist. Not at all."

"Oh? And what's your image of a scientist?"

Maldonado considered the question.

"An ugly dude."

"Well, I can assure you that there are some cute ones, too. And not all of them are 'dudes.'" She smiled. But he'd turned serious and stopped joking.

"There's something else that intrigues me about you. You're at the top of your class, you're guaranteed a scholarship to the best place in the world, your future couldn't be brighter ... As if that weren't enough, you just finished college and you could ... I don't know, sleep for twenty hours straight, climb the Alps, do anything you wanted. But instead, you march right out and take a killer exam to get one of twenty spots in David Blanes's summer course. I mean, this Blanes guy must be pretty spectacular."

"He is." Elisa's eyes lit up. "He's a genius."

Maldonado scribbled something down.

"Do you know him personally?"

"No, but I admire his work."

"Most public universities in this country hate him. Did you know that? That's why he had to teach this course at a private institution..."

"The world is full of envious people," Elisa said. "Especially the world of science. But, yeah, I've heard that Blanes can be difficult."

"Would you like to do a dissertation on him?"

"Obviously."

"Anything else?"

"What?"

"I asked you if you'd like to do a dissertation on him and you said, 'Obviously.' Is that all you have to say?"

"What else do you want me to say? You asked me a question and I answered it."

"That's the problem with you physicists," he lamented, making more notes. "You take everything so literally. What I wanted to know is, what's Blanes got that everyone's so into him? I mean ... I know they say he's a fucking genius, he's been nominated for the Nobel Prize, and if he wins he'll be the first Spaniard to win the damn Nobel in physics. I know all that shit. But what I want to know is, what's his deal? You know? His course is called …" He looked at one of his papers and read, falteringly, "'The topology of time strings in visible electromagnetic radiation.' That doesn't exactly clear a lot up for me."

"You want me to sum up the whole of theoretical physics to you with one answer?"

Maldonado seemed to seriously weigh the possibility.

"OK," he replied.

"Fine. Let's see. I'll try to summarize …" Elisa was in her element. She liked explaining as much as she liked understanding. "You know about the theory of relativity?"

"Yeah, Einstein. 'Everything is relative,' right?"

"The theory of relativity is a little more complicated than that. But what I'm trying to say is that it works in almost every situation, except in the world of atoms. That's where quantum physics comes in. Together, those theories are the most perfect intellectual creations humans have ever conceived. They can explain *almost* anything. But the problem is, we need *both* of them. What's valid on one scale doesn't work on the other, and vice versa. And that's a big problem. For years, physicists have been trying to combine the two theories into one. Does that make sense?"

"Sure, it's like any country's political parties, right?" Maldonado suggested. "Both sides are wrong, and they still never agree on anything."

"Something like that. Anyway, one of the most popular theories that attempts to combine them is called string theory."

"I've never heard of it. String?"

"Yeah. String theory. Also called superstrings. It's an incredibly complicated mathematical theory, but basically what it comes down to is quite simple …" Elisa quickly cast her eyes around for an object, and then settled on the paper napkin around her cup. While she spoke, she folded it in half and then creased it into a sharp edge with her long fingers. Maldonado watched, intrigued. "According to string theory, the particles that make up the universe, you know, electrons, protons ... all of those particles are not little balls, like we learned to visualize in elementary school, but are actually elongated, like strings ..."

"Things like strings ... ," Maldonado pondered aloud.

"Yeah. Really fine strings, because the only dimension they possess is longitude. But they have a special property." Elisa raised her hands to Maldonado's eye level, holding the napkin taut so that he was looking at the crease. "Tell me what you see."

"A napkin."

"That's the problem with you journalists. You worry too much about appearance." Elisa smiled playfully. "Forget what you already think it *is*. Just tell me what you think you *see*."

Maldonado squinted and stared at the sharp edge that Elisa held up before him.

"Um ... A line. A straight line."

"Good. From your perspective, it could be a string, right? A thread. Well, the theory states that the strings that make up matter only look like strings from certain angles. But if we look at them from another perspective ..."—Elisa flipped the napkin up and held the rectangular surface before him—"then they have other dimensions, and if we could unroll them, or 'open' them ..."—she unfolded the napkin all the way now, so that it became a large square—"then we could see even more dimensions."

"What a trip." Maldonado looked impressed. Or else he was a good faker. "So, have those dimensions been discovered?"

"Ha! Not even close," Elisa replied, balling up the napkin and stuffing it into her cup. "'Opening' a subatomic string requires machines we don't have yet: incredibly powerful particle accelerators ... But that's where Blanes and his theory come in. He thinks there are some strings that can be opened with low levels of energy. Time strings. He's mathematically proven that time is made up of strings, just like everything else. But they can be opened with accelerators that already exist. It's just very difficult to carry out the experiment."

"So what you're talking about, in practical terms"—Maldonado was scribbling furiously—"is time travel? Going back to the past?"

"No. The idea of traveling back through time is total science fiction. Basic laws of physics make it impossible. There's no way to go back to the past, sorry. Time can only travel forward, into the future. But if Blanes's theory were correct, there would be another possibility ... We could open time strands and *see* the past."

"See the past? You mean ... Napoléon, Julius Caesar? Sorry, kiddo, but *that* sounds like science fiction."

"You're wrong. It's very possible." Elisa looked at him, amused. "Not only is it possible, it's run of the mill. We see the past every day."

"You mean old movies, faded photographs, all that?"

"No. We're seeing it right now." She laughed at his expression. "Seriously. You want to bet?"

Maldonado glanced around.

"Well, OK, some of those professors have seen better days, I'll grant you that."

Elisa laughed and shook her head.

"You being serious?"

"Completely." She looked up, and Maldonado did the same. Night had fallen. A blanket of shimmering stars shone brightly in the black sky. "The light from those stars takes millions of years to reach the earth," she explained. "They may no longer exist, but we'll still be seeing them for a long, long time. Every time we look at the sky, we go back millions of years. We can travel through time just by looking out a window."

They were both silent for a moment. The sounds and lights of the party faded away for Elisa, who was much more interested in the magnificent silence that rose above her like a vaulted cathedral. When she looked back down, and then over at Maldonado, she realized he felt the same thing.

"Physics is a beautiful thing," she murmured.

"One of many," he responded, staring at her.

They continued their conversation, though at a more relaxed pace. Then he suggested they stop and get something to eat, and she put up no resistance (it had gotten late and she was hungry). Maldonado jumped up and headed for the bar.

While she was waiting for him, Elisa glanced around indifferently. There were still plenty of hangers-on at the party, enjoying the warm summer temperatures. An old Umberto Tozzi song was playing, and here and there groups of students and professors stood chatting animatedly beneath the party lights.

Then she noticed a man watching her.

He was a completely anodyne fellow, standing on the embankment's lower deck. His checked, short-sleeved shirt and well-pressed trousers were wholly unremarkable. His hair was graying, and his only distinguishing feature was a big gray mustache. Elisa guessed he was a professor, though he wasn't speaking to any colleagues. Or doing anything else, for that matter.

Except staring at her.

His gaze intrigued her. She wondered if she knew him from somewhere, but concluded that he must be the one who recognized her. Maybe he'd seen her picture in the paper, too.

Suddenly, he whipped his head around quickly (too quickly) and vanished behind one of the groups of gathered professors. She was more disturbed by his rapid departure than his staring. It was like he was faking it, like he'd realized that Elisa had become aware of him. *Caught me, damn it.* But when Maldonado returned with two big, paper-wrapped sandwiches, a bag of potato chips, and beer and another Diet Coke for her, she forgot the incident. It wasn't the first time an older man had stared at her, after all.

ON the ride back to Madrid, they were mostly silent, but Elisa felt entirely at ease in the car, being driven home by a boy she hardly knew. She somehow felt at ease in his company. Maldonado made her laugh from time to time with his ironic quips, but he'd stopped asking questions, and Elisa was glad about that. She took advantage of the situation by asking *him* questions instead. His life was quite straightforward: he lived with his parents and sister, and he was into traveling and sports (two things she loved, too). It was almost midnight when Maldonado's Peugeot pulled up in front of her apartment building on Claudio Coello.

"Some building," he said. "Is being rich a requirement for making it as a physicist?"

"For my mother, it's a requirement for anything."

"We haven't even talked about your family ... What does your mother do? Mathematician? Chemist? Genetic engineer? Inventor of the Rubik's Cube?"

"She owns a beauty salon two blocks from here," laughed Elisa. "My *father* was a physicist, but he died in a car crash five years ago."

Maldonado looked genuinely distraught.

"I'm so sorry."

"Don't worry, I hardly knew him," Elisa replied easily. She climbed out and closed the car door. "He was never home." She bent down to look in at Maldonado. "Thanks for the ride."

"Thanks for your help. Hey, if I have ... more ... questions ... could we, uh ... go out sometime?"

"Sure."

"I have your phone number. I'll call you. Good luck tomorrow on the first day of class with Blanes."

Maldonado waited courteously for her to reach the door to her building. Elisa turned to wave.

And froze.

Across the street, a man was staring at her.

At first, she didn't recognize him. Then she saw his graying hair and big gray mustache. She felt a chill, as if her body were full of holes and a gust of cold wind had just blown through her.

Maldonado drove off. Another car drove by. Then another one. Then the street was empty, and the man was still standing there. *I must be confused. This man isn't wearing the same clothes.*

Suddenly, he turned and walked around the corner.

Elisa stood staring at the spot where he'd been just a few seconds ago. *That must have been another guy; they just looked the same.*

Nevertheless, she was sure that this man, too, had been watching her.

05

"THIS is not going to be a fun class," David Blanes said. "We're not going to talk about amazing, extraordinary things. We're not going to answer any questions. If you're looking for answers, go to church or back to school." Nervous laughter. "What we're going to see here is reality, and reality has no answers, and it's not particularly amazing."

He stopped abruptly when he got to the back of the room. *Must have realized he can't walk through walls,* Elisa thought. She stopped looking at him when he turned back around, but she was hanging on his every word.

"Before we get started, I want to clear something up."

Taking just two steps, Blanes strode over to the slide projector and turned it on. Three letters and a number appeared on the screen.

"There you have it: $E = mc^2$. Probably the most famous equation physics has ever produced. The relativistic energy of a particle at rest."

He clicked to the next slide. A black-and-white photograph of a young Asian boy, his left side destroyed. You could see his teeth through his cheek. People whispered. Someone said, "Jesus." Elisa couldn't move. She shuddered in horror at the image. She was also riveted.

"This, too, is $E = mc^2$, as they know in every Japanese university."

He switched off the projector and turned to face the class.

"I could have shown you one of Maxwell's equations and the electric light of an operating room where someone is being saved, or the Schrödinger wave equation and a cell phone, which enables a doctor to save the life of a suffering child. But instead I chose Hiroshima, which is slightly less optimistic."

When the murmuring died down, Blanes went on.

"I know what a lot of physicists think about our profession, not just contemporary physicists, and not just bad ones, either: Schrödinger, Jeans, Eddington, Bohr—they all agreed. They thought all we worried about were symbols. 'Shadows,' Schrödinger used to call them. They think that differential equations are not reality. Hearing some colleagues speak, it's as though theoretical physics was just playing house with plastic building blocks. This absurd idea has gained currency, and now people seem to feel that theoretical physicists are little more than dreamers locked away in ivory towers. They think our games, our little houses, bear no relation to their everyday worries, their interests, their problems, or their welfare. But I'm going to tell you something, and I want you to take it as a ground rule for this course. From now on, I will be filling this board with equations. I'll start in one corner and end in another, and I promise you I'll make good use of the space because I have small handwriting." People laughed, but Blanes wasn't joking. "And when I'm done, I want you to do the following: look at those numbers, all those little numbers and Greek letters on the board, and repeat to yourselves, '*This* is reality,' repeat it over and over ..." Elisa swallowed. Blanes added, "Physics equations are the key to our happiness, our fears, our lives, and our deaths. Don't forget it. Ever."

He jumped up onto the dais and raised the screen, grabbed a piece of chalk, and began scribbling on the left-hand side of the board, just as he'd promised. And for the rest of the class, he made no mention of anything besides complex noncommutative algebraic abstractions and advanced topology.

DAVID Blanes was forty-three years old, tall, and appeared to be in good shape. His gray hair was receding and thinning on top, but it just made him look interesting. Elisa had also noticed some things that weren't as obvious in the many photos she'd seen of him: the way he half closed his eyes when he was concentrating; his pockmarked cheeks, no doubt the result of teenage acne; his nose, which was so bulbous in profile it was almost comical. In his own way, Blanes was sort of attractive, but only "in his own way," like so many men who are not famous for their looks. He was dressed in an absurd explorer getup, with camouflage vest, baggy pants, and boots. His voice was hoarse and quiet, and didn't seem to fit his constitution, but he gave off a certain air of authority, a certain desire to rattle people. Maybe, she thought, it was a defense mechanism.

Everything Elisa told Maldonado the day before was 100 percent true, and now that was becoming obvious. Blanes' disposition was "special," more so than the other big names in the field. But it was also true that he'd had to take a lot more flak and faced a lot more prejudice than the others. First, he was Spanish, which meant that for an ambitious physicist (as she and her classmates were all perfectly aware) he was already a fish out of water and at a serious disadvantage. Not because of any discrimination, but because of the pathetic state of physics in Spain. The few achievements made by Spanish physicists had all taken place abroad.

Then, Blanes had made it. And that was even more unforgivable than his nationality.

His success was the result of a few hurried equations that fit on one side of a piece of paper. That's what science comes down to: a collection of short, timeless strokes of genius. He'd written them in 1987, while he was working in Zurich with his mentor, Al-

bert Grossmann, and his colleague Sergio Marini. They were published in 1988 in the prestigious *Annalen der Physik* (the same
journal that, more than eighty years earlier, had published Einstein's article on relativity) and shot him to an almost ridiculous
level of fame. The kind of bizarre celebrity that only very rarely
do scientists achieve. And that in spite of the fact that the article,
which proved the existence of time strings, was so complex that
few specialists, even, understood all of it. Despite its mathematical perfection, it would take decades to obtain any significant experimental proof.

Be that as it may, European and North American physicists reacted to his findings with awe, and that awe filtered through to the
press. The Spanish papers didn't get too excited at first (SPANISH
PHYSICIST DISCOVERS WHY TIME ONLY MOVES FORWARD and
TIME LIKE A SEQUOIA, SAYS SPANISH PHYSICIST were the most
common headlines), but Blanes's popularity in Spain derived more
from the spin put on the news by less-respected publications,
which had no qualms about making declarations like "Spain takes
lead in twentieth-century physics with Blanes's theory," "Professor Blanes affirms that time travel is scientifically possible,"
"Spain could be the first country to a build time machine," and so
on. None of it was true, but it worked. The public ate it up. Magazines began to put his name on the cover next to naked women,
associating him with the mysteries of time. One esoteric publica-
tion sold hundreds of thousands of copies of their Christmas edition with the headline WAS JESUS A TIME TRAVELER? and then, in
smaller type below, "DAVID BLANES'S THEORY DISCONCERTS THE
VATICAN."

Blanes was no longer in Europe to gloat (or take offense). He'd
practically been beamed over to the United States. He gave lectures
and worked at Caltech, and, as if he were following in Einstein's
footsteps, at the Institute for Advanced Study at Princeton, where
great minds strolled through silent gardens with plenty of time
to think and plenty of paper to write on. But in 1993, when Con-

gress voted to terminate the Superconducting Super Collider project in Waxahachie, Texas, aborting construction on what would have been the biggest and most powerful particle accelerator in the world, Blanes suddenly cut short his honeymoon with the United States. His comments became somewhat notorious in the American press shortly before his return to Europe. "This country's government would rather invest in arms than in scientific development. The United States reminds me of Spain, in that it's a country full of talented people ruled by disgusting politicians." Since he'd insulted both countries and their governments equally in his comparison, his assessment managed to offend everyone and please almost no one.

After concluding his U.S. tour, Blanes returned to Zurich, where he lived a life of quiet solitude (his only friends were Grossmann and Marini; the only women in his life, his mother and sister—Elisa admired this monastic existence) and his theory took a real beating, since people had stewed for ages and the results of their long-festering ire appeared regularly in print. Curiously, some of the most vehement rejections of his theory came from the Spanish scientific community. Endless university experts came out of the woodwork to blast the "sequoia theory," as it was being called at the time (in reference to the time strings coiled within particles like the tree rings within a sequoia's ancient trunk used to date them), claiming that it was a beautiful theory but totally inaccurate. Perhaps because he was from Madrid, critics there took a little longer to get going, but perhaps for the same reason, once they did, they really let loose. One famous professor from the Complutense even called his theory "a fantastic pile of poppycock with no basis in reality." Things weren't much better abroad, although at least specialists in string theory like Edward Witten at Princeton and Cumrun Vafa at Harvard claimed that it could still turn out to be an intellectual revolution comparable to the one set off by string theory itself. Stephen Hawking, from his Cambridge wheelchair, was one of the few who came out in

Blanes's defense (albeit not wholeheartedly) and helped circulate his ideas. When they asked him about it, the famous physicist would answer with one of his typical ironic quips, emitted in the cold, inflexible tone of his voice synthesizer. "Though many people want to chop it down, Professor Blanes's sequoia still provides plenty of shade."

Blanes himself was the only one who kept quiet on the subject. His strange silence lasted almost ten years, during which he ran the lab that his friend and mentor Albert Grossmann (now retired) had left in his charge. Due to its great mathematical beauty and fantastic possibilities, the sequoia theory still interested scientists, but no one could prove it. So it slid into the "let's see" category that science so often uses to place ideas in history's freezer. Blanes refused to speak in public about it, and many people assumed he was embarrassed by his errors. Then, in late 2004, his course was advertised—the first one in the world he'd ever give about his "sequoia." He had chosen Spain, of all places, to teach it: Madrid, to be exact. As a private institution, Alighieri would cover all the costs and was willing to accept the scientist's rather odd demands: that the course be taught in July 2005, in Spanish, and that twenty places be awarded strictly on the basis of scores on a rigorous international exam on string theory, noncommutative geometry, and topology. In theory, they'd only accept graduate students, though graduating seniors would be allowed to take the exam if they had a letter of recommendation from their theoretical physics professors. That was how people like Elisa had been able to give it a shot.

Why had Blanes waited so long to give his very first classes about sequoia theory? And why now? Elisa had no idea, but she didn't really care, either. What mattered to her was that she was there. She felt lucky to be in that unique position, in the kind of class she'd only dreamed about.

By the time that first session was over, however, she'd changed her mind considerably.

SHE was one of the first to leave. Without even stopping to stuff her notes into her backpack, she slammed her books and notebook shut and sped out of the room.

As she was walking down the steep road toward the bus stop, she heard a voice.

"Hey ... Excuse me ... Can I give you a ride somewhere?"

She was so pissed off she hadn't even realized there was a car beside her. Víctor "Lennon" Lopera was poking his head out from within it, like an awkward turtle.

"Thanks anyway, but I've got a long ways to go," Elisa said disinterestedly.

"Where to?"

"Claudio Coello."

"Well ... I could take you if you want. I ... I'm going back to Madrid, anyway."

She didn't feel like talking to him, but she thought he might distract her.

She climbed into his messy car, which smelled like mildewed upholstery and was littered with loose papers and books. Lopera drove the way he spoke, slowly and cautiously. But he seemed pleased to have Elisa as a passenger and gradually began to warm up. As with all great introverts, his chatter would at one point suddenly get out of control.

"What did you think of what he said right at the start, about reality? 'Equations are reality' ... Well, if he says so ... I don't know, I thought it was pretty reductive, a real positivist oversimplification ... I mean, that right there is rejecting the possibility of revealed truths and intuitive truths, the foundations of religious belief and common sense, for example ... And that's not right ... I mean, I suppose he says it because he's an atheist ... But in all honesty, I don't think religious faith has to be incompatible with scientific proof ... It's just on another level, like Einstein said. You can't just ..." He stopped at an intersection and paused, waiting for the road to clear before he drove or spoke again. "You can't just convert metaphysical experiences into chemical reactions. That would be absurd ... Heisenberg said ..."

Elisa tuned him out and stared at the road, grunting from time to time. But then later, he murmured, "I noticed it, too, you know. How he treated you, I mean."

She felt her cheeks burn, and thinking about it made her want to cry all over again.

Blanes had asked a few questions in class, but he called on someone sitting two seats to her right to answer them every time. Someone who raised his hand as soon as she did.

Ric Valente Sharpe.

Then, at one point, something happened. Blanes asked a question and she was the only one to raise her hand. Yet instead of calling on her, he prodded the rest of the class to answer. "Come on, what's wrong? Afraid they'll take away your degrees if you're wrong?" A few tense seconds went by, and then Blanes pointed to the same seat once more. And Elisa heard that smooth, soft voice, the almost amused tone, the slight foreign accent. "There's no geometry that's valid on that scale because of the quantum foam phenomenon."

"Very good, Mr. Sharpe."

Five years in a row at the top of her class had turned Elisa into a fiercely competitive woman. There was no way to be number one in the world of science if you didn't possess a predator's instincts, the desire to pick off you rivals, one by one. And that made Blanes's bizarre disdain for her totally insufferable. She didn't want to expose her injured pride, but she couldn't hold it in anymore.

"It was like he couldn't even *see* me," she muttered, holding back her tears.

"Well, the way I see it, he couldn't *stop* seeing you," Lopera replied.

She looked at him.

"I mean, it seems like ... I think he saw you and thought, you

can't have a girl who looks so ... well ... you can't be both ... Well,
I mean, no matter how you look at it, it's sexist. Maybe he doesn't
realize you're the one who came in first on the exam. He doesn't
know your name. He thinks Elisa Robledo is ... well, that she
couldn't be like you."

"And what am I like?" She didn't want to ask that question, but
she no longer cared if she was being cruel.

"Well, there's no reason it's incompatible, really ...," Lopera
blathered on, without addressing her question, as if he were talking to himself. "Though genetically it *is* unusual ... Beauty and
brains, I mean ... They don't often go together. Of course there are
exceptions, Richard Feynman is very good-looking, right? That's
what they say, anyway. And Ric is, too, in a way, don't you think?
A little?"

"Ric?"

"Ric Valente, my friend. I've called him Ric ever since we were
kids. I pointed him out at the party yesterday, remember? Ric Valente."

Just hearing his name was enough to make her gnash her teeth.
Valente Sharpe, Valente Sharpe ... The name took on a mechani-
cal sound in her brain, like an electric saw shredding her pride.
Valente Sharpe, Valente Sharpe...

"He's good-looking and very smart, too, like you," Lopera went
on, oblivious, it seemed, to her feelings. "But he also knows how
to wrap people around his finger, you know? He's a real snake
charmer with his professors ... Well, with everyone, really." His
throat gurgled in what was seemed a bizarre laugh (Elisa would
hear that laugh for many years to come, and would come to find it
charming, but right then she found it repulsive). "Girls, too. Yep,
girls, too, yessiree."

"You act like you're not friends."

"Like we're not ...?" She could almost hear Lopera's hard drive
whirring into action as he processed the banal comment. "Of
course we are ... Or, at least, we were ... We met in grade school,

and we were going to go to college together. But Ric ended up getting one of those killer scholarships and went off to Oxford, lucky duck, to Roger Penrose's department, and we sort of fell out of touch ... He wants to go back to England when Blanes's course is over ... if Blanes doesn't take him back to Zurich, that is."

Lopera gave a fleshy smile with that last sentence, and Elisa disliked it intensely. Her darkest thoughts crept back and she felt totally and utterly dejected, almost comatose. *Blanes will choose Valente Sharpe, obviously.*

"We haven't really seen each other the last four years ...," Lopera went on. "I don't know, maybe I feel like he's changed. He's more ... more sure of himself. I mean, he's a genius, there's no doubt about that, a genius to the third degree, since his father and grandfather are geniuses, too. His father's a cryp ... a cryptographer who works in Washington at some national security organization or something ... His mother's American, she's a math teacher in Baltimore. She was nominated for the Fields Medal last year." Elisa was impressed, against her will. The Fields Medal was awarded in the United States every four years in recognition of outstanding mathematical achievement in the best and most promising mathematicians in the world; it was almost like a Nobel. She wondered how she'd feel if *her* mother had been nominated for the Fields Medal. But right then, all she felt was rage. "They're divorced. And his mother's brother ..."

"Wait, let me guess ... Won the Nobel Prize in chemistry?" Elisa quipped, feeling petty. "Or maybe Niels Bohr is his uncle?"

Lopera emitted that weird sound again; it had to be a laugh.

"No. He's a programmer for Microsoft in California ... What I meant is that Ric's learned a lot from all of them. He's like a sponge. When you think he's not paying attention, he's actually analyzing everything you do and say ... He's a machine. How far up Claudio Coello do you want me to drop you off?"

Elisa told him not to take her all the way home, but he insisted. Stuck in a lunchtime traffic jam in Madrid, they had plenty of time to stop arguing and stew in silence. She spied a couple of books on top of the glove compartment, half hidden under some dog-eared folders. She read the title of one: *Mathematical Games and Puzzles.* The other one was weightier: *Physics and Faith: Scientific and Religious Truth.*

As they were making their way up Claudio Coello, Lopera broke his silence.

"You sure pissed Ric off when he saw you beat him on the entrance exam." And he burst out with another gurgle-giggle.

"Really?"

"God, yes. He's a sore loser. A very sore loser." Suddenly Lopera's expression changed. It was as if he'd thought of something else, something he hadn't considered until right then. "Be careful," he added.

"Of what?"

"Of Ric. Be very careful."

"Why? Can he sway the Fields Medal selection committee, so I'll never get the award?"

Lopera ignored her sarcasm.

"No. He just doesn't like to lose." He stopped the car. "Is this your building?"

"Yeah, thanks. Hey, listen, why do you say I should be careful? What do you think he'd do?"

Instead of looking at her, he stared straight ahead, as if he were still driving.

"Nothing. I just meant that ... he was surprised you came in first, that's all."

"Because I'm a girl?" she asked hotly. "Is that it?"

Victor seemed embarrassed.

"Maybe. He's not used to ... coming in second." Elisa bit her lip to keep from answering. *Me either,* she thought. "But don't worry," he added, trying to cheer her up, or maybe to change the subject. "I'm sure Blanes will appreciate you. He's too good not to see that *you're* good."

That softened her a little, and she resolved not to hate Lopera. When she got to the door of her building, she thought that maybe she'd been rude to him and turned back around to wave, but he'd already driven off. She stood there a minute, lost in thought.

The scene made her recall the night before, with Javier Maldonado. She glanced up and down the street, almost as a reflex, but no one was spying on her. She saw no graying men with big mustaches. *Albert Einstein. Of course! Einstein is Valente's grandfather, and last night he was spying on me. That must be it.*

She smiled and walked to the elevator, deciding that it had been a coincidence. Coincidences were not only possible, they were mathematically probable. Two men with similar features stare at her in one night. Why not? You'd have to be paranoid to stress out about that.

While she was riding up to her floor, she thought about Víctor Lopera's weird warning.

Be careful of Ric.

It was absurd. Valente didn't even know she was alive. He hadn't looked at her once.

06

THE date was set for Saturday afternoon; they were meeting at a café she'd never heard of, near Atocha Street. "You'll like it," Maldonado had promised.

He was right. It was a relaxed place with dark walls and felt like an old theater, mainly because of a red velvet curtain hanging next to the bar. She loved it.

Maldonado sat waiting for her at one of the few occupied tables. Elisa couldn't deny that she was thrilled to see him after the wretched week she'd had.

"I called you a bunch of times yesterday, but the line went dead every time someone picked up."

"The phone wasn't working. It's fixed now, though."

The phone company said it was a "systems failure," but, said Elisa, the one who really had a "systems failure" was her mother, who had been climbing the walls, her restrained voice slightly louder than usual as she threatened to sue them for damages ("I have very important clients who call me at home, in case you didn't realize …"). They assured her they'd send out technicians that very Saturday, and they'd kept their word. And only then did Marta Morandé calm down.

Elisa ordered a Diet Coke and watched, amused, as Maldonado pulled a stack of papers from his backpack.

"More questions?" she joked.

"Yeah. Do you mind?" She told him she didn't as soon as she realized he was serious. "I know it's a pain in the ass," he apologized, "but this is what I do, what can I say? And I really appreciate your helping me out, honestly ... Good journalism is the product of accurate information, patiently compiled," he recited in a dignified tone of that surprised her.

"Of course. I'm sorry ..." *I screwed up,* she thought. But Maldonado's shy smile dissipated her fears.

"No, *I'm* sorry. I'm just a little uptight because the year's almost over and I have to hand in my report ASAP."

"Come on, then," she said encouragingly. "Let's get a move on. Ask away, leave no stone unturned."

Still, their conversation was forced and unnatural at first. He asked formulaic questions about her free time, and she replied hesitantly, as if it were an oral exam. Elisa realized they were both sorry they'd had to start the night with such a different tone than they had at the party. But once Maldonado became interested in her active lifestyle, things picked up. Elisa told him she did everything she could, which was true: weight lifting, swimming, aerobics ... He stared at her.

"Well, that explains your physique."

"What's up with my physique?"

"It's a perfect *physique* for *physics.*"

"That was terrible," she groaned.

"You asked for it."

Then they talked about her childhood. She told him she'd been a lonely child and that she'd lived inside her head, even when she was a little girl, even when she was playing. She'd had no choice, since her parents hadn't wanted any more kids and never paid much attention to her, preferring to spend their time working on their own problems. Her father ("He was a Javier, too") had become a physicist during times when things were "even worse" than they are now. Elisa remembered him as a friendly guy with a dark, bushy beard, but that was about it. He'd spent part of his life in England and the United States researching weak interaction, the force emitted by some atoms when they disintegrate, which was (at least in physics) all the rage in the seventies.

"He spent a long time studying something known as 'CP symmetry violation' caused by kaon … Come on, don't give me that look," Elisa laughed.

"Who me?" Maldonado asked. "I'm just taking notes."

"That's kaon, with a 'k,'" she corrected, pointing to Maldonado's notes.

She was getting more and more into this. Unfortunately, she had to talk about her mother, too. Marta Morandé, a mature, attractive, magnetic woman, owner and operator of Piccarda. *Uncover your beauty … at Piccarda.*

She found it hard to talk about her mother and feel even slightly amused.

"She comes from a family that's always had money, always traveled. I swear I wonder what my father ever saw in her. The thing is, I'm sure that if my mother had been a different kind of person, my father wouldn't have left me alone so much. She was always saying that she had to 'enjoy' life, that she couldn't lock herself up and throw away the key just because she'd married a 'brainiac.' That's what she used to call him. Sometimes even in front of me. 'The braniac's coming back tonight,' she'd say." Maldonado had stopped scribbling. He was listening intently. "I think my father decided it was too much of a hassle to go through with a divorce. And, besides, his family was very Catholic. So he just pretended not to notice, and let my mother get on with her life." Elisa looked down at the table, smiling. "I have to confess, I decided to study physics to annoy my mother, who wanted me to go into business and help her run her famous beauty salon. And boy did I annoy her! That really got her. She stopped speaking to me and moved to her summerhouse in Valencia while my father was out of town. So I was left in Madrid, alone except for my paternal grandparents. When my dad heard, he came straight back and told me he'd never leave me. I didn't believe him, though. A week later he went to Valencia to try to get my mom to sign an agreement. On his way back, a drunk driver crashed into him head-on, and that was the end of that."

She was cold and rubbed her arms. She wasn't actually uneasy talking about it and thought it had probably done her good. After all, who had she ever been able to talk to before this?

"Now I'm back living with my mom," she added. "But we've carved out our own spaces at home, and we both try not to cross the line into each other's territory."

Maldonado was doodling. Elisa realized that their initial tension could easily creep back in and decided to take another tack.

"But still, the time I spent on my own in Madrid did me a lot of good. It gave me the chance to really get to know my grandfather, who was the greatest guy in the world. He was a teacher and he loved history. He'd tell me all about ancient civilizations, and show me books ..."

Maldonado seemed more interested in this topic and started taking notes again.

"Do you like history?" he asked.

"Thanks to my grandfather, I love it. Though I don't actually know that much about it."

"What's your favorite historical period?"

"I don't know," Elisa thought about it. "The ancient civilizations fascinate me: the Egyptians, the Greeks and Romans. My grandfather was really into Imperial Rome. You start thinking about those people, they left so many things behind and then they disappeared forever, and ..."

"And what?"

"I don't know. I like it."

"You like the past?"

"Who doesn't? It's like something we've lost forever, you know?"

"By the way," Maldonado said, as he'd just remembered. "We haven't discussed your ideas about religion. Do you believe in God, Elisa?"

"No. Like I said, my father's family was very Catholic, but my grandfather was smart enough not to burden me with all that. He just instilled me with his values. I never believed in God, not even as a little girl. And now ... this will probably sound weird, but I think of myself as more of a Christian than a believer. I believe in helping others, in sacrifice, liberation, in just about everything Christ advocated, but not in God."

"Why would that seem weird to me?"

"Doesn't it?"

"You don't think Jesus Christ was the son of God?"

"No way. I don't even think there is a God. What I think is that Christ was a really great guy, and really brave, and he knew how to teach people values ..."

"Like your grandpa."

"Yeah. But he wasn't as lucky as my grandfather. He was killed for his ideas. And that's something I do believe in: dying for your ideals."

Maldonado took notes. Suddenly, it occurred to her that those questions were so specific that he must be asking them for personal reasons rather than for his report. She was about to say something when suddenly he put his pen away.

"That's it for me. Do you want to take a walk?" Maldonado asked.

They strolled up to the Puerta del Sol, the very center of Madrid. It was the first Saturday in July; the evening air was warm, and the plaza was crowded with people pouring out of the closing big department stores. After walking in silence, Elisa pretending to be more concerned with avoiding the crowds and gazing at the statue of King Charles III than with talking. Maldonado finally said something.

"So how're things with Blanes?"

That was what she'd been afraid of. If she was going to be honest, she'd have to say that her pride had been not just wounded
but almost slain, that it now lay abandoned in some intensive
care unit in the depths of her personality. She was no longer trying to shine; she wasn't even bothering to raise her hand, no matter what the question was. She just listened and learned. Valente
Sharpe, on the other hand, (who still hadn't even deigned to look
at her), shone more each day. Classmates had started asking *him*
questions, as if he were Blanes, or at least his right-hand man.
And if he wasn't yet, it was only a matter of time, because even
Blanes himself asked for his opinion on things. "Valente, nothing
to say about this?" And Valente Sharpe would respond with glorious exactitude.

Sometimes she thought it was just envy. *But that's not it; it's
more a void. I'm deflated. It's as if I trained for a marathon and
then wasn't allowed to run it.* It was quite clear who Blanes was
going to take with him to Zurich. So all she could do was try to
learn as much as possible about that beautiful theory and come
up with another plan for her professional career.

She wondered if she should tell Maldonado all this, but then
thought she'd probably already told him enough for one night.

"Good," she said. "He's an excellent teacher."

"Still want to do your dissertation with him?"

She hesitated before answering. An enthusiastic yes would
just be a lie, but a curt no wouldn't be honest, either. Emotions
were like quantum uncertainty, she thought.

"Of course," she said coolly, leaving her true feelings hanging
in the air.

They'd walked across the plaza to Madrid's famous statue of
the bear and the strawberry tree—*"el oso y el madroño"*—the symbols of the city. Maldonado asked her if they could stop at one of
the ice cream parlors there to indulge one of his few "weaknesses,"
a chocolate-dipped cone. She laughed at his childlike tone when
he ordered it, and even more at his obvious delight in devouring
it. As they stood there in the plaza, Maldonado savoring his treat,

he suggested they have dinner at a Chinese restaurant. Elisa accepted immediately, glad that the evening was not yet over.

She spotted the man just then, purely by chance.

He was standing by the entrance to the ice cream parlor. Gray hair, big gray mustache. He was holding an ice cream cone, nibbling at it every little while. This guy didn't look as much like the second man as he did the first one. In fact, he looked like he could be the brother of the man from the party. Or maybe— she couldn't be sure—it was actually the same guy, just dressed differently.

No, it couldn't be. Now she saw that his hair was curly, and he was thinner, too. It wasn't the same man.

For a second she thought, *This is not unusual; there's nothing wrong with this picture. It's just a guy looking at me who looks like some other guys who were looking at me.* But suddenly it was as if the floodgates had opened and a whole slew of irrational thoughts rushed into her mind, making a racket and causing a scene, like coked-up party crashers. *Three different men who all look the same. Three men watching me.*

"What's wrong," Maldonado asked.

She couldn't lie. She had to say something.

"That man."

"What man?"

When Maldonado turned around, he wiped his hands on a napkin and no longer looked at Elisa.

"The guy standing by the ice cream parlor. He was giving me a weird look." She really didn't want Maldonado to think she was seeing things, but now she couldn't stop herself. "He looks a lot like another guy I saw at the party at Alighieri, who was also watching me. It could be the same guy."

"Really?"

Just then, the man turned and strode off toward Alcalá Street.

"I don't know, I just got the feeling he was spying on me ..." She tried to laugh it off but couldn't. Maldonado wasn't laughing, either. "Maybe I'm wrong."

He suggested they go to some quiet bar and talk it over. But there were no quiet bars around there, and Elisa was too jittery to walk far. So instead they decided to go to the Chinese place and have dinner. It was still early, and there weren't that many people in the restaurant yet.

"Now. Tell me exactly what happened the other day. Every detail," he said once they'd sat down at a quiet, out-of-the-way table. He listened carefully, and then asked her for a detailed description of the man she'd seen at Alighieri. But before she could finish giving it, he interrupted her. "Hang on ... Gray hair, mustache. I know that guy. It sounds like Espalza; he's a statistics professor. He gave some guest lectures in my sociological stats class, but I know him more because he's in the teachers' association and I'm in the students' association ..." He paused and then adopted that mischievous look that she loved. "He's also divorced and has a reputation as a perv. He's always ogling gorgeous students. He must have really been slobbering over you ..."

She suddenly wanted to laugh.

"You know what else happened, that same night? When you dropped me off at home, this other guy with a mustache was staring at me ..." Maldonado widened his eyes comically. "And that guy today had a mustache, too."

"Why, it's a ... a mustachioed conspiracy!" he murmured, feigning alarm. "A-*ha,* now I see!"

Elisa burst out laughing. How could she have been so stupid? There was only one explanation: finishing college and starting Blanes's course had taken a toll on her nerves. She laughed until tears streamed down her face. Maldonado's expression changed abruptly as he stared at something behind her.

"Good God!" he said, sounding scared. "The waiter!" Elisa turned to look, wiping the tears from her cheeks. The waiter was Asian, but (and this struck Elisa as unusual for an Asian man) he wore a big, black bushy mustache. "Another mustache. And this time it's a Chinese mustache!"

"OK, OK," she laughed again. "Enough already."

"Let's get out of here, we're surrounded," he whispered.

Elisa had to hide her smirk with a napkin when the waiter actually came to take their order.

SHE was still giggling when she got home that night.

Javier Maldonado was a great guy. Really great. He'd made her laugh all night, telling stories about professors and classmates, including Espalza and his tendency to pick up anything young with boobs. Hearing those banal stories had been like a breath of fresh air for Elisa, after having spent too long in a sea of books and equations. And what was more, when she'd finally had enough, he picked up on it instantly and took her right home. He hadn't driven, but he rode back with her on the metro to Retiro, the closest stop to her house. His mischievous face stayed with Elisa as she got off the train, and she kept picturing it on the walk back.

She came to the conclusion that although it was unfair to say she'd come very far in her relationship with Maldonado, she had taken a few steps. She was no fool; she been through this before. One of the advantages of her solitary lifestyle was that she'd learned to depend solely on herself. She'd been out with a few boys, especially when she just started college, and she thought she knew what she wanted. What she had with Maldonado was a friendship for now, but things seemed to be moving along.

The apartment was dark and silent. When she turned on the entry-hall light she saw a note her mother had taped to the door-frame: "I WON'T BE BACK TONIGHT. THE CLEANING GIRL LEFT YOU SOME DINNER IN THE FRIDGE." The cleaning "girl" was a robust forty-five-year-old Romanian, but her mother had called every maid she'd ever had a "girl." She turned the living-room light on and the entry-hall one off, wondering why her mother felt the need to inform her of the obvious. Marta Morandé took every weekend off; even the society pages knew that. Most times she didn't come back until Monday. There were plenty of gentlemen who invited her to spend a few days at their luxurious abodes. She shrugged. What did she care what her mother did?

She turned the living-room light off and the hall light on, knowing there would be no one there. The "girl" had Sundays off and always spent Saturday nights with her sister in the apartment she rented in the outskirts of Madrid. Elisa loved those nights when she had the whole house to herself, knowing she wouldn't be interrupted by her mother's annoying presence or the maid hovering around.

She walked down the hall, turned the corner, and headed for her room. Out of the blue, she recalled the "mustachioed conspiracy" and laughed out loud. *Watch, now there'll be another one waiting in my room. Or hiding under the bed.*

She opened the door. The coast was clear of mustaches. After closing it behind her, Elisa hesitated for a moment and then locked it, too.

Her room was her little bunker, her fortress, the place in which she lived and studied. She'd had many a fight with her mother about it, insisting that she mind her own business and keep out. She'd been cleaning her own room, making her bed, and changing her own sheets for ages. She didn't want anybody rummaging through her things.

Elisa kicked off her shoes, took off her jeans, threw them on the floor, and then turned on her computer. She thought she'd check her e-mail, since no messages had gotten through while the phone line was down.

As she logged on, she wondered what to do that night. She wasn't going to study, she knew that for sure. She was tired, but didn't feel like going to bed yet. Maybe she'd look at some of the erotica she kept on her hard drive, or visit a chat room or one of her "special" pages. Electronic sex had been the fastest and most antiseptic way for her to handle her long period of hibernation while she studied around the clock. She decided she really didn't feel like it right then, though.

She had two unread messages. The first was from an electronic math journal. The second one had no subject line and showed the little paper-clip icon, indicating it was sent with an attachment. She couldn't place the address:

mercurio0013@mercuryfriend.net.

It had "virus" written all over it. Deciding not to open it, she selected the message and hit "delete." Immediately, her screen went dark.

For a second, she thought it was a power outage, but then she realized that her lamp was still on. She was going to crawl behind her desk to check the cables when suddenly the screen came back on; one photo filled it entirely. A couple seconds later, it clicked to another one. Then another.

Elisa sat there, speechless.

They were black-and-white drawings, old-fashioned looking. She guessed the style dated from the early twentieth century. They were all pretty similar: nude men and women, with other nude men and women sitting astride them, riding them. Beneath each one, in red capital letters, the question "DO YOU LIKE IT?"

She watched the little parade of images, unable to do anything to stop it. Her keyboard wasn't responding; the computer seemed to have a will of its own.

Bastards. She was sure that, somehow, despite all her precautions, it was a virus. Then she froze.

The slide show ended, and the screen now showed a black background with big red capital letters that resembled bloody claw marks. She saw the sentence before another electronic flicker made it disappear, and then her regular e-mail page came back up.

The message was gone. As if it had never existed.

She contemplated the words and shook her head.

That can't have referred to me. That was some random ad.

What it said was:

THEY'RE WATCHING YOU

07

THE following Tuesday, she again heard from "mercuryfriend." Configuring her e-mail software to block the address did nothing. She turned off her computer, but when she rebooted, the message opened automatically and filled her screen with similar drawings and identical words, though this time rather than early twentieth-century artworks, they appeared to be modern graphic art: airbrushed bodies and three-dimensional computer-generated reproductions. They were still all men and women, this time walking or running, wearing boots and harnesses and carrying other people on their shoulders. Elisa stopped looking.

She had an idea. She searched the Web for mercuryfriend.net and was not surprised to find that it had unrestricted access and she could get onto the page with no trouble. Tons of banners for bars and clubs with bizarre names flashed on a hideously loud purple background. Abbadon, Euclid, Gobbledygook, Mister X, Scorpio—they all seemed to be very colorful places offering live shows, opportunities for swingers, and outrageous "hosts" and "hostesses." So, that was it, then. Just as she'd suspected, it was some sort of ad. Somehow she had inadvertently given those pigs her address, and now they were bombarding her with spam. She'd have to find a way to deal with it; maybe she'd have to change her e-mail address. But she was relieved to know that there was nothing personal in the messages.

She'd made her peace with the Mustache Mob, too. She'd hardly even thought about them since Maldonado had calmed her fears. Hardly. A couple of times she'd seen gray-haired men with mustaches on the street and felt a little shiver run through her. Sometimes she could spot them from a long way off. But she understood that, subconsciously, her brain searched them out. None of them seemed to be spying on her or following her, and by the time the weekend rolled around again she'd even forgotten about them. Or at least stopped thinking they were somehow meaningful.

She had other things on her mind.

ON Friday, she decided it was time to take a different tack in Blanes's class.

"How do you think we might solve this?"

Blanes pointed to one of his equations, scribbled on the board in his tiny chicken scrawl. Elisa and the rest of the class were more than used to his writing, though, and they could read those symbols as easily as if they'd been written as words and not numbers. They expressed the fundamental question of the theory: How can we identify and isolate finite time strings if they have only one end?

It was a mind-blowing concept. Mathematically, it could be proven that time strings only came to an end on one side. To use a simile, Blanes drew a line on the blackboard and asked them to imagine that it was a loose thread on a table: one end would be the "future" and the other the "past." The thread would move in the direction of the future, which he indicated with an arrow. He couldn't do it any other way, since according to the equations, the "end" of the past, that is, the left-hand end of the thread, simply didn't exist (this was the famous proof of why time moved only in one direction, which had brought Blanes so much fame). He represented this fact by drawing a question mark. There was no loose end that could be identified as "past."

(past) ? _____ → **(future)**

The most incredible thing about it, however, the thing that defied logic, was that despite the fact that the string had only one end, *it was not infinite.*

The "past" side ended, but that end wasn't an end.

That paradox made Elisa's head spin. She loved it. She always got that feeling when she had insights into how weird and wonderful the world was. How was it possible that all of reality, the most personal things in our lives, could be made up of something as crazy as tiny little strings whose ends *weren't ends?*

At any rate, she was convinced she knew the answer to the question Blanes was asking. She didn't even have to write it down. She'd worked it out at home, and she had the answer in her head.

Swallowing hard, yet sure of herself, she decided to take a chance.

Twenty pairs of eyes were glued to the board, but only one hand shot up.

Valente Sharpe's.

"Tell us, Valente," Blanes smiled.

"If there were curls in the middle of each string, we could identify them, even isolate them using discrete quantities of energy, if that energy were enough to separate the curls. What I mean is ..." There followed a torrent of mathematical language.

No one said a word. The whole class, including Blanes, was left speechless.

Valente, however, wasn't the one who had answered. As if he were a ventriloquist's dummy, he'd opened his mouth, but another voice two seats to his left had interrupted him and stolen the show.

Everyone stared at Elisa. She looked only at Blanes. She

could hear her heart beating and feel her cheeks burning, as if she'd whispered sweet nothings rather than math equations. She awaited the consequences of her actions, feeling his half-closed eyes on her (it was a typical Blanes look that reminded her of Robert Mitchum) and yet managing to remain unbelievably calm all the same. Her hotheadedness, which under normal circumstances she thought of as her number one defect, now worked to her advantage: she was sure she was right and was prepared to fight for it, regardless of who her opponent was.

"I don't recall having called on you, Miss . . . ," Blanes said in a tone as inexpressive as his face, though she felt a hard edge to his comment. The silence grew thick.

"Robledo," Elisa replied. "And you didn't see me raise my hand because I didn't. I've been trying every day for over a week and you never seem to see me, so this time I decided to speak."

Everyone turned to watch Blanes and Elisa, as if they were tennis pros in a match that had come down to the final seconds of the deciding set. Then Blanes turned back to Valente and smiled.

"Please, go ahead, Valente," he asked again.

Valente, sitting there primly, with his thin lanky body and white skin, looked like an ice sculpture seated at a desk. He answered immediately, in a loud, clear voice.

As she watched his emaciated profile, Elisa had to admire one simple detail: even though Valente gave *the same reply* as her, he did it in his own way, using his own words, somehow making it seem as if that was what he'd been thinking all along, before he'd even heard her, even making a slight mistake with his variables that Blanes quickly corrected. *Defending his territory, like me,* she thought, pleasantly surprised. *So now we're tied, Valente Sharpe.*

When Valente finished his elucidation, Blanes said, "Very good. Thank you." Then he looked down and stared at a spot between his feet.

"This course is for theoretical physics graduates," he proceeded quietly, his voice hoarse. "For adults. If any more of you are planning to have childish outbursts, I would kindly ask you to leave the room first. Please keep that in mind." Then, looking up again, this time neither at Valente nor Elisa but at the whole class, he added in the same hushed tone, "Aside from that, Ms. Robledo's solution is brilliant."

She felt a chill. *He's naming me because I was the first one to say it.* She recalled something one of her optics professors used to say: "In science, you're allowed to be a complete asshole; just make sure you're the *first* asshole." She didn't, however, feel any great pleasure, or even glee. In fact, a wave of shame swept over her.

Out of the corner of her eye, she watched Valente Sharpe's inexpressive profile. *Congratulations, Elisa. Today you were the first asshole.*

She looked down and shielded her eyes with her hand to hide her tears.

WHEN Elisa got home, she was so flustered by the morning's events that she didn't even care about the new e-mail from mercuryfriend in her inbox. Since she knew the attachment would kick into action and fill her screen no matter what she did, she just went ahead and opened it. The slide show began.

She was about to look away when she noticed a difference.

Mixed in among the erotic drawings were others: a man walking, hunched over under the weight of a stone on his shoulders; a World War I soldier carrying a girl in a little chair on his back; a male dancer on another man's shoulders ... Finally, in the same red letters on black background, appeared a new, enigmatic proclamation: "IF YOU ARE WHO YOU THINK YOU ARE, YOU'LL KNOW."

What was that about? Uncomprehending, Elisa shrugged and turned off her computer. But she had a strange feeling and stood motionless in front of the screen a few more seconds.

She decided it must have been some random detail, something

she'd forgotten and was trying to remember. Sooner or later, it would come to her.

Next she took off her clothes and took a long, hot shower to help her relax. By the time she emerged from the bathroom, she'd forgotten all about the message and was thinking about what had happened in class. Blanes's scorn spurred her on. *The harder I try, the more he hates me.* Without even getting dressed, she spread her towel on the bed and stretched out on it with her notes and books, planning to make a few calculations that she thought might help her with the project she had to hand in.

There were only five days of class left. The last one was planned to coincide with a two-day international symposium at the Palacio de Congresos that some of the world's best physicists would be attending, including Stephen Hawking and Blanes himself. By that date, each student had to hand in a study examining possible solutions to the problems thrown up by the sequoia theory.

Elisa tried out a new idea. The results were unclear, but just knowing she had a path to follow made her feel better.

Unfortunately, she lost her cool in no time flat.

Leaving her room to get something to eat, she bumped into her mother, who was dutifully doing her best to make Elisa's life difficult.

"Well! I didn't even know you were back. You just lock yourself up in your room and don't even say hello ..."

"Well, now you know. I'm back."

They'd met in the hallway. Her mother, impeccably dressed and perfectly coiffed, smelled like the kind of perfume that has full-page ads in fashion magazines, ads generally picturing naked women. Elisa, on the other hand, had thrown on an old robe and knew she looked like a mess. She guessed her mother would comment on it, and she wasn't wrong.

"You could at least put on some pajamas and brush your hair. Have you had lunch yet?"

"No."

She headed for the kitchen, barefoot, and remembered to tie her robe shut when she saw the "girl." Dishes of food, covered in Saran Wrap, were (as usual) artistically prepared and presented. That was how Marta Morandé, baroness of Piccarda, insisted things be done. Elisa had given up on requesting simple food that she could eat with her fingers to save time; trying to go against her mother's wishes was like banging her head against a wall. Today was risotto. She ate until her stomach stopped grumbling, and then suddenly was struck by another idea. Elisa played with her fork as she sat in the kitchen drinking water, stretching her long, bare, tan legs while her brain tackled the equations in question from various angles. She was unaware of Marta Morandé's presence and only registered that her mother was standing there when she spoke.

"... a very nice person. She says her friend's son was one of your classmates at college. We talked all about you."

She stared at her mother, glassy eyed.

"What?"

"You won't recognize her name. She's a new client, and very, *very* well connected ..." Her mother paused to pop one of the diet pills that she always took with a full glass of water at lunchtime. "She asked me if I was your mother. 'They say your daughter's a genius,' she said. I know you don't like it, but I was very proud to brag about you. Of course, I didn't have to do much bragging; this woman already thought you walked on water. She wanted to know what it was like to live with a mathematical mastermind ..."

"Oh." Elisa suddenly realized why her mother was so happy. She cared only about her daughter's achievements when they came in handy at the beauty salon. Especially when she could use them to show off in front of a new "client," and even more so if she was "very, *very* well connected." It bugged her that the word "mastermind," lexically speaking, referred explicitly to men. Who ever said "mistressmind"?

"'And not only that,' this woman said, 'but I've heard she's gorgeous.' I told her you were. 'She's the perfect girl,' I told her."

"Save the irony."

Leaning against the fridge, Marta Morandé turned to look at her.

"I'm being serious ..."

"Well, don't, please."

"Can I just say something?" Elisa didn't answer. Her mother stared at her. "When people talk about you like that, like this woman did today, I feel so proud. It's true, I do. But I can't help thinking what it would be like if, on top of *being* perfect, you just made a little effort to *look* the part ..."

"Why bother when you're around?" Elisa replied. "After all, you're ... what does your Christian psychology book call it? 'Virtue incarnate'? I wouldn't want to step on your toes."

But Marta Morandé blathered on as if she hadn't heard.

"While I was listening to that wonderful woman sing your praises, I was thinking, 'What would she think if she knew how little effort my daughter puts into anything?' She even said she bet you were getting job offers left and right, now that you've finished school."

Elisa went on guard. This was a slippery slope that inevitably led into the abyss of a bitter argument. She knew her mother wanted her degree to "get her somewhere," wanted her to get an important post in some company. Marta Morandé's mind could conceive of nothing theoretical.

"Where are you going?"

Elisa, who'd started out of the room, didn't stop.

"I have stuff to do." She pushed through the swinging doors and got out of the kitchen, but not in time to to avoid hearing her mother's parting shot.

"I have stuff to do, too, you know, but every once in a while I'm considerate enough to spend a little time with you."

"That's your problem."

She practically ran through the living room, bumping into the "girl" when she reached the hall. Elisa realized that her robe was hanging open, but she didn't care. She heard heels clicking behind her and decided to face up to her mother.

"Leave me alone, will you?"

"Of course," her mother said coldly. "There's nothing I want more in the world. But you should start thinking about leaving *me* alone, too ..."

"I try my best."

" ... and in the meantime, I remind you that you're living under my roof and you will obey my rules."

"Whatever you say." There was no use; she didn't have the energy to keep fighting. She started to turn back around, but stopped in her tracks when she heard her mother say, "People would change their minds about you if they knew the truth!"

"Yeah? And what's that?" she challenged.

"That you're a child," her mother replied calmly. The woman never raised her voice. Elisa was good at calculating equations, but there was no one like Marta Morandé when it came to calculating emotions. "That you're twenty-three years old and you're still a child who doesn't care about her appearance, or about getting a job, or about other people ..."

A child. She felt like she'd been punched in the stomach. *What could you expect from a child but childish outbursts in class?*

"Do you want me to pay rent?" she asked through clenched teeth.

Her mother stopped in her tracks. But then, perfectly calm, she replied, "You know that's not it. All I want is for you to come back down to planet Earth, Elisa. Sooner or later, you'll realize that there's more to life than sleeping in that pigpen of a room, studying math, and strutting around the house half naked while you eat your—" She slammed the door in her mother's face, cutting the tirade short.

For a while, she leaned against the door, as if she thought her mother was going to break it down. But all she heard were expensive heels, clicking away into the distance. In order to calm herself down a little, she looked at her notes and the books spread all over her bed. Just seeing them relaxed her.

She soon became engrossed with another matter far more important to her.

Elisa understood the meaning of those messages from mercury-friend.

SITTING at her desk, she grabbed a piece of paper, a pencil, and a ruler.

Bodies carrying other bodies on their backs. The soldier and the girl.

She made a sketch using the same pattern: a stick figure, with another on its shoulders. Then, using a finer pencil, she traced three squares around the figures, leaving a triangle in the center. She contemplated the result.

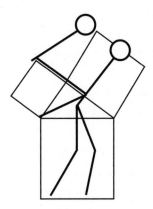

Next, she carefully erased the stick figures, trying to leave the lines she traced beneath them intact. Then she retraced the places she'd accidentally erased.

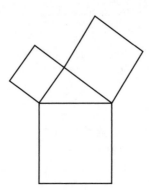

Any math student worth their salt knew that diagram by heart. It was Euclid's Postulate 47, from the first book of *Elements*. In it, the brilliant Greek mathematician proposed an elegant means of proving the Pythagorean theorem. It was easy to demonstrate that in a right triangle like the one above, the sum of the squares of the lengths of the sides is equal to the square of the length of the hypotenuse.

Over the centuries, Euclid's proof had become popular among mathematicians using allusive drawings, the most famous of which was a soldier carrying his girlfriend in a chair on his back. That drawing, known as the "sweetheart seat," had given her the key. She realized that the rest of the figures must have been taken from some sort of art book related to math (not erotica!), and even remembered having seen one once.

If you are who you think you are, you'll know.

She shivered. Could it be?

No one without a great deal of mathematical knowledge would have been able to make that kind of connection among the drawings. The anonymous sender wanted to tell her that only someone like her could come up with the solution. She had to conclude that it wasn't a coincidence.

That message is for me.

But what did it mean?

Euclid.

That new realization and all the possibilities it held made her feel dizzy.

She turned on her computer and went online. Directing her browser to the mercuryfriend.net page, she looked at the ads for the bars and clubs it listed.

Her mouth ran dry.

The ad for Euclid, on first glance, looked much like the rest. The club's name in big red letters, and beneath that the words "classy place for intimate encounters." But something else was written below:

Friday, July 8, 11:15 p.m.
Special reception. Come down and we'll talk.
You'll be interested.

She couldn't breathe.

Today was July 8.

08

"I didn't know you were going out tonight," her mother said, flipping through a magazine as she half watched the television. She stared at her daughter from over the tops of her reading glasses.

"I'm meeting a friend," she lied. Or maybe it wasn't a lie. Who knew?

"That journalism student?"

"Yeah."

"I'm glad. It's good for you to get to know people."

Elisa was surprised. Last week she'd made a comment about Javier Maldonado, just something banal to fill the silence that always stretched between them. She thought her mother hadn't even registered it, but now she saw how wrong she was. She was intrigued by this sudden maternal interest; she'd always assumed that neither of them could care less what the other did, or with whom. *What's the difference? It's all a lie.* She heard her say one more thing (it might have been "Have a good time") as she walked out. She smiled, since she had no idea what kind of time she was going to have. She didn't even know exactly where she was going.

Because Club Euclid didn't exist.

The address was correct—a narrow street in the Chueca neighborhood—but she'd found no reference to a bar or club with that name in any guidebook or listings of any kind, there or anywhere else in Madrid. Paradoxically, that reassured her. Elisa was convinced that July 8 was intended specifically for her.

She reasoned that if the place had been easy to find, then the whole string of coincidences (the message, the Web page, Euclid's theorem, the club's existence) would have been too much. But the fact that it wasn't listed anywhere, in any paper or guidebook, piqued her curiosity, especially after she verified that the other places *were* for real. Maybe that meant that it was all just a fantasy. Or maybe it was a sign that her messenger had hatched a clever plan, using Euclid's name to draw her to a specific place at a specific time. But why? Who could it be and what did they want?

When she got off the subway at Chueca and walked out into the warm night air amid throngs of young people of all races, there was so much noise pouring out of so many different bars that she couldn't help but feel uneasy. Not for any reason in particular (because she neither hoped for nor feared anything specific), but she had this feeling, this slight tingling sensation on her back, under her T-shirt and cardigan. She was glad that her outfit, complete with ripped jeans, didn't attract any attention there.

The address she had was for the end of one of the narrow streets that led off the plaza, between two other doorways. It was either a bar or a club, or both, though it wasn't called Euclid. The neon sign was missing some letters, but Elisa didn't care about that. She did notice, though, that it had smoked glass and swinging doors. Aside from that, it didn't appear to be any secret hideout or clandestine gambling den that relied on mathematical subterfuge to attract gorgeous young physics graduates in order to subject them to cruel, humiliating acts. People came and went, the Chemical Brothers blared over the sound system, and there didn't seem to be any bouncers at the door. Her watch said ten past eleven. She decided to go in.

There was a spiral staircase, and as she wound her way down, she saw a fairly nice scene. The small dance floor was packed, making it look even smaller. The only lights (red) were coming from the bar at the far end of the room, so all she could make out were random arms, thighs, hair, and backs, all tinged with the same reddish glow. The music was so loud that Elisa was sure that if it were turned off now, everyone's ears would continue to ring for hours. At least the air-conditioning seemed to be working. *So, what else do I have to do, Mr. Euclid?*

When she got to the bottom of the stairs, she blended in with the shadows. It was hard to make her way anywhere without touching people or being touched. *Maybe we're supposed to meet at the bar.* She headed for it, using her hands to help clear a path.

Suddenly, someone used his hands on *her.* A firm grasp on her arm.

"Come on!" She heard the voice. "Hurry up!"

She was shocked, but she obeyed.

THEN came a quick succession of images. They made their way to the back of the bar where the bathrooms were, went up another staircase, narrower than the one she'd come down, and then down a short hallway that led to a door with a metal push bar and a pneumatic closer and an Exit sign above it. When they reached the door, he pushed the bar and opened it a few inches. After peering out, he closed it again and then turned to her.

Elisa, who had followed him as if she'd been on a leash, wondered what was going to happen next. Under the circumstances, it could be anything. But even she wasn't expecting his question and assumed she'd misheard.

"My cell phone?"

"Yeah. Do you have it on you?"

"Of course."

"Give it to me."

Speechless, she shoved her hand into her jeans pocket. She'd barely managed to extract it when he snatched the phone away from her.

"Stay here and keep a look out."

He snuck into the alley and she stood by the door, peeking through the crack just in time to see him cross the narrow street and (she could hardly believe this) throw her phone into a trash can tied to a streetlight. Then he came back and closed the door.

"Did you see where I left it?"

"Yeah, but what the . . ."

He put a finger to his lips.

"Shh. They'll be right here."

In the silence that followed, she watched him and he watched the street.

"Here they come," he said suddenly. He'd lowered his voice to a whisper. "Come over here—slowly." Again she felt compelled to obey him, despite the fact that she had no desire to stand right next to him. "Look."

Through the crack in the door all she could see was a car tearing down the narrow street, its engine roaring, and a man across the street, reaching into the trash. Another car drove by, and then another. When they'd gone and her line of sight was clear, she saw that he'd extracted something from the trash and was shaking it off angrily, cleaning it. She didn't have to squint to see what he held. It was her phone, there was no doubt. The man opened it and its little blue screen lit up. She'd never seen the guy before. He was bald and wore a short-sleeved shirt and (she was almost surprised) had no mustache.

All of a sudden, he turned toward them. Then she couldn't see.

"We don't want them to see us, now, do we?" the man whispered in her ear, after closing the door. "That would ruin the plan . . ." Then he smiled in a way that made Elisa very uncomfortable. "I should check to see if you're wearing a wire . . . Maybe underneath your clothes, hidden on your body . . . But there'll be plenty of time later on tonight for me to give you a thorough search."

She said nothing, unsure of what shocked her more: the guy she just saw digging through the trash for her cell phone, or him, with his incredible cold blue-green eyes and voice layered with that mocking tone. Still, when he barked another order, she obeyed immediately.

"Let's go," said Valente Sharpe.

"**HOW** could anyone have put a transmitter in my phone?"

"Are you sure you didn't leave it anywhere? Or lend it to anyone, even for a second?"

"Positive."

"Did anything break at home recently? Washing machine? TV? Anything that would require a serviceman to come to your house?"

"No. I ..." Then she remembered. "The phone line. Last week they came to fix it."

"And you were home, of course. And your cell phone was in your room."

"But it hardly took any time ... They just ..."

"Oh," Ric Valente smiled. "They had enough time to bug your toilet seat if they wanted to, I can assure you. They might be clumsy, but this is one thing they do all the time; they've got it down pat."

They'd reached the Plaza de España. Valente turned toward Ferraz. He drove slowly, serenely, accepting the customary Friday night traffic. He'd told Elisa that the car they were in was "safe" (a friend had lent it to him for the night), but added that the last thing he wanted was to get pulled over by the cops and have them ask for his ID. Elisa listened, thinking that considering all that had happened (and was happening), a ticket was the last thing on her mind. Her brain was like a Gordian knot. Every little while she looked over at Valente's aquiline profile and wondered if he were insane. He seemed to realize this.

"I know this is hard for you to believe, sweetheart. Let's see if I can't give you a little more proof. Have you had the feeling that people were following you recently? People who looked the same? I dunno, redheads, or cops, or street sweepers?"

Elisa was stunned. She felt like she'd just awoken from what she thought was a nightmare only to find someone telling her that she had never been sleeping. When she told Valente about the men with gray mustaches, he gave a hollow laugh as he braked at a red light.

"Mine were beggars. In the industry, they're known as decoys. Red herrings. They're not really watching you at all; in fact, just the opposite. All they're trying to do is get you to notice them. You know, like in the movies, there's always some guy that the protagonist notices, sitting there pretending to read the paper or wait for a bus, all the while actually spying on him. But in real life, all you ever see are the decoys. Believe me, I know what I'm talking about," he added, turning his pasty face toward her. "My father is a surveillance specialist. He says decoys are used for purely psychological reasons. If you think there are men with gray mustaches watching you, your brain will seek them out unconsciously and discard anyone who doesn't fit the bill. Then you convince yourself that you're being paranoid, lower your guard, and stop noticing other strange coincidences. Meanwhile, the real spies have a field day. Though my guess is that we've given them the slip for the eve."

Elisa was impressed. What Valente was saying was *exactly* what she'd been feeling over the past few days. She was going to ask another question when she realized he'd pulled over. He parked quickly beside a big Dumpster and began walking down toward Paseo de Pintor Rosales. She kept pace with him, still feeling dazed, having no idea where they were headed (she'd already asked and he hadn't answered, and she had too many other important concerns to repeat the question). So now she followed him without complaining as she tried to fit the pieces of that mind-boggling puzzle together.

"You say they're watching us, but who is 'they'? And why?"

"I'm not sure." Valente's hands were jammed down into his pockets, and though he appeared calm, she felt like he was walking awfully fast. She had trouble falling in with his meticulous steps. "Have you ever heard of ECHELON?"

"It rings a bell. I read something about it awhile ago. Some kind of ... international surveillance system, right?"

"*The* surveillance system, the most important one in the world, sweetheart. My father used to work for them, that's how I know. Did you know that everything you say on the phone, or buy with a credit card, or search on the Internet is tracked, examined, and filtered by computers? ECHELON tracks all of us, every citizen in the country, and ranks us according to our perceived threat. If the computers decide we're of interest, up goes a red flag, and then they really start to trail us: decoys, bugs, the whole shebang. That's ECHELON, the global Big Brother. We have to watch our asses, they say, so we don't end up sitting on broken glass. September 11 in New York and March 11 in Madrid brought us right back to Adam and Eve days. We're stark naked, and they're watching. ECHELON isn't Spanish, though. It's American. My dad once told me that Europe has something comparable, a surveillance system that uses similar tactics. Maybe that's who's watching us."

"I'm hearing you loud and clear, but I have to say ... this all seems ... I mean, why would ECHELON, or anybody, care about us?"

"I don't know. But I have an idea. And that's what we're going to find out."

"What's your idea?"

"They're watching us because we're the top two in Blanes's class."

Elisa laughed out loud. It was true that great physicists tended to be a little weird, but Valente appeared to be a total freak.

"You *must* be joking."

Valente stopped short and looked at her, hard. He was wearing, as usual, flamboyant clothes: white jeans and an off-white sweater with such a wide neckline that it almost slid off one of his bony shoulders. His straw-colored hair fell into his eyes. She heard the irritation in his voice.

"Listen, sweetheart. I went to a lot of trouble to organize this little meeting. I've spent a whole week sending you little drawings and hoping you were smart enough to decipher the message, OK? If you don't believe me, that's your problem. I'm not going to waste any more time with you."

He turned around and banged on a door. Elisa thought life with Valente Sharpe must be anything but dull. The door opened, revealing a dark hallway and the shadowy features of a man. Valente went in and turned to her.

"If you want to come in, hurry up. Otherwise, fuck off."

"Come in?" Elisa glanced into the darkness. The olive-skinned man watched her, a strange glint in his eye. "To where?"

"My house." Valente smiled. "Sorry it has to be the service entrance. Still standing there? Forget it." He turned to the man. "Slam the door in her face, Faouzi."

The heavy wood door closed in her face with a resounding boom. But almost immediately, it opened again, and Valente's amused face peeked out.

"By the way, have you already answered the questionnaire? How did they get you to do it? Was it that guy talking to you at the party? Who did he say he was, a journalist? Student? Admirer?"

That was it. It was as if someone had handed her the missing piece of the puzzle, the thing she'd unconsciously been searching for right from the start. And now she could see it all so clearly.

It was so obvious, so clear, so appalling.

Valente burst out laughing, though it was an almost silent laugh: all he did was open his mouth wide, giving her a quick glimpse of his pharynx, and squint.

"Judging by the idiotic look on your face, anyone would think that ... Don't tell me you *liked* that guy!" Elisa stood very still, unblinking, not even breathing. Valente seemed to come to life, as if her expression delighted him. "Unbelievable. You're even dumber than I thought! You might be good at math, but you have the social skills of a hippopotamus, hey, sweetheart? How disappointing! For both of us." He made as if to close the door again, and then asked, "Are you coming in or not?"

Elisa didn't move.

09

THE place was strange and creepy, like its owner. Her first impression turned out to be right: it wasn't a house, but an apartment building. Valente confirmed this as they climbed up what must surely have been the building's original stone staircase.

"My uncle bought all the apartments. Some of them belonged to his father, some to his sister and his cousin. He totally renovated them, and now he has more space than he needs. I, on the other hand," he added, "don't have *as much* as I need."

Elisa wondered how much space Valente thought he needed. She realized that this damp, dark den buried in the middle of Madrid was three times the size of her mother's apartment. But, as she followed his footsteps up the stairs, she was sure of one thing: she could never live there, in that murky darkness that smelled like mildewed brick.

From someplace on the first landing came a ghostly voice; it sounded like a starving man, repeating different versions of the same word over and over. She could vaguely make it out: "Astarte," "Venus," "Aphrodite." Neither Valente nor his butler turned a hair, but when they reached the first floor, Faouzi, who was ahead of them, stopped and opened a door. While she was crossing the hall toward the next flight of stairs, she couldn't help but try to see through the door. It was an enormous room, and she spied a man in pajamas sitting beside a lamp. The butler approached him and spoke loudly, with a strong Moroccan accent. "What's the matter with you today? Why so much complaining?" "Kali." "Yeah, yeah, Kali, I know."

"That's my uncle. My father's brother," Ric Valente said, still climbing up the stairs two by two. "He used to be a philologist. Then he went senile, and now he spends all day reciting goddesses' names. I wish he'd die. The house is his; I have only one floor. As soon as he dies, I'll get the whole thing. It's already been decided. He doesn't recognize anybody, doesn't care about anything, doesn't even know who I am. So his death will benefit everybody."

He'd said it with such indifference, without even hesitating. It wasn't just the words themselves, which she'd immediately thought were cruel, but the cold way he'd pronounced them that Elisa intensely disliked. She remembered Víctor's warning *(Be careful with Ric)*, but when she stood at the door being insulted, moments ago, she'd decided that she wasn't going to back out. She wanted to know what Valente had to tell her.

The sheer size of the house dumbfounded her. The landing they were on, which seemed to be the last one, opened out onto a foyer with two doors on one side and a hallway straight ahead, with several more doors coming off it. This floor smelled different than the other ones, like books and wood. There were wall lights with dimmers, and it was clear that this whole part of the building had been recently remodeled.

"Is this ... your floor?"

"Yep, all of it."

She would have liked him to give her a tour of the bizarre museum-like house, but Ric Valente did not appear to be a man concerned with niceties. She watched him stride down the labyrinthine hallway and stop at the other end, grabbing a door handle. All of a sudden, he seemed to change his mind and opened the double door on the other side, reaching in to flick on the lights.

"This is my headquarters. It's got a bed and table, but this isn't where I sleep or eat, just where I come for entertainment."

Just that room alone, Elisa thought, would have been the biggest bachelor pad she'd ever seen in her life. Though she was used to her mother's domestic luxury, it was obvious that Valente's wealth was on a whole different scale. This room was like a loft, with two different levels and incredibly high ceilings, white walls, an industrial column shooting up the middle of it, and a spiral staircase that led to a platform with a bed. The lower level was full of books, speakers, magazines, a whole slew of cameras, two strange stages (one with red curtains, the other with a white screen), and several spotlights.

"This is fantastic," she said. But Valente was already gone.

She tiptoed out, as if she were afraid to make any noise, and went into the room to which he'd originally made his way forward.

"Sit down," he ordered, pointing to a blue sofa.

This room was of a more normal size, and had a laptop sat open on a small desk. There were several framed pictures, mostly black and white. She recognized some of the Hotshots: Albert Einstein, Erwin Schrödinger, Werner Heisenberg, Stephen Hawking, and a very young Richard Feynman. But the biggest picture, and certainly the most conspicuous, was very different. The last picture was a brightly colored drawing of a man wearing a suit and tie, stroking a naked woman. The expression on her face made it clear that this was not a pleasant situation for her, but she couldn't do much about it given that her hands were tied behind her back.

Elisa thought that if Valente had noticed the look she'd had on her face ever since she walked in, he certainly wasn't letting on. He sat down at the computer, but turned the swivel chair to face her.

"This is a safe room," he said. "What I mean is it's not bugged. Actually, I haven't found any bugs in the whole house, but they put a transmitter in my cell and they've been tapping my phone, so I'd rather talk here. When they tagged me, they tried to claim that the electricity was down. But I sealed this room off and gave Faouzi strict instructions. When they came, we convinced them that this was just a storage room with no outlets or anything. And I have a few surprises. You see that thing in the corner cupboard that looks like a radio? That's a microphone detector. It picks up all frequencies from fifty megahertz to three gigs. These days you can get them on the Internet. The green light means we can speak freely." He rested his pointy chin in his hands, fingers laced together, and smiled. "We really ought to decide what we're going to do, sweetheart."

"Well, I still have a few questions." She was irritated and anxious—not just by everything he'd told her, but also by the loss of her phone, which she was now starting to regret (though he hadn't even mentioned it). "How did you even get in touch with me, and why did you pick me to begin with?"

"OK. I'll tell you what happened. First, they made me fill out the questionnaire at Oxford; that was what first got me suspicious. They said it was a 'vital prerequisite' in order to attend Blanes's course. When I got to Madrid, I started seeing beggars everywhere, and it seemed as if they were spying on me, and then came the power outage ... But I'm forgetting something. Weeks before that, a bunch of U.S. universities called my parents to ask questions about me, claiming to be 'interested' in me. Did that happen to you? Did anyone ask your family about your life, or your personality?"

"One of my mother's clients," Elisa recalled, growing pale. *Very, very well connected.* "She just told me about it today."

Valente nodded at her approvingly, as if she were a diligent student.

"My father had already told me about that. They're well-known strategies, though I never thought they'd try them on me. Anyway, so I made a simple deduction: all of this started happening after I decided to sign up for Blanes's course, so the surveillance must be related to the course. But then I spoke to Vicky ... Oops, my mistake"–he gave a childlike, apologetic look and corrected himself–" ... to my friend Víctor Lopera, I think you know him, we've been friends since we were kids and I really trust him. But don't call him Vicky or he'll get really pissed off. Anyway, when I asked him about it, he said they hadn't made him fill out any forms. I was curious to find out if I was the only one who was being spied on, so the next logical step was to ask you, since we got ... about the same score on the entrance exam." She smiled to herself, thinking that those four one-hundredths of a point really killed him, but she kept quiet. "Then I saw you talking to that guy at the party at Alighieri, and that pretty much clinched it. But I couldn't just stroll right up to you and say, 'Hey, are they watching you, too?' I had to prove it to you, because I was sure you were an innocent little lamb and wouldn't believe me just because I told you to. I had to discard the possibility of any normal form of communication ..."

He paused, stood up and walked toward the corner of the room, where there was a tiny basin, a faucet, and a glass. He turned on the faucet and filled the glass.

"All I can offer you is water," he said. "And we have to share it. I'm an appalling host. I hope you don't mind putting your lips on the same glass as me."

"I don't want any, thanks," Elisa replied. She was starting to get hot and took off her cardigan. All she had on underneath was a sleeveless T-shirt. He glanced at her for a split second as he drank and then returned to his seat.

"So, then I remembered a trick my father taught me. 'When you want to send a secret message, use porno.' That's what he told me. Only idiots send secrets in inconspicuous e-mails. In his world, anything 'inconspicuous' is conspicuous. But nobody really investigates spam, especially pornographic spam. So that's what I did, but I had an ace up my sleeve. I was sure that some pictures based on Euclid's diagrams would look like porno to anyone who didn't have comprehensive knowledge of math. And as far as the ad and 'mercuryfriend,' those were just arbitrary details, like hacking into your computer."

"Hacking into my computer?"

"Easiest thing in the world," Valente said, scratching an armpit. "Your firewall is Stone Age. Or should I say Abacus Age? Besides, I'm a pretty decent hacker. I've even started creating my own viruses."

Despite being impressed by his brilliant plan, Elisa felt exceedingly uncomfortable. *So that's it. He has no scruples about rummaging around in my private life and he wants me to know it.*

"So why bother to tell me? Why would you care whether or not I knew I was being watched?"

"Oh, believe me, I wanted to meet you," Valente said, adopting a serious expression. "I find you very interesting, as does almost everyone else ... Yeah," he admitted after a second, "I'm sure Blanes finds you interesting, too, even though he always calls on me. There aren't too many girls in theoretical physics, and at Oxford there are even fewer than in Madrid, believe me, and even fewer like you. I mean, I've never seen a girl who knows as much as you do *and* has a hooker's mouth, with tits and ass to match."

Though Elisa had heard him perfectly, her brain took a moment to process the information. Valente's tone hadn't changed one iota; it was almost hypnotic. And her trancelike state was not helped by his marshy eyes, staring out from that gaunt, lean face. When she finally realized what he had said, she didn't know how to respond. For a second, she felt paralyzed, like the woman in the painting, with her hands tied. Certain people, like certain snakes, had that power over others.

At the same time, though, she was sure that he wanted to offend her, and deduced that he would chalk up a victory for himself if she reacted to his vulgarity. She decided to bide her time.

"I'm serious," he continued. "You're fucking hot. A little weird, like me, but hot. I have a theory about it. I think it's all organic. The best physicists have always been pathological. Admit it. The

Homo sapiens brain can't take in all the profundities of the quantum or relativistic world without serious side effects."

He got up again and pointed to his portraits, one by one, as he spoke.

"Schrödinger: sex fiend. Discovered the wave equation while screwing one of his many lovers. Einstein: psychopath. Left his wife and kids and married another woman, and when she died he said he was glad, because he could work in peace without her around. Heisenberg: Nazi. Active collaborator and the father of the H-bomb project under the Führer. Bohr: neurotic. Obsessed with Einstein. Newton: vile wretch. Mediocrity incarnate. Lied and falsified documents just to offend anyone who criticized him. Blanes: mentally disturbed misogynist. You must have seen how he treats you. Probably jacks off thinking about his mother and sister. I could keep going for hours. I've read about all of them, even me." He smiled. "Yeah. I've kept a diary since I was five, and I'm a very meticulous recorder. I like to reflect on my own life. I swear we're all the same. We come from good families (some, even aristocratic ones, like de Broglie); we have an innate ability to reduce nature to pure math. And we're all freaks. And I don't mean just mentally. Physically, too. For example, I'm dolichocephalic, and so are you. In case you didn't know, that means we have long heads, like cucumbers. Schrödinger and Einstein, too. My body is more like Heisenberg's, though. I'm not kidding, I think it's genetic. And you. Well, who knows who the hell you take after, with a body like that. I'd like to see you naked. Your breasts are a little weird, sort of long, too, like your head. 'Dolicomammaries,' we could call them. I want to see your nipples. Why don't you take off your clothes?"

Elisa surprised herself, wondering if she should. Valente's voice was like radiation: you suffered the consequences of it before you even knew you'd been affected.

"No, thanks," she said. "How else are we weird?"

"Our families, maybe," he said, sitting back down. "My parents are divorced. My mother even wanted to kill me. By having an abortion, I mean. My father finally managed to convince her to have me, and my aunt and uncle took me in. So I came to Madrid and lived in this house for a long time before I went to Oxford. And even if you don't believe me, I have actually spent quite a bit of time with each of my parents." He smiled broadly, showing his eyeteeth. "Turns out that once I was far enough away, mom and dad realized they loved me. Let's just say we're good friends now. What about you?"

"Why ask me if you already know?" she replied.

Valente snickered.

"I know some stuff," he admitted. "That you're the daughter of Javier Robledo, that your father died in a car accident. Just what's in all the interviews."

She decided to change the subject.

"You were saying we should do something. Why don't we go to the police? We have proof that they're spying on us."

"You don't get it, do you, sweetheart? The police are the one's who're doing the spying. Not just the regular police, or even the secret police. The *authorities*. Bigwigs."

"But why? What have we done?"

Valente gave that irritating laugh again.

"One of the things you learn with my father is that you don't have to have done anything wrong for them to keep tabs on you. In fact, most of the time, if you're under surveillance, it's because you've done too many things *right*."

"But why us? We're students, we just graduated ..."

"It has to do with Blanes, somehow. I'm sure of that." Valente turned around and typed something on his laptop. A series of equations appeared, equations from the sequoia theory. "Something to do with him or his class, but I have no fucking idea what. Maybe he's working on some project. At first I thought it was because of his theory, some kind of practical application or some experiment related to it, but it can't be that ..." He flicked his index finger continuously, scrolling down through them. "The theory is beautiful, but totally impractical." He turned toward her. "Like some girls."

Once again, she resisted the temptation to get angry.

"You mean the trouble with solving the equation?"

"Of course. There's an insurmountable predicament. The sum of the 'past' end tensors is infinite. I've already calculated that, see? So, despite your ingenious response about curls this morning (which I had already thought of, by the way), there's no way to isolate the strings as individual particles. It's like asking if the sea is made of one single drop or trillions of them. In physics, the answer is always the same: it depends on how you define a drop. Without a concrete definition, it makes no difference whether the strings even exist or not."

"Well, this is how I see it," said Elisa, leaning forward to point to the equation on the screen. "If we take the time variable as infinite, the results are paradoxical. But if we use a limited delta t, no matter how great it is—say, from the big bang to the present—then the solutions are fixed quantities."

"But that's basing it all on a false premise," Valente retorted immediately. "You yourself are creating an artificial limit. That's like just changing a number when you're doing sums to make the figures add up to the total you need. It's absurd. Why pick the start of the universe as your time and not any other time? It's ridiculous ..."

A marked change had overcome him. Elisa noticed that he'd lost his sneer and his cold tone, and now he was speaking animatedly. *Now I've got you by the balls.*

"You just don't get it, do you, *sweetheart?*" she replied calmly. "If we can select the time variable, we obtain concrete solutions. It's a renormalization process." Valente pulled a face and she continued, excited. "I'm not proposing we use the big bang as the variable; what I mean is, we have to use *some* variable as a reference, just to renormalize the equations. For example, the time that's passed since Earth began, about four billion years. The 'past' end of the time strings of Earth's history end there. They are discrete, calculable longitudes. In less than ten minutes you can get finite solutions by applying the Blanes-Grossmann-Marini transformations; I've already tried."

"And what good is that?" Valente's tone was aggressive now. His normally pale cheeks had turned red. "What good is your stupid localist solution? That's like saying, 'I can't live on the salary I earn, but look, I found a few cents this morning!' What the fuck good does a partial solution applied to Earth do? It's stupid!"

"Tell me something," Elisa said calmly. "Why do you just sit there insulting me when you can't prove anything yourself?"

Pause.

Elisa savored Valente's expression. She thought that although he might well be a clever snake in the world of human relations, she was a shark in the world of physics, and she would be happy to prove it to him. She knew she didn't have all the optimal knowledge (after all, she was just an apprentice), but she also knew that no one could bring her down with insults.

"Of course, I can prove it," he spluttered. "What's more, I'll have the proof very soon. The course is over in a week. Next Saturday, there's an international meeting of the minds: Hawking, Witten, Silberg ... they're all coming. And, of course, Blanes will be there. Rumor has it that there's going to be some kind of mea culpa about the sequoia theory. Where we went wrong and why. And before that, we'll have handed in our projects. We'll see which one of us is wrong."

"Fine by me," she said.

"Why don't we make a bet?" Valente suggested, smiling once more. "If your partial solution is acceptable, I'll do whatever you want. For example, I'll give up my plan to go with Blanes and you can have my spot, if he picks me, that is. Or you can order me to do anything you want. I'll do anything, no matter what it is. But if I win, and your partial variable solution doesn't solve shit, then

I'll be the one doing the ordering. And you'll do whatever I say. No matter what."

"I don't accept," Elisa said.

"Why not?"

"I have no interest in giving you orders."

"Oh, I don't know about that."

Valente tapped a few keys on his screen and the equations were replaced by pictures.

Seeing them right after the cold numbers was quite a shock, like the contrast between the naked woman and the portraits of famous physicists. One by one, the images flashed by, and all Valente did was turn to watch her face, smiling.

"That's a very interesting collection you have there on your hard drive ... Those chat rooms you go into are pretty kinky, too ..."

Elisa was speechless. She couldn't believe he'd violated her privacy that way, but the fact that he boasted about it to her was even more humiliating.

Be careful with Ric.

"Don't get me wrong," he said, as a year's worth of her private files flashed up on the screen like old dirty laundry—or dirty lingerie. "I couldn't care less what you do to relax in your free time. Let me make myself perfectly clear: I don't give a shit if you jack off or not, if you get your rocks off alone, whatever. I've got a private photo album myself. In fact, sometimes I even *take* the pictures. You saw my studio in the other room, right? I've got friends, girls who will do anything ... But up until now I'd never met anyone who took ... Oh, I love this one," he said, pointing to the image on screen. Elisa looked away.

Be careful.

"Who took such extreme pleasure in passion, if you know what I mean," he continued, stopping the slide show with a click. The equations returned. "Imagine. I've found a soul mate, someone whose mind is as warped as mine, and that makes me very happy, because honestly, I thought all you liked to do was show off in front of Blanes like a snot-nosed little girl, like you did today. So. You're wrong. You *do* want to give me orders. For example, you could order me to stop snooping. Or to not tell anyone else how to get into all your private files."

What the hell? What kind of sicko is this guy? she wondered. She looked at his pointy face, white as a skeleton, his feminine nose and lips, his huge green eyes, half hidden behind that wispy, blondish hair. Revulsion was the only thing she felt for him. And suddenly she realized that she'd overcome one of his magic powers: she was now able to react.

"So, do you accept?" he asked. "Your will against mine?"

"I accept."

She realized Valente hadn't expected that answer.

"I warn you, I'm being serious."

"I can see that. So am I."

Now he seemed more hesitant.

"You really think your partial solution is correct?"

"I know it is." Elisa pursed her lips. "And I can think of a fair few things I'd like to order you to do."

"Like what?"

But Elisa just shook her head. She realized, all of a sudden, that she understood something about Valente and stood up without looking at him.

"You didn't tell me we're being watched to *help* me," she said. "You told me to *hurt* me. But there's something I still don't understand ..."

Instantly, Ric stood, too. She noticed that they were the same height. They stared at each other.

"Well, now that you mention it," he replied, "I did lie. I don't exactly think it's 'surveillance.' The questionnaire, the questions people asked our families about us. It's pretty obvious. They're not spying on us in order to track us; they're doing it to get to know us. It's a secret selection process. They want to pick one of us, to participate in something. I don't know what, but judging by how much effort they've put into it, it must be very important and very unconventional. In this type of case, if they realize you know they're watching you, it automatically disqualifies you from the selection process."

"So *that's* why you threw out my cell phone," she murmured as the penny dropped.

"I don't think that's a particularly decisive detail, but yeah, it's possible they might be a little pissed at you. Maybe they think you're hiding something and they already struck you off the list."

Elisa felt a sort of calm descend, listening to him. *So now I know what you really want.*

But she was wrong. He didn't only want to shove her off the path that led to Blanes. That became clear when, with no warning whatsoever, he reached his bony fingers out to touch her breasts.

Every fiber in her body screamed, ordering her to jump back. But she didn't. Nor did Valente touch her. His hand slid through the air, millimeters from her T-shirt, down to her hips, outlining her with his hand. She stood stock-still, not breathing for the duration of that humiliation.

"My orders won't be easy to fill," he said, "but they'll be a lot of fun."

"Right. Can't wait." She grabbed her cardigan. "Can I go now?"

"I'll show you out."

"I can find the way, thanks."

On her way back down the dark stairs, listening to that ancient voice moan ("Ishtar ..."), she felt tense and nervous. Once back out on the street, Elisa stopped to take in some air, opening her mouth wide to gulp it in.

Then she looked at the world as if for the first time, as if she'd just been born under the city's dark shadows.

10

TIME is a strange thing.

Its strangeness derives, paradoxically, from the fact that it seems so familiar. Not a day goes by that we don't think about it. We measure it, but we can't see it. It's as fleeting as the soul, and yet it's a universal, demonstrable, physical phenomenon. Saint Augustine summed it up thus: *Si non rogas, intelligo* ("If you don't ask, I understand").

Scientists and philosophers have debated it without ever coming to any agreement. And that's because time seems to take on different forms depending on how we study it, even how we experience it. For a physicist, a second is defined as 9,192,631,770 oscillations or cycles of the cesium atom's resonant frequency. For an astronomer, a second might be that unit divided by 31,556,925.97474, which is the time it takes Earth to make a complete 360-degree revolution—that is, a tropical year. But, as anyone who has ever waited for a doctor to announce whether an operation has been successful or not, whether a loved one has lived or died, knows, a cesium second and an astronomical second are not always a second. To our minds, seconds can stretch on for ages.

The idea of time as a subjective phenomenon is not something foreign to either science or to ancient philosophy. The wise ones have never had a problem accepting that psychological time could vary from subject to subject, and yet they were sure, at the same time, that physical time was immutable, the same for everyone.

But they were wrong.

In 1905, Albert Einstein dealt the definitive blow to that belief with his theory of relativity. There is no *one* privileged time; there are as many times as there are perspectives, and time and space are inseparable. It is not a question of subjectivity or entelechy, but an indispensable component of matter.

This finding, however, still comes a long way from clearing everything up about our evasive Father Time. Think, for example, about the moving hands of a clock. Intuitively, we know that time moves forward. "It goes by so quickly," we complain. But does that really make any sense? If something moves forward, it does so at a certain *speed.* So how fast does time go? High school students sometimes fall into the trap of trying to answer that question with this deceptively simple sentence: "At one second per second." But, of course, that makes no sense. Velocity always relates a measure of distance to a measure of time. So it's impossible for a second to travel "at one second per second." Although our enigmatic friend Father Time *moves,* we can't seem to agree on how fast he travels.

And what's more, if time really is the fourth dimension, as relativity claims, it's a lot different than the other three. Because in space we can travel up and down, left and right, and back and forth. But in time, we can travel only forward. Why is that? What keeps us from being able to go back and live what's already been lived, or see it? In 1988, David Blanes's sequoia theory tried to answer some of these questions, but he barely scratched the surface. We still don't know almost anything about this "indispensable" element of reality that travels in only one direction, at an unknown speed, and which we only seem to understand if no one asks what it is.

Very odd.

With those words, Reinhard Silberg, professor of the philosophy of science at Berlin's Technischen Universität, began his opening remarks at the UNESCO hall in Madrid's Palacio de Congresos, where the international symposium "Modern Theories on the Nature of Space-Time" was being held. The modest hall was overflowing with attendees and journalists who were hanging on his every word, and waiting to hear from Witten, Craig, Marini, and the two "stars" of the show: Stephen Hawking and David Blanes.

Elisa Robledo had other reasons to be there. She wanted to know if her theory of local variables had any chance of success and, if not, she wondered what Ric Valente planned to try to make her do.

She was almost sure of two things: first, that she'd lose the bet, and second, that she'd refuse to do whatever it was.

THE whole week had been a race against time. Which was ironic, given that she'd spent the whole time *studying time.*

Passion and intellect went hand in hand in Elisa. After the emotional upheaval that her encounter with Valente had turned out to be, she sat down to reason things out and made a very simple decision: whether or not she was being watched, and regardless of any bet, she was going to do her homework. She'd already given up all hope of coming out first in Blanes's course. But she still didn't want to slack off at the end, especially on her final project.

She wholeheartedly threw herself into her work. For several nights in a row, she didn't sleep more than a few hours at a time. She felt sure she wasn't going to be able to prove anything with her local time variable hypothesis and became increasingly convinced that Valente had been right when he questioned her premise, but she didn't care. A scientist had to fight for her ideas even when no one accepted them, she thought.

At first, she didn't think about the bet. In fact, although she thought for a second that she might faint when she had to face Valente in class that Monday (they didn't look at each other, they didn't say hi, and both acted as if nothing had happened), and despite the fact that she was aware of his slimy presence at every second—like a persistent odor—at no point did it occur to her to worry about what might happen (or what she would agree to do in order to keep her word) if she lost. She'd met few people as arrogant and churlish as Ricardo Valente Sharpe and she was not impressed with the vile, juvenile hacking into her computer he'd done or the way he tried to blackmail her with her own bedroom secrets.

Or at least that was what she was trying to convince herself of, at all costs.

She wasn't even sure she was being watched, as Valente claimed. On Tuesday afternoon, the police had called. They scared the living daylights out of her, but it turned out they only wanted to tell her they'd found her cell phone. An upstanding citizen had found it Friday night when he threw out the paper cup from his ice cream on a narrow street in Chueca. Since he had no idea whose it was, he left it at the downtown police station. After a few inquiries (an abandoned cell phone was suspicious, even alarming these days, the police had told her), they had tracked down the owner: Elisa.

That afternoon, after stopping by the station, Elisa used a tiny screwdriver to pry it open. She didn't know exactly what the inside of a cell phone was supposed to look like anyway (pen and paper were more her style), but she couldn't see anything that seemed particularly out of place. The man who'd found it could be the same guy who she'd seen from the back door of that bar; maybe it was just a coincidence, and Valente had taken advantage of it.

Wednesday, she went to the registrar's office at Alighieri to get her certificate of attendance for Blanes's course, and while she was there she asked a few questions. The girl behind the counter verified everything she wanted to know: Javier Maldonado *was* a student there, he *was* studying information science, and there *was* a statistics professor named Espalza. Didn't sound like much of a conspiracy, then.

She started to think that maybe Valente himself was responsible for the whole charade. It was clear that he wanted some kind of "special" relationship with her (given that he found her—what had he said?—"so interesting"). He was very clever, there was no doubt about that. So he'd probably taken advantage of certain co-incidences and spun that tale about surveillance just to scare her. Curiously enough, Elisa wasn't the slightest bit scared of him.

She handed in her project on Friday. Blanes took it without a word and then said good-bye to the class, summoning them to the symposium the following day, where they would talk about "some of the thornier aspects of the theory, like the paradox of the 'past' end of the strings." He didn't say anything about the possibility of resolving the paradox. Elisa turned to look at her rival. He sat there smiling without looking back at her.

Fuck Valente Sharpe.

So there she was, at the symposium, waiting to hear what the Wise Ones had to say about it all and to find out who'd win the bizarre bet.

Things, though, were about to take a totally unexpected turn.

SHE'D been listening to late twentieth-century physics mumbo jumbo for hours, and it was all old hash: Branes, parallel universes, black-hole fusion, Calabi-Yau spaces, tears in reality ... Almost every speaker at least mentioned the sequoia theory, but no one talked about any possibility of identifying isolated time strings as a means of resolving the "past" end paradox with local variables. Sergio Marini, the experimental physicist and Blanes's collabora-tor in Zurich, whom Elisa had been anxiously waiting to hear, de-clared that it was essential to accept the theory's contradictions, and as an example put forward the infinite results of relativistic quantum theory.

All of a sudden, amid an expectant, respectful silence, she caught a glimpse of Stephen Hawking, making his way toward the stage in his electric wheelchair.

Pressing himself against the back of his chair, the illustrious Cambridge physicist (who held the same post Newton had held centuries before him) looked like little more than a sickly man. But Elisa knew that he was not only blindingly intelligent and surprisingly witty (his eyes, hidden behind enormous glasses, radiated personality), but also that he had an iron will that enabled him to become one of the world's foremost physicists of all time, and this despite suffering from a crippling motor neuron disease. Elisa realized that she didn't admire him nearly enough. Hawking was living proof that you should never give up on anything in this life.

Using the controls on his voice synthesizer, Hawking transformed written text into intelligible speech. The audience was instantly captivated. People laughed heartily at his scathing, witty commentaries, pronounced in a mechanically precise English. However, to Elisa's displeasure, he spoke only about the possibility of recovering information lost in black holes, barely even mentioning Blanes's theory in passing at the very end of his talk.

He concluded, "The branches of Professor Blanes's sequoia stretch toward the future in the sky, while its roots bury themselves in the unreachable ground of the past." The electronic voice paused. "Nevertheless, as long as we're hanging on to one of those branches, nothing stops us from looking down at the roots."

That sentence made Elisa think. What was Hawking talking about? Was it just a poetic closing statement, or was he trying to cast doubt on the possibility of identifying and opening isolated time strings? At any rate, it was clear that the sequoia theory had lost a lot of cachet among the great physicists of the world. All that was left was to wait for Blanes himself, but it wasn't looking too hopeful.

When the lunch break was announced, everyone in the auditorium stood as one to head for the exits, causing an almighty traffic jam. Elisa got in line just in time to hear a voice whisper in her ear.

"Ready to lose?"

She'd been expecting something along those lines and turned her head to reply.

"Are you?"

But Ric Valente had already slipped into the crowd. Elisa shrugged and thought about the answer to that question. Was she ready? Maybe not.

But she hadn't lost yet.

VÍCTOR Lopera asked her to have lunch with him and she gladly accepted, actually looking forward to his company. Despite his obsession with religion, which she felt was a slippery slope (and one that made him talk too much), Lopera was a good conversationalist and an all-around likable guy. Getting a ride home from him had become part of a routine they both enjoyed.

They bought vegetarian sandwiches at the conference center's self-serve cafeteria. Víctor had ordered his with double mayo. Elisa had a feeling that mayonnaise was one of the only things that could get her friend off the topic of Teilhard de Chardin, or when Monsignor Lemaître discovered that the universe was expanding and Einstein didn't believe him. He devoured it with such relish that he ended up with big globs of the white stuff on his lips and around his mouth, and then, like a cat, flicked his long tongue to lick them off and clean himself.

They couldn't find a free table so they ate standing up, talking about the speakers' presentations (he'd loved Silberg's) and waving to professors and classmates (the place was like a catwalk, and Elisa had to smile at people every five seconds). At one point, without warning, he complimented her, turning red in the process. "You look very pretty." She thanked him, though not totally sincerely. That Saturday she'd decided, for the first time in a week, to wash her hair and fix herself up a little, putting on a sky-blue blouse and dark-blue cotton trousers instead of her standard ripped jeans, which were so dirty they could have stood up and walked by themselves, as her mother liked to say. But she wished Víctor had complimented her on something besides her looks.

Nevertheless, on that occasion, she felt like his interest in her was special. She realized it before he brought it up, catching the sidelong glances he gave her when he thought she wasn't looking. It was clear he had no future as a criminal: he was the most obvious guy she'd ever met.

After taking his last bite of sandwich and licking the remaining bits of mayo off with his tongue, Víctor said in a conspicuously casual tone, "I talked to Ric the other day." She watched his Adam's apple bob up and down. "Sounds like you guys have become ... friends."

"That's not true," Elisa replied. "Is that what he told you?"

Víctor smiled apologetically, as if he were begging forgiveness for having misinterpreted her relationship with Valente. But in no time he became serious again.

"No. Just what I deduced. He told me he liked you, and that ... he'd made a bet with you."

Elisa stared at him.

"I have my opinion about Blanes's theory," she said finally, "and he has his. So we made a bet to see who's right."

Víctor waved his hand away, as if to dismiss the topic.

"Believe me, I don't care what you're up to." Then he added, so quietly that Elisa had to lean in just to hear his words in the noisy cafeteria, "I just wanted to warn you ... Don't do it."

"Don't do what?"

"Whatever he tells you to do. It's not a game for him. I know him. We used to be really good friends. He was always ... Let's just say he's very perverse."

"What do you mean?"

"It's too hard to explain right now," Víctor glanced at her sidelong and changed his tone. "I mean, I don't want to exaggerate or anything. I'm not saying he's ... he's crazy or anything like that ... I just mean he doesn't respect girls very much. I'm sure some

of them like that about him. Not all of them, of course, but ..."
He'd turned red as a beet. "I feel like an idiot telling you this. It's
just that I like you, and I wanted.... Well, anyway, you do what
you want. I just wanted ... I didn't know you two had spoken, so I
thought I should warn you."

Elisa was tempted to make a sarcastic comment. Something
along the lines of "I'm twenty-three years old, Víctor, I can take
care of myself, thanks." But she realized that Lopera, unlike her
mother, wasn't trying to teach her a lesson. He was being completely sincere and thought he was helping her out. She didn't
want to ask him what else Valente had told him about their conversation. At that point, she no longer cared what Mr. Four One-
Hundredths Less could say or do.

"Valente and I aren't friends, Víctor," she insisted. "And I have
no plans to do anything I don't want to," she said very seriously.

Víctor still didn't seem satisfied, as if he'd realized that the
only one who'd come off poorly after all that was him. He opened
his mouth to say something else, but then closed it again and
shook his head.

"Of course not," he replied. "That was idiotic of me ..."

"No, I appreciate it, really."

Then came the call for them to return to the auditorium; the
symposium was about to resume.

Elisa spent the next several hours completely engrossed,
though not by the conference. Half of her brain was concentrating
on the speakers' words; the other half contemplated Víctor's im-
mature warning. But then she abruptly forgot all about Víctor and
even Valente, and sat up in her seat.

David Blanes was making his way to the stage. If it had been
a courtroom, the silence that greeted him would have made clear
that this was the accused.

Blanes took up where Hawking had left off, with the comment
about the tree.

"The sequoia is leafy, but it doesn't bear fruit," he began.

In less than ten minutes, Elisa knew that she'd lost the bet.

BLANES spoke for another half an hour, but he spent his time talking about how new generations of physicists would discover as-yet-undreamed-of means of solving the problems presented by the "past" end of the strings. He mentioned various possible solutions, including local variables and another one that hadn't occurred to Elisa using imaginary numbers. But he branded them all "elegant but pointless, like wearing a tux in the desert." She could tell that he was depressed, tired, and probably sick of defending himself from his adversaries' attacks. Despite the applause, Elisa was sure the audience was disappointed with what he was saying. She felt disdain for the man who'd once been her idol. *You don't want to fight for your ideas. Well, I do.*

Blanes's had been the last talk of the day, but there was still a roundtable scheduled for after the coffee break. Elisa stood and lined up with everyone else, and made her way out into the lobby. She heard the voice behind her, just as she had at lunchtime.

"Go to the men's room and wait there."

"I haven't lost yet," she said, whirling around.

As she saw him try to slip into the crowd, Elisa stuck out her hand and grabbed onto his shirt. *This time you're not getting away.*

"I haven't lost," she repeated.

Valente backed up, but he couldn't get away. They walked to the exit together and headed for the lobby. As always, Elisa thought his appearance was about as subtle as a neon sign that read "Valente Sharpe here!" Bright-red denim shirt buttoned all the way to the neck, maroon belt and trousers, red leather boots, gold chain, and earrings. He wore his nametag (Elisa had stuffed hers into her pocket) over what was probably his nipple. His blond bangs were carefully combed over his right eye. The displeasure in his voice was clear.

"I've given you your first instruction: go to the men's room ..."

"No."

She saw a gleam in his eye, as if he was mocking her, but his face remained impassive.

"Well, Ms. Robledo, that's very cowardly of you, going back on your word like that."

"I'm not going back on my word, Mr. Valente. I'll keep my word if I lose."

"You've already lost. Blanes already said your local time variables are about as valuable as a piece of dogshit on the bottom of your shoe."

"That's an opinion," she objected. "He hasn't proven anything; he's expressed an opinion. But as you know, physics is not a matter of opinion."

"Oh, come on ..."

"There's a lot at stake here. I just want to make sure that you're right and I'm wrong. Or are you the one who's afraid to lose?"

Valente stared at her without batting an eye. She did the same. Finally, he sighed.

"What do you propose?"

"Well, I'm not going to get involved in a discussion with Blanes during question time, that's for sure. But I have a plan. Everyone knows that Blanes is going to pick the person to accompany him to Zurich based on the final projects we handed in. I'm sure that if he thinks my idea merits examination, he'll pick me. If not, and he thinks it's stupid, he won't. So let's wait and see."

"He's going to pick me," Valente said quietly. "Accept it, sweetheart."

"Well, all the better for you, then. But he doesn't even have to do that. If he just *doesn't* pick me, I'll concede defeat."

"What do you mean by 'concede'?"

"I'll go wherever you tell me to, do whatever you ask me to."

"I don't believe you. You'll just find another excuse."

"I swear," she said. "I give you my word. I'll do whatever you want if he doesn't pick me."

"You're lying."

She stared at him, eyes flashing.

"I take this more seriously than you think."

"What? The bet?"

"No. My ideas. I couldn't care less about your bet, or any of the bullshit you told me the other night. There's no one 'watching' us, nobody's spying on us. The whole cell-phone thing was a coincidence: I got it back the other day. I think you're just trying to make yourself out to be interesting. And I'll tell you something." Elisa smiled wide enough to show off her white teeth. "Be careful, Mr. Valente, because now I'm interested."

Valente gave her a strange look.

"You're a very unique girl," he said quietly, almost to himself.

"You, on the other hand, with your 'meet me in the bathroom' crap, are proving yourself to be more and more a cliché."

"The terms are decided by the winner."

"Agreed," said Elisa.

Suddenly, he began to laugh, as though he'd been keeping himself from doing so throughout their conversation.

"You're unbelievable. Literally, you're un-fucking-believable! I just wanted to test you, see what you'd do. I'd have laughed my head off if you'd actually gone to the men's room." Then he looked at her, serious once more. "But I accept your challenge. I'm totally sure Blanes is going to pick me. In fact, sweetheart, I'd say he already has. And when that becomes clear, I'm going to call your cell phone. Just once. I'll tell you where you have to go, and how, what you can wear and what you can't, and you'll listen and obey every word like a dog in a dog show. And that will be just the beginning. I'm going to have the time of my life, I swear. Like I said, you're unique, especially with that temper. I'm curious to see how far you'll go. Or maybe I'll just prove what I already suspect: that you're a liar and a coward."

Elisa calmly stood there and let him shower her with insults. Her heart though, was pounding and her mouth was dry.

"You want to back out?" he asked with feigned seriousness, staring at her with his left eye (the right hidden behind a curtain of hair). "This is your last chance."

"I've made my bet," Elisa smiled. "Now, if *you* want to back out, that's another story ..."

Valente looked like a kid who'd just been given a new toy.

"Great," he said. "I'm going to have a good old time with you!"

"We'll see. Now if you'll excuse me ..."

"Wait," Valente said, looking around. "I already told you I'm sure I'm going to win. But I want to be totally honest with you. There are a few things at this conference that make me feel like things are not what they seem. Blanes and Marini seem a little too keen on proving that their 'sequoia' has turned into a 'bonsai,' and I noticed something strange." He motioned her to follow as he began to walk away. "Come with me if you want to see."

THEY walked through the lobby toward the registration tables, dodging people left and right: foreigners and Spaniards, professors and students, people in suits and others in jeans, folks who were trying to imitate their idols (Elisa had to laugh at the physicists sporting Einstein-style hair) and those who just wanted to touch them (Hawking's wheelchair had disappeared in a swarm of admirers). Suddenly, Valente stopped.

"There they are, all together like a happy family."

She followed his gaze. Indeed, they did form a separate group, as if they'd wanted to isolate themselves from the rest of the pack. She identified David Blanes, Sergio Marini, and Reinhard Silberg, in addition to a young experimental physicist from Oxford who'd spoken after Silberg, Colin Craig. They were all chatting away.

"Craig was one of my mentors in particle physics," Valente explained. "He's the one who encouraged me to take Blanes's admission test. Silberg is a professor of the philosophy of science with a PhD in history. And check out that tall woman in purple next to Craig ..."

It would have been hard not to, Elisa thought, given that she was absolutely stunning. Her long brown hair fell straight down to her waist like a pencil, and her form-fitting clothes were elegant yet simple. Standing with her was a girl who seemed much younger, with long, remarkable albino hair. Elisa didn't recognize either one of them.

"That's Jacqueline Clissot, from Montpellier. She's a world-famous paleontologist and anthropologist. The one with white hair must be one of her students."

"What are they doing here? They weren't on any of the panels."

"That's just what I was thinking. I think they're here to meet up with Blanes. This symposium has been like a big family reunion. Meanwhile, Daddy Blanes and Mommy Marini are put in charge of telling the scientific community that the sequoia isn't going to bloom this year. It's as if their main objective is to lay their cards on the table and prove that no one's cheating. Weird, isn't it? And that's not all."

He walked off, hands in his pockets, and Elisa followed him, intrigued despite her best efforts at indifference. They crossed the lobby, the summer light still streaming in through the large windows.

"This is the strangest thing," he continued. "I bumped into Silberg and Clissot at Oxford a few months ago. I had to take care of some stuff with Craig, so I went to his office. He opened the door, but he was busy. I recognized Silberg and wanted to know who the hottie with him was. But Craig didn't introduce me. In fact, he seemed annoyed that I was even there. But being on friendly terms with the secretaries has its advantages, and Craig told me all about it later on. It seems Clissot and Silberg had been in conversation with her boss for a year or so, and finally they were meeting up in Oxford."

"So? They were probably just working on a project," Elisa said.

Valente shook his head.

"I got pretty tight with Craig, and he used to tell me all about the projects he was working on. Besides, what kind of project would a guy like Craig, who deals with particle accelerators, be working on with a historian like Silberg and a dead-chimp special-ist like Clissot? Add Blanes and Marini into the mix, and what do you get?"

"A mess?"

"Yeah. Or a sect of devil worshippers." Valente lowered his voice. "Or something much more ... exotic."

Elisa stared at him blankly.

"What are you thinking?"

He just smiled. A musical chime announced the resumption of the symposium, and the public was drawn back to the hall like iron filings to a magnet. Valente jerked his head in their direction.

"There they all go. Look at them. Little ducklings waddling along behind Momma Duck: Craig, Silberg, Clissot, Marini ... Blanes is paying for it all, but it's not his money." He turned back to her. "Now you'll see why I'm so sure they've been 'watching' us. Check this out ..."

He'd stopped beside one of the signs propped up on an easel. It read, in English, "First International Symposium. Modern Theo-ries on the Nature of Space-Time. July 16–17, 2005. Palacio de Con-gresos, Madrid." But Valente was pointing to the smaller print.

"Sponsored by ...," he read aloud.

"Eagle Group," Elisa finished. She made out the artistic logo. The "g" in "Eagle" was used in the word "Group," too.

"You know what that is?" Valente asked.

"Of course. They're a pretty new conglomerate, but they've made a big splash. Some EU consortium that finances scientific development ..."

He smiled at her.

"My father once told me that the equivalent to the Americans' ECHELON in Europe is called Eagle Group," he said.

11

ON Sunday, after the last morning session, Víctor went to find Elisa to ask her to lunch. Wanting to speak to him, she agreed. Something strange had happened.

Ric Valente hadn't shown up that morning. Neither had Blanes. And that double no-show made her uneasy. It was true that Sunday's panels were devoted to experimental physics, which was not Blanes's field, but Elisa couldn't help but think that the disappearance of the sequoia theory creator and of Valente Sharpe had to be related. Nevertheless, she didn't want to seriously consider the suspicions she'd been harboring just yet.

They found a table at the back of the crowded cafeteria and ate in silence. As Elisa sat there wondering how to broach the topic, Víctor wiped the mayonnaise from his chin and then said, "Blanes called Ric this morning; he asked him to go with him to Zurich."

She couldn't swallow.

"Oh," she murmured.

"Ric called to tell me. He said he wasn't going to come today because they had to meet up and plan."

She nodded idiotically, gagging on a wad of dry bread that her mouth seemed unable to send down her throat. She asked Víctor to excuse her, got up, and went to the bathroom, where she spat that ball of sawdust into the toilet. After splashing her face in the sink, she reconsidered. *Well, wasn't that what you were expecting? So what's the big deal?* She'd considered the possibility during long sleepless nights, and she'd been more than aware that it was the most likely outcome. After all, Ric Valente had been Blanes's favorite right from the start. She dried her face with a paper towel, returned to the table, and sat down opposite Víctor.

"I'm happy for him," she said.

And she supposed she really was. She was glad about everything that had happened, now that the competition was finally over. The sequoia theory was still knocking at her door, tempting her with its amazing mathematical beauty, but soon it would get tired and leave, and she'd be in peace once more. There were other fish in the sea, scholarships to MIT and Berkeley that she'd applied for in case Zurich didn't come through. She was sure she'd end up doing her dissertation with one of the world's best physicists, no matter what. She was ambitious and knew that her drive would take her far. Blanes was one of a kind, but he wasn't the *only one* who was one of a kind.

"I'm happy for him too," Víctor spluttered. "I mean, not entirely. Well, for him I am, but not for you. I mean ..."

"I don't care. Honestly. Blanes and his sequoia aren't the be-all and end-all."

She felt better after that blow. She'd always tried to adapt to new situations, and this was no exception. And since she'd now actually have some time to relax, she decided she'd reorganize her life. She might even call her own private "spy," Javier Maldonado, and return his dinner invitation, asking him a few questions, just to clear up some things she'd been brooding over since Valente had spoken to her. *Have you been spying on me? Do you work for Eagle Group?* She could just picture his face.

Then she remembered the bet.

Well, that was OK, she was pretty sure Valente would forget about it. *When Blanes said, "Come with me," he probably forgot all about bets and trotted after him like a puppy.*

But what if he didn't? What if he wanted to play this thing all the way out? She considered the possibility, and it made her very nervous. There was no way that she was going back on her word. She'd do whatever he said. But she also had to assume, or at least hope, that he wouldn't go too far. She'd give in, hoping he'd do the same. She was almost sure that Valente was more interested in humiliating her than anything else, and if she was casual about it and gave in to his demands, he'd lose all interest.

I'm going to call your cell phone. Just once. I'll tell you where you have to go, and how, what you can wear and what you can't...

All of a sudden, she felt uncomfortable with her cell in her pants pocket. It was like having Valente's hand on her thigh. She pulled it out and looked to see if she'd missed any calls. None. Then she placed it on the table like a gambler staking it all on one number. When she looked up, she could see the alarm in Víctor's eyes; he seemed to read her thoughts.

"I think I crossed a line yesterday," he said. "I'm sorry. I shouldn't have spoken to you like that. You probably misunderstood me. I ... I didn't mean to scare you."

"You didn't scare me," she replied, smiling.

"Well, I'm glad to hear you say that," Víctor said. But his expression showed that he was anything but. "All day yesterday, I kept going over it in my head, thinking I'd been a little over the top. I mean ... Ric's not the Devil incarnate or anything...."

"I'd never thought he was. But thanks for clearing it up; Satan might have been offended."

Something about that comment charmed Víctor. Seeing him laugh, Elisa did the same. Then she glanced down at her almost untouched sandwich, her cell phone lying next to it. She added, "I just don't understand how you two ever became friends. You're so different."

"We were just kids back then. When you're a kid you do a lot of things that, later on, you'd never have done."

"I suppose you're right."

And then, out of the blue, Víctor began to talk. It was like a torrent or a violent storm, his sentences like thunder rolling from his lips, but the thoughts that impelled them were more like lightning, striking from deep within him. Elisa listened carefully since, for the first time since she'd met him, he was talking about something other than physics or theology. He stared off into space, reeling off his tale as he did.

As always, he spoke about the past. About that which has taken place and continues to take place, as Elisa's grandfather had once explained it to her. Things that once were and therefore still are. He spoke about the only thing we ever really speak about when we're honest, because it's impossible to go into detail about anything other than our memories. And as she listened, the cafeteria, the conference, and her professional concerns melted away. For Elisa, all that existed right then was Víctor's voice and the story he told.

It had taken her several years to realize, but she saw that her grandfather had been right when he once said, "Other people's past might be our present."

TIME is, indeed, strange. It carries things off to remote places we have no access to, and yet still has a magical effect on us. Víctor turned back into a child, and she could almost see both of them: two lonely boys who were both incredibly intelligent, maybe had the same tastes, were ruled by their curiosity and thirst for knowledge, but also by interests that other boys their age wouldn't dare express. The two of them did, though, and that's what made them different. Ric was the leader, the one who decided what had to be done, and Víctor—Vicky—complied, perhaps fearful of what might happen if he didn't, or perhaps just hoping for his turn.

The thing he liked most about Ric was also his biggest shortcoming: his solitude. Abandoned by his parents, raised by an uncle who was increasingly remote and indifferent, Ric had no boundaries, no rules of conduct, and he thought of nothing but himself. He saw everyone and everything around him as a theater whose only purpose was to delight him. Víctor became a regular in the audience of that theater; but when he got older, he stopped attending the fantastic performances.

"Ric was unlike anyone else. He had an incredible imagination, but he was also very down to earth. He didn't delude himself. If he wanted something, he'd give it his all, do anything to get it, regardless of who or what stood in his way. At first, I liked that. I suppose that's what happens to anyone who meets a guy like that. Back then, Ric's world revolved around sex. But he was always cynical. For him, girls—all girls—were always inferior. When he was a kid, he used to cut out pictures of the girls in his class and paste them over the centerfolds' faces in girlie magazines—which he had a ton of. Which was funny at first. But then I got tired of it. I really couldn't stand the way he treated girls like objects. They were just things he could get pleasure from. He never loved any of them; he just used them. He liked to take pictures, film them naked, in the bathroom. Sometimes he paid them, but a lot of times they didn't even know they were being filmed. He had hidden cameras."

He paused for a moment to look at Elisa, searching for some sign that he should stop. But she motioned for him to continue.

"As if that wasn't enough, he had the money and the space to do whatever he wanted. We spent summers at Ric's family's summerhouse near a town in Andalusia called Ollero. Sometimes we brought girls there. It was just the two of us, and we thought we owned the world. Ric would take raunchy pictures. And then, one day, something happened." He smiled and pushed his glasses up on his nose. "There was this girl I liked, and I think she liked me, too. Her name was Kelly. She was from England and she went to our school ... Kelly Graham ..." He lingered over the name for a minute. "Ric invited her over to the house, but I didn't mind. I was sure that he knew Kelly was off limits. But one morning ... I found them ... Ric and Kelly ..." He gazed at Elisa, nodding slowly. "Well, anyway, I'm one of those guys who only gets mad once in a blue moon, but ... but ..."

"But when you do, all hell breaks loose," Elisa helped him.

"Yeah. I called them every name in the book. I mean, looking back on it, it was just a little kid's tantrum. We were only ten or eleven years old. But seeing them ... kissing and ... *touching* each other ... Well, let's just say it was a shock to me. Anyway. We argued, and Ric pushed me. We were outside, on some rocks by a river. I fell and hit my head. I was lucky there was a man there who'd come to go fishing. He picked me up and took me to a hospital. It wasn't anything serious: a few stitches. I think I still have the scar. But what I wanted to tell you was ... I was out for a few hours. And when I came to that night, Ric was there with me, begging me to forgive him. My parents told me that he had sat by my side the whole time. The whole time," he repeated, his eyes misty. "When I woke up, he started crying and saying he was sorry. I think it's important to have friends when you're a kid, to really know what friendship is. That day, I was closer to him than ever. Does that make any sense? You asked me what brought us together ... Now, when I think about it, I think it was things like that that brought us together."

He fell silent and sighed deeply.

"I forgave him, of course. In fact, I thought we'd be friends forever. But then things changed. We grew up, our lives took different paths. We didn't stop speaking, but somehow it was worse than that. We put up barriers. He still kept trying to get me to be like him. He told me he kept inviting girls to Ollero. He'd film them secretly, sometimes while they were making love. Then he'd show them his home movies and blackmail them. 'You think your parents would want to see this? Or your friends?' he'd say. And he'd make them pose some more." After another pause, he added, "Of course, he never got in trouble with the police or anything. He was very careful, and they'd always keep their mouths shut ..."

"Did you ever see it?" Elisa asked. "The whole blackmailing side of things, I mean."

"No, but he told me about it."

"I'll bet you he was just showing off."

The way Víctor looked at her, it was as if she were someone he really admired who'd just really let him down.

"You don't understand … You have *no idea* how Ric treated them…"

"Víctor, Ric Valente might be a pervert, but deep down he's just a third-rate clown. I know that for a fact."

"You think you could disobey him?" he asked sharply, suddenly. His slow manner of speech instantaneously evaporated. "You think that if you accepted his terms, you'd be able to get out of anything he ordered you to do?"

"What I think is that you still admire him, despite it all." Now she was fed up. "Valente is an idiot who's never so much as been slapped by his parents, and you think he's an unscrupulous sadist who'd commit the most heinous acts imaginable without batting an eye. Or maybe you just *like* to think that…" She shouldn't have said that, and she knew it. Immediately, she wished she could take it back. Víctor stared at her, totally solemn.

"No," he said. "You're wrong about that. I don't like it at all."

"What I meant was…"

The cell phone rang. Almost frightened, Elisa snatched her cell off the table to look at the screen. Unknown number.

For a second, she recalled Valente's words the day before, his watery eyes taking her in from behind his bangs. *I'll tell you where you have to go, and how, what you can wear and what you can't, and you'll listen and obey every word … And that will just be the beginning. I'm going to have the time of my life, I swear …* For a second she was afraid to answer. It was like her phone's insistent ring was inviting her to enter a different world from the one she'd previously known, a world in which her talk with Ric Valente and Víctor's whole story were just the preamble. Maybe—she thought—it would have been better to be a coward or to lie than to accept his sinister invitation…

She looked up hesitantly and glanced at Víctor, who seemed to be begging her with his hangdog eyes not to answer.

And that was precisely what made her mind up, that private fear she perceived in him. She wanted to prove to Ric Valente Sharpe and Víctor Lopera that she had mettle. No one and nothing was going to scare her off.

At least that was what she believed back then.

"Hello?" she picked up, her voice steady, having no idea what she was about to hear.

And when she heard it, she froze.

After she hung up, she stared at Víctor, mouth agape.

HER mother, astonishingly, canceled all of her appointments at Piccarda and took her to Barajas International Airport on Tuesday morning. She was very obsequious, openly exclaiming how happy she was. Maybe—she thought—what she was happy about was the fact that her little chickadee was finally going to fly away and leave the expensive nest. *OK, let's not be so negative, especially not now.*

Her greatest joy was seeing Víctor. He was the only one who came to see her off. He didn't give her a kiss, but he patted her back.

"Congratulations," he said, "though I still don't understand how you did it."

"Me neither," she admitted.

"It was only logical, though. That he pick both of you, I mean. You were the top two students in the class …"

She felt a knot in her throat. Her happiness was absolute; she wasn't even thinking about Valente, whom she would no doubt meet up with in Zurich. After all, neither of them had won the bet. As usual, they'd tied.

There was still over half an hour before her plane took off, but she wanted to wait at the gate. So before going through security, mother and daughter looked at each other in silence, as if deciding which of them would take the next step. Suddenly, Elisa held out her arms and hugged the elegant, perfumed body before her.

She didn't want to cry, but tears slid down her cheeks despite her best effort. Taken by surprise like that, Marta Morandé kissed her daughter's forehead. It was a light, cold, discreet peck.

"I hope you're very happy and that it all goes really well for you, honey."

Elisa waved and put her bag through the X-ray machine.

"Call me, and write me, don't forget," her mother said.

"Lots of luck, lots and lots ...," Víctor repeated. Even after she could no longer hear him, watching his lips move, it seemed that he still repeated the same thing again and again.

And then Víctor and her mother's faces were gone. She watched Madrid out of the plane's window, and, from so high up, she felt as if she were opening a new chapter in her life. *He called me. He wants me to go to Zurich to work with him. It's unbelievable.* Everything changed for her. She'd stopped being "Robledo Morandé, Elisa" and entered a new world, totally different from the one she'd feared. A world that seemed to be waiting for her, winking at her from up in the sky. She smiled and closed her eyes, enjoying the feeling.

Years later, she would think that had she even remotely suspected what that trip held for her, she would never have boarded the plane, or even picked up her cell phone that Sunday.

If she'd had any idea, she would have run home and locked herself in her room, sealing the doors and windows forever.

But at the time, she didn't have a clue. Not the slightest idea.

THREE

The Island

"The isle is full of noises ..."

SHAKESPEARE

12

A pair of eyes watched her as she moved, naked, throughout the room.

That was when she first got the feeling that something was wrong. It was just a vague premonition of what was to come, though at the time she didn't know what it was. Only later did she come to realize that those eyes were just the beginning.

Those eyes weren't really evil; they were just the door to evil.

SHE didn't start to feel uneasy until they took her to the house.

Right up until then, everything had seemed normal, even fun. Having a man in an expensive suit waiting for her at the airport in Zurich, holding a sign that bore her name, seemed like a charming confirmation of Swiss meticulousness. She stifled a giggle when she realized, rushing to keep up with his long strides, that she'd assumed he was a colleague and was about to start discussing physics. Actually, he was the chauffeur.

The ride in the dark Volkswagen was enjoyable, and she stared out the window at the lush landscape, so utterly different from the wide-open golden fields surrounding Madrid. She saw a thousand different shades of green, and it reminded her of the colored pencils she'd used in her sketchbooks as a girl (actually, weren't those Swiss pencils?). She'd been to Switzerland before: in college, she spent a few weeks at CERN, the European Organization for Nuclear Research, in Geneva. Now, they were going to the Technical Research in Physics laboratory in Zurich, where she had a room reserved. She'd never been to the famous lab where the sequoia theory was born, but she'd seen countless pictures of the building.

That's why she frowned when it became clear that, in fact, this was not where they were taking her.

They were probably a few kilometers north of Zurich (she'd seen "Dübendorf" on a sign), on what looked like a farm with pretty trees, a well-manicured lawn, and fancy cars parked at the entrance. *The producer's house. They're filming a movie.* The chauffeur opened the door for her and grabbed her suitcase. *Is this where I'm going to stay?* But she didn't even have time to think. A man who'd clearly been to the same tailor as the chauffeur asked her to take off her jacket and then patted under her arms and down her legs with some sort of metal detector. He found her house keys, cell phone, and loose change, all of which were returned intact. Then he led her through the silent house, in which the hardwood floors shone so deeply they seemed to reflect the water from the lake. Finally, he left her with another man who said his name was Cassimir.

If his name and broken Spanish hadn't already given him away, Cassimir had plenty of other qualities that made it clear he was not from the Iberian Peninsula. He was blond and built like a house, and his pasty Anglo-Saxon skin tone contrasted sharply with the black turtleneck and gray trousers he wore. He was obviously in charge of welcoming her. He asked all the requisite questions. Had she had a good flight? Had she ever been to Switzerland before? And so on. As he asked her these and other questions, he led her to a bright office and asked her to have a seat at a hardwood desk made of what looked like cherry. Behind Cassimir's chair, a large window opened onto the clear, sunny Swiss day, and to Elisa's left (Cassimir's right), a long mirror reflected a double of the room, showing another Elisa with wavy black hair, a pink tank top that underscored her tan skin and white bra strap (her mother couldn't stand that she let her bra strap show; she found it "vulgar"), tight jeans, and tennis shoes. Also reflected was an enormous Cassimir clone in silhouette, his fingers laced together. She stifled a laugh, recalling an erotic video she'd downloaded off the Internet once, in which a girl was asked to take off her clothes in the office of a (porno) film producer, while from the other side of the two-way mirror, someone watched her. *I know someone is watching me from the other side of that mirror. This is white slavery, and they're assessing the goods before they accept them.*

"Professor Blanes isn't here." Cassimir had taken out two sets of papers, one blue and one white. "But as soon as you read and sign these, you'll be meeting with him. These are the general provisions. Read them carefully because there are some things we weren't able to set up before you got here. If you have any questions, just ask. Can I get you a coffee, a refreshment?"

"No, thanks."

"How do you say it in Spanish? Is it 'refreshment' or 'refreshing'?" Cassimir asked with giddy curiosity. And when Elisa cleared it up for him, he explained agreeably, "I mix those up sometimes."

The papers were all written in perfect Spanish. The white ones bore the notation "work-related," but the blue ones said only "A6." Cassimir clarified what that meant.

"The blue ones are the confidentiality agreement. Why don't you read that first?"

She saw her name in capital letters surrounded by a sea of text and was overcome by another wave of apprehension. She hadn't been expecting her name to be written in the same font as the rest of the document. She'd expected something pro forma with her name handwritten on a dotted line. Upon seeing ELISA ROBLEDO MORANDÉ typed out just like the rest of it, she was shocked. It was as if this had been made out expressly for her, as if they'd gone to too much trouble over her.

"All clear?" Cassimir asked solicitously.

"Well, here it says that I can't publish anything ..."

"For a time, yes, but that only applies to the research you carry out with Professor Blanes. Read down below, Clause 5c ... This prohibition applies only to said research for a period of at least two years, but that doesn't stop you from publishing studies with Professor Blanes or any other professor, as long as it's on a different subject. And then look at the following clause. You have the chance to do your PhD with Professor Blanes as long as it's not directly related to your time here ... If you read the white papers, where it says, 'Amount of Stipend,' you'll see it's very generous. And that doesn't include your housing, which is free. You only pay for food and personal expenses. You get paid every month, like a salary, through December of this year."

The voice speaking to her about the blue papers, which were full of headings she barely understood ("Post-contractual Confidentiality Clause," "Norms of Investigation for EU State Security," "Penal Code for Revealing State Secrets and Classified Information"), was much colder. But it wasn't the legalese that concerned her; it was Cassimir's good-natured insistence, the way he kept trying to smooth things over so she wouldn't worry, his persistent attempts to cut everything into bite-sized chunks for her, so she could swallow it all without complaining.

"If you prefer, I can leave you alone so you can take your time and read everything carefully. Please take your time."

She looked up and blinked at the sun glaring through the window, noticing something she (absurdly) hadn't seen until just then. Cassimir was wearing glasses. When had he put them on? Had he been wearing them the whole time? She became fixated on that detail and other questions, her mind swirling in confusion.

"What exactly does the job consist of?"

"Helping Professor Blanes."

"Helping him do what?"

"Research."

She forced herself not to be sarcastic. From the mirror, the other Elisa scowled back at her.

"What I'm getting at is, what *kind* of research will I be carrying out with Professor Blanes?"

Cassimir smiled. "Oh, I couldn't tell you anything about that. I'm not a physicist."

"Well, if you don't mind, I'd like to know what I'm going to be doing."

"You'll find out very soon. We'll get things going the same minute you accept the conditions. 'The same minute?' Is that right? No, 'the very minute,'" he corrected himself.

"What conditions?"

"As soon as you sign, I mean."

This is absurd. We're going around in circles. If her mother were there, she thought, she would have pointed out the unmistakable Elisa-Robledo-Pissed-Off-Smile. But Mr. Cassimir wasn't her mother, and he was smiling, too.

"Look. I'm not signing anything until I find out what I'm going to be doing."

Cassimir (and his mirror-reflected image) feigned irritation.

"I told you. You're going to be helping Professor Blanes with his research ..."

"What's EG SECURITY?" Elisa decided to change tactics and pointed to a line on one of the white pages. "It's all over the place. What is it?"

"Oh, they're our main financial backers. They're some sort of consortium of different research firms ..."

"Does EG stand for Eagle Group?"

"Oh, I don't work for them, and I don't know what the initials stand for."

Oh, you're so clever, Mr. "Oh!" Elisa decided to cut the politeness crap and go for a full-frontal attack on Mr. Oh.

"Are you the ones who've been keeping tabs on me the past few weeks? Who put a transmitter in my cell phone and made me respond to all those questions on the questionnaire?"

She enjoyed watching his smile vanish, seeing the disconcerted look on his face. It was obvious that Cassimir was used to dealing with more passive clients, or maybe he'd just underestimated her, thinking that a young woman would be easier to manipulate.

"Excuse me, but ..."

"No, excuse *me*. I think you already know plenty about lil' old me. Now it's my turn to get some answers."

"Miss ..."

"I want to speak to Professor Blanes. After all, I'm going to be working with him."

"I told you, he's not here."

"Well, somebody had better at least tell me what it is I'm going to be doing."

"You're not allowed to know," a different voice said, in perfect English.

A man had just emerged from a door beside the mirror, behind Elisa. He was tall and thin, and wearing an impeccably tailored suit. His blond hair was graying at the temples and his mustache was carefully groomed. Another man, short and stocky, was with him. *So they* were *spying on me.* Her heart was pounding.

"You speak English, don't you?" he continued in a mellifluous voice, walking over to her. Unlike Cassimir, he neither offered his hand nor extended any sort of courtesy. His eyes freaked Elisa out a little. They were cold and blue, like cut glass. "I'm Harrison. This is Carter. We're in charge of security. I repeat: you are not allowed to know anything. We ourselves know nothing. This project is considered classified, it's top secret. Professor Blanes needs young scientists on board, and you were chosen as one of them."

He stopped speaking when he stopped walking. He'd reached Elisa, and his blue eyes bore into her like needles. After a short pause, he added, "If you accept, sign. If not, you'll return to Spain and that's that. Any more questions?"

"Yes. Several. Have you been keeping tabs on me?"

"Of course," he replied disinterestedly, as if it were the most mundane thing imaginable. "We've spied on you, we've tracked your movements, we've given you a questionnaire, and delved into your private life … just like all the other candidates. It's all legal; these practices are upheld by international conventions. This is utterly routine. When you apply for a job, any job, you send your résumé, answer questions, have an interview. And none of that seems improper to you, does it? Well, this is what happens when you apply for a job that's been deemed classified matter. Anything else?"

Elisa stopped to think for a moment. Her mind flashed with images of Javier Maldonado and the sound of his voice. *"Good journalism is the product of accurate information, patiently compiled." Fucker.* But in a second she calmed down. *OK, he was just doing his job. And now it's my turn to do mine.*

"Can you at least tell me if I'll be staying in Zurich?"

"No, you won't. As soon as you sign, you'll be taken someplace else. Have you read the section titled 'Isolation and Security Filters'?"

"Second page of the blue set," Cassimir piped up, speaking for the first time since Harrison and Carter entered the room.

"You'll be working in complete isolation," Harrison said. "All of your telephone calls, e-mails, all of your contact with the outside world, will have to go through a security filter. As far as the rest of the world knows, including your friends and family, you'll still be in Zurich. Any unforeseen event that might arise due to this arrangement will be our responsibility. You won't have to worry about anyone trying to visit you unannounced and finding that you're not here; we'll take care of all of that."

"Who's 'we'?"

For the first time, he smiled.

"Mr. Carter and I. Our mission is to ensure that all you have to think about are equations." He looked at his watch. "Question time's over. Are you going to sign, or would you prefer to get on the next flight back to Madrid?"

Elisa stared at the papers on the table.

She was scared. At first she thought her fear was normal, that anyone in her position would feel the same, but then she realized that her fear contained something more, as if a voice inside her were shouting, *Don't do it!*

Don't sign. Leave. Go home.

"Can I read through this more carefully and have a glass of water?"

MYSTERIOUS experiences are often unforgettable, but sometimes, paradoxically, what we remember most about them are the inane, jumbled details. Anxiety and agitation etch certain things in our mind, but those things are rarely the most accurate details used to describe what's happening objectively.

From that first trip, so nervous she was almost sick, Elisa stored up a whole host of trivial scenes. For example, she recalled the argument that Carter, the stocky one (who was the one who accompanied her; she didn't see Harrison again for a long time), had with one of his subordinates as they boarded the little ten-seater plane at Zurich airport that afternoon. It revolved around whether "Abdul was at his post" or whether "Abdul left" (she never found out who Abdul was). And there were Carter's big, hairy, veiny hands as he sat across the aisle from her leafing through a file he'd taken from his briefcase. And the smell of flowers and diesel (if there could be such a mix) at the airport where they landed (which they told her belonged to Yemen). And the exhilarating moment when Carter had to show her how to put on a life jacket and helmet when they boarded the helicopter awaiting them on an out-of-the-way runway. "Don't worry, this is standard procedure for longer trips on military helicopters." And Carter's crew cut and sparse beard, speckled with gray. And his gruff manner, especially when he gave orders over the phone. And how hot it was with the helmet on.

Each and every one of these insignificant details were what made up her experience of the shortest day and longest night (they were traveling east) of her life. This was all she had to cling to over the years, when she tried to reconstruct the five-hour plane and helicopter journey.

But of all the memories that time's acid slowly dissolved, there was one that remained indelible, crisp and vivid, and she thought about it every time she recalled the trip.

It was what she saw written on the file folder that Carter had pulled out of his briefcase.

More than anything else, that was a visual for her; it summed up that day. And the events that followed would never, ever let her forget it.

"Zig Zag."

13

"**IMAGINE** wanting to understand all that I saw." That strange sentence was written, in English, below a drawing of a man gazing at two circles of light in the sky. She was searching for some clothes to put on when she noticed the sticker on the headboard of her bed, which she hadn't seen until just then.

That was when it happened.

It wasn't a rational thought but more of a physical sensation, a sort of heat at her temples. She was naked, which made her panic even more. She turned around and looked at the door.

And that's when she saw the eyes.

IT wasn't that she hadn't been expecting it. She'd been warned about that possible eventuality. She wasn't exactly going to have her beloved privacy there on New Nelson, Mrs. Ross had told her the night before, when she came out to greet her on the sandy ground where the helicopter had landed (or maybe it was that same night, she couldn't keep time straight). Mrs. Ross had been very nice, affectionate even. Her smile, as she stood waiting by the helicopter, was so wide it almost spread to her clover-shaped earrings. She held out both her hands.

"Welcome to New Nelson!" she exclaimed in enthusiastic English, once they were far enough away from the deafening roar of the chopper's blades. It was as if this were all a giant celebration and Mrs. Ross were in charge of seeing to the guests and organizing the party games.

But it was no party. It was a very dark, steamy place, an incredibly dark, steamy place, with reflectors lighting up a barbed-wire fence. A sea breeze like none she'd ever felt blew through her hair, and, despite her earplugs, she could make out strange sounds.

"We're about a hundred and fifty kilometers north of the Chagos Archipelago and three hundred kilometers south of the Maldives, smack in the middle of the Indian Ocean," Mrs. Ross continued, striding through the sand. "This island was discovered by a Portuguese man named La Gloria, but when it became a British colony they changed the name to New Nelson. It used to be part of the BIOT—that's the British Indian Ocean Territory—but since 1992 the island has formed part of the land acquired by an EU consortium. It's like heaven, you'll see. A tiny slice of it, anyway. It could practically fit in the palm of your hand; it's barely eleven square kilometers." They'd walked through a gate in the fence that a soldier (not a cop; a *soldier* armed to the teeth) held open for them. She'd never been so close to someone with that many weapons. Elisa turned to see if Carter was still with them, but all she could see were another couple of soldiers, standing by the helicopter she'd just climbed out of. "You'll be able to explore tomorrow. You must be exhausted."

"Not really." In fact, Elisa couldn't remember what being tired felt like.

"Aren't you sleepy?"

"*En mi casa*—" Elisa stopped short, realizing that she'd responded in Spanish, and quickly switched into English. "At home, I always go to bed late."

"I see. Still, it *is* four thirty in the morning."

"What?"

Mrs. Ross gave a friendly laugh. And on realizing her mistake,

Elisa laughed, too. According to her watch, it wasn't even eleven at night. She made a quick joke, not wanting Mrs. Ross to think she was an inexperienced traveler (which, in fact, she was not). But her nerves were playing tricks on her.

They walked to the furthest of three barracks, where Mrs. Ross opened a door to let them into a hallway illuminated with the tiny bulbs used in movie theater aisles after the lights are turned down. Immediately, Elisa noticed a marked change in temperature and even atmosphere. Instantly, the climate went from the thick, sticky outdoor air to the climate control of those portable buildings. Mrs. Ross opened another door, stopped again at the first one on the left, turned the handle without using a key, and flipped on the light inside.

"This will be your room. It's hard to see it right now because at night they only leave the bathroom lights on, but ..."

"It's great."

She'd thought she would be in a tiny cell, but this was spacious. Later, she'd be able to tell that it was about ten feet long by fifteen feet wide and was neatly furnished with a dresser, a little desk, and a bed and night table in the middle of the room. On the far side of the bed, the room was only half as wide, since the rest of the space was taken up by a wall to another room. "The bathroom," Mrs. Ross said, opening the door.

Elisa nodded and made polite conversation, saying it was all fine, but Mrs. Ross didn't beat around the bush. She launched into an interrogation, "woman to woman": How many changes of clothes had she brought? Did she use any particular shampoo? What kind of sanitary napkins did she want? Did she sleep in pajamas or not? Had she brought a bathing suit? And so on. Then she pointed to the door, and Elisa noticed that it had a rectangular glass peephole, like the kind you see in movies where a dangerous lunatic is locked up in a cell and under observation. It gave her the creeps. There was another, identical one in the bathroom door, which also had no lock.

"Security requirements," Ross said. "They call them 'grade two low-privacy stalls.' In practical terms, what it means for us is that any old pervert can spy on you, but luckily we're surrounded by decent men."

Elisa smiled, unable to help herself despite the fact that this loss of privacy made her feel a whole host of strange and unpleasant feelings. But it seemed like with Mrs. Ross by her side, nothing bad could happen.

Before her hostess left her, Elisa examined her in the bathroom light: she was plump and matronly, maybe fifty or so, and wore a silver sweat suit and athletic shoes. She was also wearing full makeup, her hair looked as though she'd just come from the beauty salon, and she had on gold rings, bracelets, and earrings. Pinned to her sweat suit was a photo ID that read "Cheryl Ross. Scientific Section."

"I'm sorry to have made you get up in the middle of the night," Elisa said.

"That's what I'm here for. Now, you need to get some rest. Tomorrow at nine thirty (well, in about four hours, actually) there's a meeting in the main room. You can have breakfast in the kitchen before that. And if you need anything at all while you're here, just contact Maintenance."

That last sentence made Elisa suspect that Mrs. Ross was begging a question, and she decided to indulge her.

"Where's Maintenance?"

"You're looking at it," the woman replied, obviously pleased.

"IMAGINE wanting to understand all that I saw," the sticker said. She'd bent over to read it, and that was when she realized she wasn't alone.

The reptilian eyes were staring at her fixedly.

She realized that there was no need to get so ridiculously upset about it, but she couldn't help jumping back to try to cover her breasts and crotch with one hand each as she wondered where the hell she'd left her towel. The indulgent part of her mind was able to understand her reaction. She hadn't slept a wink during those few hours, due to the stressful circumstances *(yesterday I was in Madrid saying good-bye to Víctor and my mother, and this morning I'm naked on an island in the Indian Ocean, for God's sake).* Exhaustion had taken a toll on her nerves.

Still, despite everything, she felt enthusiastic. She'd gotten up far earlier than necessary, as soon as she saw the light begin to filter in through the glass rectangle on the far wall, and had been astonished when she walked over to the window. It was one thing to *know* you were on an island, and another thing entirely to *see* the dark waves crashing violently on the horizon, so close you could almost reach out and touch the water, just beyond the barbed-wire fence, palm trees, and beach.

She decided to take a shower, and pulled off her T-shirt and underwear without thinking about the peepholes or any other type of surveillance. The bathroom had just enough space so that she could sit on the toilet without banging her knees against the wall, but she didn't care. The water pouring down over her in that tiny, curtainless metal cubicle felt delicious, and it was just the right temperature. She found a towel and dried off. Emerging from the bathroom with her towel, she glanced at the glass peephole: it was dark. She didn't want to be on display, but she also wasn't going to change her routine just because the peephole was there. She threw the towel down somewhere *(fuck, where was it?)* and unzipped her suitcase to find some clothes.

That's when she saw the sticker on the headboard. There were several, in fact, and postcards, too. They seemed to have been placed there to give a more homey air to the aluminum rectangle that was her room. She leaned in to examine the most interesting-looking one and then, suddenly, got that weird feeling and saw the eyes at the peephole.

It was then.

As she jumped back, her hands flew to cover herself like an affronted damsel.

And then, for the first time, she had a portent of the evil she was soon to discover.

"**WELCOME** to New Nelson, though I imagine you've already heard that."

She recognized him before he barged in. She'd know those greeny blue eyes anywhere, be it in the middle of the Indian Ocean or the North Pole. The same went for the voice.

Ric Valente walked in and closed the door. He was wearing a matching green T-shirt and Bermuda shorts that went well together but were nothing like the kind of clothes he normally wore (as if he, too, had been caught off guard by this island location, she thought). He held two small carafes of something steamy. His bony face relaxed into a smile.

"I asked for a queen-size bed, but they didn't have any left. Still, I'll be happy just to see you like that every morning. By the way, if you're looking for your towel, it's right here on the floor." He pointed to the other side of the bed but made no move to pick it up for her. "Sorry to scare you, but as you know, privacy is prohibited by decree. This is a sex commune; everyone screws everyone. The temperature helps, of course. At night, they turn off the AC." He left the carafes on the desk and took two paper cups and four triangles of cut-up, cellophane-wrapped sandwich from his roomy pockets.

Standing by the window, still covering herself with her hands, Elisa felt dispirited. Valente was a thorn in the side of her being there. He was the same as ever, with the same interest in humiliating her as ever, and seemed to be in his element, perhaps because he'd made her blush so easily. But she'd known she'd have to see him sooner or later (though she hadn't anticipated being naked when the time came), and she had a lot of things to think about besides whether he'd seen her without her clothes on.

Sighing, she lowered her hands and walked as casually as possible to where her towel lay. Valente watched, amused. Finally, he nodded, assessing.

"Not bad, but I'm certainly not prepared to give you a ten, or even four one-hundredths less. Seven, tops. Your body is ... how can I describe it? Too overwhelming, too exuberant. Too glandular, too muscular. And if I were you, I'd definitely do something about that bikini line."

"Nice to see you, Valente," she replied indifferently, turning her back to him once she had the towel wrapped around her. She kept rummaging through her luggage. "I think there's a meeting at nine thirty."

"It would be my pleasure to accompany you to it, but I thought you might not want to have breakfast with a bunch of strangers, so I opted to come here and have it just with you. Do you want the ham and cheese, or the chicken sandwich?"

He was right about breakfast. She was starving, but she had no desire to begin her day by having to greet a bunch of people she didn't know.

"When did you get here?" she asked, choosing the chicken.

"Monday." Valente held up the carafes. They were half full of coffee. "Do you take sugar?"

"No."

"Me neither. We're equally bitter."

Elisa had pulled out a tank top and a pair of shorts that, luckily, she'd stuck in her bag for what she thought would be her days off in Switzerland.

"What is all this about?" she asked. "Do you know?"

"I told you, it's a sex camp. And we're the guinea pigs."

"I'm being serious."

"So am I. We have no privacy, and we're all staring at each other's asses inside some metal cages on a tropical island in the Indian Ocean. Sounds like sex to me. Aside from that, I don't know any more than you. I thought Blanes was in Switzerland, and being brought here was a complete surprise to me. Then I was even more surprised to find out you were coming, too. Now I'm used to surprises. They're just part of island life." He raised his carafe. "To our bet."

"The bet's off," Elisa said. She sipped her coffee; it was excellent. "We tied."

"Not on your life. I won. Blanes told me yesterday that your idea about the local time variables is ridiculous, but that you were too hot to leave behind, and I didn't object. And now that I've seen it all, I can say he wasn't mistaken."

She began scarfing down her sandwich.

"Would you just shut up and tell me what you know?"

"All I know is that I know nothing. Or hardly anything." Valente devoured his sandwich in two bites. "I know that I was right all along and that whatever this is, it's a big deal. So big they want to keep it all secret. That's why they wanted people like us, students, unknowns who won't get in their way. Got it, sweetheart? As for the rest of it, I'm guessing this nine thirty meeting will fill in the blanks. But, as God said to King Solomon, what exactly do you want to know?"

"What do we do with our dirty clothes?"

"That I can tell you. We wash them ourselves. There's a washing machine, a dryer, and an ironing board in the kitchen. We also have to make our own beds and clean our rooms, wash our dishes, and take turns cooking. And I warn you, the girls have extra duties at night; they have to please the men. Seriously, Blanes's experiment was all about seeing if people could stand married life without losing their minds. You're putting on a bra? Please! All the girls go braless here. We're on an island, sweetheart."

Paying no attention to him, Elisa went into the bathroom to change.

"Tell me one thing," she said, zipping up her shorts. "Am I going to have to put up with you the whole time I'm here?"

"This island is eleven square kilometers including the lake, so don't worry. There's enough room for us to stay out of each other's way."

She walked back into the room. Ric was lying on the bed, sipping his coffee and watching her.

"Well, now that my dream of seeing you naked has come true, maybe it's time to own up," he admitted. "Blanes wasn't the one who called me on Sunday. It was Colin Craig, my friend from Oxford. I was his choice. He'd already picked me, though I didn't know it. That's why they were watching me. They were also keeping tabs on you as a probable candidate for Blanes, though he hadn't picked you yet. But after he read your project, he made up his mind." He smiled at her look of surprise. "Yep. Looks like you're Blanes's girl."

"What?"

Amused, Valente added, "You were right, sweetheart. The local time variable was key, and we didn't have a clue."

THE sun and most of the sky were hidden behind huge clouds that resembled bulging sacks of grain. But it wasn't cold, and the air was thick and sticky. The landscape in this new world was fascinating: fine sand, heavy palm trees, a jungle beyond the heliport, and a grayish sea that surrounded everything.

As they walked to the second barracks, Valente explained that New Nelson was horseshoe shaped, open on the south side where the coral reefs were, and enclosed a saltwater lake that was five square kilometers. The island was an atoll. The science station was on the very north tip, on the most solid ground, and between it and the lake lay the jungle they now contemplated.

"We could go for a hike one day," he added. "There's bamboo, palm trees, even liana. And the butterflies are amazing."

Walking across the sand, Elisa was overcome by a sort of giddiness she'd never before experienced. And that, despite the barbed-wire fence and the rest of the paraphernalia, which didn't exactly fit in with the natural beauty of the setting: satellite dishes, antennae, makeshift garrison, and helicopters. Right then, she

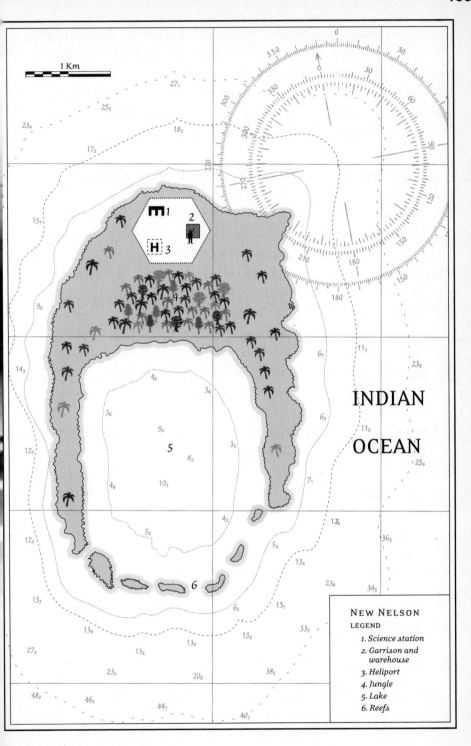

1 Km

INDIAN

OCEAN

NEW NELSON
LEGEND
1. Science station
2. Garrison and
   warehouse
3. Heliport
4. Jungle
5. Lake
6. Reefs

didn't mind the two soldiers who appeared to be on sentry duty, or even Valente's irritating presence, small yet persistently bothersome, like a pimple. She supposed her giddiness emanated from someplace very private, maybe even subconscious. It was like the Garden of Eden. I'm in paradise, she thought to herself.

That feeling lasted exactly twenty seconds, the time she spent outside.

As soon as she walked into the second barracks, which was bigger than the other one and full of artificial light, metal walls and glass windows showed a functional dining room. Her paradise evaporated. All that was left was her professional pride, on recalling Valente's words. *My solution was right.*

"The science station is also horseshoe shaped, or maybe fork shaped," Valente explained, drawing in the air. "The first barracks is closest to the heliport, and that's where the labs are; the second one is the main artery, and that's where the screening room, dining room, and kitchen—with a trapdoor down to the pantry—are; and the third one is for the bedrooms. The perpendicular one is the control room, or at least that's what they call it. I've only been in there once, but man, it's *full* of state-of-the-art computers and a fucking amazing particle accelerator, a new kind of synchrotron. Right now we're going to the screening room."

He pointed to an open door on the left. She could hear people speaking English. Until that moment, Elisa hadn't bumped into anyone. She guessed the team was pretty small. Suddenly, Cheryl Ross appeared at the door, dressed now in jeans and a T-shirt, but still sporting the same hairdo and identical smile as last night. Elisa cast off her Spanish as soon as she saw her.

"Good morning!" Ross sang. "I was just coming to find you! The boss doesn't want to get started until we're all here; you know how he is ... How was your first night on New Nelson?"

"Slept like a log," Elisa lied.

"I'm glad."

The room looked like a home theater, set up for twelve. Seating consisted of three rows of chairs, and there was a console with keyboard on one wall and a ten-foot screen on the other.

But Elisa was more interested in the people. They all stood up and made a tremendous racket in the process, their chairs scraping the floor. Then there was a frenzy of handshaking and cheek kissing when Valente introduced her as "the missing member." Forced to think in English, Elisa just let herself be carried along by the course of events.

She recognized Colin Craig, a young, good-looking man with short hair, round glasses, and a neat beard. She remembered that the beautiful woman with long brown hair was Jacqueline Clissot, who was quite reserved and only held out her hand. Nadja Petrova, the girl with albino hair, on the other hand, was downright effusive. She gave her an affectionate kiss and made her laugh by attempting to say, "I'm a paleontologist, too," in Spanish.

"Pleased to meet you," she said, adding, *"Me alegro de conocerte,"* and Elisa truly appreciated the girl's effort to speak her language.

Valente, unsurprisingly, made a big song and dance of introducing the other lady, a skinny, mature woman with a gaunt, lined face and a big freckled nose. He threw his arm over her shoulder with forced camaraderie, causing her to flash an embarrassed smile.

"Allow me to introduce you to Rosalyn Reiter of Berlin, Reinhard Silberg's beloved disciple; she studied history and philosophy of science and currently specializes in a very remarkable field."

"Which one?"

"History of Christianity," Rosalyn Reiter replied.

Although Elisa didn't change her chirpy, polite tone, her mind was definitely elsewhere. Looking at the faces of the people she'd be working with, she speculated. *Two paleontologists and a Christian historian ... What does that mean?* Just then, Craig pointed at something.

"And here comes the Counsel of Wise Men."

David Blanes, Reinhard Silberg, and Sergio Marini filed in. Marini closed the door behind him.

It reminded Elisa of some sort of selection committee, sitting around deciding everyone's fate. Who will go to heaven and who gets expelled. Who earns eternal glory and who stays here on earth. She counted them: ten, herself included.

Ten scientists. Ten chosen ones.

Everybody sat down in silence. Only Blanes remained standing before them, his back to the big screen. Elisa watched the papers he held flutter and thought she must be dreaming.

Blanes was trembling.

"Friends, we waited until all the participants in Project Zig Zag were present to give you the explanations that, no doubt, you've been waiting for ... But let me say this. Those of us who are here today in this room can consider ourselves very fortunate. We're going to see things no human has ever seen before. That's not an exaggeration. On some occasions, we'll see things that no creature, living or dead, has *ever* seen, since time immemorial ..."

Elisa got the chills. She was petrified.

The sea I sail has never yet been passed.

She sat up straight in her chair, preparing to dive, along with her nine astonished colleagues, into the uncharted scientific waters that would seal her fate.

FOUR

The Project

Everything that is, is past.

ANATOLE FRANCE

14

It was almost there.
Those eyes were the prelude.
Next would come the shadow.

THOUGH she didn't know it yet, the darkest evil she would ever encounter in her life had already been born.

And it was just around the corner, waiting for her.

SERGIO Marini was everything Blanes wasn't: elegant and seductive. Thin, with dark, wavy hair, tan skin, a smooth shave, and a disarming smile, he knew how to project his basso voice and captivate his Milanese students. Born in Rome, he studied at the prestigious Scuola Normale Superiore in Pisa, where bigwigs like Enrico Fermi had earned their PhDs in physics. After the obligatory stint in the United States, Grossmann had called him to Zurich, where he met Blanes, and together they developed the sequoia theory. "Together" meant—in the words Marini himself always used to refer to those years of collaboration—that "I let him calculate in peace and rushed over every time he wanted to tell me the results."

He had something Blanes lacked: a sense of humor.

"One night in 2001 we filled a glass to the halfway mark. Then we left it on the lab table for thirty hours straight. After the time was up, David smashed it on the floor. That was as far as his actual experimentation went." He looked at Blanes, who was laughing along with everyone else. "Don't get upset, David. You're the theoretician, I'm the hammer-and-nail man. Anyway ... our idea was ... Oh, you explain it. You're better at this stuff."

"No, no, go ahead."

"Please, you do it; you're the father."

"And you're the mother."

Both of them were trying to improvise, to put on a show, and it was pretty much working. They were like a cheap cabaret act: the bumbler and the wise guy; the lady-killer and the geek. Elisa watched them and could relate to their years of solitary, fruitless toil, and the uncontainable excitement at their first success.

"Well, OK, looks like it's my turn," said Blanes. "Anyway, let's see. As you know, the sequoia theory states that every particle of light has time strings coiled up inside it like the rings in a sequoia's trunk. Those that grow out from its center. The number of strings is not infinite, but it is gigantic and inconceivable: it's the number of Planck times that have transpired since the origins of light ..."

There was some murmuring, and Marini whined, "Professor Clissot wants to know what a Planck time is, David. Don't disregard those who aren't physicists, even if they deserve to be!"

"A Planck time is the smallest possible interval of time," Blanes explained. "It's how long it takes for light to cross a distance equal to a Planck length, which is the shortest length in existence. To give you an idea, if a single atom were the size of the universe, a Planck length would be the size of one tree. The time that it takes light to cross that distance is called Planck time. It's approximately one-septillionth of a second, and there is nothing in the universe that takes *less* time than that."

"You've never seen Colin eating foie gras sandwiches," Marini quipped. Craig raised his hand in acknowledgement. That was the first time she'd ever seen Blanes burst out laughing, although he did get serious again almost immediately after.

"Every time string equates to one specific Planck time and contains *everything* that was reflected by light in that briefest of intervals. With some necessary mathematical adjustments to our equations (using local time variables, for example), the theory told us it was possible to isolate and identify the strings chronologically, even open them. It didn't require a *lot* of energy, but it did take an *exact* quantity. Sergio called it 'supraselective.' If the appropriate supraselective energy was used, the strings from a determined time period could be opened, showing us the images from that period. Now then, this, of course, was just a mathematical finding. And for over ten years, that's all it was. But eventually, a team led by Professor Craig designed the new synchrotron, and using it we were able to obtain the kind of supraselective energy we needed. But we didn't get any results until the night we broke that glass. You continue, Sergio. This is the part you like."

"Well, we videotaped the image of the broken glass and sent it to a particle accelerator," Marini went on. "As you know, a video is nothing but a beam of electrons. We accelerated those electrons to obtain a level of energy that was stable to within a few decimals and we made them collide with a stream of positrons. The resulting particles should have contained the open strings from a period equivalent to two hours before the breaking of the glass. We then reconverted those particles into a new beam of electrons, made them collide against a television screen, used a special software program to profile the image. And when we turned on the screen, what did we see?"

"A broken glass on the floor," said Blanes, and laughter erupted once more.

"Well, yes, that's what happened the first hundred or so times we tried it," Marini admitted. "But that night in 2001 was different. We managed to receive an image of the *unbroken* glass on the table. And we had never filmed that image. Do you see what I'm getting at? It came from the past. Specifically, from two hours before we began filming ... Guys, that night we went out and got blind drunk. I remember being in a pub in Zurich with David, three sheets to the wind, when an equally drunk Swiss guy says to me, 'Why so happy, friend?' 'Because the glass is unbroken,' I said. And the guys says, 'Lucky you; I've already broken three tonight.'

"No joke, that really happened," Blanes insisted as laughter rang out in the small room. Even Valente, who was always so superior when people made run-of-the-mill jokes (Elisa thought) seemed to think it was hilarious.

"When we showed that image to the people with the big bucks," Marini continued, "jeez! Offers for financial backing started to flood in ... Eagle Group took the reins and started construction on this scientific station here on New Nelson. And, well, Colin will tell you the rest." Colin Craig got up, and Marini took his seat. People were still giggling and making comments. Nadja's face was flushed from laughing so hard, and Mrs. Ross (who had unexpectedly gone into hysterics with the tale of the man in the Zurich pub) was still wiping tears from her cheeks. Everyone seemed happy and relaxed.

Still, Elisa picked up on something.

Something different, something incongruent.

She thought she could see it in the glances that Marini, Blanes, and Craig exchanged. It was as if they were thinking, "May as well let them have fun for a little while."

Maybe the rest won't be so enjoyable, she surmised.

"**SO** I was in charge of coordinating all the practicalities for the project," Craig said. "In 2004, a dozen satellites were secretly launched in geosynchronous orbit; that is, they were programmed to rotate at a rate that matched the speed of the earth's rotation on its axis. They were equipped with cameras that could produce multispectral imagery at up to a half-meter resolution and focus on a twelve-kilometer area. They could record telemetric sequences of anyplace on the planet, using the coordinates received from New Nelson. And those images are retransmitted to our station in real time (which is why the project is called Zig Zag; the signal boomerangs back and forth from the earth to the satellite and back to the earth again), where they're processed by a twenty-two-bit computer, isolating the geographic zone in question. Now, that's not quite precise enough to allow us to count every hair on Sergio's head …"

"But it is on David's, since he's got so few left," Marini interjected.

"Precisely. In a word, we can see whatever we want, whenever we want, just like military spy satellites. Let me give you an example." Craig strode over to the computer console, gently pushing his wire-rimmed glasses up on his nose as he did. Elisa thought he possessed such a natural elegance that he could attend a reception at Buckingham Palace in the jeans and T-shirt he was wearing right now without attracting attention. He quickly typed something and the screen came to life, showing a rough sketch of the Egyptian pyramids. In one corner stood two mummies. Their faces had been covered with cutouts from photos of Marini and Blanes. People giggled. "Let's suppose we ask the satellites to capture a sequence of the Nile delta. They do it, send it to us, and a computer processes it and obtains a series of maps of the pyramids. After streaming the beam of electrons through our synchrotron, we recover the recently formed particles, and then another computer reconstructs them and captures the new image. If we've used the right amount of energy, then we'll be able to see the same place, the Egyptian pyramids, but, say, three thousand years earlier … With a little luck, for a few seconds, we'd be able to see a pyramid being built, or a pharaoh's burial ceremony."

"Amazing," Elisa heard Nadja murmur, two seats to her left.

Marini stood abruptly.

"Hey, Colin, I think it's time to convince our audience that this isn't just a pipe dream."

Craig typed something into the console. A blurry but identifiable image—pale rose, almost sepia in color, like an old photo—appeared on the screen.

A sudden hush overcame the room.

Elisa felt a strange, ambiguous emotion; she wanted to laugh and cry at the same time. Valente, sitting next to her, leaned forward with his mouth open, like a little kid unwrapping the present he's been dreaming of, the one he thought no one was going to give him.

The photograph wasn't particularly interesting. It was just a close-up of a glass, half full of water, sitting on a table.

"The amazing thing about this image," said Marini calmly, "is that *it was never photographed.* We extracted it from a twenty-second clip of the same table, but what we filmed showed the glass broken on the floor two hours later. So what you have before you is the *first* real image of the past ever seen by the human eye."

Elisa's eyes began to moisten with emotion.

That was what science was, she thought. *True* science, the kind that changes the course of history forever, was precisely that: seeing an apple fall from a tree, and weeping.

Or an unbroken glass sitting on a table.

IT was Reinhard Silberg's turn. When he planted himself in front of the screen, he gave the impression (the *correct* impression, Elisa thought) of being enormous. He wore a short-sleeved shirt and cotton trousers with a leather belt, and was the only one there wearing a tie, though it was loosened. Everything about him was imposing, and maybe that's why he sometimes seemed to be trying to lighten up, giving a smile that looked almost childlike on his clean-shaven, pudgy, bespectacled face.

Right then, however, he wasn't smiling. Elisa guessed the

reason. *Maybe he's the one who's here to give us the catch.* The German scientific historian's first words made clear that she was right.

"I'm Reinhard Silberg, and I specialize in the philosophy of science. I was recruited for Project Zig Zag as a consultant for all matters that are not physics related, but are still of great importance." He paused and moved a foot, as if he were tracing something on the metal floor with a toe. "As you know, this project is top secret. No one knows we're here. Not our colleagues, not our friends, not our families, not even most of the managers at Eagle Group. Naturally, we can't fool the scientific community, but with the articles we've published and conferences we've put on, we've dangled a few carrots. They know that the sequoia theory has potential, if you'll pardon the expression, but not how potent it really is. This project is one of a kind, at least up until now. We've been selected after a rigorous study of our lives, hobbies, friends, and concerns. We'll be working on something that no one has any prior experience with. We're pioneers, and we need special security measures ... for several reasons."

He paused again and looked down at his foot, which was still jiggling.

"To begin with, don't even *think* that we'll be watching movies on this screen. When we go to the movies, we see Caesar's murder, for instance, as if it had been filmed by a home-movie buff straight from the time of the Roman Empire. But the images we obtain from open time strings are not movies, not even "true" or "real" films of the past: they *are* the past. We can watch them on a screen like movies, record them onto DVD like movies, but you must always remember that these are *open time strings* that we've extracted information from. When we see Caesar's murder it will *be* Caesar's murder, just exactly as it happened and was recorded in the actual particles of light reflected at the time, which is to say in the real past. This gives rise to certain consequences. We don't know, for example, what would happen with events or people who form part of our culture, part of our ideals. Some secret studies have been carried out, but they've been pretty inconclusive. For example, what would happen if we saw Jesus Christ, or Muhammad, or Buddha? Just seeing them and knowing, for certain, that it was actually them ... Not to mention what could happen if we discovered aspects of their lives that went against the teachings of the churches and creeds that claim to follow these founders. What these churches have been making millions of people—including several of us, most likely—believe for centuries. Well, clearly, that's more than enough reason for Project Zig Zag to be considered classified. But ... there's also another reason." He paused and blinked. "I'd like to explain it to you using another image. It's the only one we've been able to obtain, with the exception of the Unbroken Glass. Most of you don't even know it exists. Jacqueline, you're going to be quite surprised ... Colin, would you?"

"Sure."

Craig typed something else. This time the screening room lights went dim. In the darkness, someone (Elisa thought it was Marini's voice) said, "Fast forward through the ads, Reinhard." But this time, no one laughed. Silberg began speaking, and his silhouette was visible in the dim light emanating from the computer console.

"This was obtained using the system that Colin just explained to you about before. A satellite sent the images, we calculated the energy needed to open the time strings and processed it ..."

The screen lit up. Washed out, reddish forms appeared.

"The faded color is due to the fact that the 'past' end of the string is located, in spatial terms, almost a million light-years away from us, and it keeps getting farther," Silberg explained, "so it fades to this reddish hue in the same way other celestial bodies do. But this, in fact, comes from Earth ..."

It looked like a landscape. The camera was flying over a mountain range that seemed approachable, almost diminutive, and had circular valleys and spherical rocks between the mountains. The whole of it looked like a great baker had frosted it with an enormous load of whipped cream.

"My God," said Jacqueline in a shaky voice.

Leaning forward, Elisa uncrossed her legs. She felt weird. She couldn't put her finger on what she felt, but she knew it was related to the image she was seeing. It was like a shift toward uneasiness.

Something vaguely threatening.

But where was the threat coming from?

"Immense glaciers …," Clissot murmured, absorbed, "glaciers with U-shaped erosion … Look at those cirques and nunataks. Look, Nadja, what does it remind you of? You're the real paleogeologist …"

"Those mounds are drumlins," Nadja replied in a tiny voice. "But they're enormous. And those moraines on either side of them … It looks like a ton of sediment has been washed in from really far away."

What's going on? Elisa gave a nervous giggle. It was absurd, but she couldn't help it. There was something very disturbing about those red-tinged snowy summits. She felt faint and confused.

She saw Nadja tremble and wondered if it was just excitement at these findings, or if something similar was happening to her. Valente looked like he'd been affected, too. She heard someone gasp.

This is ridiculous.

But it wasn't. There was something very strange about that landscape.

"There seem to be signs of water in the crevasses," Nadja whispered, disconcerted.

"My God, that glacier is melting!" Clissot cried.

Silberg's voice, anxious and barely audible yet steady and clear, came from beside the screen.

"Those are the British Isles, eight hundred thousand years ago."

"The Günz glaciation ...," she whispered.

"Exactly. Pleistocene. The Quaternary period."

"Jesus, Mary, and Joseph," Clissot whispered. "Oh my God, oh my God, oh my God!"

Nausea. It's nauseating.

But *what?*

When the lights went on, Elisa realized she'd been hugging herself tightly, as if she'd been naked in public and was trying to hide.

"**THIS** is the second reason that Project Zig Zag has to be kept a secret. We don't know what creates it. We're calling it 'Impact.'" Silberg wrote the word on a small whiteboard on the wall, beside the screen. "We always write it like that, 'Impact,' with a capital I. Everyone experiences it, to a greater or lesser degree. It's an unusual reaction to images from the past. I could venture a theory to explain it. Maybe Jung was right; we have a collective unconscious that's full of archetypes, sort of like the species' genetic memory, and the images from the open time strings somehow disrupt it. Keep in mind that this particular part of our unconscious has been inviolate for generations, and, suddenly, for the first time, the door opens, light filters into the darkness ..."

"Why didn't we feel anything with the Unbroken Glass?" Valente asked.

"Well, in fact we did," said Silberg, and Elisa realized that this could explain part of her excitement when she saw that image. "Just with less intensity. It seems that the strongest Impacts come from the remote past. The symptoms we've detected so far include anxiety, depersonalization, a disconnect from reality—that is, the feeling that we are unreal, or that the world around us is—insomnia, and, occasionally, hallucination. That's why I started off by telling you that this isn't like the movies. Opening time strings is a much more complex phenomenon."

Elisa saw Nadja rubbing her eyes. Clissot had sat down with her and was whispering into her ear.

"We still don't know if there are other, more important side effects or not," Silberg continued. "Grave Impacts, I mean. And that means we have to set out a series of security measures that we must all obey. The most important one is this: when we see an image for the first time, we'll always do it as a group, just like today. That way we can observe each other's reactions. In addition, our behavior outside this room, even in private, will be subject to certain controls. That's why there are peepholes on our doors and no locks. It's not about spying on each other. It's so that no one is isolated. If the Impact affects any of us especially strong, the others need to know as soon as possible. Still, there's a margin of unknown risk. We're confronting something totally new, and we can't predict all of the effects it will have on us."

At first, people muttered, but shortly thereafter the general atmosphere changed. The project that lay before them made everyone undeniably excited. Elisa's eyes were welling up and she had a knot in her throat. *I've seen a landscape from the Quaternary period. Good God. And I'm still here, this isn't a dream ... I've seen Earth, the planet I inhabit, almost a million years ago.* Sergio Marini's voice rang out good-naturedly above the rest.

"Well, now we've heard the cons. What are we waiting for? Let's get to work!"

Elisa stood up, inspired. But just then Valente whispered, "They're hiding things, sweetheart. I'm absolutely sure they're not telling us the whole truth."

15

THE night of July 25, Elisa saw the shadow for the first time.

Later on, she realized that it was another sign: Mr. White Eyes had arrived.

Here I am, Elisa. It's me.

I'll never leave your side.

LIGHT and silent, like a soul on one of those "astral voyages" that her mother believed in, it floated for a second in the peephole at her door and then disappeared. She smiled. *Someone else who can't sleep.*

It didn't seem strange. The room was comfortable, but you couldn't really think of it as a home. It was hot within those metal walls because, as Valente had said, they turned off the air-conditioning at night, and her window was one of those tilting ones that didn't open all the way. Wearing only her panties, Elisa lay sweating on the bed, in a mix of light and darkness: to her right, the glare of the spotlights on the fences; to her left the faint rectangle cast by the peephole.

She'd seen it head toward the door that separated the two wings of the barracks, so it was probably one of her colleagues, Nadja, Ric, or Rosalyn. Everyone else slept in the other wing.

Where was it going? She strained to hear. The doors weren't creaky, but they were metal, after all, so she assumed that in a few seconds she'd hear some sort of click.

But she didn't.

The silence intrigued her. It made her think it was more than sheer consideration for those who were sleeping. It was as if the insomniac in question were being cautious.

She got out of bed and walked over to the peephole. She could see the faint emergency lights in the hallway, which looked empty, although she was sure she'd seen a silhouette go past.

She put on her T-shirt and walked out. The door that connected the barracks' two wings was closed. Someone, though, must have opened it just a second ago. It wasn't a ghost.

She hesitated for a second. Should she try to find out if someone was missing from his or her bed? No, but she knew she wouldn't be able to rest easy if she did nothing. She opened the door that led to the next wing. Before her stretched the darkened hallway, feebly lit by tiny bulbs. To the right, the bedroom doors. To the left, the way to the next barracks.

She felt uneasy.

She wanted to laugh. *They ordered us to spy on each other, and that's exactly what I'm doing.* In her T-shirt and undies, barefoot in the hallway, it was like…

A noise.

This time she was sure, though it was far off. It could have been coming from the next barracks over.

She walked toward the end of the hallway that led to the second barracks. Her anxiety refused to leave, like the last guest at a party, but she hid it well. She was a fairly calm person. Being an only child had taught her how to walk alone on dark, quiet nights.

But she was about to lose that ability entirely.

She reached the hallway and peeked in.

About six feet away, a strange creature that seemed to be made of shadows held its arms out wide, waving them around, and staring at her with an intense, all-consuming look. And the worst thing (later she would realize that this was another warning) was seeing that it had no face, or at least she couldn't make out any of its features in the darkness.

"Be quiet!" a gruff voice said in English. There was a flash of light and she realized, now, that she'd been screaming. "I'm sorry to have scared you ..."

She had no idea the soldiers patrolled the inside of the barracks at night. The flashlight he turned on cleared up the mystery. His rifle was what she'd thought were outstretched arms; the "intense" look came from his infrared visor; the lack of face was some sort of walkie-talkie that covered his mouth. He wore a nametag on his shirt front: Stevenson. Elisa knew him. He was one of the five soldiers on the island, and one of the youngest and cutest. Until that moment, she'd never spoken to any of them. All she did was wave when she saw them, aware of the fact that they were there for her safety and not the reverse. Now she felt deeply embarrassed. Stevenson lowered his flashlight and raised his infrared visor. She could see that he was smiling.

"What were you doing wandering around the hallways in the dark?"

"I thought I saw someone outside my room. I wanted to know who it was."

"I've been here for an hour and I haven't seen anyone." She thought she could detect an edge to his voice.

"Maybe I made a mistake. Sorry."

She heard the sound of other doors, people alarmed by her ridiculous scream. She didn't even want to know who they were. Apologizing once more, she went back to her room, got into bed, and, thinking she'd never be able to fall asleep, promptly fell asleep.

THE next day, Tuesday, July 26, 6:44 p.m.

She yawned, got up, and put her computer into sleep mode.

She'd programmed it to keep working on the complicated calculation by itself.

The Shadow in the Night Incident was still floating around in her head. She decided she'd tell Nadja about it at the beach, at least for entertainment value. For the moment, she needed to rest. She'd been on New Nelson for only six days, but it felt like months. She wondered if she might be getting sick from exhaustion. *No problem, though. I've got the hospital right here.* She looked at the paleontologist's silent lab, which doubled as a clinic and even had an examining table. If she didn't feel better soon, maybe she'd ask Jacqueline for some kind of pep pill. "I've used up all my energy on calculating energy," she'd joke.

She left the lab and went back to her room, grabbed her towel and bikini, and walked out of the barracks and into the fading sunlight. It was one of those rare days during the monsoon season when it hadn't rained, and she wanted to take advantage of that. Seeing the soldier on guard duty at the fence reminded her of the previous night's incident again, but this time it wasn't Stevenson but Bergetti, the stout Italian that Marini sometimes played cards with. She said hi to him on her way past (she was terrified of those human porcupines, so heavily armed), walked through the gate, and then wandered down the gentle slope to the most amazing beach she'd ever seen.

Over a mile of golden sands, a sea that on good days was an amazing array of blues, and foamy waves that could make Nadja's skin look as tan as hers. The powerful waves were brutal, totally unlike any of the piddling, domestic undulations on civilized beaches. What was more, as if the god of that paradise didn't want to create any disturbances, the strongest waves broke far enough offshore that she could walk out for ages in shallow water, even swim with ease.

Nadja Petrova waved to her from their usual spot. In just a few days, she'd formed an easy, intense friendship with the young Russian paleontologist, the way people often do when forced to live together in isolated places. They had several things in common, in addition to their ages. Enthusiastic personalities, sharp wit, and a way of climbing the achievement ladder, step-by-step. In this, in fact, Nadja was ahead of her. Born in St. Petersburg, she'd emigrated to France as a teenager and worked nonstop until she obtained a highly coveted scholarship to do her PhD with Jacqueline Clissot in Montpellier, where she became Clissot's number one disciple. And all of that without having a rich mother who paid for everything, including her time. But when she spoke to Nadja, she never seemed bitter or jaded. In fact, she always got the impression that she was an open, friendly girl, with snowy skin and almost-white hair, who put all of her time and energy into smiling. Elisa thought she could never have found a better companion.

"Mmm. The water looks so tempting today," Elisa said, dropping her towel and bikini on the sand, then starting to undress. "I think I'll go in and see if I drown."

"So, you still haven't got it," Nadja said, smiling from underneath enormous black sunglasses that covered half of her sheet-white face.

"What I *did* get was depressed."

"Repeat after me. 'Tomorrow, I'll get it. Tomorrow will be the day.'"

"Tomorrow, I'll get it. Tomorrow will be the day," Elisa obeyed. "Can I alter the mantra slightly?"

"What do you have in mind?"

"Well, what about 'One of these days, I'll get it,' for example." Elisa pulled the bikini bottom up over her hip and grabbed the top. "That way I can keep hope alive but still not get bored."

"But the key to a mantra is getting a little bit bored," Nadja declared, giggling.

After she had her top on, Elisa placed her clothes in a pile and weighed them down with one of the countless bottles of lotion her friend always brought with her. Then she spread out her towel and used more bottles to weigh down each corner. The wind didn't seem as strong today as on other days, but she didn't feel like spending her downtime chasing her panties or towels across the sand.

Nadja lay facedown. Elisa glanced at her thin body, beneath a curtain of white hair, and saw the pink lines of her bikini strap. On the first day, they'd laughed when they tried on the bathing suits Mrs. Ross had found them (neither of them had thought they'd need a bikini in Zurich). She got the pink one and Nadja the white one, but she had bigger breasts than Nadja and the white suit was bigger and fit her much better. They decided to switch right away.

"Still stuck in the same place?" Nadja asked.

"Ha! I wish. Every day I go farther backward, it seems. I'm going to end up at the beginning." Elisa planted her elbows in the sand and stared out at the sea. She turned to her friend, who was wagging a bottle at her and smiling graciously.

"Oh, sorry, I forgot."

"Yeah, sure," Nadja said, untying her top. "More like you think putting lotion on my back is undignified."

"Well, I'm better at that than at doing calculations, that's for sure." Elisa poured lotion into the palm of her cupped hand and began to spread it over Nadja's back.

Her skin glimmered under the ton of protection she wore, despite the fact that she never came to the beach before late afternoon. Elisa felt bad about her friend's "almost albino" condition. It was such a disadvantage, given her profession. "I'm not an albino, I'm *almost* albino," Nadja had explained. "Strong sunlight can really do me damage, even cause cancer. And you might imagine that, as a paleontologist, I have to be outside a lot, sometimes in the tropical sun or in the desert." But, given her personality, she made light of it. "I go out at night in search of merocanites and cephalopods. I'm like a vampire paleontologist."

"Your friend Ric is stuck, too. But he doesn't take it to heart so much. He says he's going to beat you."

"He's not my friend. And he always wants to beat me."

They'd divided the work between two groups. Valente had joined Silberg's team and she was on Clissot's. Her job was to find the exact energy required (the solution required at least six decimal points) to open a time string from 150 million years ago, which was four thousand seven hundred billion seconds before she and Nadja had plunked their bottoms down on this beach in the Indian Ocean. "A sunny, jungle day in the Jurassic period," Clissot said. If they managed, the results would be amazing, inconceivable. They could see the first ever images of a living ... (no, don't say it, we don't want to jinx ourselves).

She and Nadja dreamed of it.

Elisa, who had always loved dinosaur movies as a kid, thought there was nothing she wouldn't do to achieve that goal. If her work could help obtain the image of some great prehistoric reptile doing *anything at all* (even if it was just peeing on the grass!), then she would have seen and accomplished everything she ever wanted to do. *Jurassic Park* was a joke compared to this. *Eat your heart out, Steven Spielberg.* She could die happy.

But it was an incredibly complex, tedious task. In fact, she and Blanes had split it up between them. While he tried to calculate the energy needed to *start* opening the time strings, she was searching for the final energy push. Then they'd compare and double-check each other's work to try to make certain they were the correct quantities. But she'd been lost in a forest of equations for days, and although she hadn't given up, she was afraid Blanes was regretting his decision to bring her on board.

"I'm sure you'll get it soon," Nadja said encouragingly.

"Yeah, I hope so," Elisa wiped her hands on her thighs to get the remaining lotion off. "Anything new with the Perennial Snows?" she asked.

"Are you joking? I don't even know where to begin. Every time she sees the image, Jacqueline discards twenty more paleogeological theories. It's unbelievable. Those few seconds are enough to write a whole treatise on the Quaternary period." Still facedown,

Nadja bent her knees and lifted her legs in the air, touching her toes together. Her dainty feet were pretty and elegant. "You spend half your life studying glaciation, you find proof in the subsoil of Greenland, you dream about it … But then suddenly you see England under tons of snow and you say, 'All the science and all the work of all the professors in the world can't compare to this.'"

"It must be the Impact. You're losing your mind," Elisa joked.

Surprisingly, her friend took her seriously.

"I don't think so. Though I *have* been sleeping really poorly the past few nights."

"Have you mentioned it to Jacqueline?"

"Yeah. She's not sleeping well, either."

Elisa was about to say something when, out of the corner of her eye, she noticed one of those fighting crabs with one huge claw sidling up to her left leg. Her friend had told her that in the jungle and at the lake (which she had yet to visit) there were other species "of great paleontological importance."

"Quick question," Elisa said. "Is this creature that's about to pinch my calf of great paleontological importance, or can I smash it to smithereens?"

"Poor thing," Nadja laughed, sitting up. "Leave it alone. It's a fiddler crab."

"Well, he can go play his music somewhere else!" She threw a fistful of sand at it, changing its course. "Go on. Scram!"

When the "danger" had passed, Elisa turned over and rested her chest on the towel. Nadja did the same. They were very close and stared at each other (Nadja at her, and she at herself in the reflection in Nadja's glasses). She couldn't help but notice the contrast in their bodies: cappuccino brown and vanilla ice cream white. The breeze, the waves, and the afternoon temperatures relaxed her so much she thought she was going to fall asleep.

"Did you know that Professor Silberg has lots of different images saved?" Nadja asked, nodding at Elisa's dumbfounded expression. "It's true. They'd already done a lot of other experiments. The

Unbroken Glass and the Perennial Snows aren't the only ones. But don't get excited; the rest of them are all blurry due to incorrect energy calculations. They call them 'diffusions.'"

"How did you find that out? And why haven't they told us?" Suddenly, Elisa recalled Valente's words. Was it true that they were hiding things?

"Jacqueline told me. But Silberg swears you can't see anything in any of them. 'I seenk I smell somesink feeshy, comrade,' she joked, affecting a terrible German accent. "But seriously, haven't you ever wondered why they brought us to an island?"

"The project's top secret. You heard Silberg."

"But there's no strategic reason that we have to work from an island. We could do this from Zurich. In fact, we'd attract less attention there."

"Well then, why do *you* think we're here?"

"I don't know. Maybe they want to keep us isolated," Nadja ventured. "It's like ... like they're afraid we might ... I don't know, become dangerous or something. Have you seen how many soldiers there are?"

"There's only five. Six, if you count Carter."

"Well however many there are, it's too many."

"You're a little paranoid, you know?"

"I don't like soldiers." Nadja looked at her from over her sunglasses. "I saw them all the time in my country. And I can't help but wonder if they're here to protect us, or to protect everyone else from us." The wind blew her hair into her face.

Elisa was about to reply when they heard a shriek.

Someone in a T-shirt and shorts ran across the sand, about a hundred feet away. Another figure, in red Bermudas, chased after the first with long strides. The person running away didn't seem very intent on escaping; the second one caught up in no time. For a few seconds, they stood very close, backlit by the sinking sun. Then they dove onto the sand, laughing hysterically.

"New experiences, new friends," Nadja quipped, winking.

Elisa wasn't surprised. She'd seen them talking together several times already in Silberg's lab, him gazing at her with those watery, reptilian eyes and her staring back with the same sour expression she always wore, as if the world owed her an immense favor that could never be entirely paid back. *Poor Rosalyn Reiter.* She didn't like seeing Valente taking control of that quiet, homely woman so easily. She felt like giving the German historian a few pointers about her new Latin lover.

"Some of us seem to be searching for energy levels in all sorts of new ways," she joked.

"Yes, and very energetically!"

Valente and Reiter were working with Silberg to open time strings from sixty thousand million seconds ago, capturing images from Jerusalem. If all went well, the Jerusalem time strand could prove more groundbreaking then the Jurassic time strand. Much more important for them, and for the rest of humanity.

They'd see Jerusalem during Christ's lifetime. Specifically, the last years of his life.

They might catch a glimpse of some historical or biblical event.

Maybe a very unique event.

Although their chances were about the same as having one shot to hit a millimeter-wide bull's-eye set from a thousand miles away ... maybe they'd see *him.*

A tyrannosaurus, Napoléon and Caesar, would be child's play in comparison. Anything *would be child's play in comparison.*

Elisa had told Maldonado the truth when she said (and now his questions about her beliefs made perfect sense) that she was an atheist. But still, not even an atheist could remain passive at the idea of *seeing him,* even for an instant.

Let she who remains indifferent cast the first stone.

And one of the people in charge of trying to make that miracle come true was currently sticking his red-shorted butt high in the air, no doubt thrusting his tongue into the mouth of a mature, frustrated historian who appeared to be at his beck and call.

Nadja seemed to be having a blast, watching the show. She glanced over at Elisa, one cheek on her towel, her face red.

"They spent the night together the other night."

"Seriously?" Elisa wasn't sure how she felt about that. Images of her visit to Valente's house in Madrid flashed before her, along with the warnings he'd given her regarding their bet. She imagined him humiliating Rosalyn Reiter.

"Don't say anything about it," Nadja laughed. "I shouldn't tell you, it doesn't really concern me."

"Me neither," Elisa said quickly, hoping her friend wouldn't change her mind.

"It was Sunday night. I heard some strange noises and got up. I looked through Ric's peephole and ... his bed was empty! Then I looked through Rosalyn's, and I saw both of them in there." Nadja laughed quietly, showing her white teeth, which had spaces between them. "Are all the men in Spain like that?"

"What do you think?" Elisa snorted, and her friend burst out laughing, maybe on seeing how serious she'd grown. "I saw something last night, too. I was going to tell you. There was someone wandering around the hall. It turned out to be a soldier, but he scared me to death, the asshole."

"Are you serious? She sleeps with soldiers, too?" The young paleontologist's face, just inches from hers, was so red Elisa thought she was going to explode. She threw some sand on her shoulder.

"Shut up, you Russian pervert! I'm going to take a dip and cool off. Their show is getting me all hot and bothered."

She walked to the shore without glancing over at the couple stretched out on the sand a hundred feet away.

THAT night she heard noises. Footsteps in the hallway.

She jumped out of bed and looked out the peephole. No one.

The footsteps stopped.

Grabbing her watch from the nightstand, she pushed the button that illuminated the clock's face. It was 1:12 a.m., still early, but not for the customs and traditions of the scientific community of New Nelson. They ate dinner at seven, and by nine thirty everyone was in their rooms. Lights-out was at ten. Elisa still had insomnia. She thought about the soldiers who glided around silently, about shadow-soldiers with no faces slipping down the darkened hallways, passing by her room ... And about Valente and Reiter, though she wasn't sure why.

Footsteps. Yes, now she could distinguish them clearly. In the hallway.

She half opened her door and peeked out, turning her head left and right.

No one. The hall was empty, and the door to the next wing was closed. The steps had stopped again, but she thought of a possibility. *They're coming from his room. Or hers.*

Unable to resist a sudden impulse ("you're such a child," her mother would say), she dashed out into the hall without even getting dressed. First, she stopped next door at Nadja's room and peeked in through the peephole. Nadja was in bed. In the light streaming in from outside, her white hair was as bright as a neon sign. Her position, and the sheets tangled up around her legs, indicated that she'd been asleep for some time. She looked like a fetus tucked inside a uterus. Elisa smiled. She recalled a conversation they'd had at the beach that weekend.

"I'd like to be a mother," Nadja had declared in a burst of sincerity.

"What on earth are you talking about?"

"Just something that happens to female paleontologists from time to time. After being inseminated by a male, they breed and then carry embryos in their wombs."

"Well, I've decided to be a drone, myself," Elisa replied, dozing on her towel.

"You really don't want kids, Elisa?"

Elisa couldn't believe the question. But she also couldn't believe that she couldn't believe the question.

"I haven't really given it much thought," she said, and Nadja assumed she was joking.

"It's not a math problem, you know. You either want to or you don't."

Elisa bit her lip, the way she did when she *was* working on a math problem.

"No. I don't want kids," she said after a long silence, and Nadja shook her head slowly, that angel hair of hers swishing back and forth as she did.

"Do me a favor," she'd said. "Before you die, leave your brain to the University of Montpellier. Jacqueline and I would love to study it, I can assure you. There are very few female examples of *Fisicus extravagantissimus*."

She came out of her daze. She was in the hallway, in the middle of the night, spying on her colleagues in her underwear. *What if they get up and catch the* Fisicus extravagantissimus *in her underwear peeking through their peepholes?* She couldn't hear the footsteps anymore. Still smiling, she tiptoed up to Ric Valente's door. The metallic floor was cool on her feet, a nice contrast to the heat she felt everywhere else. She looked through his peephole.

Her theory was disproved. Under the light filtering in through the window, she could clearly make out the skinny contours of Valente Sharpe stretched out in bed, his bony back, his white underwear.

She watched him for a moment, and then went on to the last room. That ball curled up under the sheets had to be Rosalyn Reiter; Elisa even thought she could make out her highlighted hair.

Shaking her head, she returned to her room, wondering what she'd been expecting. *Nosy.* She realized that all the work she'd been putting into her first project on the island was starting to take a toll. In a normal situation, she knew how to deal with that kind of stress. She'd take a walk, exercise, or even explore her erotic fantasies. But on New Nelson, with such a lack of privacy, she felt like she'd lost her bearings.

She got back into bed, faceup, and sighed deeply. No more footsteps. No noise at all. If she strained, she could make out the sounds of the ocean; but she didn't feel like straining. After debating it for second, she slipped under the sheets, even though it was very hot. She wasn't trying to get warm, though. She sighed again, closed her eyes, and let her fantasies take her wherever they wanted to go.

She was afraid she knew where that might be.

Valente was still Valente Sharpe: a stupid, vacuous boy with a brilliant mind and the body of a sickly child. A daddy's boy. But somehow, almost against her will, her fantasy (which was probably also sickly, she guessed) inevitably drove her to him. This was the first time it had happened, and she was taken aback.

Fisicus hornissimus.

She imagined him walking in just then. She could see him clearly, now that she'd closed her eyes. She slipped her hand under the sheet and pulled down her underwear. But he didn't think that was submissive enough, so she tugged them all the way off, balled them up, and threw them on the floor. She imagined that even that wouldn't be enough for Valente Sharpe. *Well, fuck you, then, because I'm not pulling the sheet down.* She slid her hand down to the exact burning spot and began to stroke herself, squirming and panting. She could imagine exactly what he'd do: stare at her scornfully. And she'd say...

Just then, she heard footsteps right beside her bed.

A feeling of budding pleasure exploded in her brain, like fragile china being trampled by an elephant.

She opened her eyes, moaning quietly.

No one.

That fear, abruptly interrupting the climax of her sexual excitation, had been so intense that she was almost glad just to be alive. It was like yellow fever or malaria, something that left you stiff and shivering. Somewhere she'd even read that fear like that could actually kill you, give you a heart attack no matter how young you were or how clear your arteries.

She sat up, holding her breath. Her door was still closed. She hadn't heard it open at any point. But the footsteps, she was sure, had been *inside* her room. And yet there was no one there.

"Hello?" she called out to the dead.

The dead responded with more footsteps.

They were coming from the bathroom.

At the time, Elisa was sure that she would never be more scared than she was right at that moment. That she could never she feel more fear than what she felt at that moment.

Later, she found out just how wrong she was.

But that was later.

"Um, hello?"

No reply. The steps faded in and out. Was she wrong? No. They were definitely coming from the bathroom. She didn't have a lamp on her nightstand, and they cut the lights at night anyway, except for the bathrooms. She'd have to get up in the dark and walk over there to turn it on.

Now she couldn't hear anything anymore. They'd stopped again.

All of a sudden, she felt like a complete idiot. Who the hell could have gone into her bathroom? And who would possibly be moving around in there in the dark, without saying anything? The steps must be coming from someplace else and just echoing against the walls.

Despite that reassuring conclusion, the idea of actually pulling back the sheet, getting up *(don't even dream about stopping to put on your underwear; besides, if you're about to die, what the hell difference does it make if you're stark naked?)*, and walking over to the bathroom seemed like a superhuman feat. She realized that the bathroom door, which she couldn't see from bed, was closed, and the peephole was completely dark. She'd have to open the door and then reach in and turn on the light.

She turned the handle.

As she pushed it open as slowly as humanly possible, revealing more and more darkness within, she could hear herself panting. She panted as if she were still in bed with her fantasies. No, louder than that. As loud as a steam train. Her moaning in bed was a joke compared with this.

She opened the door all the way.

She could tell even before she turned on the light. It was empty, of course.

Relieved, she exhaled, not knowing what she'd expected to find. Then she heard the steps again, but this time quite obviously distant, maybe in the professors' wing.

For a second, she stood there, naked in the doorway of the lit bathroom, wondering how on earth those steps could have echoed beside her bed just moments earlier. She knew her senses weren't playing tricks on her, and she wouldn't be able to sleep until she arrived at a logical solution to the problem, even if it was just so she didn't feel like an idiot.

Finally, she thought of a possibility. Crouching down, she put her ear to the metal floor. She thought she heard the steps with more intensity and deduced that she was right.

There was one place in the science station she'd still never been: the pantry. It was underground. On New Nelson, they had to save both space and energy, and storing supplies in the subsoil fulfilled both of those objectives since, given the subterranean temperature, the refrigerators worked on an energy-save mode and many provisions could simply be kept on shelves with no additional refrigeration needed. Cheryl Ross went down there some nights (there was a trapdoor that led down from the kitchen) to make lists of all the supplies that had to be replenished. The cold store was close to her room, and the footsteps of whoever was in there must have been able to be heard easily due to the metal paneling on the walls. She thought she could hear the steps *in* her bathroom, but really she must have heard them *below* it.

That must have been it. Mrs. Ross was probably in the pantry.

When she finally felt calm enough, she turned out the bathroom light, closed the door, and went back to bed, after first finding her underwear and putting them back on. She was exhausted. After that unbelievable fright, the sleep she so longed for began to wash over her.

But as she drifted off, before slumber dragged her all the way into its blackness, she thought she saw something.

A shadow slipping past the peephole on her door.

16

From: tk32@theor.phys.tlzu.ch
To: mmorande@piccarda.es
Sent: Friday, September 16, 2005
Subject: hello

Hi Mom,
Just wanted to send you a few lines to tell you I'm OK. I'm
sorry I can't write (or call) more often, but we're working
flat out here in Zurich. Which I like (you know me), so I can't
complain. Everything I see and do is incredible. Professor
Blanes is amazing, and so are the other people I'm working
with. We're on the verge of a really important breakthrough,
so please don't worry if I'm not back in touch for a while.
Take care. And say hi to Víctor for me if he calls.

Love, Eli

YEARS *later it occurred to her that she, too, was to some degree
responsible for the horror.*

*We tend to blame ourselves for the tragedies we suffer. When
catastrophe overcomes us, we withdraw into the past, searching
for some sort of mistake we might have made, something to ex-*

plain it all. Often, that tendency is absurd. In this case, though, she thought it was only fair.

Her tragedy was overwhelming. And perhaps her mistake had been, too.

When had she made it? At what exact moment?

Sometimes, at home alone, standing before the mirror, as she counted the agonizing seconds to go until her nightmares would start up again, she thought that her biggest mistake had also been her greatest success.

That Thursday, September 15, 2005, was the day of her great breakthrough.

Her day of reckoning.

MATH problems are like anything else. You spend weeks banging your head against the wall and then suddenly one day, you wake up, have some coffee, watch the sunrise, and there, right in front of you, blindingly obvious, is the solution you've been searching for.

On the morning of September 15, Elisa sat stock-still before her computer screen, pencil in mouth. She printed out her results and dashed off to Blanes's office, paper in hand.

Blanes had an electronic keyboard in his private office and he often played Bach. A lot of Bach. In fact, Bach was all he played. His office and Clissot's were connected, and sometimes the crystalline sounds of a fugue or the *Goldberg Variations* aria filtered through the walls like ghosts on the lonely afternoons that Elisa spent working in solitude. She didn't mind. In fact, she found it sort of comforting. She imagined, despite her ignorance of all things musical, that Blanes was a decent pianist. Nevertheless, that morning she had her own tune to play him, and she was pretty sure that if it was the right one he'd be happy to hear it.

His hands hovering motionless above the keys, Blanes stared at the trembling sheet of paper before him.

"It's perfect," he said impassively. "We've got it."

Blanes no longer seemed "amazing," as she liked to tell her mother, but he wasn't average, either; he wasn't even an asshole. If Elisa had learned anything in twenty-three years, it was that nobody, absolutely nobody, could be easily pigeonholed. Everyone is something, but they're all also something else, and maybe even the opposite of what they are, too. People, like electron clouds, are hazy. And Blanes was no exception. When she met him at Alighieri during his summer course, she thought he was some sexist jerk, or maybe an introverted sicko. Then, when they'd first come to New Nelson, she decided that she just didn't even figure on his radar screen, that maybe the problem was her deeply rooted belief that all male professors would somehow treat her differently, not just because she was smart (very smart) but because she was also hot (very hot), and she knew it, and was used to working it to her advantage. But with Blanes, she felt like he was saying, "I couldn't care less about your geometric intuitions, your original methods of integrating, your legs, your shorts, or the fact that you often go braless."

Later, Elisa realized that he did care. That he always looked at her with those squinty Robert Mitchum eyes as if he were about to fall asleep when actually that was the furthest thing from the truth. That when she was on her way back from the beach half naked and bumped into him in the hall, he did, of course, gawk, even more than Marini (and that was saying something) and Craig (and that was not). But she suspected that Blanes's mind, like her own, was elsewhere, and that he probably suspected a few things about her, too. She sometimes thought that maybe they should just sleep together and see if that cleared the air. This is how she pictured it: they'd both be standing there, naked, staring at each other. After a few minutes, he'd suddenly say, "You mean you really don't mind if I touch you?" and she'd say, "You mean you actually *want* to touch me?"

"Let's wait for Sergio to finish," he said, and went back to playing Bach for a change.

Blanes's idea was to take both light samples—the Jurassic and

Jerusalem—on the same day, since the geographic area they were investigating was more or less the same. But Marini and Valente were behind on their calculations, just like last time, so there was nothing to do but wait.

With nothing to work on, Elisa spent her time vegging out and doing things like writing her mother the e-mail she'd send the next day (after going through the requisite security filters, of course). Then she thought about that morning in early August, a month and a half ago, when she'd interrupted another one of Blanes's recitals to show him her first answer. She'd been tormented after that, and Nadja had saved her.

She'd just had one of her worst encounters with Valente and thought she finally understood just how much he hated the fact that he kept coming in "last" in the supposed race they were having (in his mind, at least). Ironically, at the time, both of their solutions were incorrect.

This time it was going to be different. She was sure that this time she'd hit the nail on the head. And she was right.

She also believed that if her calculations were correct, she'd be the luckiest person alive.

And there, she was wrong. Dead wrong.

THE previous month had certainly not been the best in Valente Sharpe's life. Elisa barely saw him around the station, not even in Silberg's lab, which is where he supposedly worked. But there was no doubt that he *was* working. Sometimes she needed to tell him something and she'd find him in his room, sitting on his bed with his laptop, so into his work that she was almost inclined to consider him a "soul mate," as he'd once called it. He'd even stopped his little flirtation with Reiter (and it was clear that Rosalyn was a lot more upset by it than he was). Now he seemed to seek out the company of Marini and Craig, and it wasn't unusual to see the three of them returning from a long walk on the beach or by the lake in the late afternoons. It seemed clear to her that Ric had entered a new phase in which he really wanted to shine at all costs. He wasn't satisfied with being *one of* the only people chosen for the project; he wanted to be *the only* one. He wanted to beat not just Elisa, but everyone else, too.

At times, she found that more disturbing than the tales of his perversion she'd heard from Víctor. The period of forced coexistence on the island had let her see that beneath his apparently calm, disdainful surface lay a churning volcano of desires to be the best, to be number one. *That's the sole purpose of every single thing he does or says.* She realized obsession was eating away at him, and not only from inside. He had developed new tics; his lips and right leg twitched convulsively whenever he sat at the computer; his naturally anemic skin tone had grown even paler; and the bags hanging under his eyes were so big they could have been nests. *What's the matter with him? What is he up to?*

He was so fixated that she felt sorry for him. And she knew that feeling even the tiniest speck of pity for Valente Sharpe meant she was at least halfway to earning a place in heaven, maybe well on her way to having done so. But she'd grown so used to his presence that she did feel sorry for him.

At least until that day she met him on the beach.

On the afternoon of Wednesday August 10, one day after she'd handed in her first attempt at a calculation for the Jurassic time strand, Elisa went down to the beach. Nadja wasn't there yet. In her place on the sand stood a white statue that someone had clothed with a few rags that flapped in the wind.

When she realized who it was, she was dumbstruck.

Valente stood stock-still. In fact, he was petrified. And he was staring at something. It must have been the sea, because she looked in the same direction and all she could see was a glorious horizon of green waves, blue sky, and clouds. He didn't even realize that she was there.

"Hey," she ventured. "What's up?"

That seemed to shake him from his stupor, and he turned around. Elisa felt a chill run down her spine. For a brief moment, the expression on his face reminded her of an old classmate of hers, a physics major who was schizophrenic and had to drop out of school altogether. She was pretty sure he didn't even recognize her.

In a split second, though, his face changed completely and the old Ricardo Valente Sharpe peered down at her.

"Well, looky here," he murmured, his voice hoarse. "If it isn't little Elisa, the prick tease. What's up, Elisa? How you doin', Elisa?"

"Listen, asshole," she said, quickly switching from fear to anger. "I realize we're both under a lot of pressure, but I'm not going to let you stand there and insult me. I've had about enough. I'm serious. We work together, like it or not. And if you insult me again, I'll file an official complaint with Blanes and Marini and get you thrown off the project."

"*Insult* you?" The sun was in Valente's face, and he squinted as if he were sucking lemons. "What are you calling an insult, sweetheart? I'm merely stating fact. I can see your body through that T-shirt, and I can practically see up your shorts, and it gets me hard; that's teasing my prick, as far as I'm concerned. A raised temperature and a sudden stiffness in the male member, that's what I'm talking about. And it's not my fault. That's like accusing me of saying that the first law of thermodynamics applies to heat engines. I'll make an official note of that, too. Wait, where do you think you're going?"

Valente blocked her way.

"Let me go," Elisa said, trying to dodge him.

"I know where you're going. You're going to strip on the beach and increase the temperature of my member even more. If you weren't such a prick tease, you'd put on your bikini in your room, like your friend, but since you're such a fucking prick tease you get naked right here on the beach so we can all watch you. Isn't that right?"

Elisa dodged him again. She was now incredibly sorry she'd

wondered if he was OK a minute ago. And it was about to get even worse.

He stood in her way once more.

"So you're going to report me for telling you what you technically and scientifically are?" Suddenly, she realized that this wasn't one of his jokes. Valente was livid, even more irate than her. "That would be like me accusing you of something unthinkable, something monstrous, like ... fantasizing about me when you jack off. Something impossible ..."

She froze. All of a sudden, she had no desire to go for a swim, to be with Nadja or anything else. She wasn't embarrassed or humiliated; she was scared.

"It would be like accusing me of bestiality just because I like your tits," he continued in the same tone, as if it were all part of the same joke. "You're such a drama queen. If you don't want to hear the truth, then don't go asking for it ..."

He saw me. He must have seen me. But that's impossible. He's just saying it. She tried to see through the mocking gleam in his eye to the truth, but she couldn't. Two weeks had gone by since that night she'd been touching herself in her room, and she was sure that nobody had seen her. *But then, how ...?*

"Let's all just calm down," he said. "You think you've got the solution, don't you, sweetheart? That all your calculations have paid off. Well, then, let the rest of us dimwits do our work and stop flaunting yourself around like the tease you are ..."

He turned and stalked off, leaving her standing there. Nadja arrived a minute later, but she was gone by then. It was several days before she felt like going back to the beach, and from then on she always changed into her bikini in her room. She didn't bother telling her friend what had made her change her routine.

Afterward, when she looked back on things with some perspective, she saw that she *had* been a little dramatic. She considered Valente's attacks from a competitive perspective and realized that it was clear he couldn't *stand* seeing her get results before he did.

What was more, she took him too seriously; there was no need to shrink back in his presence. Valente might seem like some indescribable, bizarre, freakish being, but when it came right down to it, he was a total dick who happened to be really smart and got off on trying to hurt her whenever he saw the chance. But that was more because she let him than because he was so great.

She was sure that what he'd said was just bluster. There was no way anyone could have seen her, not even through the peephole, and she'd already cleared up the mystery of the footsteps. Mrs. Ross had been down in the pantry that night; she'd told Elisa the next day. So that was all cleared up. Valente was taking shots in the dark just to see if he could rile her. *He'll get over it. Maybe this will make him realize he'd be better off spending his time working and not sleeping with his colleagues.* She thought no more about it. In fact, she felt remarkably relaxed. Since she'd finished her calculations, she slept like a log and had stopped seeing shadows and hearing noises.

On Thursday, August 18, the energy for the Jerusalem time strand was placed on Blanes's desk on a clean sheet of paper. They set up the experiment for the next day. After Craig and Marini obtained the sample images and made them collide at the level of energy they'd calculated, the whole team began to endure a nail-biting wait.

Elisa was on cleaning duty, which had suffered some neglect over the past few days, and she was glad to have something to do. She and Blanes were in the kitchen together. Seeing Blanes wash dishes was not something she ever thought she'd experience, especially back when she was in his classes at Alighieri. But this was the kind of thing that happened when you lived together on an island.

Suddenly, there was silence. Several long faces stood in the kitchen doorway. Colin Craig was the one who told them.

"Both images diffused."

"Don't cry," Marini tried to joke. "But that does mean you'll have to go back to the drawing board and start calculating again."

No one cried right then. But maybe alone, in their rooms, they did. Elisa was sure they cried. *She* did. And the next day, everyone had red-rimmed eyes, puffy faces, and no desire to talk. Mother Nature seemed to be in mourning, too, and the last days of August were filled with thick clouds and a warm, driving, almost horizontal rain. It was monsoon season, Nadja said, something a majority of the planet experienced. "The summer months are when the southwest winds—the *hulhangu*—blow, and when driving rain is almost a daily occurrence, like in the Maldives." Elisa had never seen anything like it. It didn't look like drops, but like strings. Millions of strings being pulled by furious puppeteers and hammering down on rooftops, windows, walls. It didn't patter; it sounded more like a low, guttural, constant snore. Sometimes Elisa looked up and stared out the window, zombielike, at the fury the elements were unleashing. She thought it accurately reflected her state of mind.

The first Monday in September, after an unpleasant argument with Blanes, who upbraided her for working so slowly, she felt an odd, cloying bitterness. She didn't cry. She didn't do anything at all. She just sat motionless in front of the computer in Clissot's lab, thinking she'd never get up again. Time passed. Maybe a few hours, she wasn't really sure. And then she smelled perfume and felt a hand on her bare shoulder, as soft as a leaf drifting down from a tree.

"Come," Nadja said.

If she'd done anything else to try and convince her, if she'd hurled abuse (like her mother) or tried reasoning with her (like her father), Elisa would never have obeyed. But her smooth movements and sweet voice cast a spell on her. She got up and followed her friend, like one of the Pied Piper's rats.

Nadja was wearing sturdy pants and boots that looked too big.

"I don't feel like going to the beach," Elisa said.

"We're not going to the beach."

She led her to her room and pointed to a pile of clothes and another pair of boots. Elisa laughed when she realized that the clothes actually fit her pretty well.

"You have a soldier's physique," Nadja said. "Mrs. Ross says those boots and pants are for Carter's men."

Thus disguised, she smeared on a strange-smelling lotion that Nadja called "mosquito repellent"; Elisa thought it was just plain *repellent*. Then they went outside and walked toward the heliport. It wasn't actually raining, but she had the impression that the monsoons were just lying in wait, camouflaged, biding their time. Elisa's lungs filled with humidity and the smell of vegetation. The north winds brought in a constant flow of quick-moving clouds that hid and uncovered the sun every other second, producing an almost strobe-light effect.

They left the heliport's landing pad behind. In front of the soldiers' garrison, Carter stood talking to the Thai soldier, Lee, and the Colombian, Méndez, who was on guard duty at the gate that led into the jungle. Elisa liked Lee because he always smiled at her, but Méndez was the one she spoke to most. Right then he was smiling widely, his white teeth contrasting with his dark skin. She was no longer as afraid of the soldiers as she had been. She'd realized that beneath their metal and leather exteriors, they were just people. And now, she tried to concentrate more on what was underneath, not on, their uniforms.

They passed the warehouse where the munitions, weapons, technical equipment, and water purifier were stored, and Nadja took a path parallel to the jungle wall.

The famous rain forest, which to Elisa had seemed like no more than a smattering of trees and mud, was absolutely magical once she was inside it. She jumped up and down like a little girl on enormous, mossy tree roots; she marveled at the size and shape of flowers, and listened to the endless sounds of life. At one point, what seemed like a black-and-white model plane buzzed past her.

"Giant dragonfly," Nadja explained. "Or a damselfly. Those black spots on its wings are pterostigmas. In some parts of Southeast Asia they believe they're the souls of the dead."

"I can see why," Elisa agreed.

Suddenly, Nadja crouched down. When she stood back up she was holding a little red, black, and green bottle in her hand. It looked like a witch's potion, and had six jet-black handles. "This is a *Cetoniidae*. Or maybe it's a *Chrysomelidae,* I'm not sure. Beetles, for normal folks." Elisa was amazed. She'd never seen a beetle so brightly colored. "I have a French friend who's an expert in coleoptera who'd love to be here right now," Nadja added, placing it back on the ground. Elisa made a joke about the kind of company her friend kept.

Nadja also showed her a family of stick insects and an unbelievable pink mantis. Nothing they saw was larger than an insect (except for one brightly colored lizard), but according to Nadja that was often the way in jungles. The creatures that inhabited that place hid from each other, blended in, or camouflaged themselves in order to save their own lives or to take others'. The jungle was a place of fearsome disguises.

"If we came at night with infrared goggles, we might see lorises. They're nocturnal lemurs. Have you ever seen pictures of them? They look like teddy bears with huge, scared eyes. And those noises ...," Nadja said, and then froze like an ice sculpture in that green cathedral, " ... are probably gibbons ..."

The lake was large, and the north side of it was marshy, full of mangroves. Nadja showed her the tiny marsh creatures: crabs, frogs, and snakes. In the late afternoon light, the water looked dark green. They walked along the shore until they got to the coral reefs, where they came across a pool so bright it looked as if it were lined with emeralds. After looking around cautiously, Nadja took off her clothes and invited Elisa to do the same.

There are times when we have the feeling that everything we've ever done in life up to that moment has been false. Elisa had felt something like that when she viewed the Unbroken Glass and the Perennial Snows images, but now it was different. Splashing around in that warm, crystal clear water, as naked as nature had intended and in the company of her friend, also naked, she felt it again, maybe more intensely. The life that she lived surrounded by computers and equations seemed as fake to her as her velvety reflection on the water's surface. Her skin, her pores, her whole body submerged in that cool water—all seemed to be telling her she could do anything, that nothing stood in her way, that the world lay at her feet.

She looked at Nadja and could tell she felt the same way.

They didn't do anything out of the ordinary, though. For Elisa, just the *thought* was enough to make her happy. It occurred to her that the (subtle) difference between heaven and hell could be as simple as not acting on all the impulses that pop into your head.

It was an unforgettable afternoon. Maybe not the kind you'd tell your grandkids about, she guessed, but definitely the kind that, when it happens, makes you realize that every fiber in your body had been crying out for it.

Half an hour later, without even waiting to dry, they got dressed and headed back. They didn't talk much as they walked back; in fact, they were pretty much silent. Elisa intuited that their relationship had reached a new level, a deeper level, and that they no longer needed words to bond them together.

And after that day, things got better for her. She went back to the lab, to her calculations. Days passed almost without her realizing it, and then on September 15 she experienced a déjà vu when she interrupted Blanes and his music to show him her results once more. The figure was almost identical to the one she'd come up with the first time, except for the last few decimal points.

TWO days later, the energy for the Jerusalem time strand was handed in, too, but they had to wait for Craig and Marini to finish tinkering with the accelerator. Finally, on Friday, September 24, the whole team congregated in the control room (Marini called it "the Throne Room"). A vast hall almost a hundred feet wide and 120 feet long, it was New Nelson's prêt-a-porter architectural gem. Unlike the barracks, it was made of brick and cement and reinforced with insulation to minimize the chance of a short circuit.

That was where the four most powerful computers were, as well as SUSAN, the supraselective accelerator that was Colin Craig's baby. It was a steel doughnut 45 feet in diameter and 3 feet thick. The magnets that produced the magnetic field that accelerated the charged particles were attached to "her" circumference. SUSAN was Project Zig Zag's great technological triumph. Unlike most accelerators, she only needed one or two people to operate her and make all the endless adjustments necessary. The energy levels produced inside her weren't high, but they were extraordinarily precise. On either side of SUSAN were two small doors with skulls and crossbones that led to the station's generator rooms. One stairway, which you reached through the left door, led up above the doughnut so that whoever needed to could "touch our little girl's private parts," as Marini said with his typical macho southern humor.

Sitting at the telemetric screens, Craig anxiously tapped in the coordinates of two groups of satellites so they would capture the images of North Africa and send them down to New Nelson in real time (time strings could be opened only in real time—or "fresh time," as the ever-imaginative Marini called it—since storing them in any way distorted the results). The geographic area selected was about twenty-five square miles, and was nearly the same for both experiments. From that, they could obtain the images of Jerusalem and Gondwanaland, the megacontinent that 150 million years ago was formed by South America, Africa, the Hindustan peninsula, Australia, and Antarctica. When they received the images, the computers identified and selected them, and Craig and Marini started up SUSAN to accelerate the electron beams and make them collide with the calculated energies.

While all this took place, Elisa watched her colleagues' faces. They were all tense and eager, though each with their own idiosyncrasies: Craig, contained as always; Marini, exultant; Clissot, reserved; Cheryl Ross, mysterious and practical; Silberg, worried; Blanes, expectant; Valente, as if he couldn't care less; Nadja, thrilled; Rosalyn, staring at Valente.

"That's it," Colin Craig said, getting up from his seat by the mainframe. "Within four hours, we'll know if the images are visible."

"If you're a believer, this would be the time to pray," Marini added.

No one prayed. They did, however, attack the food. Everyone was starving, and lunch was relaxed yet quick.

While they waited for the image analysis, Elisa recalled her magical afternoon with Nadja two weeks ago and laughed, thinking that her friend had been her own "accelerator." She'd given her enough energy to open up and to realize that she still had a lot to offer. At the time, she thought they'd have more afternoons like that for as long as they remained on the island.

Later on, it became clear that their little excursion had been her last happy moment before the shadows began to engulf everything.

"**THERE** are images."

"From both samples?"

"Yes." Blanes held up a hand to silence their comments. "The first one is from three or four isolated strings on solid ground, about four thousand seven hundred billion seconds ago, which is a hundred and fifty million years."

"The Jurassic period," affirmed Jacqueline Clissot, as if in a trance.

"That's right. And that's not even the best news. You tell them, Colin."

Colin Craig, who even over the past few exhausting days had not stopped looking like a dandy in jeans and T-shirt, pushed back his glasses and gazed at Jacqueline Clissot as if he were about to ask her on a date.

"Our analysis shows there are very large, living creatures."

The computer used to digitalize the images captured from the strings was set to detect shapes and the movement of objects, with the aim of picking up on the presence of living organisms.

For a second, no one spoke. Then something rather remarkable happened. Clissot, an amazing, fascinating woman—perfect, Nadja called her—whose outfits gave the strange impression that she wore more metal than cloth (unlike Ross, she wore steel accessories: watch, bracelets, rings, pendants), took a deep breath and whispered a single word that sounded more like a moan.

"*Dinos* ..."

Nadja and Clissot hugged and people applauded, but Blanes interrupted their displays of joy, raising his hands.

"The other image corresponds to Jerusalem, a little over seventy-two thousand million seconds ago. Our computations situate that in early April, the year AD 33."

"The Hebrew month of Nisan," Marini said, winking at Silberg. Now everyone stared at the German professor.

"There are also living creatures in this one," Blanes added. "And they are well defined. According to the computer, there is about a ninety-nine point five percent chance they're human beings."

This time there was no applause. The feeling that overwhelmed Elisa was almost wholly physical. She was trembling, and it felt like it was emanating from her bone marrow.

"One or more people walking through Jerusalem, Reinhard," Craig said.

"Or one or more trained chimpanzees, if we consider the remaining point five percent." Marini smiled, but Craig shook his head.

Silberg, who had taken off his glasses, looked at them one by one, as if daring anyone to be as happy as he was.

AFTER a quick, noisy celebration with real champagne served in real champagne flutes that Mrs. Ross found in the pantry, they all met up in the screening room.

"Ladies and gentlemen, take your seats!" Marini shouted. "Come on, hurry up! '*Le vite son corte!*' as Dante said. '*Le vite son corte!*'"

"To your posts, everyone," Mrs. Ross cried, clapping her hands.

"And fasten your seat belts!"

Almost reluctantly they began scooting their chairs, asking questions ("Do you mind if I sit here?"), calling the person they each wanted sitting next to them when the lights went down. *As if it were a scary movie,* Elisa thought. Cheryl Ross held everyone up by insisting they all finish off their champagne first and take the glasses out to the kitchen, which, of course, led to more jokes ("Anything you say, Mrs. Ross. I'm more afraid of you than of Carter," Marini said) and delays. Elisa sat by Nadja, in the second row. Blanes had already begun speaking.

"... don't know what we're going to see on this screen, friends. I don't know if what awaits us will make us happy or not, if it will teach us something new or just confirm things we already know. All I can say is that this is the most important moment of my life. And I thank you for it."

"Reinhard, please, I know you want to say a few words, too, but wait until the end," Marini begged when the applause died down. "Colin?"

Craig, who was tapping things into the keyboard at the back of the room, gave a thumbs-up.

"All set to go, *Padrino,*" he joked

"Can you hit the lights?"

Elisa saw one last thing before the room turned black: Reinhard Silberg, crossing himself.

All of a sudden, without knowing why, she wished she'd never come to New Nelson, never signed those papers, never been right in her calculations.

More than anything, she wished she wasn't sitting there, awaiting the unknown.

17

"WHY?"

"Because history is not the past. History is what happened already, but the past is still taking place. If this table had never been built by a carpenter, it wouldn't be here now. If the Greeks and Romans had never existed, you and I wouldn't be here, or at least we wouldn't be the same. And if I hadn't been born sixty-seven years ago, you wouldn't be fifteen right now or be the dazzling young lady that you are. Don't ever forget that: you are because others were."

"But you're not the past, Grandpa."

"Oh, yes I am. And your parents are, too. And you yourself are your own past, Elisa. What I mean is that the past is what makes up our present. It's not just 'history'; it's something that happens, something that is happening. We can't see it, or feel it, or modify it, but it's always with us, like a ghost. And it determines our life, and maybe our death. You know what I think sometimes? It's a little strange, but with all that math you do, I think you're intelligent enough to understand. People often say, 'The past isn't dead,' and that scares them. But you know what really scares me, Eli? Not that the past isn't dead, but that it could kill us …"

THE black turned to blood. An impenetrable, blinding, almost sticky color.

"There's no image," Blanes said.

"But there's no evidence of diffusion," Craig pointed out from the back.

The scream scared them all, leaving a trail of hasty words in the air.

"My God, yes, there *is* an image! Can't you see it?" Jacqueline Clissot was almost out of her front-row seat. She bent at the waist, as though she wanted to climb into the screen.

Elisa realized she was right. The red was still opaque at the center, but now it looked like it had a halo around its edges. The meaning of that didn't become clear until the camera jumped a few seconds later.

"The sun. It's the sun! Reflected in the water!" Clissot said.

The image kept moving. With the new angle, the glare was no longer blinding and the dark curve of a shoreline became visible on the lower half of the screen. Everything was cast in red. There were different shades and varying degrees, but it all looked red, including those long, twisted shapes. Elisa held her breath. *Is that them?* If so, they were the weirdest creatures she'd ever seen. They looked like giant snakes.

But according to Clissot, they were just trees.

"A Jurassic forest. Those are probably *Equisetum,* commonly known as horsetails. Or tree ferns. My God, they're so tall! And those plants floating on the lake, or whatever it is ... Maybe giant amphibian lycopodiums?"

"The palm trees are cycads," Nadja interrupted. "But they look shorter than we thought they were."

"Ginkgos, araucarias ..." Clissot was still listing. "And those biggies over there are sequoias ... David, it's a symbol of your theory." The image skipped to another time string and kept moving along the shore. "Wait, wait ... One of those branches might be ... It could be ..." The paleontologist waved her arms angrily. "Colin, would you just *stop the damn movie!*"

"We don't want to freeze any of the images yet," he replied calmly.

It skipped again.

And there they were.

When they appeared, Blanes, Nadja, and Clissot stood up, forcing the rest of them to do the same if they wanted to be able to see. It was like the most exciting motion picture ever, and the crowd's emotion had reached fever-pitch.

"Their skin," Elisa heard Valente whisper from the row behind her. He'd said it in Spanish: *la piel.*

"Is that their *skin?*" Marini cried.

It was really a rather remarkable sight. Their cervical and dorsal muscles looked like jewels, and so did their extremities. Huge Fabergés, glimmering gems, wobbling in the sun. They reflected so much light that it was hard to look at them without being blinded. Elisa could never have imagined anything like it. Nothing had prepared her for that image. She thought they must have become extinct because nothing that beautiful could possibly survive alongside human beings.

There were two of them, standing still, photographed from above. Seeing their enormous heads and long bodies, something very strange occurred to her: those creatures were somehow related to her; they weren't just animals but dreams she'd once had (dreams about devils, because that was what they looked like, with those huge horns). It was as if by watching them, everyone was now seeing inside her.

The picture jumped again. One of them was now at the water's edge. She could make out its unbelievably pointy, speckled tail in the reddish glow. Jacqueline Clissot was gesturing wildly and shouting in French. She looked like a presidential candidate on the campaign trail.

"Antennae! How could anyone have guessed? No, wait. Retractable feelers?"

"**HOW** many toes did they have? Did anyone count them? They could have been megalos ... No, not with those protuberances. They were probably allosauruses. They were eating something ... Nadja, we have to see what they were eating! And those feelers, my God!" Clissot, now the center of attention, was blathering almost uncontrollably. She hadn't let up since the moment the images began. "Feathers on their tails and feelers on their heads! The allosauruses' crania show supraorbicular slits that have always been the object of debate. People said they were sexual, but no one ever thought ... No one could have guessed they had some sort of retractable feelers, like snails! What would they be used for? Maybe they're olfactory organs, or a sensory organ to help them navigate the jungle ... And those feathers prove that they used much more complicated mating rituals than we'd ever suspected ... How could we have guessed? I'm so nervous. I need a glass of water ..."

Mrs. Ross was already on top of it, clearing a way between Silberg and Valente. The lights were on, now, and Elisa couldn't quite believe they'd just seen those earth-shattering images in a shabby little home theater, complete with prefab walls and twelve plastic chairs.

"How could it have been so shiny?" Marini asked.

"What a shame we couldn't see the original colors!" Cheryl Ross lamented.

"The red deviation was very intense," Blanes agreed. "Those time strings were located a hundred and fifty thousand light-years ago ..."

"So many things we didn't know." The paleontologist gulped down the glass of water in one go and wiped the back of her hand across her mouth. "So, so many. Fossils, most of the time, just show us the bones. We knew that some of them had feathers ... In fact, dinosaurs are the ancestors of birds. But no one ever imagined that dinosaurs that big could have had feathers ..."

"Giant carnivorous chickens!" Marini said, giving a nervous laugh.

"Oh God, David!" Clissot gave Blanes an impulsive hug, which seemed to throw him off.

"We're all very happy," Mrs. Ross chimed in.

Not everyone.

Elisa was unable to define exactly what she felt. It seemed like some sort of *traction,* a force displacing her center of gravity, making her want to fall. It was like vertigo, but it didn't just affect her balance. It knocked her off her emotional balance as well, and even her *moral* equilibrium was threatened. She wanted to listen to Clissot's explanations, but she couldn't. She leaned against the wall, intuiting that if she allowed it to win, she'd fall into an abyss, and only by standing could she save herself.

Not everyone is affected the same.

She'd felt it when she hugged Nadja. Rosalyn and Craig, too. Curiously, despite her enthusiasm, Clissot seemed somehow neutral. Valente, too. The Impact. This time it's our turn.

The rest of the team was joyful, but Silberg, sweating profusely (though seemingly incapable of removing his tie) called them together in his booming voice.

"Please … Just a minute … We forgot about the effects of the Impact. I'd like you all to tell me what you're feeling." Elisa would have liked to, but she couldn't. She saw Blanes watching her and fled the screening room through the side door, running for her room. When she got there, she closed herself in the bathroom. She wanted to throw up, but all she managed to do was dry heave. Elisa held onto the walls as if she were below the deck of a boat with no crew being tossed by the waves. She knew she'd fall if she remained standing, so she fell to her knees and felt an intense pain as her kneecaps slammed into the metal floor. There on all fours, her head hanging down, she felt as though she was waiting for someone to come and take pity on her. *No! God, don't let anyone to see me!*

And then, abruptly, it was over.

It ended as suddenly as it had come on. She got up and splashed her face. Glanced at herself in the mirror. She was still Elisa. Nothing was wrong. What were those bizarre thoughts that had crept through her mind like spiders? She couldn't make any sense of it.

And she didn't want to miss the next transmission for anything in the world.

IT was a city, not that remarkable in and of itself. Big, made of stone, not very pretentious. However, just like with the dinosaurs, she found herself amazed at how beautiful it was. There was forethought and *desire* in those forms, in the wall that surrounded the city, in the tangle of streets and the rooftops, in the placement of the towers. And all of it was stunning to her eyes. A wild, physical perfection, so far from the world she inhabited. Did ancient things—objects, cities, animals—really used to be so beautiful? Or was it just that now everything was so ugly? It occurred to her that maybe, in part, the Impact was this: a yearning for lost beauty.

"The temple ... We can't see Solomon's Portico ..." Silberg was a cicerone in the dark. "Antonia's Fortress ... And that over there must be the Praetorium, Rosalyn ... It's hard to tell because it's all so new ... That's right. New. That semicircular building is a theater. There are things hanging from the windows ..."

"Roman standards," Rosalyn Reiter said in an almost sorrowful voice.

Elisa was holding her breath. She knew they wouldn't see him. They couldn't possibly be that lucky. That would be like finding a needle in a *million and one* haystacks.

Silberg agreed. They'd have more chance of seeing him on the cross than walking through the streets. But in any case, he and Reiter had still counted the days. According to the synoptics, he died on Nisan 15; according to John, it was the fourteenth. Silberg tended to agree with John, which meant a Friday in April. Pontius Pilate had ruled from the year AD 26 to the year AD 36, which left two probable dates: April 7, AD 30, and April 21, AD 33. But there was something else to consider: Sejanus, commander of the Prae-torian Guard in Rome and a man who showed no love for the Jews, had died in AD 31, and Emperor Tiberius had been manifestly op-posed to his firm-hand policy. If Sejanus was already dead, then Pontius Pilate's reluctance to condemn the Hebrew carpenter made more sense. Which made AD 33 seem the more likely year.

Silberg and Reiter had chosen a very precise moment (a "wa-ger," Silberg called it): the days leading up to April 21, AD 33.

"He was just one person in a city of seventy thousand, but he made quite a splash ... Perhaps ... we might see something indi-rectly ... be able to decipher something based on people's comings and goings ..."

But there were no people anywhere. The city was desolate.

"Where is everyone?" Marini asked. "The computer saw people ..."

"There are other strings open, Sergio," Craig said. "We don't know which exact time this string is from ... Maybe everyone's ..."

But when the image skipped, Craig fell silent. The camera de-scended on a steep street and then jumped again. The silence in the room became sepulchral.

On the left side of the screen they could make out a motionless silhouette.

It was black as a shadow and wore what appeared to be a veil over its head. There was something white in its hands, maybe a basket. They couldn't make it out clearly, even with the zoom. In fact, the image was partially dissolved. That blurry, black shape just standing there in sharp contrast to the light all around it was terrifying. But there was no doubt about it.

"It's a woman," Silberg pronounced.

Elisa forced herself not to shiver. Nothing in the world could make her close her eyes right now: not red-hot pokers coming straight for her eyeballs, and certainly not any fear of the Im-pact. She devoured it; she treasured the image with hungry eyes, tears streaming down her face. *The first human being we've seen from the past.* Just standing there, on the screen. *A real woman who really lived two thousand years ago.* Where was she going? To the market? What was in her basket? Had she seen Christ preach? Had she seen him enter the city on a donkey and wave a palm branch?

The image skipped to another nonconsecutive string and the figure jumped several feet, to the center of the screen. She was still motionless, draped in dark clothing, but her posture seemed to indicate that she'd been photographed from above while walking from left to right down the steep road.

It skipped again. This time the figure stayed put. Had she stopped? The computer did an automatic zoom and focused on her upper half. Silberg, who had started speaking, instantly fell silent again.

Then something made Elisa lose her breath.

After another jump, the figure turned sideways, head raised, as though she was looking at the camera. As though she was looking *at them.*

But that wasn't what made people scream, knocking down chairs and bumping into each other in the dark.

It was her face.

BLANES was the only one who remained calm, sitting still on one edge of the table. Marini, at the other end, was playing with a marker, like a magician practicing an old trick. Clissot was drumming her fingers on the table. Valente seemed more concerned with the landscape out the window, but it was easy to see that he was upset, because he changed positions constantly. Craig and Ross were finding excuses to make trips to the kitchen (taking out dishes, bringing them in). Silberg didn't need an excuse. He paced like an angry bull in a tiny corral.

Elisa, sitting in front of Marini, looked at the room, each person in turn, taking in the details, their gestures, watching to see how each one reacted. It helped her not think.

"It must be some sort of disease," Silberg said. "Leprosy, would be my guess. Back then it was epidemic, devastating. Jacqueline, what do you think?"

"I'd have to watch it again, slower. It could be leprosy, but it seems odd ..."

"What does?"

"Well, that her eyes and most of her face were missing, and yet she walked as though she could see perfectly."

"Jacqueline, I'm sorry, but we have no idea whether or not she walked 'perfectly,'" Craig pointed out politely, standing before her. "The images were skipping. There could have been two seconds between each one, or fifteen. She may have been stumbling, for all we know."

"That's true," she agreed, "but still, the damage was much more severe than what we associate with leprosy. Though maybe back then–" "Now that you mention seeing," Marini interrupted. "How could she have been ... looking at us? Didn't she give you that impression?"

"She had no eyes," Valente chirped, smiling hideously.

"What I mean is, it was as though she knew we were there, as though she had some sort of presentiment ..."

"That's a two-thousand-year 'pre-.' Don't you think that's a pretty long 'pre-'?"

"She didn't have any presentiment, Sergio. That's what it looked like to us, but it's totally impossible," Silberg intervened.

"I know, all I mean is that–"

"The thing is," Silberg cut him off, "we saw what we wanted to see. Don't forget about the Impact. It makes us more apprehensive."

A shadow crossed Elisa's line of vision. It was Rosalyn. *Poor Rosalyn. How are you taking it?* Both Nadja and Rosalyn had gone to lie down after the Jerusalem images produced nervous reactions in them. Nadja had started crying hysterically, and the historian had gone completely stiff. Elisa would never forget Rosalyn Reiter's appearance when the lights were flipped back on: standing, arms at her sides, she looked like a statue. Nadja looked *scared,* but Rosalyn looked *scary.*

She still did, a little bit. Rosalyn walked into the dining room and stood before them all like a servant awaiting orders.

"How do you feel?" Silberg asked.

"Better." She smiled. "I feel better."

She glanced over at Valente, who was the only one not looking at her. Then she walked into the kitchen. Through the open door, Elisa saw her adjust her shorts and smooth her hands over her face and hair, as though she was trying to decide what to do next.

"We should figure out a way to measure the Impact's effects," Blanes suggested.

"I'm devising a psychological test," Silberg informed them, "though it won't be as simple as responding to a few questions. We still might not know all the consequences. It might be like sub-liminal advertising, something that only comes out later. We don't know yet, and there's no way to tell right now."

Mrs. Ross suddenly jumped into action.

"I'm going to see how Nadja's doing," she said.

Mrs. Ross's absence left them all feeling empty, as if she'd whisked their spirits away on her way out. Valente stood at the window; it started to rain heavily again.

"Now, I know this is absurd, so please don't laugh," Clissot began, "but ... thinking about Sergio's idea, I'm wondering ... Isn't it possible that there is somehow some form of communication between past and present? What I mean is ... Well, why couldn't that woman have somehow sensed our presence?" Elisa was horrified at the possibility. "I know you've explained it several times already, but I still don't understand the exact physics behind opening time strings. If what you're doing is making a hole to be able to see back in time, why couldn't the people from back then see forward through it, too?"

Silence. Blanes and Marini exchanged a quick glance, as if deciding who should tackle the question. Or *how* to tackle it.

"Anything is possible, Jacqueline," Blanes said, finally. "The 'exact physics behind opening time strings,' to use your expression, is a mystery to us all. We're moving in such a tiny field that the laws governing it are, to a large degree, unknown. In quantum physics, there's a phenomenon known as entanglement, by which two particles, even if they're billions of kilometers apart, have a mysterious connection, and what happens to one of them affects the other *immediately*. That's known as nonlocal behavior. And in the case of time strings, we think that without the temporal distance there would be a higher chance of quantum entanglement. That's why we don't want to do any experiments on the recent past."

"Guess I skipped physics class that day," Clissot said, smiling.

Blanes made as if to stand up, but Marini beat him to it.

"I've got the dry-erase, maestro." He strode to the whiteboard on the wall and drew a horizontal line with his left hand—Marini was quite elegant for a southpaw. "Imagine that this is a time line, Jacqueline. The right end represents the present, and the left one is an event that occurred, say, a thousand years ago. When we open their time strings, we create a sort of passageway called a 'wormhole,' which is a tunnel of particles that connects the past to the present, at least for the instant that the opening takes place. The same thing would happen if we opened strings from five hundred years ago, although in this case the bridge would be much shorter. See?"

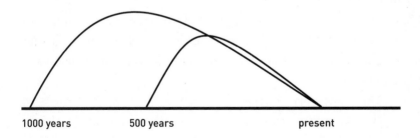

1000 years   500 years   present

Clissot nodded. Elisa judged his explanation so far as superb.

"But, what would happen if we opened strings from, say, seventy years ago? If you look at our diagram, the tunnel would be tiny. And if we tried it with a period like ten years, five years, one year ..." Marini drew other lines representing these time frames. The last one was just a fat vertical line. The illustration left no room for doubt.

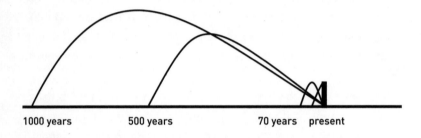

1000 years   500 years   70 years   present

"I see. There would be no tunnel. The two events would merge."

"Exactly. An entanglement." Marini pointed to the vertical line. "The shorter the temporal distance, the greater the possibility of interacting with our present. This is a crude illustration, because the real proof is mathematical, but I think it might help you understand ..."

"Perfectly."

Ric Valente left his post at the window and walked into the kitchen. He and Rosalyn began a heated discussion. Elisa couldn't hear what they were saying.

"That's why we're not concerned about experimenting with events that took place five hundred or a thousand years ago, but we don't want to repeat what happened with the Unbroken Glass," said Blanes.

There was a brief silence.

"Did something we don't know about happen with the Unbroken Glass?" Clissot asked.

"No, no," he said quickly. "All I mean is that we don't want to take any risks."

There was a slight commotion coming from the kitchen. When everyone turned to look, Valente smiled at them from the next room, and Rosalyn, her face red as a beet, stared angrily.

"Just a friendly disagreement," Valente said, holding up his palms in a sign of peace.

The dining-room door opened. Elisa expected to see Nadja, or maybe Ross, walk in, but it was neither of them. A voice she hadn't heard for many days boomed across the room.

"Can I have a word with all of you?" asked Carter.

"**HOW** do you feel?"

"Better."

Nadja Petrova's room was almost dark. One small, battery-powered lamp on her nightstand cast a faint glow. Elisa guessed that Mrs. Ross, who was bustling around in the bathroom, must have brought it. She was glad to see that her friend did, indeed, look better, and she was obviously happy that Elisa had come to see her (Nadja was not one to hide her emotions). She sat on the edge of the bed and smiled at her friend.

"I don't like this one bit; look at these lights." Mrs. Ross, ever cheerful, emerged from the bathroom carrying a stepladder. "Not only have the bulbs burned out, the whole light fixture is singed. When did you say it happened, Nadja? Last night? Odd. The same thing happened in Rosalyn's room the other day. They must be faulty connections. I'm sorry it's not something I can fix right now."

"Don't worry, this lamp will be fine for now. Thank you."

"You're very welcome, darling. I'll talk to Mr. Carter. I bet he knows something about sockets and such."

After Mrs. Ross closed the door, Nadja turned to Elisa and stroked her arm affectionately.

"Thank you for coming."

"I wanted to see you before I went to bed. And to give you the latest gossip." Nadja arched an almost-white eyebrow and pricked up her ears. "Carter just came to inform us that he received some news via satellite. There's a serious storm headed for New Nelson, a typhoon. It should hit us by midweek, but the worst of it will be Saturday and Sunday. This rain is just the buildup. The good news is that we have a compulsory vacation. We won't be allowed to use SUSAN or receive any new telemetric images, and on the weekend we won't even be allowed to boot up our computers, in case the generator fails and we have to switch onto emergency power." Her friend looked alarmed. "Don't worry, silly. Carter is sure we won't lose power ..."

Nadja's expression wiped the smile off her face. When she spoke, her voice was unrecognizable, as though someone was forcing her to repeat the words against her will.

"That ... woman ... was ... *watching* us, Elisa."

"No, hon, she wasn't ..."

"And her face ... It was like someone had filed it down and then scraped off all her features ..."

"Nadja, come on now ..." Overcome by compassion, she hugged her friend. They remained like that for a while in the poorly lit room, protecting each other from something they couldn't comprehend.

Then Nadja pulled away. The redness of her eyes was all the more obvious against her snow-white skin.

"I'm a Christian, Elisa. When I responded to the questionnaire, I said I'd give anything to be able to ... to see him ... But now I'm not so sure ... I don't know if I want to!"

"Nadja." Elisa grasped her shoulders and wiped the hair out of her face. "A lot of what you're feeling is a result of the Impact. That suffocating feeling, the feeling you can't breathe, the panic, the idea that it's all somehow related to you ... I felt the same thing with the dinosaurs. It took everything I had to overcome it. Silberg says we'll have to study the Impact's effects more, to find out why it happens to some of us with some images and not others. But regardless, you have to understand that it's a psychological side effect. You mustn't think that ..."

Nadja was crying into Elisa's shoulder, but her sobs slowly subsided. After a while, all that could be heard was the humming of the air conditioners and the drumming of the rain.

Part of Elisa couldn't help but share Nadja's horror. With or without the Impact, the image of that faceless woman was sickening. Just recalling it, the room seemed suddenly colder, the darkness denser.

"Didn't you like the dinos?" she joked.

"Yeah ... Well, not entirely. That shiny skin. Why did you think that was so beautiful? It was disgusting ..."

"Here we go. You like the bones, not the packaging."

"That's right, I do. I'm a paleo ..." Nadja struggled to pronounce it in Spanish.

"*Paleontóloga*. You got it. A paleontologist."

They both smiled. Elisa smoothed her white hair and kissed her forehead. Nadja's doll-like hair fascinated her.

"Now you should try to get some rest."

"I don't think I'll be able to sleep." Fear distorted her face. Her features weren't especially beautiful, but with that look, she reminded Elisa of a damsel in distress out of some old painting. "I'm going to hear more noises. Don't you hear them anymore? Those footsteps?"

"I told you, that's Mrs. Ross ..."

"Not always."

"What do you mean?"

Nadja didn't reply. She seemed to be thinking about something else.

"Last night I heard them again," she said. "I got up and looked in Ric and Rosalyn's doors, but they were in their beds. Didn't you hear anything?"

"I slept the sleep of the dead last night. But it was probably Carter. Or Mrs. Ross in the pantry. She does a weekly inspection. I asked her. She told me."

Nadja shook her head.

"No. It wasn't her. And it wasn't a soldier."

"How do you know?"

"Because I *saw*."

"Saw who?"

Nadja was pale as a sheet.

"I told you I got up and went to look. Well, I looked in Ric and Rosalyn's rooms, but I didn't see anything out of the ordinary. So I turned around to go to your room ... and I saw a man." She squeezed Elisa's arm tightly. "He was standing by your door, with his back to me so I couldn't see his face. At first, I thought it was Ric, so I called out, but then I realized that it was someone else ... someone I'd never seen."

"How could you know that?" Elisa whispered, terrified. "The hall is always so dark ... and you say he had his back to you ..."

"But ..."–Nadja's lips were quivering, her voice a petrified whimper–" ... when I got closer I realized that he was ... he was facing me ..."

"What?"

"I saw his eyes. They were white. But his face was empty, blank. He had no face, Elisa. I swear it. Please believe me!"

"Nadja, you're being affected by the image of the Jerusalem Woman."

"No, I saw her for the first time *today*. This happened *yesterday*."

"Have you told anyone?" Nadja shook her head. "Why not?" When her friend made no reply, she continued. "I'll tell you why. Because deep down, you know it was a dream. Right now you can't see that, because of the Impact ..."

Her explanation seemed to calm the young paleontologist down. They looked at each other for a moment.

"Maybe you're right ... But it was such an awful dream."

"Do you remember anything else?"

"No ... He came to me and ... I think I fainted when I drew near ... Then I woke up in my bed ..."

"See?" Elisa said. Nadja squeezed her arm again.

"Don't you think there could be someone else here, besides Carter, the soldiers, and us?"

"What do you mean?"

"On the island ... Someone else on the island."

"That's impossible," Elisa said, shivering.

"But what if there *were* someone else, Elisa?" Nadja insisted, clutching her arm so hard it hurt. "Someone we were never told was here."

18

SERGIO *Marini liked to do magic tricks. He could pull a dollar out of your ear, rip it in half, and put it back together, all with his right hand, as though he reserved the left for more serious tasks. Colin Craig had copies of Manchester United's greatest matches stored on his laptop, and he and Marini used to watch the international games when they were broadcast. Jacqueline Clissot liked to show everyone pictures of her son Michel, who was five, and send him funny e-mails; then she'd sit down with Craig, who was going to be a first-time father next year, and give him practical advice. Cheryl Ross had been a grandmother for two years, but she didn't knit or bake cookies; instead, she discussed politics and took great delight in criticizing "the bloody buffoon," Tony Blair. Reinhard Silberg had recently lost his brother to cancer and he collected pipes, though he rarely smoked. Rosalyn Reiter read John Le Carré and Robert Ludlum novels, though during the month of August her favorite pastime was named Ric Valente. Ric Valente worked and worked, all the time and everywhere; he'd stopped spending time with Rosalyn, and even taking walks with Craig and Marini, and all he did was work. Nadja Petrova chatted and smiled: what she liked best was not being alone. David Blanes wanted to be alone so he could play Bach's labyrinths. Paul Carter worked out (free weights and sit-ups) by the garrison. That they had in common,* *though she preferred running on the beach and swimming, rain and wind permitting. Bergetti played cards with Marini and Stevenson, and his fellow Brit, York, watched soccer with Craig. Méndez was a comedian and liked to make Elisa laugh by telling stories that, had anyone else told them, would have come across as moronic. Lee was into New Age music and electronic gadgets.*

That's what they were like. That's what the only seventeen inhabitants on New Nelson between July and October 2005 used to be like.

She'd never forget the banal hobbies that defined them, that gave them history and identity.

She'd never forget. For many reasons.

ON the morning of Tuesday, September 27, Elisa got some very exciting news. Mrs. Ross (who according to Marini was "like the tax man" because she knew everything about everyone) told her at lunch. Elisa spent the rest of the meal debating whether she should do it, and imagining all the possible outcomes.

In the end, she opted for long pants. It might seem silly ("childish," her mother would say), but she didn't want to go see him in shorts.

When she got to his office that afternoon, she could hear the pecking of two little birds skipping across the keys. She cleared her throat. She knocked on the door. And when she opened it, she swore to herself that she'd never forget the image of the scientist sitting there at his electric keyboard, his face reflecting some form of private ecstasy in which even physics had no place. She stood in the doorway, listening, until he stopped.

"The prelude to the first suite in B-flat major," Blanes said.

"It's lovely. I didn't want to interrupt."

"Oh, don't be silly. Come on in."

Though she'd been in his office several times before, she felt very tense. She always felt tense when she went there. The size of the room (it was tiny) was partially to blame, and the huge number of objects piled up (including a plastic whiteboard teeming with equations, a desk with his computer and electric keyboard on it, and a bookshelf) didn't help.

"I wanted to congratulate you, Professor Blanes," she murmured, still standing with her back against the door. "I was very happy to hear the news." She saw him frown, squinting his eyes as if she were invisible and he was making every effort to figure out what kind of incorporeal creature was addressing him. "Mr. Carter told Mrs. Ross . . ." She wiped her lips and was suddenly struck by a thought. *Oh, shit. He doesn't know yet. I'm going to have to be the one to tell him.* "An unofficial source at the Swiss Academy leaked the news this morning . . ."

Blanes looked away. He seemed to have lost all interest in the conversation.

"I'm just a 'strong candidate,' as they call it. Happens every year." And he banged out a chord to end the conversation, as if to say he'd rather go back to his music than keep talking drivel.

"You'll get it, Professor Blanes. If not this year, then next."

"Sure. I'll get it."

Elisa didn't know what else to say.

"You deserve it. The sequoia theory is an astounding breakthrough."

"An *unknown* breakthrough," he corrected, his face to the wall. "One of the defining features of our generation is that everyone knows the meaningless breakthroughs, a few people know the important ones, and no one knows the astounding ones."

"Well, they're going to find out about this," she replied sincerely. "I'm sure there are ways to reduce the Impact, or control it. And I have no doubt that in the end, everyone will find out what you've achieved, Professor Blanes."

"Enough 'Professor Blanes' already. Me: David; you: Elisa."

"OK." Elisa smiled, despite the fact that she felt a little uncomfortable with the fuss she had unwittingly caused. All she'd wanted was to congratulate him and leave; she wasn't even looking for any thanks. But it seemed obvious that Blanes didn't give a damn either way.

"Take a seat, if you can find one."

"Oh, I just wanted to ... to congratulate you, that's all ..."

"Just sit down, for Christ's sake."

Elisa found a place to perch on the table, by the computer. It was quite narrow, though, and the edge was sticking into her butt. Good thing she was wearing long pants. Blanes was still staring at the wall. Elisa suspected he was about to launch into a tirade about the injustices that a poor Spanish physicist like himself suffered in the face of society. But instead, what he said made her stomach tingle.

"Do you know why I never let you respond in class, Elisa? Because I knew you knew the answers. When I lecture, I don't want to hear answers; I want to *teach*. And with Valente, I was never sure."

"I see," she said, swallowing hard.

"Then, that day when you so foolishly answered without being called on, I changed my opinion about you."

"Yeah."

"No. It's not what you're thinking. Let me tell you something." Blanes rubbed his eyes and then stretched. "Don't take this the wrong way, but you have one of the biggest damn flaws anyone in the world can have: you seem flawless. That was what I least liked about you, right from the start. Remember this: it's always better—much better—to have people make fun of you than it is to have them envy you. But then that day when you burst forth with your injured pride, I thought, 'Aha, that's it! She might be gorgeous, intelligent, and hardworking, but at least she's an arrogant little fucker.' At last I'd found a flaw."

They sat there staring intently at each other, and then suddenly they both smiled.

Friendship isn't as hard as people often think. We tend to believe that the things that really matter don't happen overnight, but sometimes friendships or love just emerge, like the sun from behind the clouds: one second it was all gray, and the next, there's blinding light.

In that one second, Elisa became David Blanes's friend.

"So I'm going to tell you something, to help you hold onto that defect," he added. "In addition to being an arrogant little fucker, you're also a fabulous coworker, the best I've ever had. And that excuses you from having come to congratulate me."

"Thanks. But ... didn't you want to be congratulated?" she asked hesitantly.

Blanes answered with another question.

"Do you know what the Nobel means to someone like me? It's a carrot. The sequoia theory officially still hasn't been proven, and we can't publicize or even talk about the experiments we've been doing here on New Nelson because they're classified. But they want to pat me on the back. Say, 'Blanes, the scientific community admires you. Keep working for the government.'" He paused. "What do you think of that?"

She considered the question.

"I think it sounds like the opinion of an *arrogant little fucker*," she said, imitating his "cruel" intonation.

This time they both burst out laughing.

"Touché," Blanes replied, blushing. "But I'll tell you why I think I'm right." He ran his hand over his face, and Elisa knew that they'd reached the serious part of the discussion. There were no windows in the room, but the sound of the rain and the humming of the air-conditioning filtered through the metallic walls. For a moment, that was the only sound. "Did you ever meet Albert Grossmann?"

"No, never."

"He taught me everything I know. I love that man like a father. I've always thought the teacher-disciple relationship is much more intense in our field than in others." *And how,* thought Elisa. "We idealize our mentors to unbelievable extremes, but at the same time, we feel this imperious need to outshine them. I think that's because this is such a solitary job. In theoretical physics, we're like monsters locked up in cages. We change the face of the earth—at least on paper. I mean, my God, we're really *dangerous* ... But I'm getting off track ... Grossmann is a strong man, a real Teuton, full of energy. He's retired now. Recently diagnosed with cancer ... No one knows that, so keep it to yourself ... I'm just telling you that so you see what kind of man he is. He's totally unconcerned about it, says he's got a lot of years left in him, and I believe him. He looks better than me, I kid you not. He was already retired back in 2001, but the night we obtained the image of the Unbroken Glass, I went over to his house and told him about it. I thought he'd be thrilled, thought he'd congratulate me. Instead, he looked at me and said, 'No, David,' so softly I thought maybe I'd imagined it. But he repeated it. 'Don't do it, David. The past is off-limits. Don't touch what's off-limits.' I think that was when I realized why he'd retired. A theoretical physicist retires when he starts believing that discoveries are off-limits." He was staring intensely at the black-and-white keys of his keyboard. After a pause, he added, "Anyway, maybe Grossmann was right about something. Back then, we still didn't know anything about the Impact. But there's more to it than that. There's also the company financing Project Zig Zag."

"Eagle Group," Elisa said.

"Yes. Eagle Group. But they're just the tip of the iceberg. Who's really behind all this? Have you ever wondered? I'll tell you: the government. And behind them? Big business. The Impact is just an excuse. The thing Eagle Group really wants to hide at all costs is the military interest in the project."

"*What?*"

"Think about it, Elisa. Do you really think all the financial backing for Zig Zag stems from their passion for Troy, or ancient Egypt, or the life of Christ? Don't be naive. When Sergio and I showed them the Unbroken Glass, lightbulbs started flashing in their heads. 'How can we use this against the enemy?' was the first thing that popped into their little brains. 'And how can we keep the enemy from using it against us?' was the second. As far as Jesus, the pharaohs, and the emperors go, well, they're interesting, but not a decisive part of the final equation." Elisa blinked. This had never occurred to her before. She couldn't even see how the ability to see the remote past could be of use to the military. But Blanes began ticking off the ways on the fingers of his right hand, as if he could read her thoughts. "Espionage. Space imaging that shows not only what's happening now but what happened ten months or ten years ago, when the enemy had yet to even *imagine* we were spying. That's a good way to get information on terrorist training camps, which are always dissolving, always on the move. Here one day, gone the next, without a trace. Or assassination attempt investigations. Doesn't matter that the bomb already exploded: film the area and figure out what happened on the days leading up to it, the exact methods used ..."

"My God ..."

"Indeed. My God." Blanes mouth twisted. "The eye of God is watching all of it. Time, the original Big Brother. Then there's industrial espionage, political espionage, searching for proof of this or that scandal so they can oust this or that president. It's a race against time between Europe, which is financing the project, and the United States, which must already have its own personal Project Zig Zag on some island in the Pacific right now. We've proven that with a simple video camera you can see everything that happened, anytime, anyplace in the world. Zig Zag has stripped humanity naked, and the military wants to be the first Peeping Tom. And you know what? There's only one tiny yet bothersome thing stopping them." He pointed to his chest. "Me."

Elisa didn't think it was conceit talking. He really didn't seem to want the role at all. And what he said next confirmed that.

"To paraphrase an old bolero, 'I'm just a little thorn in their side,'"he warbled. "I don't like being a pain in the neck, honestly. The reason I left the States was because they were putting more money into arms than accelerators, and I'll leave Europe if Zig Zag gets used for military purposes, but I'm also aware of the fact that the reason I'm here is because they're paying me. I want to deliver, I want to give them what they've asked for. I really do. But I *refuse* to experiment with the recent past." His voice suddenly became edgy. "I told them there were risks and there are, Elisa … lots of them. Believe me. But that's a matter of personal opinion. Sergio, for example, is more daring, even though in the end he agreed with me. That's why they want us to carry on with our little games, to see if we can come up with something less risky they can use."

"They didn't tell me anything about all this when they hired me," Elisa said, taken aback.

"Of course not. You think they told me everything? Ever since September 11, the world stopped being divided into truth and lies. Now all we have are lies. The rest, we'll never know."

They were both silent. Blanes stared at a spot on the floor. Somewhere in the distance, the rain fell in sheets.

"You know what the worst thing is?" he asked suddenly. "If I'd refused, if I'd listened to Grossmann and abandoned the whole thing, we would never have seen a Jurassic forest, or the dinosaur's feelers, or a woman walking down a street in Jerusalem during the time of Christ. None of that excuses my actions, but it does explain them. It's like having the best present in the world and not being able to share it with anyone. So. If they award me the Nobel, you can have it, OK? You want it?" He pointed at her.

"I don't think so." Elisa scooted off the table and pulled down her cropped T-shirt to cover her midriff, smiling. "You can keep it."

"Hey! As my disciple, part of your job is to take all the things I turn down. What else do you suggest? Throwing it in the trash?"

"Give it to Ric Valente. I'm sure he'd be thrilled."

They laughed.

"Ric Valente," Blanes said slowly. "One strange kid. An extraordinary student, but too ambitious ... I tried to get to know him at Alighieri, and I realized I didn't like him. If it were up to me, he wouldn't be here, but Sergio and Colin think he walks on water."

Elisa stared at him for a minute. Then, before leaving, she said, simply, "Thanks."

Blanes looked up.

"What for?"

"For sharing your gift with me."

As she walked back down the hall replaying fragments of the conversation in her head, she sensed that the rain had intensified. It must have been the buildup to the typhoon. But she wasn't worried about the approaching storm. Carter had assured them that it presented no danger, and they'd already taken "the necessary precautions."

And he was right. The typhoon would prove to be the least dangerous thing of all.

THAT downpour made any outdoor activity impossible and forced the scientists to their bedrooms, trapping them in a gloomy, gray lethargy. Elisa and her colleagues were harder hit by that apathy since it was now Clissot, Silberg, Nadja, and Rosalyn who had things to do, while the physicists sat back, idly. She often met up with Clissot and Nadja in the lab after breakfast to pass the time and watch them study the image of the Lake of Sun (as they'd baptized it, rejecting Marini's chosen name: Lake of the Carnivorous Chickens) inch by inch. At first she was enthralled, but slowly the paleontologists' meticulous work began to bore her. "Examine A's first extremity, Nadja. Now compare that to B's homolateral. A has only one phalange, but B has two." Elisa yawned. *If anyone had told me a couple days ago that I would get bored of this, I'd have laughed. Just goes to show...*

Nadja was feeling much better. She'd started sleeping better, and she was far less anxious. Though she was going to have a psychological checkup with Silberg the following week, nothing kept her from her daily routine at the computer.

Every time she saw her, Elisa thought about what Nadja had told her the day of the screenings. It seemed so absurd, just a figment of her imagination, but she had some doubts. Could there actually be someone else on the island they didn't know about? Why not? She'd been there two and a half months, and although she thought she knew each and every inhabitant, including the soldiers, choppers came and went with supplies all the time. Surely it was possible that a new soldier had come to replace someone and was staying with the rest of them in the garrison. But if that were the case, why wouldn't he have introduced himself? And what was he doing exploring the barracks at night, out of uniform? *Ridiculous. Nadja'd had a really intense nightmare. And the effects of it were intensified by the Impact.*

Still, she couldn't get that horrible idea out of her head: a man with white eyes, staring at her from the darkened hallway.

The night of Saturday, October 1, after playing (and losing) several hands of poker with Craig, Marini, and Blanes after dinner, Elisa went back to her room. By nine o'clock, she was in bed, and the lights went out at ten o'clock sharp.

The typhoon seemed to be getting worse. It sounded like the beginning of Judgment Day, like one of those Dantesque apparitions—an eagle or a cross—was flying over them. But with all those layers of insulation, it was easy to feel like you were in a metal bubble. Nothing moved. Everything was still and quiet. Still, Elisa couldn't get off to sleep.

She pulled back the sheet and got up, deciding to go for a walk. She could go to the kitchen and make herself a cup of tea. Then she remembered that Carter had forbidden them to use any electric appliances. And he was right to do so, because lightning flashed silently, momentarily lighting up parts of her room. She still liked the idea of going for a walk, though. The emergency lights in the hall would do. And besides, she was sure she could walk the entire barracks with her eyes closed.

Then she noticed something.

She looked toward the window when she saw it. At first, she wondered if she was dreaming.

It was a gap. On the upper-left-hand side of the wall, where the ceiling met the bathroom wall. It was elliptical, and if she'd tried she could have fit through it. The silent flashes weren't coming from the window but from that opening.

She was so upset at not having noticed something so obvious that she missed another strange detail.

Silent flashes.

Silent.

She was surrounded by silence. Total silence. Where had the storm gone?

But there wasn't, in fact, *total* silence. Something behind her made a noise.

This time they weren't footsteps echoing through the walls, but sounds that indicated a concrete presence, very nearby. The squeak of rubber soles, someone's breath. Someone in her room, *inside* her room, with her.

Her skin felt like it was being peeled off. It was as though each pore was an iron filing and she stood beside a powerful electromagnet that pulled each and every one, from the nape of her neck right down to the soles of her feet. It took her an eternity to turn around and look behind her. And when she finally managed to, she saw a figure.

It stood stock-still by the door, a little farther than she'd guessed by the sound of its breathing. The flashes partially revealed tennis shoes, Bermudas, and a T-shirt. But its face was enveloped by shadow.

A man.

For a second, she thought her heart was going to explode from sheer terror. Then she recognized him and almost laughed.

"Ric ... What are you doing here? You scared the daylights out of me ..."

The figure made no reply. Instead, he advanced toward her, slowly, lightly, like clouds covering the moon.

She had no doubt it was Valente. The build, the clothes. Well, she was *almost* sure. But if it was him, what did he think he was doing? Why didn't he say anything?

"Ric?" She never thought that one little word could be so hard to get out. Her throat constricted as she said it. "It *is* you, Ric, right?"

She took a step back, then another one. The man walked around the bed and kept approaching, expressionless, in complete silence. He was taking his time. The flashes lit up his Bermudas and dark T-shirt, but his face was still dark beneath a curtain of hair.

It's not Ric. There's someone else on the island that we don't know about.

Her back was pressed up against the metal wall. She felt the cold metal make contact with her skin. That was when she realized she was stark naked. She couldn't remember having taken off her clothes, which made her suspect this wasn't actually happening. She was dreaming. It had to be a dream.

But regardless, watching that silhouette draw closer and closer in dead silence was insufferable. She screamed. When she was a little girl and had nightmares, she always woke up the moment she screamed. She always thought, in fact, that screaming was what shattered the nightmare, ended the horror.

Now, it did nothing. She opened her eyes and the man was still there, advancing slowly. If she reached out, she could touch him. His face was like an abandoned building. All she could see were the hollow walls of his cheeks and, behind that, the laddered ridges of his vertebra. Aside from that there was no flesh or bones; it was totally unreal, an empty space between two parentheses, a completely black void ...

His head is a rat's nest, and the rat gnawed up his face and is living in his brain. There's someone else on the island that we don't know about...

... black void, except for his eyes.

His name is White Eyes, and he's come to see you, Elisa. To see all of you, actually.

A short visit, but one that will change everything.

Eyes empty, like abscesses.

It wasn't a dream. He immobilized her. He was about to...

Eyes like enormous moons that, when she looked into them, drew her into their luminescence, blinding her with their ashy vacuousness.

Please help me someone please help me this is not a dream oh god please...

That was the moment when the darkness no longer hid in shadows. It was unleashed.

THE darkness had an absurd voice.

It sounded like a schoolboy who'd just had his ice cream cone stolen by the big kids on the playground. It was a high-pitched whine. It was Ric Valente; Elisa had really pricked his pride, no matter how aloof he thought he was. His cries were so deafening that Elisa wanted to tell him to shut up or she'd prick him again, or burn his feathers, because now that she looked closer, he had feathers on his backside and feelers on his head, and he was moving back and forth on top of her. Actually, it was a carnivorous chicken of great paleontological importance, opening its beak and squawking. "But I can't laugh because this is a nightmare."

Or at least in part. She'd made love for the first and last time in her life when she was seventeen. Bernardo was his name. She'd been so traumatized by the experience that she never wanted to repeat it. Bernardo had been friendly, sweet, shy, and romantic, but the second he penetrated her he began firing on all cylinders. He grabbed her ass, gurgled, grunted, pushed, and foamed at the mouth. She'd gone to the movies with a human being and found herself in bed with a rabid dog that just kept stabbing his thing in between her legs and roaring, "Mmmmfff," "Uuuuff." She really didn't like it, truth be told. Her vagina burned and she most *definitely* did not come. When it was over, he shared a cigarette with her and said, "That was unbelievable." She coughed.

A couple of months later, on the way back from Valencia, her father was killed by a drunk driver.

It's not as though the two things were in any way related. She was sure tragedy wouldn't strike every time she got laid. But she had no desire to put it to the test.

So ... how did she end up with that man in her bed? He was much worse than Bernardo, more ferocious and with worse intuition. She'd once seen a movie (what was it called again?) in which the protagonist sleeps with the Devil himself, a being that smelled like sulfur and had white eyes and (one supposed) an enormous cock. *I know it's ridiculous but I can't help it, here, now, with this thing on top of me ... its eyes bright white like lights, and someone who isn't me (but must be me) screaming their head off, practically making me go deaf ...*

She woke up in the dark. There was no one on top of her, underneath her, or anywhere else. She wasn't naked. She wore the same T-shirt and undies she'd worn to bed. And, of course, there was no gaping hole in the wall. But she hurt inside, and it felt like it had the first time. She couldn't think about that, though, because there were too many other disturbing things going on.

There were no flashes. There were no searchlights on the station, no station on the island, maybe no island in the sea. Just that awful wailing sound, a demented howling piercing her eardrums. *An alarm.*

She sat up, refusing to feel scared, and then she heard voices in the sound not filled by the vibrating bell. The voices brought fear the way a breeze brings in the smell of carrion. Screaming in an

English she didn't need to translate in order to understand that something terrible had happened, because there comes a time in any emergency when people understand everything they hear without deciphering it. Catastrophe is multilingual.

She lunged for the door, thinking that it must be a fire, and almost crashed straight into a horrifying ghost, white as the X-ray of a human body pinned to the wall.

"All the lights have gone out! The lights! All of them! Even my flashlight!"

It was true, not even the tiny emergency lights in the hall were on. They were surrounded by impenetrable darkness. She put an arm around Nadja's trembling shoulders, trying to console her, and the two of them ran up the hall, feeling their way together, barefoot.

A wall kept them from going any farther. They could hear Reinhard Silberg's voice from beside it, his silhouette outlined in the murky glow of a flashlight. Standing on tip-toes to see past him, Elisa could also see Jacqueline Clissot, lit up from underneath, and Blanes, struggling with the person holding the flashlight (a soldier, maybe Stevenson) at the door to the hallway that led to the next barracks. *I want to get through! You're not allowed! I have a right! I'm telling you ...! I'm the scientific director ...!*

She realized Nadja had been shouting something for some time.

"Ric and Rosalyn aren't in their rooms! Have you seen them?"

She tried to come up with something longer than no when suddenly it went quiet. The silence was absolute.

And then, breaking it, the voice of Marini (in the distance, coming from the next barracks), relieved: "Damn, it's about time." The alarm, no longer sounding, was still ringing in Elisa's ears with such intensity that she didn't realize that someone else was coming down the hall beside Stevenson. An enormous hand emerged from the dark, a stony face that confronted Blanes.

"Calm down, Professor," Carter said without raising his voice.

"Everyone, just calm down. The main generator short-circuited, and that set off the alarm. That's why the lights went out."

"Well, why didn't the backup generator kick in?" Silberg asked.

"We don't know yet."

"Is all the equipment OK?"

Elisa would never forget Carter's reply, the way he averted his gaze, his squared jaw contrasting with the pallor of his cheeks and the way he lowered his voice.

"The equipment is, yes."

19

"SORRY, does anyone want more tea or coffee? If not, I'm going to take the cups out to the kitchen."

Mrs. Ross's voice piped up unexpectedly, as if she were the kind of person who never spoke up. Elisa noticed that she was the only one eating (a yogurt, spooning it calmly but ceaselessly into her mouth). She was sitting at the table and looked better than might be expected, given not only the circumstances but also the fact that she hadn't had time to get dressed and put on all the jewelry she normally wore. A short time earlier, she'd made tea and coffee, passed out cookies like a practical mother who thinks that breakfast is the essential ingredient necessary to discuss death.

No one wanted anything else. After smoothing down her hair, she went back to her yogurt.

They'd congregated in the dining room: a collection of pale faces, bags under their eyes. Marini and Craig weren't there; they were checking on the accelerator. Jacqueline Clissot, too, was off taking care of something she was trained to do but had no idea would be required of her until the tragedy.

"The way I see it," Carter said, "Miss Reiter must have gotten up in the middle of the night, walked down to the control room, and gone into the generator room for some reason. She touched something she shouldn't have, triggered a short circuit, and ...

well, you know the rest. When the doctor is finished with her examination, we'll know more. She doesn't have the right tools to do an autopsy, but she promised she'd give us a report."

"And where is Ric Valente?" Blanes asked.

"That's the second part of the mystery. I don't know yet, Professor. Ask me again, later."

Silberg was seated at the table in his pajamas, with the bewildered expression shared by all very nearsighted people who don't have their glasses on (he'd left them in his bedroom and still hadn't been allowed to go back for them), tears streaming down his cheeks. He held his hands out imploringly and spoke softly.

"The generator room? Wasn't it locked?"

"Yes, it was."

"So how could Rosalyn get in?"

"With a copy of the key, most likely."

"But what would Rosalyn want with a copy of the key?" Elisa couldn't make sense of it, either.

"Just a minute," Blanes said. "Colin told me that he had to wait for *you* to turn off the alarm in the generator room, because you're the only one with the key. Right?"

"That's right."

"That means it was locked from the *outside*. Which means that Rosalyn was locked *in*. How could she do that by herself?"

"I didn't say she did it by herself," Carter conceded, scratching his graying beard. "Someone locked her in."

That statement took things to a new level, and gave the situation a whole different spin. Blanes and Silberg glanced at each other. There was an uncomfortable silence, which Carter broke.

"We can't rule out the possibility of an accident. She could have tripped in the dark, or accidentally touched some wires ..."

"Wasn't there light in the generator room?" Silberg asked. "She was the one who caused the short, right? So there would have been light at least until she touched the wires. Why wouldn't she turn it on?"

"Maybe she did."

"Well, did she or didn't she?" Blanes took over. "Was the light switch up or down?"

"I didn't notice, Professor," Carter replied, and for the first time Elisa thought she sensed irritation in his voice. "Still, if someone locked her in, she could have gotten flustered and not have been able to find the switch."

"But why lock her in to begin with?" Silberg looked disconcerted. "Even if someone wanted to hurt her ... why do that? There are too many things that don't add up ..."

Carter quietly laughed.

"In great tragedies, things don't add up, that's for sure. But what happened has a simple explanation. In real life," he said—stressing the word *real*—"things are almost always quite straightforward."

"Maybe in the real life you know," Blanes objected, "but not me. What about Ric's disappearance? Nadja, tell us again what you found in his bed."

Nadja nodded. Elisa, sitting beside her at the table, could tell without touching her that she was trembling and held her hand protectively.

"When I heard the alarm I got up and went out into the hall ... I was alone, no one else had gotten up yet and, well, I wanted to wake them. So I looked in and saw that Rosalyn's bed was empty ... And in Ric's bed was ... well, not exactly a doll, it was more basic than that, just a pillow and a couple of round backpacks, really. His sheet was on the floor," she added.

"Why would Ric do that?" Blanes asked.

Carter looked as if he'd just thought of something. "He probably didn't think any of you would make good detectives. He thought you were just physicists."

"Physics is based on hypothesizing, following clues, and finding proof, Mr. Carter. That's what we're trying to do right now."

Blanes gave Carter that sleepy look he had that Elisa knew so well. "Do you think Ric is hiding somewhere in the station?"

"He'd have to be the Invisible Man. We've searched everything top to bottom. There aren't many places he could be hiding here. On the island, yes, but inside the station? I don't think so."

The door opened and Marini, Craig, and the Thai solder, Lee, filed in one by one. Both Lee and Craig were literally soaked, as if someone had sprayed them down with a pressure washer. Stevenson, the soldier who had barred their way that morning, and who was now standing guard in the living room, was also dripping wet.

"All in order," Marini said, though his face seemed to indicate the opposite. He wiped his hands on a rag. "The computers are all fine, and the screens are still picking up signals from the satellites ..."

"SUSAN is fine, too," Craig confirmed. "No one touched anything."

Who would have touched anything anyway? Elisa wondered distractedly.

"Lee?" Carter asked.

"Nothing wrong with the backup generator, sir." Lee wiped sweat from his face with the back of his hand—or maybe that was rain, too. His uniform was unbuttoned, revealing a scrawny white chest beneath his undershirt. "There's plenty of electricity. But the main generator is kaput, completely burned out. No way to repair it."

"Why didn't the backup kick in when the main one burned out, then?" asked Blanes. Carter conveyed the question to Lee by shrugging and raising his eyebrows at the soldier.

"The ignition wires burned out, so all the backup generator could do was trigger the alarm. But I just rewired it."

"Does it make sense that the *backup* ignition wires get burned out by a short circuit in the *main* generator?" Blanes queried.

An electronic bleep interrupted them. Carter took the walkie-talkie from his belt and they heard static and indistinct words.

"York says they've made it to the lake and there's no sign of Mr. Valente," he explained, after listening to the communiqué. "But they still haven't searched the rest of the island."

"And what are we supposed to do in the meantime?"

Carter raised a hand to his thick neck and paused, though he didn't seem particularly bothered by the question. It was as though he wanted to create suspense, as though the time had come to show the know-it-alls what was what. He stood beneath the only dining-room light that was on (two of the three had been turned off to prevent another possible short, he said); all eyes were on Carter. His robust figure seemed to be saying, "Trust me." In a way, Elisa was glad there was someone like him there with them. She'd never think of going dancing with Carter, or to a French restaurant or even for a walk in the park with him. But in that situation, she liked having him around. Guys like him were good in tragic circumstances.

"This is all set out in the contracts you signed. I'm assuming command, and calling off the project until further notice; there will be no more scientific investigation, and we can all start packing our bags. By noon, the weather should have improved a little, and the choppers at our nearest base might be able to come pick us up. By tomorrow night, no one but the search team should be left on New Nelson."

The announcement was expected, maybe even wished for, but it was met with somber silence.

"The project is off...," Blanes said. Despite what had happened, Elisa understood why he sounded so distraught.

"Paragraph five, confidentiality appendix," Carter recited. "'In any situation entailing unknown risks to personnel, the security team may call off the project indefinitely.' I think the death of one colleague and the disappearance of another qualify as unknown risks, don't you? But we're talking about a break here; this doesn't mean we're terminating the project indefinitely. What I'm worried about right now is finding Valente. So for the time being, get going. Pack your bags."

ELISA didn't have much to pack. She quickly stuffed everything in her room into her suitcase, but when she went to get her stuff from the bathroom, she found that the lights had burned out, probably after the short. The bulbs and sockets were black, as if they'd been singed. She decided to find Mrs. Ross and see if she could get a flashlight from her.

Questions raced through her head as she wandered down the hall. *Why did he run away? What made him hide? Did he have anything to do with what happened to Rosalyn?* She didn't want to think about Valente. Picturing him made her think of her bizarre dream, and that made her feel like she couldn't breathe.

Never in her life had she ever had a dream as horrifying, disgusting, and at the same time realistic. She'd even gone so far as to examine her body, searching for some sign of the rape experience. But aside from a faint yet persistent pain, there was nothing, just a sensitivity that eventually went away. She tried to convince herself that the alarm, combined with the story Nadja had told her the week before, caused her nightmare. She could think of no other explanation.

Elisa found Ross in the kitchen, taking inventory.

"That's odd," the woman replied on hearing her request. "The same thing happened to Nadja last week ... But I don't think it has anything to do with the short circuit, because my bathroom light is fine. Must be the sockets. Anyway, as for a flashlight, let me think ... Lately, demand is far outweighing supply!" And she gave that low, open laugh that Elisa had heard the first time the night she arrived on the island. Almost immediately, though, Ross became circumspect, as though she knew any sign of joy was out of place that morning. "I'd lend you mine, but I'm about to go down to the pantry, and if the lights go out again, I don't want to be banging my shins against those refrigerators. Hmm. You could ask Nadja ... No, wait ... She told me hers broke this morning ..."

"Never mind, it's no big deal," Elisa said.

"How about this? If you're not in a rush, I'll try to find some more in the pantry. I was planning to go down as soon as I finished taking inventory here anyway. We need to know exactly how much we're leaving behind, because I'm sure we'll be back soon."

"Can I give you a hand?"

"Well, since you're offering, that would be great. Thank you, honey. If you could just tell me what's up in that high cupboard, since you're tall enough not to need a chair to stand on ..."

Elisa stood on her tiptoes and began to list the products. Mrs. Ross asked her to stop at one point, to give her time to jot it all down. Elisa filled the silence.

"Poor Rosalyn, you know? Not just the way she ... Not just the accident, but everything she went through over the past few days."

It didn't take long for Ross to offer her theory. Mrs. Ross loved devising theories about people and events; she'd always done it as part of her job ("I used to be a consultant," she'd once said, without specifying what kind or for whom). In her opinion, Valente was hiding somewhere on the island and would reappear before they left. And why was he hiding? Ah, that was a whole different story.

"Mr. Valente is a very odd young man," she pointed out. "In fact, he could probably win the Weird Scientist Award. He might make some women's hearts flutter, but a lot of his attraction resides in his eccentricity. That was all Rosalyn saw in him. He dominated her, and she liked that ... Can you reach those bags at the back there? Pull those out for me, would you?" Ross helped her, sticking the papers in her mouth to free her hands. "Didn't you think it was strange that Nadja found the sheet in Ric's room on the floor? If he wanted to make out that he was in bed, why would he leave it on the floor? Seems like someone else went in there before Nadja and found him out, don't you think?"

Elisa realized that Mrs. Ross was more perceptive than she let on.

"I'll tell you what I think," Cheryl Ross continued. "Rosalyn was frantic because he'd stopped paying any attention to her, so that night she got up and went to his room to talk to him, but when she pulled back the sheets he wasn't there. So she searched the station and found him in the control room. That must be where he was, because the door was ajar when I got there, and I was the first one to arrive, before the soldiers even. I'm a light sleeper, and that alarm had me out of bed in a flash. Anyway, so … Maybe they argued, like they did in the kitchen that day last week, remember? Maybe they were shouting and went into the generator room so no one could hear them. Then she got an electric shock and he got spooked, took off, and locked the door behind him. I'm sure he had a copy of the key. Men are sneaky like that, you'll find that out one day. And it doesn't take a five-hundred-volt shock for them to hit the road and leave you stranded, either."

"But why would Ric leave a pillow in his bed? What do you think he was up to?"

Mrs. Ross winked.

"That I can't say. But I bet you it was something underhanded."
Just then, Stevenson interrupted them. The helicopters would be arriving sooner than expected. Mrs. Ross headed for the pantry's trapdoor. "Thank you for your help, honey. I'll bring you up a flashlight in a little while."

Elisa went back to her room to survey her luggage. Her brain bubbled over with questions. *Why did he want people to think he was still in bed? And where is he now?* She was so lost in thought that she didn't hear the door open behind her.

"Elisa."

It was Nadja. The expression on her face (she could read it easily) made her forget all about Valente and steel herself for another dreadful surprise.

"**LOOK** at this edge ... See? And now ..."

Nadja's hands were shaking on the keyboard. They'd been locked in Silberg's lab for the past fifteen minutes. They'd gone into his lab because Jacqueline Clissot was still examining Rosalyn Reiter's body in the other one and they didn't want to disturb her (Elisa, for her part, didn't want to help her, either). Nadja had enlarged the Jerusalem Woman's face several times, zooming in until she found what she was looking for. She refused to explain it to Elisa. She wanted her friend to find whatever it was for herself.

"I've been thinking about this nonstop since yesterday. I wanted to be sure before I said anything to you, but after they told us we'd be leaving and the images were staying behind, I couldn't wait any longer."

Carter had made it perfectly clear, despite Silberg and Blanes's protests: all of the images obtained there—the Perennial Snows, the Lake of the Sun, and the Jerusalem Woman, everything except the Unbroken Glass—were considered classified and could not leave the island. Plus, Eagle Group had decided that for security reasons, no one aside from the project's participants would see the images for now. They didn't want to expose anyone to the possible risks of the Impact, and they didn't have a clear picture of all the symptoms yet. Elisa could understand their concern, but she still thought it was terrible that images as unique as those would stay behind, especially since there were no copies.

"Hurry up already," she said.

"Give me a second ... *Oh, mierda!*" Nadja swore in Spanish. "I lost it again ... What are you laughing at?"

"Oh, *mierda?*" Elisa replied.

"Don't you say that in Spain?" Nadja asked, distracted. Then she suddenly she clenched her fists. "Got it! Look."

Elisa bent over and looked down at the divided screen. On the left side, a pretty clear close-up of the Jerusalem Woman's disgusting features, eaten away to an unimaginable degree, all the way to her brain from what Elisa could make out; her whole face was just a bloody crater. On the right half of the screen, what looked like curved sticks or broken branches that were only vaguely familiar because of the sparkling jewels covering them. She had no idea what her friend was expecting her to see.

"So?"

"Compare the two images."

"Nadja, we don't have time for ..."

"Please."

Suddenly Elisa saw it.

"The dinosaurs' legs ... are ... mutilated?"

Nadja's almost-albino head bobbed up and down affirmatively. They stared at each other in the gloomy laboratory.

"There are chunks missing, Elisa. Jacqueline thinks they're wounds caused by predators or disease. But then I thought of another idea. I knew it was absurd, but I decided to check ... You see these cuts, here and here? There are no teeth marks. They're *remarkably* similar to these here ..." She pointed to the Jerusalem Woman's face.

"That's just a coincidence, Nadja. A fluke. One of those images is from AD 33 and the other is a hundred and fifty *million* years old!"

"I know. I'm just telling you what I see. And what you yourself just saw."

"All I see is a totally ravaged face ..."

"And ravaged reptiles ..."

"Nadja, it makes no sense to try to establish a relationship there!"

"I know, Elisa."

For a minute they peered into each other's faces. Elisa smiled.

"I think we're starting to lose our minds. I'm glad we're getting out of here."

"Me, too, but don't you think it's a pretty extraordinary coinci-dence?"

"Well, it *is* odd ..."

"Let me tell you another coincidence." Nadja lowered her voice to a whisper, but her wide-open eyes were the very definition of a scream. "Did you know Rosalyn saw *the man,* too?"

Elisa didn't need to ask who she was talking about. She listened, shuddering.

"One afternoon a few days ago, I found her alone in her room, so I went in to talk to her. I don't remember how it came up; I think we were commenting on how poorly we'd been sleeping, and I told her about my nightmare ... or what you *think* was a nightmare. She looked at me and told me that she'd had a very similar ... dream. She was petrified. She had a dream about a man with no face whose eyes ..."

"Stop it, please."

"What?"

Elisa suddenly burst into nervous laughter.

"I dreamed the same thing last night ... My God ..." Her laugh-ter cracked like an eggshell and she burst into tears. Nadja gave her a hug.

They both sat there gasping, the outlines of their bodies sil-houetted in the computer screen's murky glow. Elisa was terrified. Not the vague fear she'd felt throughout the day, but a concrete fear, a *real* fear. *I dreamed about him, too. What does that mean?* She looked around at the shadows that engulfed them.

"Don't worry," Nadja said. "You're probably right, they're just nightmares ... Our fear has rubbed off on each other."

Now they could hear voices in the hallway: Blanes, Marini ... The exodus was clearly under way.

Just then, the door connecting the two labs burst open, star-tling them. Jacqueline Clissot appeared, took a few steps as if to cross the room, and then abruptly stopped. Clissot looked as though she'd dived headfirst into a swimming pool, fully clothed.

But it was obvious that the water glistening on her face, plastering her hair to her the sides of her head, and sticking her blouse to her breasts and armpits was, in fact, sweat. The paleontologist was sweating like crazy.

"Have you finished, Jacqueline?" Nadja asked, rising. "How did—?"

"Have you seen Carter?" Clissot interrupted her disciple with a stern voice. "I radioed him twice, and he doesn't pick up."

They both shook their heads. Elisa wanted to hear Clissot's verdict on the body, but she didn't have a chance to ask her. The hall door opened, and Méndez spoke to them in his accented English.

"I'm sorry. You must come to the screening room. The helicopters are arriving."

"I want to see Mr. Carter," Clissot said. She opened the trash can and threw her surgeon's mask into it. "It's urgent."

But it was too late. Méndez was gone, and Colin Craig stood in his place.

"Sorry. Any of you seen Mrs. Ross?"

"Try the pantry," Elisa suggested.

"Thank you." Craig offered a polite smile and disappeared.

"I *need* to see Carter before we go," Clissot insisted to the two women. "If you see him, let him know. I'm going to try to find him at the heliport." Then she followed Craig's footsteps and disappeared down the hall.

"She seems so edgy," Nadja murmured.

"We all are."

"Yeah, but she never was before ..."

Elisa knew what she meant. She never was *before she examined Rosalyn.*

"There you go, getting carried away with your fantasies again," she said. But she wondered what it was that Clissot could have found on Rosalyn's body that was so urgent. "Come on, we should leave everything how it was ..."

While she helped Nadja close down the computer and save all

the files, she thought about how badly she wanted to get out of there. Suddenly, the island was unbearable, with everyone coming and going, people storming in and out all the time, the soldiers making a racket. She longed for the solitude of her house. Or any house, for that matter.

"I'll be right there," Nadja said. "I still have a few things in my room."

They separated in the hallway, and Elisa headed for the exit. It seemed to have stopped raining, although the sky was still gray. The barracks were oppressive.

She walked past the dining room and was almost to the exit when she heard the screams.

THEY were coming from below her. She could almost feel them vibrate in the soles of her shoes, like the start of an earthquake. For a second, it made no sense. And then it hit her. *The pantry.* She ran to the dining room and found it empty.

Almost. Silberg had been the first to arrive (or maybe he was already there to begin with) and was headed toward the kitchen at top speed.

Her stomach did flips as she followed the German professor to the storeroom where the trapdoor leading down to the pantry was located. Silberg rushed to it and began to climb down the ladder. A shadow appeared beside Elisa.

"What's going on?" Nadja asked, panting. "Who's making that awful noise?"

Silberg stopped. Half of his body was motionless, sticking out above the trapdoor. They could hear the cries clearly now, interspersed with coughing and panting. Elisa thought it was Mrs. Ross at first, but it was a man's voice.

Then Silberg did something that horrified her. He hoisted himself up, climbed up the same top three steps he'd just climbed down, and stepped aside, his massive hands gesticulating wildly as he shook his head.

"No ... no ... no ...," he whimpered.

Seeing that enormous man sob like a schoolboy, his face a ball of wax, was more upsetting than the screams she was hearing. But what was about to happen was even worse.

Another set of gloved hands appeared above the trapdoor. A soldier. Though he had no helmet and no machine gun, Elisa recognized him right away. It was Stevenson, one of the younger ones, and he gave the impression that he was trying to escape. He ran to the corner where Silberg was and then turned and ran to the opposite side of the room, staggering like a boxer after the final, decisive blow. Then he fell to his knees and began to vomit.

The trapdoor was still open, a serene black hole, almost beckoning, seeming to call, "Who's next?" A toothless mouth waiting to be fed.

"Keep away from there!" Carter roared. He was holding a pistol. "Don't move! Nobody move!" In his other hand he held a flashlight, surely of more use than the gun, because after he climbed down the ladder he was swallowed up by darkness.

Lots of people crowded into the room now. One of the other soldiers (York), his boots and pants splattered with mud, tried unsuccessfully to comfort Stevenson; Blanes and Marini were arguing with Bergetti ... There seemed to be mayhem down below, too. Elisa could hear Colin Craig's voice perfectly. *On the wall! Right there! Are you blind? On the wall!*

It dawned on her now, amid the chaos, that it had been Craig's voice all along.

Elisa made up her mind hastily. She dodged Nadja and slipped through the trapdoor. Instinctively, she climbed down the first few rungs of the ladder.

Her way down was like reliving everything that had happened the previous night, step by step, scene by scene. She felt the same horror, heard mumbled voices, saw the confused shadows, the darkness. But there was one key difference: this time she couldn't keep going. Not because there was anything in her way. No. It was the vision before her.

She'd never forget it. Years would go by and she'd remember that scene as if for the first time, as if time itself was just a con, a disguise for the constant, immobile present.

Carter was in the back, in the cold-storage area; the only light came from his flashlight. Elisa saw his silhouette in the beam. Everything else, everything that was not Carter's dark shadow, was a dense, sticky color that covered the walls, ceiling, and floor of the room entirely.

Red.

It was as though a huge monster had swallowed Carter and he was in its stomach, about to be digested.

She couldn't go any farther. That vision paralyzed her. She stopped halfway down, just as Silberg had, and realized that someone was pulling her arm (a soldier; she saw the gloved hand). She heard a dizzying stream of commands shouted in English from below.

"Everyone keep out! Civilians, out! Get the fucking civilians out!!"

A set of hands yanked her up by the armpits and toward the light once more.

In that very instant, she heard the thunderclap and saw a huge flash of lightning.

"THAT was the moment we all died," Elisa said to Víctor, ten years later.

FIVE

The Meeting

The future torments us, and the past holds us back.

GUSTAVE FLAUBERT

20

"I lost consciousness. I remember a nightmare helicopter ride. I'd wake up, faint again ... They gave me sedatives. During the flight, they explained that the warehouse by the military compound was used to store flammable materials, and it had exploded when one of the helicopters lost control during its landing and crashed into it. Méndez and Lee, who'd been outside, were killed in the explosion, along with the crew on board the helicopter. The whole military compound was destroyed, and the control room was severely damaged. Both labs were totaled. And as for us ... well, we were 'lucky.' That's what they told us." She laughed. "We took shelter in the kitchen; that was what they considered 'lucky' ... Anyway, it made no difference, really, because by then we were already dead. We just didn't know it." She paused and then added, "Of course, they didn't tell us the whole truth."

Víctor saw her raise her left hand and stiffened.

He watched every move Elisa made, and had been since she'd asked him to pull off at the rest area and park the car. It wasn't that he didn't trust her, but the story she'd told him, the dark night, and the enormous butcher knife she was still gripped so tightly didn't exactly set his mind at ease.

All Elisa did, though, was consult her computer watch.

"I lost track of time; it's almost midnight. You probably have a lot of questions, but you need to decide one thing first ... Are you coming with me to this meeting?"

The mysterious midnight meeting. Víctor had forgotten about it, wrapped up as he was in Elisa's incredible story. He nodded his head.

"Of course I am, if you ...," he began. All of a sudden, their shadows were cast on the car ceiling by a bright light shining through the rear window. They heard the crunch of gravel under tires at the same time.

"Oh shit, drive!" Elisa shouted. "Come on, let's go!"

For a second, Víctor thought he wasn't going to be able to play the role of race-car driver, but he managed just fine. He turned the ignition and gunned the motor at almost the exact same time. The tires gripped the asphalt and burned rubber with a peal that made him imagine sparks flying out from behind them. After some skillful maneuvering, he regained control of the vehicle and they were off.

Once they were back on the Burgos highway, he had two equally satisfying realizations. First, that the van, or whatever it was that had pulled up behind them, wasn't following them (maybe it had just been a coincidence), and second, that despite the panic making him shudder like an old windup alarm clock, he was starting to feel like this was the adventure of a lifetime, and he was living it with Elisa, of all people.

The adventure of a lifetime.

That made him smile, and he decided to drive a little faster (very unlike him) than the speed limit. He didn't want to break the law, just to make an exception for one night. He felt like he was taking a woman who'd just gone into labor to the hospital. For once, he could condone it.

Elisa, who'd turned to look behind them, now twisted back around and leaned back, panting.

"We lost them. For now. Maybe we could ... Do you have autopilot?"

"Nope. I don't even have GPS or Galileo. Never wanted them. I do have a good, old-fashioned street map, though, in the glove compartment. Jeez, that was something ... I never thought I had it in me to peel out like that!" He slowed down a little and bit his lip. "Luis Lopera should have seen me!" He glanced over at her. "My brother, I mean."

But Elisa was paying no attention. For a minute, he watched her unfold the map, searching for something under the yellow map light. Bent over like that, her jet-black hair fell forward, and he couldn't see her beautiful face.

"Keep going until San Agustín de Guadalix and then take the Colmenar exit."

"OK."

"Víctor ..."

"Yeah?"

"Thanks."

"Don't say that."

He felt her fingers stroke his arm and recalled a time when he'd gone on a winter vacation with his brother's family. Sitting beside the campfire one night, the flames had given him the same sort of tingling sensation.

"The floor is now officially open to questions and requests," she murmured, folding up the map.

"You still haven't told me what *really* happened in the pantry. You said they didn't tell you the truth, but ..."

"I will. But first let me try to clear up any doubts you have about what happened up until now."

"Clear up any doubts? Elisa, right now I'm doubting absolutely everything, beginning with who I even *am*. Where do I begin? It's all so ... I don't know ..."

"So strange. Right? The strangest thing you've ever heard. And that's why we have to act strange, stranger than ever. In order to understand this, Víctor, we have to behave like strangers."

He liked that. Especially the fact that a woman like her—

wearing a low-cut T-shirt, black leather jacket, and jeans—had said it, butcher knife in hand, as they sped down the highway at 110 miles an hour. *Strangers. Yeah. You and I. Strangers in the night.* He accelerated. Then he realized there would be other people at this meeting and they wouldn't be alone, and that discouraged him slightly.

He decided to start with some preliminaries.

"Do you have any proof of all this? I mean, do you have a copy of the dinosaur images, and the woman at least?"

"I told you, they wouldn't let us take anything. And the guys at Eagle said everything was destroyed in the explosion. That could just be another lie, but to be honest, that's the least of my worries."

"Well, how is it that the scientific community knows nothing about any of this? If it happened in 2005, that was ten years ago. Things like that, astounding technological breakthroughs, they don't stay secret for that long."

Elisa thought about her answer for a minute.

"People like us, we *are* the scientific community, Víctor. And back in the forties, a lot of our colleagues knew it was *possible* to make bombs using nuclear fission, but they were just as shocked as the general public when they saw thousands of Japanese blown to smithereens. It's one thing to believe something is *possible*, and quite another to *see it happen*."

"Still ..."

"Oh, Víctor ...," she sighed, sneaking a glance at him. "You don't believe a word of this, do you?"

"Of course I believe you. The island, the experiments, the images ... It's just ... it's too much to take in all in one night."

"You think I'm hallucinating or something."

"No! That's not true."

"Do you even believe there was a Project Zig Zag?"

The question made him stop and think. Did he? She'd told him everything in plenty of detail, but had he accepted it? Had that constant stream of mind-blowing information cleared his cerebral channels? And the hardest question: had he accepted what it meant if she was actually telling him the truth? *The ability to see the past* ... the sequoia theory ... Time strings opened and viewed, their present images transformed into images from the past. It seemed ... possible ... unlikely ... fantastic ... rational ... absurd. If it were true, then the history of humankind had changed forever. But how could he believe it? Up until that moment, what he knew was what the rest of his colleagues knew: that Blanes's theory was mathematically attractive but had an exceedingly slim chance of ever being proven. And as for the rest of it (mysterious shadows, unexplained deaths, white-eyed ghosts), if it were all based on an idea that struck him as crazy, how could he believe it?

He decided to be honest.

"OK, I don't believe it all ... I mean, it's just too much to handle, the idea that for the past half an hour I've been hearing out about the greatest discovery since relativity, right here in my car, on the ride up to Burgos ... I'm sorry, I just can't ... I can't take it all in. But by the same token, I can say I believe *you*. In spite of ... the way you're acting, Elisa." He swallowed hard and then confessed all. "I have to be honest with you. A lot of things have been going through my head tonight ... I mean, I still don't even know *who* we're running from, or why you're carrying a ... a small machete around with you ... It's all pretty shocking, and frankly, I have my doubts ... about you, about me. What you're suggesting, the way you're acting, it's just all so mysterious. It's like the hardest cryptogram I've ever tried to crack. But I think I have a solution. And my solution says, 'I believe *you,* but right now I don't believe *what you believe.*' Does that make sense?"

"Totally. And I appreciate your honesty." He heard her exhale deeply. "I'm not going to do anything with this knife, I swear. I just need it right now, the same way I need you. You'll understand soon enough. In fact, if this all works out how I hope, then in a few hours, you'll understand *and* you'll believe me."

She sounded so convinced that it sent a shiver down Víctor's spine. One lonely road sign announced the turnoff for Colmenar. He got off the highway and took a narrow two-lane road as dark and perilous as his thoughts. Elisa's voice carried on, dreamlike.

"I'll tell it to you how they told it to me. After the helicopter trip, I woke up on another island, in the Aegean. It's better for you if you don't know the name. At first, I hardly saw anyone, just a few men in white coats. They told me that the Impact had made Cheryl Ross lose her mind and she'd taken her own life when she went down into the pantry in the cellar, back on New Nelson. I couldn't believe it. It was too absurd. I'd just spoken to her, and I knew it wasn't true."

Víctor interrupted her to ask the one question that was burning in his mind.

"What about Ric?"

"They refused to tell me anything about him. For the first week, they did nonstop tests: blood tests, urine tests, X-rays, sonograms, the works. And I didn't get to see anyone. I started to lose my patience. I spent most of my time locked up in a room. They'd taken my clothes and I was under constant observation. Everything I did, every move I made, it was like being in a zoo." Elisa's voice trembled. She was overcome by the sickening memory. "I couldn't get dressed, I had nowhere to hide. The excuse they gave me was that they had to make sure I was OK—this, and everything else, through a loudspeaker; no one ever came in to speak to me in person. They said it was like quarantine. I held out for a while, but by the end of the second week I couldn't take it anymore. I lost it. Kicked and screamed, the whole nine yards, until finally someone came and agreed to give me a robe, and then they brought Harrison, the guy who was with Carter when I signed the contract in Zurich. I didn't want to see him, he was such an awful man: brusque, pale, and he had the coldest look you can imagine. But he was the one who told me what he called 'the truth.'" She paused. "I'm sorry, Víctor. You're not going to like this."

"Don't worry," he said, half closing his eyes, as if they, and not his ears, were what was about to receive the bad news.

"He told me that Ric Valente had murdered both Rosalyn Reiter and Cheryl Ross."

Víctor began whispering something about God, mouthing words almost silently, perhaps commending his soul. After all, despite everything, Ric had been his best friend as a kid. *Poor Ric.*

"The Impact had affected him more than any of us. That Saturday night in October he left his room, after throwing together that dummy with the pillow to make it look like he was still in bed, and probably lured Rosalyn into the control room with a lie. Then he beat her and hurled her against the generator. And then he did something no one could have guessed. He hid in one of the refrigerators in the cellar. It must have broken down when everything short-circuited. Anyway, he hid there while the soldiers carried out their search, and no one found him. Then when Cheryl Ross went down to take inventory, he hacked her to pieces. He got a knife or an ax somewhere; that's why there was all that blood all over the place. And after he killed her, he committed suicide. Colin Craig discovered both bodies when he went into the pantry looking for her. Minutes later, by chance, the helicopter crashed. And that was that."

The news of Ric's death didn't affect Víctor Lopera; he already knew about it. He'd known for ten years, but until then the only version he'd heard and tried to picture was the "official" one. That his childhood friend had been killed in an explosion at a Zurich laboratory.

"It might sound like a pretty dubious explanation to you," Elisa continued, "but at least it was an explanation, and that was all I wanted. Besides, Ric really did die: they found his body in the pantry, they had a funeral, his parents were notified. Of course, it was all confidential. My family, my friends, and the rest of the world only heard that there had been an explosion in Blanes's lab in Zurich. The only victims were Rosalyn Reiter, Cheryl Ross, and

276 JOSÉ CARLOS SOMOZA

Ric Valente. They covered their tracks. They even produced a real explosion in Zurich—with no victims, of course—so there wouldn't be any loose ends. And we were sworn to secrecy. We weren't allowed to talk to each other, weren't even allowed to stay in contact. For a while, once we went back to our normal lives, we were under strict surveillance. According to Harrison, it was all 'for our own good.' The Impact could have other unknown side effects, so we'd be watched for a sensible length of time, just enough to make a fresh start in life. We were each given a job, a means of supporting ourselves. I went back to Madrid, did my dissertation with Noriega, and became a professor at Alighieri." At that point, she paused for so long that Víctor assumed she was done. He was about to say something when she added, "And that's how all my dreams ended, my desire to conduct research, or even work in my field."

"And you never went back to New Nelson?"

"No."

"I'm so sorry. To have to give up on a project like that, after those breakthroughs ... I understand. It must have been awful."

Elisa looked away. Her eyes narrowed, focused on the dark highway. When she replied, there was an edge to her voice.

"I've never been so happy about anything in my life."

THEY were both gazing at the flexible screen, spread out like a tablecloth on the white-haired man's legs, as the armor-plated Mercedes they were traveling in sped silently through the night on the Burgos highway. On the screen a red dot, surrounded by a labyrinth of green dots, blinked intermittently.

"Is she taking him to the meeting?" the stocky many asked, uttering his first words for several hours. His thick, gravelly voiced seemed fitting.

"Looks that way."

"Why hasn't she been intercepted?"

"Well there's no record of her having contacted anyone, and I suspect that's because she just recruited him *tonight*." The white-haired man rolled up the screen and the green glow and blinking red dot disappeared. In the darkness of the backseat, his lips stretched into a thin smile. "That was very clever of her. She managed to throw us off even though her line was tapped. Spoke in some code that only this guy understood. They're a lot sneakier than last time, Paul."

"Good for them."

That response made Harrison glance over at Paul Carter questioningly, but Carter had already turned back to the window.

"At any rate, the intrusion of ... a new element ... won't require us to change our plans," Harrison added. "She and her friend will soon be with us. And in tonight's game of chess, the only piece that concerns me is the German pawn."

"Has he left yet?"

"He's about to, but unlike her, *he* will be intercepted. Along with everything he's carrying."

And suddenly, the crisis began. It was immediate, unexpected. Harrison didn't realize it (because it was happening to him), but Carter did, though at first it was barely noticeable. All he saw was Harrison daintily unrolling the computer screen again, as though it was a delicate flower petal with a wasp he wanted to trap buzzing inside it. Then he touched it and chose an option from the menu: a beautiful face filled the screen, framed in black. Laid out floppily on Harrison's thighs, the face looked like it was melting: a hill, a valley, another hill.

It was Professor Elisa Robledo's face.

Harrison grabbed the face with both hands, and suddenly Carter knew what was happening.

A crisis.

All trace of emotion had disappeared from Harrison's face. Not just the kindness he'd shown chatting to the young driver at the airport or the coldness of his phone conversation, but literally every single sign of feeling or emotion. His features had been robbed of life. The man driving the Mercedes couldn't see them in the darkness of the car's interior, and Carter was relieved. If he'd looked in the rearview mirror and seen Harrison (or seen Harrison's face) at that moment, he'd have crashed.

Carter had witnessed several of these attacks. Harrison called them "panic attacks." He claimed he'd been dealing with "all this" for too many years, said he wanted to retire. But Carter knew there was something else to it. The attacks were always worse after certain events.

Milan. This is because of what we saw in Milan.

He wondered why he wasn't worse himself and finally deduced that it was because he couldn't possibly *get* any worse.

"There are some things that no one should see ... ever," Harrison said, recovering, rolling up the screen again and placing it back into his overcoat.

You're telling me. Carter didn't reply. He just kept looking out the window. No spectator (though there were none) could ever tell that he was affected by what he'd seen.

But he was. Paul Carter was afraid.

"**WAIT!** I think I get it!"

"No, there's no way you get it yet."

"Yes, I do ... Wait a minute. Sergio Marini's death ... The news on TV today, I was the one who called to tell you ..." Víctor opened his mouth and almost jumped out of his seat. "Elisa, you put two and two together, right? Now I see. You had a truly horrible experience, I know ... Three of your colleagues died because another one went insane ... But that was ten years ago!"

She listened carefully. And now it all made sense to him: Elisa needed his words and his comfort more than she needed him to drive her down dark, winding lanes at night. Her memories were the only thing actually after her. She was absolutely terrified of a bunch of things that were dead and gone. There was a name for that, right? Post-traumatic stress disorder. Marini's murder was just a terrible coincidence, and it had sparked the whole thing off. What should he do? The thing that would help her the most would be to make her see that.

"Think it through," he said calmly. "Ric Valente already had plenty of reasons to be unstable, and I can assure you that I'm not surprised to hear that the Impact, or whatever it was, brought his worst instincts to the surface. But he's dead, Elisa. You can't ..." Suddenly, another idea flashed through his mind. "Wait a minute ... We're on our way to meet the others, aren't we?" Her silence confirmed he was right. He decided to venture on. "The rest of the Zig Zag team. Of course ... You're meeting tonight. Marini's death made you all think that ... that another one of you had lost your minds, the way Ric did ... But if that were true, shouldn't you be trying to get help?"

"Who's going to help us, Víctor?" she asked, in the saddest, bleakest voice he'd ever heard. "No one."

"The government ... the authorities ... Eagle Group."

"They're the ones after us. Don't you see? That's who we're running from."

"But why?"

"Because they're trying to help us." With each sentence, Elisa seemed to be making less sense, getting more scrambled, mired deeper in turmoil. "When we get to the meeting, it'll all make sense. We're almost there. The exit is just after this stretch ..."

He was distracted for a moment by two curves in the road. The names of the towns they passed all blurred in his mind: Cerceda, Manzanares el Real, Soto del Real ... Faint lights were dotted throughout the black fields, sometimes clustered in what must have been little villages. The scenery would have been beautiful in the daylight (Víctor had traveled through here before), but at night it was like meandering through the ruins of a huge, haunted cathedral. It's frightening how insignificant the distance separating man from terror really is, Víctor realized. Three hours ago, he'd been watering his aeroponic plants, in his comfortable apartment in Ciudad de los Periodistas, and look at him now. Driving along a dark road with a woman who might be deranged.

"Why are you armed?" He tried to think fast. "Is Eagle Group our enemy?"

"No, our enemy is much worse ... unfathomably worse."

He took another curve, the headlights casting their beams on the trees.

"What do you mean by that? Wasn't Ric the one who—

"That was *bullshit*. They lied."

"But then—"

"Víctor," she said harshly, staring at him, "for the past ten years, someone has been murdering *everyone* who was on that fucking island ..."

He was about to reply, but as he turned into another bend in the road, his headlights shone on a car blocking their way.

21

HIS right foot took over entirely.

His mind didn't go blank. He had time to ask himself a few questions, to register Elisa's scream, invoke both God and his parents, and have a terrible realization: we're going to die.

The mass of metal blocking the highway raced toward the windshield as if *it* were moving, rather than his car. Víctor put all his weight behind his right foot as it plunged into the pedal beneath him. In his ears, Elisa's cries and the sound of tires screeching blended into one incredibly sharp, piercing note, like a chorus of terrified lunatics. There were two strokes of luck: the curve was not a tight one, and the car was a short distance away. Still, despite his sharp turn to the left, the right side of the car smashed into the driver's door of the other vehicle. For a fraction of a second, he was elated. *Whoever that asshole is, I showed him.* Then they reached the shoulder and he had a realization: beyond them were a few trees and then a steep slope. *Yes, Víctor, you're on a mountain. A steep slope. Practically a cliff.* But the world came to a halt at the safety barricade. It wasn't really a crash. The air bags didn't even deign to inflate. Newtonian inertia slightly jiggled their bodies, and then all was calm.

"God!" Víctor shouted, as if "God" were an insult to make truckers blush. He turned to Elisa. "You OK?"

"I think so …"

His legs were trembling (after having done its duty, his right foot had turned to Jell-O), but his hands were in control. He unfastened his seat belt, muttering, "Jerk … I'm going to report that idiot … He'll be sorry …" He was about to open the door when something stopped him.

For a second, he thought that the light shining through his window and blinding him was coming from the other car, but it was floating in the air and had no motor attached to it.

"It's them," Elisa murmured.

"Them?"

"The people following us."

A black leather fist banged on the window.

"Out!" the fist shouted.

"Hey, wait a minute!…

Anger was a common response for Víctor, but he was anything but angry. At that precise moment, he was terrified. He didn't want to leave the car's protective interior, but he was scared to disobey Black Fist. His fear was schizophrenic, simultaneously hissing, "Don't do it," and yet also whispering, "Do as you are told."

Dark suits with jacket tails fluttering in the wind filed past his high beams.

"Don't get out," Elisa said. "I'll talk to them."

She rolled her window down manually. An unknown face appeared, in a sliver of light. Elisa and the face spoke in English.

"Professor Lopera has nothing to do with this … Let him go …"

"He has to come too, now."

"I'm telling you …"

"Don't make this any more difficult than it already is, please."

While he witnessed that rather formal discussion, night suddenly entered his side of the car. They had somehow managed to open his door, though he didn't recall having unlocked it. Nothing separated him from Black Fist now.

"Get out, Professor."

A hand clamped onto his arm. The words stuck in his throat. No one had ever touched him like that before. His relationships were based on courtesy and a polite personal distance. The hand yanked, dragging him out. Now, mixed in with the fear assailing him, he also felt the outrage of an upstanding citizen unfairly hassled by the authorities.

"Hey! Just a minute! What right do you have– "Let's go."

There were two men, one bald and the other blond. Baldy was doing all the talking. Víctor was pretty sure Blondie couldn't even speak Spanish.

Of course, he didn't need to.

Blondie had a gun.

THE house, situated a few miles from Soto del Real, was just as she remembered it. The only changes she noticed were that the inside seemed slightly run-down now, and there was more construction in the area than there had been. But it still had the peaked roof, white walls, porch, and old swimming pool. It was nighttime, but it had been dark the first time, too.

Everything was the same, but it was all different, too, because the first time she'd felt hopeful, and now she had no hope, had resigned herself entirely.

The room they locked her in was a small bedroom that looked like it hadn't been used in years. There was no decor whatsoever, just a sheetless bed, a nightstand, a lamp with a naked bulb providing the only light, and an old wooden chest of drawers, warped with age. Oh, and a man built like a brick house, arms folded across his chest, wearing a dark suit and an earpiece while he blocked the door. Elisa had tried speaking to him, but it was like talking to a wall.

As she paced the desolate room, watched by her keeper, her thoughts were all focused on one thing, the most important of the many that should be concerning her: Víctor. *I'm so sorry. So, so sorry.*

She had no idea where they'd taken him. She guessed he was somewhere in the house, too, but the men who had ambushed them split them up, forcing Víctor into another car. She was driven in Víctor's car, after they'd confiscated that stupid knife, of course (what had she been thinking, grabbing that thing?). Nevertheless, she felt convinced they'd been brought to the same place, and that Víctor had arrived first. They were probably interrogating him at that very moment. *Poor Víctor.*

She promised herself that she'd get him out of there if it was the last thing she did. Getting her friend tangled up in this had been a tragic mistake on her part, a failing. She swore that she'd pay any price, including her life, to free him. But first she'd have to find the answers to a few questions. For example, why had she gotten *the call* if the meeting place was not secure? And how had they even found out about the meeting? Had the whole thing been a trap from the start?

Twenty or thirty minutes later the door opened abruptly, banging into the guard. A man in shirtsleeves walked in (not the Big Cheese, not yet, though she was certain he'd put in his appearance soon). The two men exchanged apologies in English, but no one said a word to her. The guy who'd been watching her nodded his colossal head at Elisa and she got up.

They crossed the living room and headed for the stairs. It smelled of freshly brewed coffee, and men in jackets and shirtsleeves walked in and out of the kitchen carrying cups and glasses. *This was all prearranged.*

They searched her again upstairs.

Not with a metal detector this time, but with their hands. They made her take off her jacket, raise her arms over her head, and spread her legs. It wasn't the regulation female officer who was allowed to touch women, either; it was a man, though she really didn't care. After so many years of surveillance and interrogations, she'd lost all sense of shame. And it was clear that *they* were certainly shameless. What were they looking for? What were they scared she might do? *They're afraid of us. Much more than we are of them.*

After a more-than-thorough patdown, the man nodded, gave her jacket back to her, and opened the door to what looked like a library.

And there, of course, was the Big Fucking Cheese.

"Ah, Professor Robledo, always a pleasure."

She felt ready for him, thought she could handle this.

She was wrong.

Suppressing her fury, she took the seat offered to her in front of the small desk. One of the men left the room, closing the door behind him; the other stood behind her, ready to take action in case she, say, decided to hurl herself at the old fogy and rip his eyes out. Which, of course, was always a possibility.

"I know why you wanted to come here tonight," the old man said in his precise English, taking a seat behind the desk. He'd obviously just arrived. His overcoat was strewn on a chair, still glistening with the damp night air. "I won't take up much of your time, I assure you. Just a friendly chat. Then you can meet up with your friends." A big lampshade hid part of his face; the man pushed it aside, revealing his smile. It wasn't exactly what she wanted to see, but she looked nonetheless.

Harrison had aged notably over the last several years, but his deep-set eyes, hidden under the narrow ledge of brows, and the smile on his smooth face (he'd given up the mustache years ago) expressed the same cold, courteous, threatening confidence as always. Maybe even more now than before. Something new seemed to bubble under the surface this time, too. Hatred? Fear?

"Where's my friend?" she asked, opting not to hide her concern.

"Which one? You have so many, and they're all so close."

"Professor Víctor Lopera."

"Oh, he's just answering a few questions. When we're finished with him, you can—"

"Leave him be. I'm the one you're interested in, Harrison. Let him go."

"Oh, Professor, Professor ... You're impatience is so ... All in good time. Would you like a cup of coffee? I won't offer you anything else, because I'm sure you've eaten dinner already. Twelve thirty is too late even for Spaniards, right?" He looked to the mystery man standing behind her for confirmation. "Ask them to bring us some coffee."

She was dying for a cup of coffee, but there was no way she was going to accept anything he had to offer her, not even if she lay dying from a snakebite and he was holding the antidote. When the lackey left, she decided to try losing her patience.

"Listen, Harrison. If you don't let Lopera go, I'll raise such a stink ... I'll raise hell, I swear to God, I will. Journalists, courts, whatever it takes. I'm not the same submissive fool I once was, you know."

"You've never been a submissive fool."

"Don't give me that. I'm serious."

"Oh, really?" Suddenly, all pretense of conviviality vanished. He sat up and pointed his long index finger at her. "Then let me tell you what we can do. We can sue you, you and your friend Lopera both. We can charge you with revealing classified material and Lopera with covering it up, of aiding and abetting. You have broken every legal agreement that you're sworn to, bound by your own signature, so maybe it's time you stopped threatening me ... What the hell is so funny?"

Elisa tucked her hair back as she laughed.

"The voice of justice, here lecturing me! You've broken into our houses, our lives, you've been spying on us for years, you kidnap us whenever the hell you want ... Right now you're trespassing on private property. I believe in both your country and mine that's known as breaking and entering. And here you are, reeling off my legal obligations!"

Just then the door opened, interrupting them, but Harrison's expression let her know that he'd changed his mind about the coffee. She congratulated herself. *Good. Just bare your teeth and don't bother with the fake smile.*

"So that's how you view the measures taken for your own protection?" Harrison replied.

"You mean the way you protected Sergio Marini?"

Harrison looked away, as if he hadn't heard her. She remembered that trick; of all her interrogator's two-faced tactics, it was one of the best. She didn't bother repeating her question.

"I've just come from Milan, Professor. I can assure you that there is no proof that what happened to Professor Marini had anything to do with Project Zig Zag."

"Liar."

"Temper, temper!" Harrison snickered. "That's the Spaniard in you. You've been like that as long as I've known you. Willful ... passionate ... and distrustful."

"You're the one who taught me to distrust."

"Come, come now ..."

Elisa picked up on something strange. It was as though behind Harrison's smiles and polite words a dangerous beast roared in fear, straining to get loose and rip her throat out.

The unforeseen possibility that Harrison's mental state might actually be worse off than her own threw her into renewed panic. She realized, then, that she preferred seeing him as executioner, not victim. *He says he's just come from Milan. So he must have seen...*

"How did Marini die?" she asked, scrutinizing his face. Once again, he gave her the fake 'Sorry, could you repeat that?' look. And this time she did. "I said, how did Sergio Marini die?"

"He was ... he was beaten. Presumably by thieves, though we're still waiting for a report ..."

"Did you see his body?"

"Of course. I already told you he was beaten to death—"

"Describe it to me."

She began to tremble when she realized Harrison was doing everything possible not to look at her.

"Professor, let's not get off track—"

"Describe the state of Sergio Marini's corpse."

"Let me speak," he muttered.

"You're lying," she whimpered, silently praying he would contradict her. But instead, he shrieked. Like an animal, almost shouting himself hoarse. It was dreadful beyond belief. He went from total tranquillity to an unbearable howling in a millisecond.

"*Shut up!*" Suddenly, he regained control and smiled. "You're ... if you don't mind my saying so ... boorishly obstinate."

She now had no doubt whatsoever. It had all happened again.

And Harrison wasn't even a threat anymore, because he was losing his mind. Like her. Like all of them.

That substantiation of the facts left her feeling more than vulnerable. She felt lifeless, spent, literally inanimate.

There are instants, airholes in our consciousness, turbulences of the soul, that are very deep. Without warning, Elisa fell into an abyss of that sort until she hit rock bottom. Harrison no longer mattered, Víctor no longer mattered, her life no longer mattered. She sank into a vegetative state, hearing Harrison's words as if they were background noise, a boring television program that was on in another room.

"Why can't you see we're all in the same boat together? If you sink, we all sink. Honestly, such a temper ... I confess I admire it, I like that part of your personality ... Don't think I'm crossing a line here. I am well aware that I'm too old and you're too young. But I'm attracted to you, I'll tell you that ... I want to help you. And yet, first I need you to describe to me the characteristics of that ... that 'danger,' let's call it. If indeed it exists ..."

And then it was over. Abruptly, she recovered and recalled the only thing she still had to fight for.

"Let Víctor go, and I'll do anything you want."

"Let him *go?* Good Lord, Professor, you're the one who brought him here!"

He was right about that, the pig.

"How long are you going to keep him?"

"However long we need to. We want to find out how much he knows."

"Well, I can tell you that. You don't have to lock him up naked in a room with a hidden camera, shoot him up with drugs, and force him to tell you about his private life in lurid detail just to find *that* out. Though maybe that's just the routine for girls, huh?" Harrison made no reply, his jaw set. "I told him about the island," she said finally. "That's it, just the island."

"That was reckless of you." He looked as though he was choosing a much more vulgar adjective, but then simply repeated, "Very reckless."

"I needed help!"

"*We* are your help—"

"That's why I needed help!"

"Don't shout." Harrison, who seemed more concerned with straightening the lampshade than listening to her, suddenly gave up, stood, walked around the desk, and zoomed in on Elisa until his face was just an inch from hers. "Don't shout," he repeated, jabbing her jacket with an admonishing index finger. "Not in front of me, young lady."

"And *you*," Elisa replied, pushing his hand away violently, "don't ever touch me again."

With the next interruption, this time from the other door, she breathed a sigh of relief. She didn't give a damn about Harrison and his index finger, but she was beginning to realize that the man leaning over her was not exactly Harrison. Or maybe it was just that it was 100 percent him and he was no longer hiding anything. No artificial sweeteners.

She recognized the guy at the door immediately. Time had not marked his stony face, had left no trace on the burly body he had managed to stuff into an elegant suit. Elisa was relieved to see that at least Carter was still Carter.

"How did I know you couldn't be far behind?" she sneered contemptuously.

"They want to see her," Carter said to Harrison, without even acknowledging her presence.

Harrison smiled in return, his courteousness magically reappearing.

"Of course. Professor, please accompany Mr. Carter. Your friends are all waiting for you. Or at least the ones who could make it ... I'm sure you're looking forward to seeing them again." As she stood up, he added, "You'll also be pleased to know that it was one of your own who let us know about the meeting." She regarded him incredulously. "Surprised? It seems not all of your friends are of the same opinion ..."

THE next room was a dark, L-shaped lounge. In it were dusty bookshelves, an old TV, and a small reading lamp bent over a small table. The lamp cast a soft beam of light like a mysterious robot searching for something hidden in the wood grain. Elisa knew it wouldn't take long for the darkness to get to her, but for the time being her encroaching fear was nothing compared to the excitement she felt at seeing everyone again.

When she did, a lump formed in her throat.

The man and woman were both sitting at the table but stood when she walked in. Their greetings were just quick, light kisses on the cheek. Still, Elisa couldn't contain her tears. She knew she was finally back with the only people who really understood her terror. Finally back with the damned.

"Where's Reinhard?" she asked, her voice quivering.

"Right now he should be taking off from Berlin," the man said. "They'll pick him up at the airport and bring him here."

So they'd cornered them all again. *Who gave us away?* She glanced at them again. *Who was it?*

It had been years since she'd seen them and she was surprised at how they'd changed, just as she had been last time. Not only had the woman not lost her looks, but Elisa thought she was even more attractive, despite the fact that she must be fortysomething by now and had lost a lot of weight. Still, her appearance was shocking. Her long hair was dyed red and hung in a thick mane down her back, and she'd powdered her face and tweezed her eyebrows. Her lips were bright red. And her clothes were striking: a spaghetti-strap top, fastened at the front, tight trousers, and high heels—all black. She also wore a very ordinary cardigan, perhaps (Elisa guessed) to tone down the mournful yet provocative air she gave off. He, on the other hand, had gone completely bald, gained weight, and wore a medium-length gray beard that matched his jacket and corduroy trousers. He had aged a lot more than she had, although she seemed wearier than him. He smiled; she did not. That was what was immediately noticeable.

One thing they had in common, though, was that their eyes both bore the same haunted look as Elisa's. It was familiar to her. *The family of the damned; we're a clan.*

"Together again," she said.

She had her back to the door and heard the footsteps approaching before the door opened. From behind his glasses, Víctor had the look of a scared rabbit. He appeared to be safe and sound, which relieved her, even though she had been sure they weren't going to hurt him anyway.

"Elisa, are you OK?"

"Yeah, are you?"

"Yeah. All I did was answer some questions ..." Just then Víctor noticed the man and his face showed a glimmer of recognition. "Professor ... Professor Blanes?"

"This is Víctor Lopera, do you remember him?" Elisa asked

Blanes. "He was in your course at Alighieri. He's a good friend. I told him a lot of things tonight ..."

The woman exhaled noisily as Víctor and Blanes shook hands. Then Elisa pointed to her.

"Let me introduce you. This is Jacqueline Clissot. I've told you about her."

"Pleased to meet you," Víctor said, Adam's apple bobbing.

Clissot just nodded. Víctor's blush and awkwardness on finding himself the unintentional protagonist of the situation might have been comical, but no one smiled.

Carter's stony voice called out from the door.

"Do you want anything to eat?"

"We want to be left alone, if you don't mind," she retorted, making no attempt to hide her disdain for the man. "You still have to wait for Professor Silberg before you can make any decisions about us, right? Besides, you can listen to everything we say with one of the hundreds of mikes you've stashed in the room, so how about you just back the hell off for a little while, and close the door behind you?"

"Please, Carter, she's right," Blanes said. "Just leave us for a while."

Carter regarded them blankly, as though he was hundreds of miles away and their words had a time delay before reaching him. Then he turned to his men.

After the door closed, the four of them sat at the table. Elisa was struck by a simile. *We're going to lay all our cards on the table.*

Jacqueline went first.

"You made a big mistake, Elisa." She glanced sidelong at Víctor, who seemed fascinated by her. Jacqueline Clissot's voice and appearance *were* both very seductive, but Elisa couldn't help thinking, as she regarded the woman, that she must be trapped in a living hell. *Maybe worse than mine.* "You shouldn't have gotten anyone else involved in ... in our business."

Jacqueline wasn't holding back any punches. Elisa had a few of her own to deliver, but she wanted to clear something up first.

"Víctor can still make up his own mind. All he knows is what happened on New Nelson, and they'll leave him alone if he agrees not to talk."

"I think you're right," Blanes concurred. "The last thing Harrison wants is to complicate matters."

"What about you?" Elisa inquired, suddenly cruel. "Haven't you ever tried to get help, Jacqueline?"

She regretted the question the second it was out of her mouth. The woman averted her eyes. She knew that not looking directly at anyone had just become habit.

"I've dealt with my life on my own for quite some time," Clissot declared.

Elisa made no reply. She didn't want to argue, especially with Jacqueline, but she couldn't stand to hear the Frenchwoman act like the only martyr in the room.

"Be that as it may," Blanes said, "Elisa brought Víctor here and we should accept it. I accept it, anyway."

"It should be *him* doing the accepting, David," Clissot replied. "We should tell him the rest and let him decide if he wants to stay or not."

"Fine by me." Blanes pressed his temples, as if to clear a new path for his thoughts. Elisa perceived a change in him, too, but it was harder to put a finger on exactly what it was. He seemed more ... confident? Stronger? Or did she just want him to be that way? "What do you think, Elisa?"

"Let's tell him and let him make up his mind." Elisa turned to Víctor and held out a hand, cautious but firm. "I don't want to force you past the point of no return, Víctor. I know I should never have gotten you mixed up in all this, but I needed you ... I wanted you to come. I wanted someone from the outside to see what's happening to us."

"Elisa, I–"

"Listen." She squeezed his hands. "I know it's not an excuse. I thought things would turn out differently, that this meeting would somehow be different ... I'm not trying to excuse my actions," she repeated emphatically. "I needed you, and I came to you. I'd do it again, in these circumstances. I'm just so scared, Víctor. We're all so scared. You still can't understand it. But we need all the help we can get … and right now *you are* all the help we can get …" *Though one of you doesn't think so,* she added to herself. She looked at them all intentionally, wondering who'd given them away. Or had Harrison just lied to cause a rift? Divide and conquer.

Suddenly, the curly-haired doll with intellectual glasses (modest physics professor frames, no longer the John Lennon wire rims) came to life.

"Hold on a sec. I got this far myself. Not because you wanted me to, Elisa, but because *I* wanted to. Hold on. Hold on." He gesticulated awkwardly, as if trying to force a large box inside another one just a couple of inches larger, testing his dexterity. Elisa was surprised at how firm his voice was. "Everyone … everyone I know always says the same thing. 'I made you do it, Víctor.' 'I'm sorry, Víctor.' But it's not like that. I'm the one who decides. I might be shy, but I *do* make my own decisions. And I *wanted* to come here tonight, I *wanted* to help you … help all of you, in whatever way I can. It was *my* decision. I don't know what I'll be able to do for you, but here I am, count me in. Yes, it scares me, I'm not good at taking risks, and I'm scared of how scared you are. But I want to be here, with you, and I want to hear … everything."

"Thank you," Elisa murmured.

"Well in any case, we should wait for Reinhard and find out what he thinks," Jacqueline Clissot insisted.

Blanes shook his head.

"Víctor's already here. We may as well tell him the rest." He glanced at Elisa. "You want to be the one?"

Now came the hard part, and she knew it. It would be awful later, finding out who had betrayed them. But for now, the idea of recounting everything she'd been hiding over the past several years (the most terrible years) seemed like an insurmountable test. Still, she knew that she was the best person to do it.

She didn't look at Víctor, or at anyone. Instead she cast her gaze toward the reading lamp's dim beam of light.

"As I said, Víctor, we accepted their explanation of what happened on New Nelson and went back to our lives, after swearing we'd follow their orders: no contact with each other, and no talking to anyone about what happened. The supposed accident in Zurich caused a little stir, but in time everything just went back to normal ... at least on the surface." She stopped and took a deep breath. "Then, four years ago, it was Christmas 2011."

She spoke in hushed tones, as if trying to send a child off to sleep.

In a way, that was exactly what she was trying to do. Cradle her own fear.

SIX

The Terror

Scientists are not after the truth;
it is the truth that is after scientists.

KARL SCHLECTA

22

Madrid
December 21, 2011
8:32 P.M.

IT was a bitterly cold night, but the thermostat was always set at seventy-six degrees. She was in the kitchen making dinner, barefoot. Her nails (fingers and toes) were painted bright red, her makeup was perfect, and her silky black hair glimmered with new salon highlights. A lilac robe hung to her knees, barely covering the sexy black lace lingerie underneath. No stockings. From the cell phone (on speakerphone) resting on an electronic pedestal came her mother's voice, prattling on. She was spending Christmas with Eduardo (her current beau) in the Valencia house and wanted to know if Elisa was coming to spend Christmas Eve with them.

"I'm not trying to pressure you, Eli, believe me. You do what you want. Though I suppose you've always done what you wanted. And I know you're not into holidays, but—"

"I'd love to, mother, really. I just can't commit for sure yet."

"Well when will you know?"

"I'll call you Friday."

She was making *escalivada,* a dish of roasted peppers, eggplant, and onions, and turned on the extractor fan as she poured the contents of her mortar into a hot pan. Angry sizzling made her step back. She had to turn up the speaker volume to hear.

"I don't want to ruin your plans, Eli, but I just thought if you don't have any ... I mean, it would be nice if you made the effort. And I'm not just saying that for my sake." She sounded hesitant. "You could use some company, you know, honey. I know you've always been a loner, but it's different now. A mother picks up on these things."

She pulled the pan off the burner and sprinkled its contents over the vegetables.

"You've been withdrawn for months, maybe years. You seem so ... distant, so off in your own world. The last time you came home, when you were here for Sunday lunch, I swear you weren't the same."

"The same as who, mother?"

She grabbed a bottle of mineral water from the fridge and a glass from the cupboard and walked into the living room, toes curling into the springy carpet. She could still hear her mother's voice perfectly from there.

"The same way you used to be, Elisa."

There was no need to turn on the lights: they were all already on, even those in the bathroom and bedroom that she wasn't using. She always flipped them all on the moment the sunlight began to fade. It cost a small fortune, especially in the winter, but she couldn't stand the dark. She even slept with a couple of lamps on.

"Well, don't listen to me," her mother said. "I didn't call just to get on your case. *Sure seems like it,* Elisa thought. "And I really don't want you to feel forced into it. If you have plans with anyone ... like that man you told me about ... Rentero ... just let me know. I won't be upset. I'll be delighted, in fact."

Oh, mother, aren't you sneaky. She placed her glass and the bottle of water on the table, in front of the flat-screen TV that was on mute, and walked back into the kitchen.

Martín Rentero had been an IT professor at Alighieri until that year, when he'd gotten a job at the University of Barcelona and moved. But he'd come to Madrid the week before for a conference, and Elisa had seen him again. He had thick, black hair and a mustache, and he knew he was good looking. Over the years at Alighieri, he'd invited Elisa out to dinner a few times and confessed how much he liked her (it wasn't the first time she'd heard that type of confession). She had no doubt that when they met up again he'd make another play. And, indeed, he did. As soon as he saw her, he suggested that they have a weekend getaway together, but she had to go to the physics party with her colleagues at Alighieri. So he tried again, telling her that he'd planned to rent a house in the Pyrenees and would love to spend the holidays with her. What did she think?

It sounded too intense, that was what she thought. She liked Martín, and she knew the company would do her good. But she was scared, too.

Not scared *of* Martín, but *for* him. Scared of what might happen with him if she broke down, if she lost her cool, if her obsessive behavior gave her away.

I'll make up an excuse, for him and *mother. I don't want to get involved with anyone.* She turned off the stove and grabbed the *escalivada.*

"You know, if you have plans, it wouldn't hurt to tell me."

"Well, I don't."

Just then, the living-room phone rang. She wondered who it could be. She wasn't expecting any other calls that night and really didn't want to talk to anybody; she'd been planning to spend a few hours "playing" before bed. She glanced at the digital clock in the kitchen and felt relieved. It was still early.

"Sorry, mother, I have to go. I've got a call coming in on my land line."

"Don't forget, Eli ..."

She hung up her cell and walked into the dining room, thinking it was probably Rentero, the source of her mother's third degree. She picked up just before the machine kicked in.

There was a pause. A soft buzzing noise.

"Elisa?" It was a young woman with a foreign accent. "Elisa Robledo?" Her voice trembled, as if coming from a place much colder than her apartment. "It's Nadja Petrova."

Somehow, across the miles of cable and the ocean of wavelengths, the chill in her voice reached Elisa's half-naked body and made her shiver.

*"**HOW** are you this month?"*
"Same as last."
"Does that mean 'good'?"
"That means 'alive.'"

THE truth was, she never forgot about any of it; it was always with her. But time was like a wool lining, something that protected her numb, naked body. Time didn't *heal* wounds; that was crap. What it did was *hide* them. The memories were all still there, intact, inside her, neither more nor less intense, but time masked them, at least to other people. It was like a blanket of autumn leaves covering a grave, or like the grave itself, hiding a mass of wriggling worms.

But she really didn't care about that. Six years had passed; she was twenty-nine and had a permanent post as professor at a decent university and taught what she loved. She lived alone, true, but she was independent, had her own place, didn't owe anybody anything. She earned enough to be able to buy whatever she wanted, and she could have traveled if she'd wanted (she didn't) or had more friends (no thanks). And as for the rest ... what else was there?

Her nights.

*"**ARE** you still having nightmares?"*
"Yes."
"Every night?"

"No. Once or twice a week."
"Could you tell us about them?"
Silence.
"Elisa? Could you tell us about your nightmares?"
"They're pretty fuzzy."
"Well, tell us what you can remember."
Silence.
"Elisa?"
"Darkness. It's always dark."

WHAT else? She had to leave the lights on all the time, of course, but some people couldn't stand being in elevators or walking through crowds. She'd had reinforced doors and security blinds installed, and electronic alarms with motion sensors. But hey, times were tough. Who could blame her?

"What about your 'disconnects'? Do you remember that term? Those episodes where you have waking dreams?"
"Yes, I still have them. But not as often."
"When was your last one?"
"About a week ago, when I was watching TV."

Once a month, a group of specialists from Eagle came to Madrid to give her a secret checkup: blood tests, urine tests, X-rays, psychological tests, and an interminable interview. She just let them do their thing. The place she went for all this wasn't a clinic, it was a nondescript apartment in Príncipe de Vergara. The blood and urine tests and X-rays they did a week earlier at a doctor's office, so the specialists already had the results by the time she saw them. Those visits were a trial: they took almost all day (psych tests in the morning, interview in the afternoon), which meant she had to skip classes, but she'd gotten used to it. In fact, on some level, she'd grown to need it. At least she could *talk* to those people.

The specialists thought her nightmares were lingering side effects from the Impact. They said that other members of her team reported the same thing, which, for some reason, relieved her.

She hadn't spoken to any of her colleagues, not only because she'd sworn she wouldn't, but also because by now, she'd stopped bothering to keep track of them. But she'd collected news clippings over the years. She knew, for example, that Blanes had disappeared from the scientific scene. His old, now-retired mentor, Albert Grossmann, had cancer, and some people said that Blanes was so traumatized by it that he could no longer work. Marini and Craig might have been swallowed up by the earth for all she knew, though she'd heard Marini no longer taught. And the last news she had about Jacqueline Clissot and Reinhard Silberg was that they'd retired from academia. Clissot, she heard, was "ill" (though no one knew what kind of "illness" she had). And Nadja, she'd lost track of her entirely. As for herself...

"You're getting better and better, Elisa. We're going to give you some good news. Starting next year, our sessions will be only once every two months. Does that make you happy?"

"Yes."

"Merry Christmas, Elisa. May 2012 bring you much happiness."

Well, there she was, that December night, dressed in Victoria's Secret lingerie and a slinky robe, ready to have her *escalivada* and then spend the rest of the night playing her Mr. White Eyes game. And then, suddenly, came this voice from the past. Nadja.

THERE was a photograph. It showed a young but haggard man with a wispy beard and wire-rimmed glasses, standing beside a pretty woman (though her face was too round) holding a blond, messy-haired boy of about five in her arms. The boy, unfortunately, had inherited his mother's too-round face. Mother and son grinned widely (the boy was missing teeth), but the man looked serious, as though forced to pose in order to avoid a tiff. The picture had been taken on a lawn, and there was a house in the background.

She imagined other, similar scenes. Needless to say, the article didn't give any details and she knew that they were just a product of her fantasy, as were Mr. White Eyes' wicked words, but still ... Those images flashed up in her mind like a slide show.

They ripped his eyes out. Tore off his genitals. Cut off his arms and legs. The boy probably saw the whole thing. They probably made him watch. "Look what we're doing to Daddy ... Do you still recognize Daddy?"

She sat on the carpet in front of the TV, legs crossed and only half-covered by her robe, as if about to adopt the lotus position. But she wasn't watching TV; she was using the attached keyboard to surf the net. She was on a British news channel, checking the breaking stories. This was the only place the story had been covered, Nadja said, maybe because it had just happened.

"My God, how awful, poor Colin ... But ..." She stopped herself before she could add, *Why are you telling me this three days before Christmas?*

"They told Jacqueline a few things that the story doesn't mention." Nadja said through the speakerphone on Elisa's cordless. "Colin's wife was found in the middle of the night, running down the road screaming. That was how they knew something was wrong. The boy was found in the backyard. He'd spent the whole night outside and had frostbite. That's what I don't understand, Elisa. Why would she leave her son at home without even calling the police, or anyone? What must have happened, for her to do that?"

"It says here that some men broke in and threatened them. Dangerous criminals, ex-cons. They were on drugs and needed money. Maybe she got away."

"And abandoned her young son?"

"The men who attacked Colin must have forced her to. Or she

just panicked. Or went crazy. Some experiences can ... can make people ..."

Blood everywhere. On the ceiling, the walls, the floor. The boy in the yard, left all alone. The mother running down the street, hysterical. "Help! Please help me! A shadow came into my house! A shadow! It's trying to devour us, and I can't see its face! Only its mouth. Its mouth is gigantic!"

"They told Jacqueline the house was surrounded by soldiers."

"What!?"

"Soldiers," Nadja repeated. "No one knows what they're doing there. Plain-clothed cops, of course, but soldiers, too. And sanitary personnel, wearing masks ... The windows have been sealed and you can't get within a mile of the place. And with the blackout, it's worse. Last night, there was a blackout all around Oxford and the electricity is still out. They said there was a short circuit at the plant that powers the city. Sound familiar, Elisa?"

Darkness descended. The Christmas tree burned out. The lights by the boy's stocking burned out. Father Christmas was going to leave presents for him there. The Craig family was all at home when darkness blew in like a cyclone.

He was still alive when they ripped his face off. His son saw the whole thing.

"With Rosalyn Reiter, the station lights went out ... and when Cheryl Ross was in the cellar, too. And there's something else, too, Elisa. Rosalyn's bathroom light, and yours, and mine ... Remember? All three of us had that dream ... and we all had the lights burn out in our bathrooms."

Coincidences. Let me tell you another coincidence.

"We can't draw any conclusions based on that, Nadja. Physics shows no relation between dreams and electric energy."

"I know! But fear is not logical. You always reason your way out of everything, and your logic does make me feel better, but when Jacqueline called to tell me about Colin,... I thought ... it's not over yet." Sniffles.

"Nadja ..."

"It was Colin this time ... like it was Rosalyn, Cheryl, and Ric last time. But it's happening again. And you know it."

"Nadja, honey ... Did you forget? Ric Valente was the one who did it! And he's dead now."

Silence. And then Nadja's voice whimpered.

"You really think it was Ric, Elisa? I mean, do you *really* think Ric killed them?"

No. I don't. She decided not to answer and ran her hands down her bare thighs. The clock flashing on the TV screen told her there was only an hour until *he* came. Her "game" was a ritual, a habit she couldn't break, like biting her nails, and she couldn't put it off. All she had to do was take off her robe and wait. *Hang up.*

"Jacqueline and I talked about something else." The change in her old friend's tone of voice alarmed her. "Tell me this. Honestly. Tell me the truth. Don't you ... get ready ... *for him?*" She froze, there on the carpet. "Elisa, please tell me, please. For my sake, for the friendship we once had. Are you embarrassed? I am, too. But you know what? I'm so scared, Elisa, that right now my fear outweighs my shame." She was listening. She couldn't move, couldn't even think, all she could do was listen. "Special underwear ... you know, sexy lingerie. And it's always black. Maybe you used to wear it already and maybe not, but now you wear *it almost all the time,* right? And sometimes you don't wear any at all. Isn't that true? Don't you go out sometimes with no panties on, even though you never used to? And at night, don't you dream ..."

No. What Nadja was saying wasn't true. Her "games" were just fantasies. They might be influenced by certain unpleasant things that happened six years ago, sure, but they were still just fantasies. And the fact that Nadja might play similar games, or that Craig was murdered last night, had nothing to do with it. Nothing whatsoever.

"Do you know ... do you know what Jacqueline's life is like

now?" Nadja continued. "Did you know she left her family four years ago, Elisa? Her husband and son ... even her job ... Do you want to know what her life's been like since then? Or mine?" Nadja was now openly sobbing. "Should I tell you what I do? Do you want to know how I live? What I do when I'm alone?"

"We're not even supposed to be talking, Nadja," Elisa interrupted. "We have monthly sessions. You can tell them ..."

"They're lying to us, Elisa! They've been lying to us for years! You know that!"

If he gets here and you're not ready ... If you're not waiting for him the way you should be...

She cast a glance at her screen saver, which showed the phases of an eerily white moon. *White, like his eyes.* A chill ran down her spine, making her shiver. She thought of her expensive hairdo, carefully applied makeup, sexy robe. *This is absurd. It's just a game! I can do whatever I feel like.*

"Elisa, I'm scared!"

In a flash, she made up her mind.

"Nadja, you said you're in Madrid, right?"

"Yes ... but I'm leaving on Friday to spend Christmas with my parents in St. Petersburg."

"Good. Let me come pick you up and we can have dinner together. My treat. What do you say?" She heard a giggle. Nadja still had that crystal clear laugh she used to when they first met.

"OK."

"On one condition. Promise me we won't talk about anything unpleasant."

"I promise. Oh, I'm so excited to see you, Elisa!"

"Me, too. Tell me where you are." She opened a computerized, interactive street map. It was an apartment in Moncloa; she could be there in half an hour.

When they hung up, she turned off the TV, put her untouched *escalivada* in the fridge, and went into her bedroom. As she took off her underwear and put it back in the drawer, she hesitated for

a moment. She almost never changed plans when she was planning to "welcome" him. *(If he gets here and you're not ready ... If
you're not waiting for him the way you should be ...)* But Nadja's
phone call and the terrible news about Colin had left her full of
questions and they needed answers.

She chose a matching beige bra and panty set, a sweater, and
a pair of jeans.

She'd go see Nadja.

They had a lot to talk about.

23

THE light came on after flickering for a moment. It was a wide, overhead light just above the bathroom mirror, so glaring that it accentuated every crack in the orange tile. Nevertheless, Nadja Petrova turned on a five-watt travel lamp with rechargeable battery, too, and placed it on a stool by the shower. She never traveled without lamps like these, and kept three flashlights in her suitcase as well.

She was glad she'd called Elisa, though it hadn't been easy, despite the fact that contacting her old friend was the real reason she'd accepted her friend Eva's invitation to come and stay at her apartment. She'd been in Madrid a week and only called Elisa after hearing about Colin Craig's death. Even then, she had her doubts. *I shouldn't have phoned. We promised not to talk to each other.* But her guilt was mitigated by the urgency of the situation. She might have been hoping to renew a friendship, but the truth was that now she needed Elisa's presence and her advice. She wanted to hear her calming words, to be reassured about what she had to tell her.

A logical explanation: that was what she needed. Something that made sense of everything that was happening.

She went into her room, where the light was, of course, already on, like those in the rest of the house. Eva would be sorry at the end of the month when her electric bill came, but Nadja was planning to leave her some money to make up for it. Two years earlier, in the Paris building where she lived, there was a blackout that had petrified her. She'd been paralyzed, curled up in a ball on the floor, for the five minutes it lasted. She hadn't even been able to scream. Ever since then she made sure to have portable battery-powered lamps and flashlights with her wherever she was, just in case. She couldn't stand the dark.

She took off her clothes, opened the armoire, and looked at the full-length mirror inside the door.

Mirrors had always made her uneasy, ever since she was a kid. She could never help imagining someone appearing behind her, some scary creature sticking its head over her shoulder, a being that could only be seen there, in the quicksilver. But, of course, that was an absurd dread.

There was nothing there now. Just Nadja herself, her milky skin, petite breasts, faded pink nipples … Just like always. Or maybe not *always,* but with a few changes. Changes she knew Jacqueline had gone through, too. And maybe Elisa as well.

She picked out some clothes and looked at the clock. She still had twenty minutes to shower and get dressed. Walking naked to the bathroom, she wondered what her friend would think about her new appearance.

What she'd think, for example, of her dyed black hair.

ELISA decided to try to avoid traffic by taking the M–30 beltway rather than drive through central Madrid in the early evening, four days before Christmas. But when she got to Avenida Ilustración she found a sea of brake lights, twinkling like rubies. It was as if all the Christmas decorations throughout the whole city had been thrown into the street in front of her. She cursed under her breath, her cell phone ringing in time with the blinking lights in front of her.

It's Nadja, she thought. And then, *No. I never gave her my cell.*

Crawling forward inch by inch, she took out her phone and answered.

"Hello, Elisa."

Emotions travel through our bodies at lightning speed. So do masses of other information. They travel through our cerebral circuits each second without producing the kind of traffic jam Elisa's car was stuck in at that moment. In a flash, her emotions traveled a considerable path: from indifference to surprise, surprise to elation, elation to apprehension.

"I'm in Madrid," Blanes explained. "My sister lives in Él Escorial, and I'm going to spend Christmas with her. I just wanted to wish you happy holidays. It's been years since we last spoke." Then he added, in a chirpy tone, "I called your house and got your machine. But I remembered you taught at Alighieri, so I called Noriega and he gave me your cell."

"I'm so happy to hear your voice, David," she said genuinely.

"Me, too. After all these years ..."

"How are you? Everything OK?"

"Can't complain. I've got a whiteboard and a few books in Zurich. I'm happy." There was hesitancy in his voice, and she knew what he was going to say before he said it. "Did you hear about Colin?"

They spoke superficially about the tragedy. In ten seconds of polite clichés, they buried their old colleague. And in that time, Elisa's car barely moved ten feet.

"Reinhard Silberg called from Berlin to tell me," Blanes said.

"Nadja told me. You remember Nadja, right? She's in Madrid, too, on vacation, staying at a friend's house."

"Oh, that's nice. How's our dear paleontologist doing?"

"She left the field years ago ..." Elisa cleared her throat. "She says it was too exhausting." *Just like Jacqueline and Craig.* She paused, those thoughts swimming through her brain, disturbing her. Blanes had just told her that Craig had asked for a leave of absence at the university. "She's got a job in the Slavic Studies Department at the Sorbonne, now, or something like that. Says she's lucky to speak Russian."

"I see."

"We're meeting tonight. She told me she's ... scared."

"Mmm."

That "mmm" made it sound as though Blanes wasn't intrigued by Nadja's state; more like he expected it.

"The details of what happened to Colin brought some things back for her," she added.

"Yeah, Reinhard said the same."

"But it's just an unlucky coincidence, right?"

"No doubt."

"No matter how much I think about it, I just can't accept that there's any relation between this ... and ... what happened ... to us ... Can you, David?"

"It's totally out of the question, Elisa."

Colin Craig's wife had been running down the street, terrified, maybe in her nightgown or robe. She saw her husband savagely attacked and tortured, her son kidnapped, but she managed to escape and ran for help.

It's totally out of the question, Elisa.

"I was just wondering," Blanes said, taking on a singsongy, let's-change-the-subject tone, "if you'd want to meet up one of these days. I know the holidays are always hectic, but, I don't know, maybe we could have a coffee." He laughed. Or rather, he made "I'm laughing" noises. "We could see Nadja, too, if she felt like it ..."

Suddenly, Elisa thought she understood why Blanes had called her, what was behind this call?

"Actually, that sounds like a great plan." She thought *plan* had been a good choice of words. "How about tomorrow?"

"Perfect. My sister is letting me use her car. I could pick you up at six thirty, if that's good for you. Then we can decide where to go."

They spoke casually. Just two friends who, after not having

seen hide nor hair of each other for years, decided to meet up one afternoon. But she got the message. *Time: six thirty. Place: let's not say it over the phone. Reason: risk. It's out of the question.*

"Tell me where I can reach you," she said. "I'll ask Nadja and call you back."

Possible reason: a frostbitten five-year-old boy, half frozen in his backyard, mouth and eyes full of snow, waiting for his mother and father to come back, but they won't, because his mother ran to get help, and his father's inside, busy with something. In danger.

Other possible reasons: soldiers, blackouts.

Yes, we have a lot of reasons.

"Fine, Elisa. Call me anytime—I go to bed late."

Traffic finally picked up on Carretera del Pardo. Elisa said good-bye to Blanes, put down her phone, and shifted gears.

Suddenly, she couldn't wait to see Nadja.

WHENEVER she took a shower, she thought she was going to die.

Over the past few years, the fear had become nearly vertiginous. Just standing naked beneath an incessant stream of warm rain seemed more like a test of courage than a hygienic necessity. Not because she wasn't used to being alone—after all, she lived on her own in Paris—but because, ironically, she suspected she never really *was* alone.

Even when there was no one there.

Don't be ridiculous. Elisa told you, what happened to Colin is horrible, but it's got nothing to do with New Nelson. Don't think about it. Get it out of your head. She scrubbed her arms. Then she soaped up her stomach, and then between her legs. She'd waxed her bikini line for years, lately opting for a full Brazilian. No hair whatsoever. At first she thought it was just a silly whim; she just felt like it, though no one had persuaded her. Then ... she didn't know what to think. After she bought all that black lingerie (she'd never liked it before; it was too much of a contrast with her almost-albino skin), and dyed her hair black, she tried to convince herself that she was just acting on her own private fantasies. She admitted that maybe they came from bad experiences. But still, it was *her* life.

Or at least that's what she thought. Until that afternoon when she spoke to Jacqueline.

The first few months after her return from New Nelson, she'd tried unsuccessfully to reestablish contact with her old professor. She called the university, the lab, even her home. The first thing she heard was that Jacqueline had been "injured" in the explosion on the island. Then they told her she'd asked for an indefinite leave of absence. The people at Eagle reproached her for those phone calls and reminded her she was not allowed to contact anyone from the project, for security reasons. But that just annoyed her, and she got worse. Then they changed tactics, started giving her updates on Jacqueline almost every month. Professor Clissot was fine, though she'd left the university. Later, she found out she'd gotten divorced. She wrote books and was an independent woman who'd decided to take a new path in life.

Nadja finally accepted that she'd never see her again. After all, she'd taken a new path, too.

Until that afternoon, a few hours ago, when her cell phone rang and she found out that her and Jacqueline's "paths" (and maybe Elisa's, too) sounded very similar: loneliness, anguish, an obsession with appearance, and certain fantasies related to . . .

She couldn't even remember which of them had brought *him* (and the things he forced them to do) up first. One of the basic rules of her fantasies was that she not talk to anyone about them. But she'd noticed Jacqueline's hesitancy, her anxiety (much like Elisa's, later on), and resolved to confess. Or maybe it was the news of Colin's death that tore down the wall of silence. And with every word, they realized just how much their nightmares bound them together . . .

Maybe there's a psychological explanation. Some sort of trauma we're suffering, after everything that happened on the island. Stop worrying so much.

A row of brightly colored birds was painted onto the orange ceramic tiles in the shower stall. Nadja examined them in an attempt to distract herself, as she aimed the shower nozzle at her back.

Stop worrying so much. You really ought to...

The lights went out so quietly, so unexpectedly that she could almost still see those brightly colored birds, even after the darkness engulfed her.

THOUGH she had almost reached the Moncloa neighborhood, her anxiety had increased. She wanted to honk the horn, scream at everyone to let her through, jam her foot down on the accelerator.

She suddenly felt anguished.

It might seem unbelievable, but she had the strange feeling—no, the *certainty*—that it was absolutely vital that she hurry up and get there.

Seeing that the building looked fine, she breathed a sigh of relief. But even the normalcy of it worried her. She found a parking spot, walked in through the building's front door, and rushed up the stairs, convinced that something terrible had happened.

But Nadja herself opened the door, smiling. The chilling apprehension that had been gnawing at her the whole way over suddenly evaporated with the warmth of her greeting. Giving her friend a bear hug, she couldn't help but start to cry. Then she held her at arm's length and looked at her.

"What the hell did you do to your hair?"

"Dyed it."

She wore full makeup and looked elegant, gorgeous even. The scent of perfume trailed behind her. She asked Elisa to come into the bright, cozy living room, where a brightly lit

Christmas tree stood in one corner. Nadja asked her if she wanted something to drink before they left for dinner, and she said she'd love a beer. Out came her friend carrying a tray with two chilled glasses that had just the right amount of froth. She set the tray down on the table, sat down opposite Elisa, and said, "I'm sorry to have troubled you. I really shouldn't have called. It was silly."

"It's no trouble, really. I wanted to see you."

"Well, here I am!" Nadja crossed her legs, a black garter belt showing through the slit of her miniskirt. She looked very sexy. Elisa realized that her Spanish was perfect; she had no accent. She was going to mention it when her friend added, "Honestly, I thought I was forcing you."

"How could you think that?"

"Well, you haven't tried to get in touch with me for the past six years. And it wouldn't have been that hard. You knew I lived in Paris ... maybe you just didn't care."

"You didn't call me, either," she said defensively.

"You're right. I'm sorry, don't pay any attention to me. I've just been so lonely." Her voice took on an edge. "So lonely. Always worried about pleasing *him*. Dressing up for *him*, looking pretty for *him*. You know how much he likes that ..."

"Yeah, I know."

That last sentence had done it. She couldn't be angry at her friend's thinly veiled reproaches. She's right: *I left home without waiting for him, like I should have.* She got up, nervous, and paced the room as she spoke.

"I'm really sorry, Nadja. I would have liked to keep in contact, but I was scared. And I know that he *wants* me to be scared. He takes pleasure in my fear. So I do it for him. I don't think there's anything wrong with that. I still have a job, I teach my classes, try to forget, and then I get ready for him, to welcome him. I do the best I can for him. It's just that I feel like I'm stuck somewhere, waiting ... But I don't know what for. And it's that expectant feeling that I can't stand. Does that make any sense to you?" She turned to Nadja. "Don't you have the same—

Nadja wasn't on the sofa anymore. Or anywhere else in sight. Elisa didn't hear her get up.

Suddenly, all the lights went out, even the lights that hung on the Christmas tree. She tried not to worry. Probably just blew a fuse. Her eyes adjusted to the darkness. She felt her way across the room and thought she could see the hallway. In the dark panic that filled the silent room, Elisa knew that something had shifted. The pleasantries of the previous minutes were no longer relevant. She knew he was there.

She called Nadja and felt sick when the echo of her own voice was the only response. She took a few more steps. Suddenly, her shoe crunched on something. Glass. A shattered crystal ball? Her own future, shattered? She looked up and thought she saw a mangled black mass where the chandelier should be. That explained the power cut.

Calmer now, she kept walking down the dark hall until she reached a sort of crossroads: an open door to the left and a closed, frosted-glass door to the right. Maybe that led to the kitchen. She turned left and then froze.

The door wasn't *open;* it had been torn down. The hinges, covered in dust or ash, jutted out from the frame like twisted screws. Beyond that it was pitch black: total darkness. She walked in.

"Nadja?"

She heard nothing but her own footsteps. At one point, the blunt edge of something banged her stomach. A sink. She was in the bathroom. She kept walking. It was gigantic.

All of a sudden, she realized it wasn't a bathroom at all. It wasn't even a house. The floor was a thick layer of what might have been mud. She reached a hand out and touched a wall that seemed to be covered in mold. She tripped on something, heard a squelching noise, and crouched down. It was white, a piece of something, maybe a broken sofa. Now, all around her, she could make out what looked like broken furniture. It was freezing cold and there was almost no odor. Just one subtle yet persistent scent, a mixture of cave and body, flesh and cavern, mixed together.

This was the place. Here. She'd arrived.

She kept walking through this forlorn devastation and tripped over another piece of furniture.

And then it dawned on her.

It wasn't furniture.

Before she could stop it, a trickle ran down her thighs and formed a puddle at her feet. She wanted to throw up, too, but the knot in her throat left no room for vomit or even words. She felt dizzy, nauseous. Reaching out a hand to steady herself, she realized that what she'd taken to be mold was the same thick sludge on the floor. It was everywhere, filling every crack, every space, every gap. It hung from the ceiling like a giant cobweb.

Another wall blocked her way, and she was surprised to find she could climb it. But no, it was actually the floor. She had fallen. She got up, kneeled, and rubbed her arms, which were bare. At some point she must have taken off all her clothes, though she couldn't imagine why. Maybe she hadn't wanted to get them dirty in all that filth.

Then she looked up and saw her.

Despite the darkness she had no trouble recognizing Nadja. She could make out her white curls (though she thought she remembered her hair had been black just a minute ago) and the shape of her body. Right away, though, she saw that something strange was happening to her friend.

Still kneeling (she didn't want to get up; she knew *he* was watching), she reached out her hands. No trace of movement in those marble legs, but she didn't seem to be paralyzed, either. Her skin was still warm. It was as if Nadja had no ability to move whatsoever.

All of a sudden, what seemed like a handful of sand fell into her eyes. She looked down and rubbed them. Something touched her hair. She looked up again and a lump of something fell onto her mouth, making her cough.

She became aware of the sickening reality: Nadja's body was crumbling before her, like powdered sugar disintegrating, an avalanche to her touch. Her cheeks, eyes, hair, breasts ... everything was flashing off, sounding like wind sweeping through a snowy bark.

She wanted to wipe that chunk of Nadja's flesh off of her face but found she couldn't. The avalanche was burying her alive, it was an onslaught, she was going to suffocate...

And then, from behind the collapsing body, *he* rose.

"HEY, lady!"

"She looks like she's on drugs ..."

"Has anybody called the police?"

"Lady, you OK?"

"Christ, would you move your car already, please? You're blocking traffic!"

People's faces and voices blurred together. Elisa was mostly concentrating on the man whose face took up two-thirds of her car window and the young woman blocking the remaining portion of the glass. The only other thing she could see was the windshield, where tiny raindrops had begun to fall in the night.

In a flash, she saw what had happened. She was stopped at a red light, though God only knew how many greens and yellows had gone by before she came to. She thought she must have fallen asleep in her car and dreamed that she was visiting Nadja and all the rest of it, including (thank God this wasn't true) the macabre discovery of her body. But no, she hadn't fallen asleep. She realized she felt her pant leg all wet with the smell of sour urine. She'd had one of her "disconnects," one of her "waking dreams." It had happened before, though this was the first time she hadn't been home (and the first time she'd peed in her pants).

"I'm sorry," she mumbled, dazed. "I'm really sorry."

She waved her hand by way of apology; the man and woman looked satisfied and moved on. The rear view mirror showed a row of irate drivers in their cars, trying desperately to overcome the obstacle in their way (Elisa). She quickly put the car in gear and accelerated. *Just in time,* she said to herself, catching glimpse of a phosphorescent vest over a dark jacket in her side-view mirror. The last thing she needed right now was a run-in with the police.

She'd reached Moncloa, but the traffic on that chaotic night in the run-up to Christmas and her own rush to get there as soon as possible seemed to have joined forces to make it take as long as possible. Soon she was stopped again, in the middle of a two-way street. People honked furiously, far-off sirens howling in the night. It was drizzling, too, which didn't help matters. She turned her Peugeot toward the curb, despite the fact that there were no free spaces. Elisa double-parked, got out, and began running down the street, clutching her purse by the strap as though it were the leash of a toy dog.

She was scared. Her fear made everything worse. It was like gambling, and having the tiniest stakes grow huge because so many people wanted in on the game. Her mouth was open, parched. Only the light rain moistened her tongue.

Nothing happened. Nadja's fine. It was just one of your crises. She's fine...

She stopped a couple of times to look at the street signs, as if they were headstones. She'd gotten mixed up. Almost screaming, she asked an old man with a jaundiced face for directions. He stared at her from a doorway, but wasn't sure about the street she wanted. He and a woman who was just leaving a building began arguing about it.

Then she heard the siren.

She left them arguing and took off.

She didn't know why she was racing so fast. She had no idea where she was going or why she had to get there right away. Still, she ran, avoiding shadows cloaked in overcoats and carrying long umbrellas that looked like swords. She ran so fast that her breath, which she could see, couldn't keep up. Turned to steam, it hit her in the face.

It was an SUV with flashing lights. It made an enormous racket as it careered through the streets, but since traffic was so dense, she didn't lose sight of it.

Suddenly, *everyone* began to run, and all the cars seemed to have lights on their roofs, sirens blaring. She found the street she was looking for, but it was blocked off by dark-colored vans. There were more of them in front of Nadja's door. Vans, ambulances, and cop cars. Men in helmets looking like the riot police were asking people to step back.

She felt like she'd been kicked in the stomach. Pushing her way to the front, she tried to get through, but a gloved hand clamped down on her arm. The man who spoke to her didn't look human. He wore a helmet and mask, and his eyes were the only identifiable life source, buried under layers and layers of law and order.

"You can't get through here, ma'am."

"My ... friend ... lives ... here ...," she panted.

"Step back, please."

"What's going on?" asked a woman standing beside her.

"Terrorists," the cop said.

Elisa tried to catch her breath.

"My friend ... I need to ... see her ..."

"Elisa Robledo? Is that you?"

It was another man, this one without armor. Well dressed, wearing a coat and tie, black hair slicked back. A stranger, but Elisa held onto his smile and kind words like a life preserver thrown to a drowning sailor.

"I recognized you," he said, still smiling as he approached her. "Let her through," he added to the masked man. "Come with me, please, Professor."

"What happened?" she asked, still out of breath as she hurried to keep up with her guide's footsteps, rushing through the deafening bedlam of lights and screeching radios.

"Nothing, really." He walked past the doorway but didn't enter the building. "We're just here ..."

"What?" Elisa hadn't heard the last sentence.

"For protection," he repeated, raising his voice. "We're here for protection."

"So, Nadja—"

"She's fine, though she's very scared. And after what happened to Professor Craig, we decided the best thing would be to move her to a secure location."

Hearing that, she felt relieved. They'd reached the end of the street; he was still ahead of her. There was a van parked on the sidewalk, its two back doors slightly ajar. The man opened them wide and disappeared inside for a second. She heard his voice.

"Miss Petrova, your friend is here."

Then he reemerged and made room so Elisa could get past. She leaned in, smiling anxiously.

Inside was another man in a white jacket, seated beside the stretcher. Which was empty.

A man covered her nose and mouth, her lips still stretched into a tentative smile.

24

"THEN *what happened?"*

"I parked the car—well, double-parked, actually—and started running..."

"Excuse me. Didn't something else happen first? Didn't you have a disconnect while you were driving?"

"Yes, I think I did."

"What did you see?... OK calm down ... And we started off so well today ... Why is it that when we get to this part, you..."

IT would have been a perfect day for a walk. Unfortunately, the courtyard was tiny. It was still better than her room, though. Through the diamond-shaped links of wire fencing she could see more fences, and off in the distance a beach and the deep blue sea. An ocean breeze rustled the hem of her gown—if you could call it a hem. It was a paper gown (*paper*, for God's sake; how cheap can you get?), but at least she was allowed to cover up this time, and the wind wasn't as cold as she'd feared. You got used to it.

They'd told her there were olive and fig trees on the western slope, which she couldn't see from there. But this landscape was enough for her: her eyes hurt from the feast of images, but it was a fleeting pain. She managed to take several steps without feeling dizzy, though in the end she had to grab onto the fence to hold herself up. Beyond the second fence, a robot moved back and forth. It was actually a soldier, but from that distance he could have passed for a movie-quality, computer-generated android. He held a pretty serious gun and moved lightly, as if to communicate that he could handle the weight with no trouble.

Then it all went dark. The transformation was so abrupt that she thought the landscape had actually changed. But it was just a cloud covering the sun.

"**LET'S** *go back to that vision of Nadja's body crumbling before you. Do you remember?"*

"Yes ..."

"Did you see anyone else? Did you see the figure you call 'him'? The one from your erotic fantasies?"

Silence.

"Why are you crying?"

Silence.

"Elisa, nothing can touch you here ... Please calm down ..."

SHE felt like she was emerging from a cave, a netherworld. The last few days had been a series of murky, unconnected shadows. Her joints hurt, and there were needle marks on her forearms. She was chock-full of them, like tiny piercings everywhere. But they'd told her the reason for all those injections. Sedating her had been their number one priority when she arrived at the base in the state she was in. They'd given her huge doses of tranquilizers.

It was January 7, 2012. She'd asked the young guy who came to get her from her room what the date was. He wore a striped suit and was very sweet. He told her she'd been there over two weeks. Then he led her to the ward.

"I don't know if you know, but 'Dodecanese' means that, in theory at least, there should be twelve islands," he said with tour-guide intonation as they traversed endless corridors that inevitably led to checkpoints where he had to show ID. "But actually, there are more than fifty. This is Imnia. I think you've been here before. It's a totally operational center: we have our own lab and heliport. Structurally, it's very similar to the U.S. DARPA bases in the Pacific—that's the U.S. Defense Advanced Research Projects Agency. In fact, we also do work with the Joint EU Department of Defense." He paused every little while to glance at her, ever attentive. "Feeling OK? Are you dizzy? How's your appetite? We'll feed you in a little while. You can eat with everyone else today ... careful, there's a step there. Your colleagues are all doing fine, so you don't need to worry. Are you cold?"

Elisa smiled. There was no way she could be cold wearing that wool sweater over her black strapped blouse. Her jeans were black, too.

"No, I just ... it's just that ... I just realized these are my clothes."

"Yes, we brought them from your house." He smiled, showing teeth so perfect that for a second she found it off-putting.

"Wow. Thank you."

From the open doors of a large salon came the labyrinthine sound of baroque piano music. Elisa shivered.

"The piano was the professor's reward. We allowed him his favorite pastime. You all know each other, so we won't waste time on introductions."

It occurred to her that his statement was only true to a point: in fact, she hardly recognized Blanes, Marini, Silberg, and Clissot, they looked so exhausted. They all had huge bags under their eyes, and their bodies, some in street clothes and others in paper gowns, showed all the telltale signs of utter fatigue. She supposed the same was true of her. When she walked in, they hardly took any notice. Blanes (who, incidentally, had grown a beard) was the only one who flashed her a weak smile after momentarily interrupting his recital.

Two more people walked in as she took a seat by the coffee table. She didn't recognize the first one straight off; he'd shaved his mustache and his hair had turned completely white. The other man, though, she knew immediately. He still had a crew cut and a gray beard, his stocky body still looked uncomfortable in business suits, and he still had that look of intense concentration that seemed to say that although few things actually interested him, those that did each received extraordinary attention.

"You all know Mr. Harrison and Mr. Carter, our heads of security," the young man said. The recent arrivals nodded their greeting, and Elisa smiled at them. Once everyone had taken a seat, the young man began by fawning over them. "Let me just say, on my own behalf, that I'm honored to have you here. And please don't hesitate to call me if you need anything at all during your stay."

After he left, following a few seconds of smiles and exchanged glances, the white-haired man turned to her.

"Professor Robledo, it's so nice to see you again. You do remember me, don't you?" It clicked. She'd never liked that man; it was probably just a personality clash. She gave him a smile, but also buttoned her cardigan up over her skimpy blouse and crossed her legs.

"Well, let's get right down to it. Paul, whenever you're ready."

Carter's speech was like boiling water, waiting to burst from his mouth.

"You'll all go home today. We call it 'reintegration.' It will be as if you never left: your bills have been paid, your meetings postponed, your immediate appointments canceled with no trouble, and your families and friends have been reassured. Because of the holidays that this operation covered, we had to use different excuses for each of you." He passed out a little dossier. "This should bring you all up to speed."

She already knew her mother had received a message on her

machine in which Elisa herself (or at least "her voice") apologized for not being able to come to Valencia on Christmas Eve. And she hadn't had to ask for time off work since classes didn't resume until after the holidays anyway.

"On behalf of Eagle Group, I'd like to apologize for having made you spend your holidays here." Harrison smiled like a rueful cashier who'd accidentally doled the wrong change. "I hope you can understand our reasons. Though I know you've been receiving *some* information over the past few days, Mr. Carter will be happy to give you the actual test results. Paul?"

"We've found no proof of any relation between Professor Craig's death and what happened in New Nelson, nor was it connected to any of you," Carter said, removing a bundle of papers from his briefcase. "As far as Nadja Petrova's suicide is concerned, unfortunately we *do* think there is a direct relationship between her death and the news of Craig's murder ..."

Elisa closed her eyes. She'd managed to *accept* the awful tragedy but couldn't help feeling a rush of anguish every time she actually thought about it. *Why? Why did she do it? Why call me and then do that?* She couldn't seem to recall many of the details of their phone conversation, but she did remember Nadja's distress, and how badly her friend had wanted to see her.

"That's precisely why we warned you not to contact one another," Harrison broke in reproachfully, staring at Jacqueline. "Professor Clissot, I'm not blaming you for anything. You did what you thought was the right thing in calling Miss Petrova. You received the news yourself and wanted to get it off your chest. Unfortunately, you chose the wrong person."

Jacqueline Clissot was sitting at one end of the table. She wore light-blue pajamas and a dressing gown but still looked incredible despite the years that had passed. Elisa did notice one thing, though: she'd dyed her hair black.

"I'm sorry," Jacqueline whispered, eyes downcast. "I'm so sorry ..."

"Don't blame yourself. Really," Harrison said. "You had no idea Miss Petrova would react that way. It could have happened to anyone. But I don't need to remind you not to do it again."

Jacqueline's head was still bowed, her beautiful lips trembling as if nothing Harrison said could stop her from believing she deserved terrible punishment for her actions. Elisa was scared. She'd talked to Nadja, too, after all.

"We've managed to reconstruct what happened." Carter passed out more sheets of paper. Photocopies of international news stories. "Nadja Petrova spoke to Professor Clissot at seven o'clock. She phoned Professor Robledo around ten. By ten thirty, she'd slit both of her wrists and bled to death in the bathroom."

"After you suggested going out to dinner together," Harrison said, pointing at Elisa. She struggled not to burst into tears.

"You can see what the press had to say about it here," Carter said, giving the floor back to Harrison. They were like actors on a stage, performing, riffing off each other.

"Obviously, they don't have the whole story. We intervened there, but I'll tell you why. When Professor Craig was murdered, we were intrigued. We sent special units to his house and put all of you back under surveillance, too. That's why we tapped your phone conversations. Miss Petrova was very upset, so we ordered one of our agents to go and make sure she was OK. When he got there, she'd already killed herself. So we cordoned off the area and decided to bring you all here to avoid another tragedy."

"Not very orthodox methods, but it was an emergency."

Harrison picked up, finishing Carter's thought.

"Not very orthodox methods, but we'd do it again if we had to. Let me make myself perfectly clear about that. We'd do it for one or all of you." He looked at them each in turn, stopping at Elisa, who looked down. Then he turned to Jacqueline, who would not meet his eyes. "Do I make myself clear, Professor?"

"Perfectly," she replied quickly.

"You've all been in isolation. For your own safety and the safety of those around you. We've been through this again and again: you all suffered from the Impact. And until we have a better understanding of what happens to a person who sees the past, we'll have to take drastic measures whenever a situation arises. I imagine you all know what I mean." He turned back at Elisa again, and she nodded. Harrison's look gave her the creeps; his blue eyes were so narrow they looked like pinpricks. "You're all educated people, intelligentsia even. So I'm sure you can grasp this."

Everyone nodded.

"But ... wasn't Colin murdered by an organized gang?" Marini suddenly shouted. Elisa was shocked by his tone: he sounded as if he *wanted* that to be true. His eyes were red and the left one twitched uncontrollably.

"There is no evidence whatsoever that points to any sort of organized crime," Carter said.

"Professor Craig was killed by criminals from eastern Europe. Scotland Yard had been after them for some time; it was an unfortunate fluke," Harrison added. "They broke into houses, tortured and then killed the inhabitants, and made off with everything of value they could lay their hands on. But they've been caught now. It was tragic, but it would have ended there had you not begun getting in touch with each other, initiating contact in states of anguish. And quite patently, Miss Petrova could not handle that anguish."

"At any rate," Carter said, "you won't be going home unprotected. We'll be watching you, at least for a few months, for your own safety. And we'll still be conducting interviews with the team of specialists—"

"What if we don't *want* to go home?" Marini cried. "We have a right to be permanently protected!"

"That's your choice, Professor." Harrison spread his hands. "We can keep you here as long as you like, in a bubble, if that's what you want. But there is no objective reason to do so. Our advice is for you to carry on with your normal lives."

The expression made Elisa grit her teeth. She didn't know what a "normal life" was anymore and suspected that—aside from Carter and Harrison—no one there could explain it.

Everyone was exhausted, and after lunch they all went back to their rooms. That evening, before they boarded the plane, their personal effects were returned to them. She looked at the calendar on her watch: Saturday, January 7, 2012.

EIGHT months later, on the morning of September 11, she received some spam on her computer watch. It was an ad that showed a map of central Madrid, with a little clock in the upper corner. The clock was what was being advertised: a prototype of a computer watch equipped with Galileo, the new European satellite navigation system. To show how it worked, the user could move the cursor anywhere on the map, and wherever there was a red circle, localized info popped up and different music played. Their slogan read "Dedicated to you." Elisa was about to delete it when she noticed something.

The music was the same for all the circles but one. She recognized it immediately: the suite he always played. She'd recognize it anywhere.

Elisa was intrigued. She moved the cursor to the only circle that didn't play that melody. She heard another one, also for piano, but this was a popular tune. Even she knew what it was.

A chill ran down her spine. *Dedicated to you.*

Then she realized that when the cursor hovered over that circle, the clock on the ad changed time from 5:30 to 10:30.

Alarmed, she decided to delete it.

Lately, everything freaked her out. She'd spent that entire summer shaking like a leaf, scared of everything. She obsessed about her looks, which were ever more spectacular, and bought clothes she'd never have considered wearing until recently. She turned down every man who wanted to go out with her (and there were many), passed on all of their elaborate plans (some of which were very suggestive), and spent her time at home, behind locked and alarmed doors, always trying to catch her breath and calm down. And although it was a pretty grim summer, by the end of it her spirits were higher than they had been after that horrible experience at Christmas. She didn't want to take a step backward.

That afternoon, she received the same message again. She deleted it. It reappeared.

By the time she got home, she was in a state of panic. That one tiny e-mail, so carefully prepared (if it was what she thought it was, and she knew it was), brought back horrible memories for her.

If it had been a phone call, she would simply not have picked up. But the message simultaneously attracted and repelled her. It was like everything was coming full circle. It had all begun with a coded message, and maybe it would all end the same way.

She made up her mind.

The time on the message was 10:30. She had almost two hours, plenty of time to get there. She dressed perfunctorily: no bra, sleeveless ivory-colored dress that fit like a glove, knee-length white boots, and a wide silver bracelet (lately, she wore lots of bracelets and bangles). She grabbed a small purse and slipped in a tiny bottle of perfume she'd recently bought, a lipstick, and some other cosmetics. She'd teased her hair and left some black curls down, to frame her face. She'd loved her naturally black hair. Before leaving, she opened the message and aimed the pointer at the circle that played that famous tune, verified the address, and walked out.

The whole way there, the song played over and over in her mind and she thought of the message: "Dedicated to you." That had been the clue.

It was Beethoven's *Für Elise*.

WITHOUT knowing why, she decided to take the metro and was so anxious that she didn't even pick up on the looks the other passengers gave her. She got off at Atocha. It was a warm night, but autumn was definitely in the air. As she walked to the spot the map indicated, she recalled another night, six years ago, when Valente had used a similar lure to get her to see that someone was putting on a show and she was one of its protagonists.

Well, things had changed now. *She* had changed.

Elisa generally paid no attention to the obscene remarks men made on the street, but just then a group of boys shouted something so brutal that she had to stop and think. She looked at herself in a storefront window: tall, slim, an ivory silhouette in high-heeled boots. She stopped, shocked. Her tube dress was so tight she might as well have been naked, and the bracelet clamped around her bicep and knee-length boots gave her an appearance very different from the one she would have liked to project.

How did this happen? How could she have gone through a 180-degree transformation? Thinking about the night she met Valente had made her reflect on all the changes her personality had gone through since then: the student Elisa didn't care about her clothes or her appearance at all; Professor Robledo acted like she was an aspiring catwalk model or some cabaret hopeful. Even her mother, elegant Marta Morandé, had said she didn't seem like herself. Seemed like a different person.

Her heart pounded as she stared into the glass. Who was she getting all dressed up for? Who had made her change so much? Then something very strange occurred to her. *Valente would have liked it.*

Stunned, she kept walking. Stunned and mystified, as if she didn't have control of her own free will. But in the end, she accepted the fact that wanting to feel desired was *her* fantasy, too. It might be enigmatic or even repulsive, but there was no doubt that the desire to feel wanted came from within her, and the Elisa of years gone by had no right to protest.

The heels of her white boots clicked on the sidewalk as she approached the meeting point. She was scared, but she also really wanted this meeting to turn out to be something *real*. Over the last few months, Elisa's fear and desire always seemed rolled into one.

It was just a street corner. There was no one there. She glanced around and was caught in the headlights of a car parking on a perpendicular side street. Feeling her pulse race, she approached. Whoever was behind the wheel opened the passenger door from inside. The car sped off immediately, heading toward Paseo del Prado. Only then did the driver speak.

"My God, I would never have recognized you. You look so ... different..."

She blushed and turned away.

"Please, let me out. Pull over and let me out."

"Elisa, they stopped watching us two weeks ago. Trust me. I know."

"I don't care. Let me out. We shouldn't be speaking."

"Give me a chance. We have to meet without their knowing. Just give me one chance."

Elisa looked at him. Blanes looked a lot better than he had at Eagle's Aegean base. He wore jeans and a loose-fitting shirt and still had his beard. All the hair once on the top of his head seemed to have migrated there. But he definitely looked different. She looked different, too. She felt ridiculous, dressed like that. Her whole fragile existence came crashing down before her. She realized he was right: they had to talk.

"I'm happy to see you. Really," he added, smiling. "I wasn't entirely convinced that my musical message would work. I know they've stopped surveillance, but I still wanted to take precautions. Besides, I had a feeling it might be the only way to get you here. We had to bait Jacqueline, too."

She picked up on the plural: *we* had to. Who else was in on this? Still, Blanes' solid presence, his proximity, was comforting. Staring out at the Madrid night, she asked about the others.

"They're fine. Reinhard took the train. One of his students

bought the ticket for him. And Jacqueline flew in. Sergio Marini couldn't make it." Seeing Elisa's raised eyebrow, he added, "Don't worry, he's fine. But he won't be coming."

The rest of the trip—across illuminated highways and dark country roads—was made in silence. The house was in the middle of nowhere, near Soto del Real, and even in the dark it looked huge. Blanes explained that it had belonged to his family: now it was his sister's and her husband's. They thought about turning it into a bed-and-breakfast. Rural tourism was all the rage. Eagle Group, he added, had no idea it existed. Or so he thought.

The sparsely furnished living room had just enough chairs so no one had to sit on the floor. Silberg stood to greet her. Jacqueline didn't. Jacqueline's appearance made her do a double take, but she forced herself to turn away when she realized that the ex-professor's reaction to her scrutiny was the same as her own when Blanes had stared at her. And Jacqueline seemed to see in Elisa a mirror reflecting her own appearance. What did all that mean? What the hell was going on?

"I'm glad you all came," Blanes said, pulling up a wrought-iron chair for her. He took another one. "Let's get right down to it. First, I should say that I'll understand your shock, even incredulity, when you hear what we're going to tell you. It's only natural. All I ask is that you try to have a little patience." No one said a thing. Blanes, lacing his fingers together and resting his elbows on his thighs, suddenly said, "Eagle Group is lying to us. They've been lying for years. Reinhard and I have proof." He pulled some papers from a side-table drawer. "I hope you'll give us your vote of confidence. The memories will come, I assure you. They came to us—"

"The memories?" Jacqueline said.

"We've all forgotten a lot of things, Jacqueline. They drugged us."

"When we were on the base in the Aegean," Silberg interjected. "And every single time the 'specialists' interview us. They drug us every time ..."

Elisa leaned forward, incredulous.

"Why would they do that?"

"Good question," Blanes replied. "First, they're trying to hide the fact that Craig and Nadja's deaths are related to Cheryl's, Rosalyn's, and Ric's. They'll go to amazing lengths to cover it up. They're spending millions on this smoke screen, and it's still slipping from their grasp. There are more and more witnesses, people they have to bring in for 'treatment,' journalists they have to throw off track. In Madrid, when Nadja died, the authorities evacuated the entire block claiming there was a bomb threat, and then leaked the news that a young Russian woman had lost her mind and killed herself after threatening to blow the whole building sky-high."

"They had to come up with a credible story, David," Elisa said.

"True. But look at this." He slid a sheet of paper over toward her. "The owner of the apartment, Nadja's friend, was on vacation in Egypt. She wanted to come straight back as soon as she heard. She didn't make it in time. Two days later, a group of kids in another apartment were playing with some sparklers they'd gotten for Christmas and started a fire. They evacuated everyone again and no one was hurt, but the whole building was burned to the ground."

"Yeah, there was a lot of speculation about that." Elisa had read the headlines. "But it was just a terrible coincidence . . ."

That's out of the question. Let me tell you another coincidence.

She glanced at Blanes apprehensively.

"There were no witnesses in Colin Craig's case, either. Not even a crime scene," he continued. "His wife killed herself at the hospital, two days later, and their son died from exposure just hours after being found. Neither Colin's family nor his wife's wanted to keep the house, so they sold it through an agent. A young IT executive at a company called Techtem bought it."

"It's an Eagle front," Silberg explained.

"They tore it down right away," Blanes finished. "Same situation in both cases: no witnesses, no crime scene."

"How did you get all this information?" Elisa asked, leafing through the papers.

"Reinhard and I have been making some inquiries."

"But this still doesn't prove any relation between New Nelson and their deaths, David."

"I know. But look at it this way. If there is no relation between what happened to Colin and Nadja and what happened on New Nelson, why go through all this trouble to demolish the actual *scene* of the crime? And why kidnap us *all,* and drug us *all?*"

Jacqueline Clissot crossed her long legs, bare to the thigh in her amazing three-piece "suit" (matching choker, tube top, and miniskirt, slits in each one). Elisa thought she looked very sexy and very made-up, her black hair up in a bun.

"What proof do you have that they drugged us?" she asked, impatient.

Blanes spoke calmly.

"Jacqueline, you examined Rosalyn Reiter's body. And after the explosion, you went down to the pantry because Carter called you in to look at something. Do you remember all that?"

For a second, Jacqueline seemed to become another person. Her face lost all expression and she visibly stiffened in her seat. Her sensual appearance contrasted so starkly with that windup doll reaction that it scared Elisa to the core. She *saw* the answer to the question in the ex-professor's fluster before she heard her speak.

"I ... think ... a little ..."

"Drugs," Silberg said. "They've erased our memories with drugs. You can do that nowadays, you know. There are even lysergic acid derivatives that can be used to create *false* memories."

Intuitively, Elisa knew Silberg was right. She thought she could recall, in the foggy haze of her mind, having received multiple injections while she confined on the Aegean base.

"But why?" she insisted. "Let's say that Colin's and Nadja's deaths *are* related to Rosalyn's, Ric's, and Cheryl's. What does that have to do with us? Why take us there, drug us, and then put us back? What information could we possibly give them? What memories do they want to erase?"

"That's the question," Silberg said. "They've drugged all of us, not just Jacqueline. But she's the only one who examined a body, and none of us has witnessed a crime ..."

"And we don't know anything," Elisa added.

Blanes held up a hand.

"That means we *do* know something. We have something they need, and the first thing we have to do is figure out what that is." He looked at each in turn. "We have to figure out what it is we all have in common, what we share without even realizing it."

"We were on New Nelson and we saw the past," Jacqueline proclaimed.

"But what information could they get from that? And what memories do they want to erase? We all remember Project Zig Zag and the images of the Lake of the Sun and the Jerusalem Woman ..."

"I'll never forget it," Silberg whispered, and for a second he looked very old.

"So what else do we have in common? What have we shared over all these years since New Nelson that they want to find out about, and then get rid of?"

Elisa, who'd been watching Jacqueline, all at once felt herself begin to tremble.

"Him," she whispered. For a second, she thought they hadn't heard her, but the sudden change in their expressions seemed to give her permission to go on. "Our dreams, the figure ... I call him Mr. White Eyes."

Blanes and Silberg dropped their jaws in unison. Jacqueline, who had turned to her, nodded.

"Yes," she agreed. "His eyes *are* white."

THAT sickening feeling. Of filthiness, Jacqueline had said. You feel it too, don't you, Elisa? She nodded in recognition. Filth was the right word. The feeling of being stained, dirty, covered in muck, as if she'd dragged her body through the scum of a huge swamp. And yet it was more than just a physical feeling: it was the *idea* of the feeling. Jacqueline had phrased it well, and Elisa realized that the paleontologist might have actually been suffering even more than she herself had.

"It's like I'm just *waiting* for something ... And I'm *part* of it, so I can never get away. I'm alone. And it calls me. It was the same for Nadja, she told me ..."

Elisa gasped. *It calls me, and I want to obey.* She wanted to say it, but it sounded so disgusting she didn't dare voice it. *A presence. A presence that wants me.*

And Jacqueline.

Maybe everyone, but mainly us.

After a long pause, Blanes looked up. Elisa had never seen him so pale, so anxious.

"You don't have to ... tell me anything ... if you don't want to," he stammered. "I'll just tell you what happened to me, and all I'm asking is that you let me know if it's the same kind of thing." He seemed mostly to be addressing the two of them, and Elisa wondered if he'd already spoken to Silberg about whatever it was he was about to say. "*He* appears in my dreams, my disconnects ... And when he does, I see myself ... doing terrible things." He lowered his voice, his cheeks turned red. "I have to do them, he makes me. To my sister ... to my mother ... awful things. Not for pleasure, though sometimes there is pleasure." The silence was thick; Elisa knew how hard it was for Blanes to talk about this. "But there's always ... torture."

"My wife," said Silberg, "is always the victim in my dreams. Though 'victim' doesn't really express it." He was a large man, but suddenly the expression on his face broke like a child, and he stood and turned his back to them. He cried for a long time, but no one could console him. Elisa was suddenly hit by another memory that chilled her to the bone. The day she'd first seen him cry, standing by the trapdoor that led down to the pantry. When he looked back at them, Silberg had taken off his glasses and his face was all wet. "We separated. We haven't gotten divorced ... we still love each other. In fact, I love her more than ever, but I can't go on living with her ... I'm so scared I'll hurt her ... scared *he* will make me."

Jacqueline had also stood up, and she walked to the window. The living room was dark and silent.

"You can consider yourselves lucky," she said without turning around, staring through the dirty panes of glass and off into the night. The thing that horrified Elisa the most about her confession was that her voice didn't change. She didn't cry, didn't whimper. If Silberg had sounded like a condemned man, Jacqueline Clissot sounded like she'd already been executed. "I never talk to anyone about this, except the Eagle doctors, but I suppose there's no reason to keep hiding it. For years now, I've thought I was sick. I thought it a year after returning from New Nelson, when I separated from my husband and son, and decided to stop teaching and leave my profession. Now I'm alone. I live in a studio in Paris that *they* pay for. And all they ask in return is that I tell them about my dreams ... and my behavior." She was standing stock-still, her body clinging to her ultrashort, outrageous outfit. Elisa was sure she wasn't wearing anything underneath. "But I don't really live alone. I live with *him,* if you know what I mean. He tells me what to do. Threatens me. Makes me want certain things, and punishes me, using my own hands. I actually thought I had gone crazy, but they convinced me it was just part of the Impact. What do they call it? 'Traumatic delirium.' That's not what I call it. When I dare to call it anything, I call it the Devil," she whispered. "And I'm scared to death of it."

No one spoke. Everyone looked at Elisa. She found it hard to speak, even though Jacqueline's story was far worse than hers.

"I always thought they were just fantasies," she said, her mouth running dry. "I imagine him visiting me every night at a certain time. I have to wait for him, and I have to be scantily dressed. Then *he* comes and tells me things. Terrible things. Things he'll do to me, or to the people I love, if I don't obey him ... He terrifies me, too. But I thought ... it was just a fantasy."

"That's the worst thing," Jacqueline agreed. "We *wanted* to think it was just us, even though we knew it wasn't."

"There has to be some sort of explanation." Blanes was massaging his temples. "I don't mean a rational explanation. We're physicists, mostly, and we know reality doesn't have to be rational. But there *has* to be an explanation. Something we can *prove*. A theory. We have to come up with a theory in order to make sense of what's happening to us."

"There are several possibilities." Silberg's voice was unrecognizable. There was something about it that seemed silent, like the house, like the countryside at night. "Let's see if we can rule them out, narrow it down. First: Eagle Group is solely responsible. They drugged us and did this to us."

"No," Blanes said. "It's true they've been hiding information from us, but they're as lost as we are."

And as scared, Elisa thought.

"OK, then. Two: the Impact. I know for a fact that the Lake of the Sun and the Jerusalem Woman had some sort of effect on all of us. And Eagle is right when they say the effects are completely unknown. Maybe it's the Impact that's making us so obsessed with ... that *thing*. Maybe it's a product of our disturbed unconscious ... Let's say Valente went crazy and found a way to kill Rosalyn and Ross ... I'm not talking about *how* he did it, just the act itself. And suppose the same thing is happening now, to one of us. Maybe Sergio, or maybe one of the people in this room right now. I know it sounds insane, but just suppose that *one of us* ... is behind Colin's and Nadja's deaths."

Silberg's idea had sown panic.

"Regardless," Blanes remarked, "the Impact could explain the similarities between our visions and the changes in our lives. Are there any other possibilities?"

"One more," Silberg replied, nodding. "A mystery. Like faith. Something incomprehensible. The unknown factor."

"In mathematics, we tend to find the value of the unknown," Blanes said. "And we'll have to find this one if we want to survive."

Jacqueline's voice got their attention abruptly.

"I can tell you one thing. Whatever it is, I'm sure that it's wicked. And it's real. Very real. It's evil. And it's stalking us."

SEVEN

On the Run

... it sometimes requires courage
to fly from danger.

MARIA EDGEWORTH

25

Madrid
March 12, 2015
1:30 A.M.

"**AND** that was it," Elisa said. "We ended the meeting, agreeing that if something happened, David or Reinhard would call the rest of us and use a code word to signal that we should meet here again, and that the house was still safe. 'Zig Zag' was our code, since that was the name of the project. We decided the meeting would be at twelve thirty on the same night as the call. Meanwhile, David and Reinhard would try to get more information, and Jacqueline and I would wait. And that was what we did. Or what I did, anyway. Wait."

She ran a hand through her wavy black hair and sighed deeply. She'd told the worst of it and felt a little calmer now.

"Of course, it wasn't easy, living like that. We knew we couldn't trust Eagle or their specialists when they interviewed us, but luckily those sessions became more sporadic. And they gradually left us alone, as if we no longer mattered. From time to time I got messages from David; he'd send me textbooks with notes hidden in the binding—'conclusions,' he called them. They were just brief memos about whether their investigation was getting anywhere … but I never knew exactly what kind of investigation they were conducting. I'm assuming he'll tell us now …" She cocked an inquiring eyebrow at Blanes, who nodded. "Anyway, time went by, and I just tried to carry on with my life. The dreams, the nightmares, they were always there. But David insisted we try to act as if we didn't know anything. I bought that huge butcher knife, not to attack anyone or to defend myself, I now know, but to quickly end my suffering when the time came. But slowly, years went by, and in the end I really believed I was safe, that the worst of it was over ..." She stifled a sob. "And then this morning in class, I saw the article about Marini in the paper. I spent all day waiting for the call. And finally the phone rang and I heard David's voice say, 'Zig Zag,' and I knew it had started all over again ... That's it, Víctor. Or at least that's as much as I know."

She paused, but it was as if she hadn't stopped speaking. No one dared interrupt. No one moved. The four of them sat at the table, gathered around the lamp's weak glow. Elisa turned to Blanes, and then toward Jacqueline Clissot.

"And now what I want to know is, which one of you betrayed us?" she said in a different tone entirely.

Blanes and Jacqueline exchanged glances.

"No one betrayed anyone, Elisa," Blanes said. "Eagle found out about the meeting, that's all."

"That's not what Harrison says."

"He's lying."

Or is it you that's lying? Still staring at her old professor, Elisa tucked her hair behind her ears and dried the tears that streamed down her face while recounting those awful memories. Blanes, she sincerely hoped, would not have been so stupid. *Either way, it's too late now.*

Blanes took over.

"What really matters right now is updating you all on what we know. Reinhard and I have found out several things. We obtained information from confidential reports that were leaked; this is secret but verifiable information—"

"David, you know they're listening in right now," Elisa warned.

"I know, but it doesn't matter. They aren't the ones I'm most

concerned about. I'm going to give you some new information. We
didn't want to tell you anything until we had proof, and we still
don't have much, but Sergio's death made us realize it was time to
lay our cards on the table. We don't have a whole lot of news, just
a few haphazard particulars, but I think everyone's case is pretty
similar. Let's start with yours, Jacqueline." He gestured toward the
paleontologist. "They brainwashed Jacqueline for the first time
when we left New Nelson. She spent a month on the Aegean base,
where they purged her memory using drugs and hypnosis. But after her second ... what do they call it?... 'reintegration' ... After
her second reintegration, she started to remember things."

"Unfortunately," Clissot threw in.

"No, not unfortunately," Blanes corrected. "The lies would have
done you more harm." He turned to the others. "At first, Jacqueline saw only jumbled, fragmented images. But when we sent her
the first autopsy reports, she began to remember concrete details.
Like the things she found on Rosalyn Reiter's body. Why don't you
tell us about that, Jacqueline?"

Clissot rested her elbows on the table and pressed her finger-
tips together, inspecting her hands under the lamp's dim glow as
if they were a fragile work of art. Then she did something that—
oddly—sent a shiver down Elisa's back. She smiled. The entire
time she spoke, she wore a tense, horrid grin.

"Fine. Well, I didn't have the proper equipment to do an autopsy on the island, but I still found ... things. At first, it just seemed
like what you'd expect: intense erythema and eschars resulting
from the joule heat—that's the heat produced from an electric
current. She had burns and markings on her right hand from the
cables, her body showed signs of metallization ... all that was
normal, considering the fact that she received a five-hundred-volt
shock. But beneath the burns, I found other markings that bore
no relation to electricity: mutilations, parts of her body that had
been cut and even ripped off ... And there were things about her
body's state of preservation that made no sense at all. I wanted to

tell Carter about it, but that's when the explosion occurred. It happened when I was on my way back to the barracks, so I wasn't hurt at all. I even helped evacuate the rest of the team."

"Keep going," Blanes prodded.

"Well, before we left, Carter asked me to take a look at ... at what was in the pantry. I'm a forensic anthropologist, but when I saw that, I lost it entirely. It was like it blinded me. I couldn't see clearly after that, until David's reports jarred my memory." Jacqueline traced circles on the table with her finger as she smiled, as if the conversation amused her. "For instance, I saw half a face on the floor, I think it was Cheryl's, and it had been sectioned, layer by layer, sliced neatly like ... like the pages of a book. I'd never seen anything like that in my life, and I have no idea *what* could possibly do that. Certainly not a hatchet or even a knife. Ric Valente? No ... I don't know who could have possibly done that, or who gutted her and smeared her blood all over the walls, the ceiling, the floor, I mean every inch of the room was covered, like paint. I don't know who, or how, but it certainly wasn't your average Joe ..." She fell silent.

"And then I sent you Craig's and Nadja's reports," Blanes was gently prodding, trying to get her to keep talking.

"Yes, then there was more. Colin's brain, for example, had been removed and sliced into thin layers. His entrails had been ripped out and replaced with other extremities that had been amputated, as though ... as though it was a game of some kind, and his blood was all over the living room, which had also been totaled. And Nadja's head had been carved. Her cranium was filed so far down it was unrecognizable ... The kind of trench of a thing that takes water years to form a rock; no machine could have done it so fast. Bizarre things like that ..."

"And there were a few surprises in those test results, too, weren't there?" Blanes asked when she fell silent again. The paleontologist nodded.

"Their livers showed no glycogen, not a trace. The lack of autol-

ysis in the pancreas and absence of lipids in the suprarenal capsules would indicate slow, lengthy agony. And the level of catecholamines in the blood confirm that, too. I don't know if this is all a bit
too technical for you, Víctor. When a person is tortured, the body
undergoes an enormous amount of stress, and the glands over the
kidneys—the suprarenal capsules—secrete catecholamines, which
bring on tachycardia, increased blood pressure, and other physical changes designed to protect us. The level of these hormones in
the blood can essentially reveal the degree of suffering the person
has endured, and tell us how long it lasted. But Colin's and Nadja's
test results were totally impossible, comparable to prisoners of
war who have undergone very prolonged torture. The suprarenal
glandular tissue was so enlarged it seemed to have been working
at capacity for an extended period of time, and that points to ...
weeks, maybe months, of torture."

Víctor swallowed.

"That doesn't make any sense." He cast a glance at the others,
disconcerted.

"It's true, it bears no relation to how fast they died," Blanes cor-
roborated, validating Víctor's shock. "For example, Cheryl Ross
had only been in the pantry for two hours. Stevenson, who was
there when Craig found her body, didn't leave his post by the trapdoor, and he didn't see or hear anything out of the ordinary while
he was stationed there. But Elisa said that she could hear someone's steps in the pantry at night. So how could Valente manage to
get in without being seen and do everything he supposedly did to
Ross that fast, and in total silence? Besides, there was no sign of
intruders, no weapons were found, nothing. And, of course, there
are no witnesses, not a single one, and I don't mean just eyewit-
nesses. No one even *heard* anything. No cries, noises, shouting,
nothing. Not even in Nadja's case, and she was savagely butchered
in a matter of minutes, in an apartment with very thin walls."

Elisa paid very close attention. Some of what she heard was
new to her, too.

"And yet ..." Blanes leaned over the table, still staring at Víctor. The lamplight accentuated his features. "Every person who saw at least one of the crime scenes, every single one, including the authorities and specialists, went into some sort of shock. That's what they're calling it, though they don't know exactly what it is. The symptoms range from a temporary state of alienation—like Stevenson and Craig in the pantry—to sudden panic and anxiety—like Reinhard at the trapdoor—to a state of psychosis that doesn't respond to any standard treatment."

"But the crimes were atrocious," Víctor protested. "I mean, *of course* people would react that way ..."

"No." They all turned to look at Jacqueline Clissot. "I'm a forensic examiner, Víctor, I do this all the time. But when I went down to that pantry and saw Cheryl's remains, I was totally traumatized."

"What we're trying to say is that the reaction is not a hundred percent related to the degree of horror," Blanes stated. "These reactions are totally abnormal, even after seeing things that disturbing. Think about it: the soldiers, for example, are experienced men ..."

"I get it," Víctor said. "Still, the reactions are unusual, but not impossible."

"I know that," Blanes said, narrowing his eyes. "I still haven't told you the impossible part. Listen to this."

HARRISON knew that perfection meant protection.

You could say he was just a workaholic, but those who knew him best (or as close to "best" as Harrison ever let anyone get) would have had the chicken-and-egg debate about it. Did he end up like that because of his job, or had he chosen his job because he was like that?

Harrison himself didn't know the answer. His professional and personal lives overlapped. He'd gotten married and divorced, spent twenty years as head of security for scientific projects, had a daughter who lived far away and whom he never saw, and all that just made him more aware of the "sacrifices" he'd made. And that awareness was exactly what made him so good at his job. Harrison knew he was doing "the right thing." He was protecting; that was what he did. If he didn't eat, or sleep, if he aged fifteen years overnight and had no free time, all that was the price you paid to "protect" others. It was a role most people on the world's stage didn't want to play, and Harrison had taken the lead.

"No cracks." That was how his superiors described him. He was a man who had no cracks. Regardless of what that expression might mean to other people, Harrison saw himself as armor plating. Just as dogs take after their owners, eventually men take after their jobs. And as head of Eagle Group's project security, Harrison knew that what he had to do was create a field of armor-plated protection around his clients. Nothing could penetrate it. Nothing in, nothing out.

And everything had been all right until ten years ago, when Zig Zag somehow managed to breach a gap.

He thought about that as he left the house in Soto del Real very late that night, accompanied by three other men. The March night was far colder in the mountains surrounding Madrid than it was in the city, but Harrison was used to far worse, and as soon as he got into the car he was comfortable once more. It was a Mercedes S-Class W Special, the body as black and shiny as a transvestite's stilettos, the windows reinforced with thermoplastic and the body with Kevlar. A 9.5-millimeter bullet fired at the windshield at three thousand feet per second would do no more damage than a kamikaze insect flying into the screen. A hand grenade, mortar, or IED *might* incapacitate the vehicle, but no one traveling in the car would be hurt too badly. Harrison felt good in that bunker on wheels. Not 100 percent safe ("Safety is knowing that you're never safe," he told his disciples), but reasonably good, which is all any reasonable man could aspire to.

The driver pulled out immediately, maneuvering skillfully between two other cars and a van parked in front of the house, and slipped into the dark night with the silence of a satellite. It was 1:45, the stars twinkled in the sky, the road was empty, and even the most pessimistic estimate put them at the airport in half an hour: plenty of time to greet the new arrival.

Harrison pondered.

After a few minutes, sitting still as a statue, he took his hand out of his jacket pocket.

"Hand me the monitor."

The man sitting on his left passed him an object that looked like a bar of Belgian chocolate. It was a five-inch flat-screen TFT monitor with high-definition resolution good enough to make you swear you had a movie theater in the palm of your hand. The menu had four options: computer, TV, GPS, and videoconference. Harrison selected the last one and then clicked on the "Integrated Systems" option. It beeped, and immediately the L-shaped room where the four scientists sat chatting popped up on the screen. In spite of the weak light, the image was extraordinarily crisp and the color of their clothes and hair was easily discernible. The sound quality was superb. Harrison could choose from two angles, since there were two different hidden cameras filming. But neither of them had a clear shot of Elisa Robledo from straight on, so he settled for a profile, from the right.

Jacqueline Clissot was speaking.

"No. I'm a forensic examiner, Víctor, I do this all the time. But when I went down to that pantry and saw Cheryl's remains, I was totally traumatized."

They were speaking Spanish. Harrison could have hooked up the automatic translator incorporated into the surveillance program, but he didn't want to. It was clear they were recounting their tales of woe and bringing Lopera up to date with what had happened.

He stroked his chin. The fact that the scientists had learned so much puzzled him, despite the fact that Carter had proof that Marini had helped them out quite a bit before he died. Could

Marini have been responsible for supplying copies of the autopsy reports? Considering the fact that Marini himself knew almost nothing about it, where could he have gotten them? Who had leaked the information? Harrison was worried.

A leak. A crack. Something that lets things in and out. A defect in the armor. His armor.

Now Blanes was talking. He couldn't stand that man's condescending superiority.

He contemplated Elisa Robledo at length. Lately, he looked at a lot of things the same way, without blinking, without even breathing, holding his breath. He was familiar with the basic anatomy of the eye and knew that the pupil was actually a tiny hole. A fissure, actually.

Leaks.

Undesirable images could slip out through that hole, like the ones he'd seen four years ago at Colin Craig's house. The ones he'd seen at Nadja Petrova's house. Or the ones he'd seen yesterday in Milan, on the coroner's slab. Images as foul and impure as the stench from a dying man's mouth. He used them to get off to sleep every night, and then he dreamed of them.

He'd already decided what to do, and the higher-ups had given their blessings. He was going to decontaminate, cut off the gangrene. He'd make sure he was fully protected and then eliminate all the rotting flesh he was staring at right now. And he'd take special, personal pleasure in eliminating the flesh that had been responsible for those cracks, those leaks.

He'd take extra special care of Elisa Robledo. He hadn't told anyone, not even himself.

But he knew what he was going to do.

Suddenly, the screen filled with jagged saw teeth. For a second, Harrison thought that the Almighty was punishing him for his evil thoughts.

"Interference," the man on the left of him said, gripping the chocolate bar. "We might not have a clear signal here."

Harrison didn't care about not being able to see or hear them. The scientists—even Elisa—were nothing more than a dim light in his private sky. He had plans, and he'd carry them out when the time came. For now, he needed his full attention on the last task of the night.

BLANES was about to continue when something stopped him.

"Professor Silberg's plane should be landing in ten minutes," Carter said, striding in and closing the door behind him.

Elisa was indignant at the interruption and jumped up out of her seat.

"Would you get out of here?" she spat. "Aren't the hidden mikes enough for you? We'd like to be alone. Get the hell out!"

She heard chairs scraping back and Víctor and Blanes asking her to calm down. But she'd passed the point of no return. Carter's stare and his rock-hard body, planted squarely in front of her, seemed symbolic: the perfect metaphor for her impotence in the face of all that was going on around her. She stood just a few inches from him. She was taller than Carter, but when she pushed him it was like pushing a brick wall.

"Are you deaf? Don't you speak English? Get the fuck out! You *and* your boss!"

Ignoring her, Carter glanced over at Blanes and nodded.

"I activated the signal blockers. Harrison already left for the airport, so he can't see or hear us now."

"Perfect," Blanes replied.

Elisa's eyes flew back and forth, from one to the other, disconcerted, not understanding a thing. Until Blanes spoke up.

"Elisa, Carter has been secretly helping us for years. He's our source at Eagle. He gave us the autopsy reports and all the test results we've got. He and I are the ones who organized this meeting together."

26

"**ALL** of my men were killed. The ones who were with me on New Nelson. There were five of them. Remember? Sickening deaths, things that make your blood run cold, just like what happened to your friends, except my men weren't so popular, were they, Professor? They weren't 'brilliant scientists.'"

Carter paused. For a second it was as though a veil had descended over his light eyes, but then his steely expression returned and it was gone. He continued in a neutral tone.

"Méndez and Lee were killed in the warehouse explosion, but the autopsy showed that someone had had a little fun with Méndez before he died. York was murdered three years ago, the same day as Professor Craig, on a military base in Croatia. And whoever or whatever is doing this ripped Bergetti and Stevenson to shreds on Monday, hours before Marini. Bergetti was on medical leave with stress-related psychological trauma; he was murdered at home. His wife threw herself off the balcony when she found his body. Ten minutes later, during a routine mission on a barge in the Red Sea, Stevenson was ripped apart. No one saw how it happened. They blinked and he was dead. I got suspicious when I found out about York's death. No one said anything to me at Eagle. I found out on my own. That was when I decided to start collaborating with Professor Blanes."

"So, Elisa, now you see. No one betrayed anyone. We arranged it this way," Blanes remarked. "If Carter hadn't informed Eagle of our meeting, we'd all be back on Imnia, drugged out of our minds. But he convinced them it was preferable to snoop on us and find out what we had to say before they made any more moves. In fact, Carter's been helping us for years. He organized our last meeting, too. Do you remember the musical message?" Elisa nodded. Now it made more sense. She'd wondered about that message; it had seemed so inappropriate coming from Blanes.

"Let me make one thing clear, though," Carter quipped. "I'm as happy about working with you as you are with me: not at all. But if I have to pick between you and Eagle, I'll take you ... and if I have to choose between you and *him,* I'll still take you." Then he added, "I don't know who or *what* he is, but he took out my men, and I suppose he's coming for me now."

"He's taking out everyone who was on the island ten years ago," Jacqueline said. "All of us."

"Do you *see* him, too?" Elisa asked Carter, trembling.

"Of course I do. Just like you, he comes to me in my dreams." He paused and then corrected himself. "I guess I don't actually see him, because I close my eyes whenever he comes."

He stepped back and loosened the knot on his tie as he spoke.

"Eagle is lying to you. They're not trying to help you at all. In fact, they're just waiting for someone else to die. I think they want to study us, to see what happens when he chooses his next victim. They did all sorts of tests on me in Imnia, too, but they trust me. And that's obviously a big advantage. So, like it or not, counting Silberg, there aren't four of you in on this, there are five. You'll have to count me in on all your plans."

"Six."

Everyone turned to stare at Víctor, who seemed as surprised as anyone at what he'd just said.

"I ..." He hesitated, swallowed, took a deep breath, and then managed to speak confidently. "You'll have to include me, too."

"Does he know everything?" asked Carter, as if doubting this new addition.

"Almost," Blanes replied.

Carter's jaw slackened.

"Well, take your time deciding, Professor. We've got time. We still have to wait for Silberg."

"I wish he were here already," Blanes admitted. "Those documents he's got are the key."

"What are you talking about?" Elisa asked.

"He's holding the explanation to what's happening to us."

Jacqueline stepped forward. Her voice betrayed new anxiety.

"David, just tell me this: does *he* exist? Is he real, or just a collective vision, a hallucination?"

"We still don't know what he is, Jacqueline, but he's real. Eagle knows that. He's definitely real." He looked at each of them as if inspecting the sole survivors of a catastrophe. Elisa picked up on the fear in his eyes. "At Eagle, they call him Zig Zag, like the project."

FOR almost the first time ever, Reinhard Silberg thought about himself.

Everyone who knew him was perfectly aware that he tended to be altruistic and selfless. When his brother Otto, who was five years older and an executive at a Berlin optical components company, called one day to tell him he'd been diagnosed with a rare type of cancer whose name he couldn't pronounce, Silberg spoke to his wife, asked for a leave of absence at the university, and went to stay with Otto. He cared for him until his death, a year later. Two months after that, he packed his bags and went to New Nelson. Times were tough, and he'd gone through some huge emotional ups and downs: back then, he thought Zig Zag was God's way of trying to show his infinite kindness and helping him recover from his brother's tragic death.

He no longer thought anything of the sort.

At any rate, until everything changed definitively, Silberg had never feared for himself. Not because he was especially brave, but because of what his wife called a "unique glandular function." He actually felt more pain at *others'* suffering than his own; that's just the way he was. "If someone in this house has to get sick, let it be Reinhard," his wife used to say, "because if it's me, then we both suffer, and he'll have it worse."

I love you so much, Bertha . . . Thinking of his wife brought her image to his mind. Anyone could see that she was no longer the slim yet curvy young woman he'd met at college almost half a century ago, but to Silberg she was still the most attractive woman on the planet. Though they hadn't been able to have children, thirty years of marital bliss had convinced him that the only real heaven on earth, the only thing that actually deserved that moniker, was living with the one you love.

For a time, though, that harmony had been threatened. Years ago, horrified by his dreams, Silberg had made a decision very similar to the one that had taken him to his brother's house. He decided to leave in order to help someone else. He packed his bags and moved into a little bachelor pad near the university that was often rented out to students. He couldn't live with his wife, scared every night that he'd wake up to find he'd actually done the horrible things he did to her in his dreams, those grotesque visions. He'd given Bertha assorted excuses: that he needed distance to get some perspective, that his nerves were shot. But then she got sick and moved heaven and earth trying to get him to come home, and he'd finally given in despite the fact that his fears were worse than ever.

He'd said good-bye to Bertha that afternoon. He didn't want anything that might happen from that moment on—regardless of what it might be—to catch him by her side. He hadn't hugged her too tight, but he'd circled his arms around her and stroked her back (lately, her back gave her so much trouble) and told her there was a new project that required his collaboration. He'd have to be away for a few days. He didn't mind telling her he was going to Madrid to meet David Blanes: he knew Eagle would have found out by now anyway, and lying to his wife would have risked the possibility of them interrogating her.

Of course, he hadn't told her *everything,* especially since he, Blanes, and the others would have to make some drastic decisions in Madrid. He knew it would be a long time before he saw his wife again (*if* he saw her again), and that was why their brief good-bye meant so much to him.

But right then he wasn't even thinking about Bertha. He was terrified—of *him, Zig Zag.* He feared for himself, for his life, for his future. He felt like a little boy who'd fallen into a deep, dark well.

The cause of his terror was in the briefcase resting on his luggage carrier.

He was flying in a private seven-seater Northwind jet with a thirty-five-foot cabin at a cruising speed of 320 miles per hour. The seats smelled of metal and new leather. The only other passengers, seated across from him, were the two men Eagle had sent to come pick him up at his small office in the Physics Department of the Technischen Universität, in Charlottenburg. For years now, Silberg had been head of a department that gave the printmakers headaches trying to find ways to fit its name on business cards: *Philosophie, Wissenschaftstheorie, Wissenschafts- und Technikgeschichte.* It was part of the Humanities Division since they studied the *philosophy* of science, but as a theoretical physicist himself (in addition to being a historian and philosopher), he also had a home in the Physics Department. That was where he'd spent the day reading, concluding, and writing up his findings, and right now they were digitally locked in his briefcase.

Silberg expected the men from Eagle, but he feigned surprise anyway. They explained that they were under orders to escort him to Madrid. He wouldn't be needing the plane ticket he had: they'd take him on a private jet. He was perfectly aware of why they wanted him on that "gilded cage." Carter had already informed him that Harrison was going to stop him at the airport and confiscate his briefcase. He trusted that Carter would be able to get it back, but even if he couldn't, he'd taken measures to ensure that his findings ended up in the right hands.

"We're starting our initial descent," the pilot announced over the loudspeaker.

He checked his seat belt and sank back into his thoughts. He wondered—not for the first time—why they were being punished this way. Maybe because they had so flagrantly disobeyed God's wishes. After expelling Adam from Paradise, God sent an angel with a flaming sword to guard the way to the Tree of Life. *You can never return. The past is a paradise not open to you.* And yet, they had tried to return. In a way, that's what they had done, even if they'd only watched it. Wasn't that a perversion? The images of the Lake of the Sun and the Jerusalem Woman (images he'd dreamed of almost every night for ten years) were the most palpable proof of their dark sin. Weren't they? Didn't they, the damned, the voyeurs of history, deserve an exemplary punishment?

Perhaps, but he still thought Zig Zag was excessive. It seemed terribly unfair.

The angel with the flaming sword, Zig Zag.

He couldn't reconcile a world created by Supreme Goodness with the suspicions he harbored. If he was right, if Zig Zag was what he thought it was, then it was all far worse than anything they'd ever imagined. If his hurried conclusions, laid out in the documents he carried, were correct, then nothing could save them. He and the rest of the "damned" were speeding straight down the road to perdition.

As the plane glided over the Madrid night like a huge white bird, Reinhard Silberg prayed to the God he still believed in that he was wrong.

LIFE had smiled on Víctor Lopera.

He had a fabulous upbringing. Two siblings who loved him and two healthy, adoring parents. Moderation was the key to his existence. There was nothing particularly remarkable about his life; he'd had a few relationships, but not too many; he didn't talk much, but he didn't want to, either; and although he wasn't a rabble-rouser, neither did he let people walk all over him. If he'd lived in a dictatorship, he still would have been pretty much the same. Víctor was highly adaptable, like his aeroponic plants.

The only outrageous thing he'd ever done was befriend Ric Valente. And even that had been a formative experience; it helped make him who he was today—or at least that's what he liked to think.

He'd ended up realizing that, as Elisa once said, Ric wasn't as diabolical as he thought; he was just a kid who'd been abandoned by his parents and scorned by his uncle. A smart, ambitious boy, in need of love and friendship. Ric was a pile of contradictions: he was an egocentric soul, yet capable of affection, as he proved after the famous fight by the river over Kelly Graham; a pleasure seeker who, when it came right down to it, was still a complete loner who liked getting off on his magazines, photos, and movies. Although seen by adults as a marginal character, he was attractive—and even instructive—to children. His friendship with Valente, he concluded, had taught him more about life than many teachers and physics books, because having befriended the Devil was actually very appropriate for someone like him, who was doing everything he could to avoid temptation.

Proof of that was the fact that when he matured enough to untangle himself from that lonely, resentful, yet brilliant boy's sphere of influence, he did it immediately. The adventures they'd shared, when he thought about them, seemed like nothing more than stages of his own growth. The bottom line was that he'd set off on his own path while Valente had simply carried on along the same one, complete with not-so-discreet perversions.

At any rate, if he viewed his life as a math equation, even with Valente thrown into it, he still came out with positive numbers.

Until that night.

If he thought about everything he'd gone through in that one unbelievable night, he had to laugh. The woman he most admired (and loved) had told him a mind-boggling tale; some random heavies had dragged him from his car, taken him to a house in the middle of nowhere and interrogated him, complete with menacing looks; and now an obviously exhausted, probably insane, bearded David Blanes wanted him to believe the impossible. These numbers were too big for mental arithmetic. Even for him.

The only thing he was sure of was that he was there to help them—especially Elisa—and that he'd do everything he could.

Despite his growing fear.

"You said there were even stranger things …," he said.

Blanes nodded.

"The mummifications. Can you explain it, Jacqueline?"

"A cadaver can be mummified by natural or artificial means," Jacqueline said. "They used artificial means in Egypt, and we know all about those. But Mother Nature can do the same thing. For example, in extremely dry places with good air circulation, like deserts, water in organisms evaporates very quickly, and that prevents bacteria from doing their job. But Cheryl, Colin, and Nadja were mummified, too, and there was no reasonable cause: it bore no relation to any known method. There was no desiccation, none of the typical atmospheric alteration, and not enough time had passed to produce it anyway. There were other inconsistencies, too. Like the chemical autolysis caused when cells die—they exhibited signs of that, but the bacterial processes that come later never occurred. The total lack of bacterial putrefaction was very unusual … as if … as if they'd been locked up for a long time someplace with no contact with the atmosphere. That's totally unexplainable, given postmortem dating. They called it 'idiopathic aseptic mummification.'"

"I know what they called it," Carter said, interrupting in clumsy yet comprehensible Spanish (Elisa had no idea he even spoke it). He leaned against the wall, arms crossed as though waiting for someone to challenge him to a brawl. "They called it, 'If anyone knows what the fuck this is, speak up.'"

"That's what 'idiopathic' means," Jacqueline said.

"But what does that point to?" Víctor wondered aloud.

Blanes took over.

"First, that the time in which the crimes were supposed to have been committed bears no relation to how long the victims were dead. Craig and Nadja were killed in less than an hour, but according to the tests, their bodies had already been dead for months. I repeat, their *bodies*. Neither their clothing nor any of the objects around them had decomposed at all, and that includes the bacteria on their skin—which explains the absence of putrefaction that Jacqueline mentioned."

No one spoke. All heads turned toward Víctor, who raised his eyebrows.

"That's impossible," he said.

"Correct. But there's more," Blanes replied. "Another thing that every case had in common was a power cut. Not only the lights, but all of the energy sources stopped functioning. Battery-operated lamps, motors ... That's why the secondary generator at the station on New Nelson, for example, never kicked in. And the same thing happened to the helicopter that plunged to the ground midflight and produced the explosion. Its motor suddenly stopped working right when the garrison floodlights went out. That was when Méndez died. And something similar happened in the pantry, with Ross's death, and at Craig's and Nadja's houses. Sometimes the power cuts are more extensive, covering a larger area, but the epicenter is always the scene of the crime."

"It could just be surges." Víctor Lopera was a physicist, and his brain had gone into overdrive. He knew nothing about cadavers, nor did he want to, but with electric circuits he was in his element. "Sometimes power surges suck all the energy out of a system."

"And the batteries from a flashlight not connected to the electricity in any way?"

"I admit that that's pretty odd."

"Indeed it is," Blanes agreed. "But somehow it serves as a point of departure for us. Zig Zag and the power cuts are related one way or another. It's as if he needs those cuts in order to act."

"The dark," Jacqueline said. "He always comes in the dark."

That seemed to spook everyone. Elisa noticed them all glance at the dim glow that the reading lamp cast over the table. She decided to interrupt the deep silence.

"OK, so Zig Zag produces power cuts, but that doesn't explain what could have been doing this to us ..." She fidgeted, anxiously smoothing out her hair. "Tormenting us, murdering us. I mean, this has been going on for years now."

"Well, as I said, Reinhard is going to give us his final analysis. But I can tell you one thing: Zig Zag is not some supernatural being, he's no devil. Physics created him. We're talking about something demonstrable, something concrete that Ric Valente created on New Nelson." Amid the stupor that this news was met with, Blanes added something even more outlandish. "Valente might even *be* Zig Zag."

"What?" Víctor noticeably paled and glanced at them all in turn. "But Ric ... Ric is dead ..."

Carter stood before them, his arms crossed.

"That was another one of Eagle's lies, the easiest one. Valente was never found guilty, and there was never any proof of his death, but they decided to blame the murders that took place on the island on him so no one would ask any questions. His parents buried an empty coffin."

Elisa stared at Carter, aghast.

"As far as we're aware, Valente is still around, though his whereabouts are unknown."

HE heard a humming noise, felt his stomach tingling, and experienced the slight dizziness of descent. His ears needed to pop. The cabin lights, dimmed for landing, gave off a soft golden glow. Any frequent flier would realize they were preparing to land.

Suddenly, the speakers crackled.

"Ten minutes to landing."

The man across from him stopped talking to his partner and gazed out the window. Silberg did the same. He saw a dark expanse, the lower part of it dotted with lights. He'd been to Madrid several times, and he loved that uniquely small "big city." He pulled back his sleeve to check his watch: it was 2:30 in the morning on Thursday, March 12. He thought of all the things that would happen after those ten minutes had passed. The plane would land, the Eagle men would escort him to the house, and from there he'd be transported with the rest of them to the Aegean base ... or who knew what remote part of the world. They'd have to work out an escape plan with Carter. Only if they managed to break free from Eagle's talons could they come up with a way to confront the *real* threat.

But what could they do? Silberg had no idea. He wiped the sweat off his face with his jacket sleeve as he felt the landing gear engage below him.

One of the men leaned over toward him.

"Professor, do you know what the ..."

That was the last he heard.

The lights went out midquestion.

"Hello?" Silberg called. He heard only his own voice.

No reply.

Nor could he hear the Northwind's engines. And his vertigo was gone.

For a second, he thought maybe he was dead. Or perhaps he'd had a brain hemorrhage and still had a sliver of consciousness left that would slowly fade out in the dark. But he'd just spoken, and he'd heard his own voice. Besides, he now realized, he could feel

the armrests, and his seat belt was still on, and he could barely begin to make out the shape of the cabin in the dark. But everything
around him was quiet and still. How was that possible?

The Eagle men must have been just a few feet away. He remembered both of them. The guy on the right was taller and pudgier,
with sideburns down to the middle of his cheeks; the one on the left
was blond and burly, with blue eyes and a marked harelip. At that
moment, Silberg would have given anything to see them again, or
at least hear them. But the blackness before him was too dense.

Or was it?

He looked around. A few meters to his right, on what must have
been the cabin wall, there was a faint glow. He hadn't noticed it
until just then. He inspected it carefully. Wondered what it could
be. *A hole in the fuselage?* A diffuse, peaceful light. *The spirit of
the Lord, floating over the water.* Nothingness. Philosophers and
theologians had tried for centuries to come to terms with what his
eyes were taking in at just that second.

As a child, Silberg's passion for Bible study had often led him
to wonder what it would be like to witness a miracle: the parting
of the waters, the sun freezing, the walls crumbling as trumpets
rang out, the body coming back to life, the placid lake in the midst
of life's storm. What did those who lived through those things
feel?

Now you know. But this isn't one of God's miracles.

In a flash, he realized what that circle of light, and the stillness
around him, meant.

Zig Zag. The angel with the flaming sword.

He'd known all along, of course, and simply refused to accept
it. It was too horrific.

So this is it. Even on an airplane.

He brought his left hand to his hip and groped for his seat belt,
but he couldn't get it unfastened. The flap and buckle seemed to
be all one piece. With increasing desperation, he yanked it forward, the belt cutting right into his flesh (he seemed to be wearing

no clothes), hurting him, making him wince and whimper in pain, but the thing wouldn't budge.

He couldn't move. But there was something far worse than that.

Worse than that was the feeling that he wasn't alone.

It was an absolutely chilling sensation on that still, eternal night. More than a feeling, it was the certainty that *someone* or *something* was at the back of the cabin, behind him, by the restrooms and the last row of seats. He looked over his shoulder, but between the darkness, the back of his seat, and not being able turn his head, he couldn't see a thing.

Still, he was certain that the presence was real. And it was approaching.

It came down the aisle.

Zig Zag. The angel with the...

In an instant, he lost the cool he'd maintained up till then. He was overcome by utter panic. Nothing—not the thought of Bertha, not his Bible study, his education, or his courage—helped him get through that moment of sheer terror. He trembled. He whimpered. He burst into tears. He struggled insanely with his seat-belt buckle. He thought he would lose his mind, but he didn't. He had a sudden realization: insanity cannot conquer the brain as quickly as anxiety. It was easier to cut off an extremity, extract entrails, or rip flesh from bone than it was to strip a healthy mind of its reason, he deduced. He intuited he was to remain mindful to the end.

But he was wrong.

A moment later, that became clear.

It turned out that in fact there were things that could strip a healthy mind of all reason, in an instant.

IT was a fragile night. A dim, black patchwork of tiny lights. The Northwind's pointed nose sliced through it like a blade of ice. The hydraulic shock absorbers took the weight of the aircraft as the brakes halted its propulsion with a deafening roar.

Harrison didn't wait for the plane to stop. He left the airport official standing there and nodded to the van parked on Terminal Three's runway. His men jumped in, silent and efficient. The last one slammed the door shut and they cruised over to the plane. There were hardly any commercial flights at that time of night, so they had no fear of interruptions. Harrison had just received a report from the pilots: no incidents to report. The first part of his mission—bringing all the scientists together—was taken care of.

He turned to his right-hand man, seated beside him.

"No violence, no weapons. Understood? If he refuses to hand over his briefcase, we'll let him hold onto it for now. We'll have time once we get back to the house. The main thing is to get him to trust us."

The van stopped; the men piled out. Wind swept across the grass around the runway and ruffled Harrison's snowy white hair. The staircase was attached, but the plane's hatch hadn't opened. What were they waiting for?

"The windows …," his man said.

For a second Harrison didn't know what he meant. But as soon as he turned to look at the plane, it dawned on him.

All of the windows aside from the cockpit, the five porthole windows on the luxurious Northwind, looked as though they'd been painted black. He couldn't recall that model having smoked glass. What were the passengers doing in the dark?

Suddenly, the windows lit up as slowly and softly as streetlights on a lonely road at dusk. Light seemed to float from one to the next. Someone was carrying a flashlight around in there. But the weird thing was the color of the light.

Red. A dirty, uneven red.

Or it looked that way because of what was covering the inside of the windows.

A tingling in his gut rooted Harrison to the spot. For a second, time stood still.

"Get onto that plane," he said. But no one seemed to hear him. He took a deep breath and gathered his courage, like a general addressing his troops before an imminent defeat. "Get onto that goddamned plane!"

It was as though everything was frozen still and only he could move. He stood there, screaming.

27

"**SERGIO** Marini planned everything. We were both fully aware of the risks, but he was …" Blanes paused for a moment, searching for the right word. "Well, maybe he was just more curious. I think I once told you, Elisa, that Eagle wanted us to experiment with the recent past, and I refused. Sergio never agreed with me about that, but when he realized he couldn't change my mind, he seemed to capitulate. I suppose I was vital to the project, so he had to fake it around me, but he spoke to Colin behind my back. He was an amazing young physicist; he'd designed SUSAN and he wanted to make a name for himself. Marini was probably saying, 'This is our chance, Colin.' They started talking about how to go about it without my finding out, and they had a brilliant idea. Why not use one of the students? They chose Ric Valente. He was the ideal candidate: a brilliant student, ambitious. Colin knew him from Oxford. At first, I'm sure they just asked him to do little things: learn how to run the accelerator and the computers, that sort of thing. Then they gave him more explicit instructions. He worked almost every night. Carter and his men knew that; they protected him."

"Those noises I heard in the hall …," Elisa murmured. "And the shadow …"

"That was Ric. In fact, he took things a step further, surprising even Marini and Craig. He had an affair with Rosalyn Reiter so that if he ever got caught lurking around the barracks at night, people would think it was because he was going to her room."

Elisa's memory returned to that bedroom on New Nelson. She heard footsteps and saw the shadow slipping by the peephole in her door. And there was Ric, again, staring down at her with that haughty, condescending smile. What she had just learned fit right in with the Ric she knew: the ambition, the need to shine even brighter than Blanes. It was all Ric to a T, especially the way he'd used Rosalyn so callously. But what kind of *thing* had he made during those nocturnal trials? What explained those dreams and those visions? How had Ric been able to devastate their lives to such a degree?

Jacqueline seemed to be reading her mind. Raising her head, she asked, "But what did Ric *do* to unleash all of this ...

"All in good time, Jacqueline," Blanes replied. "We still don't know exactly what he did, but I'll tell you what Reinhard and I think happened the night of Saturday, October 1, 2005. The night Rosalyn died and Ric disappeared."

They all sat around the table again, the reading lamp their island of light in the center. Everyone was exhausted and hungry (the only thing they'd had in the past several hours was water), but all Elisa wanted to do was hear what Blanes had to say. She knew her adrenaline was surging, and guessed everyone else's was, too, including Víctor's. Meanwhile, Carter came and went, sending messages and receiving phone calls. He'd asked Víctor for his ID, explaining that he'd need a fake passport if he wanted to accompany them. Now he spoke to someone in the hall. Elisa couldn't hear what they were saying.

"As you recall," Blanes continued, "that night they forbade us to use electrical appliances due to the storm. No one could go to the control room or turn on any equipment or computers. Ric must have thought he'd never have a better opportunity to experiment on his own, since no one would bother him. He didn't even tell Marini or Craig. He just got up and stuffed a backpack and pillow under his covers to make it look like he was in bed. But something unexpected happened. Actually, two things. First— well, at least this is what we *think*—Rosalyn went to his room to speak to him. He'd tired of the pretending, and she was desperate. When she tried to wake him up, she realized what he'd done and searched the whole station for him. Maybe they met in the control room, or maybe she didn't get there until he'd already left. Regardless, that's when the second thing happened, the one we want to prove, which is that Ric did something unusual (or maybe Rosalyn did, but it's unlikely; she probably just suffered the consequences), or did something wrong. The rest of this is just conjecture. Zig Zag appeared and killed Rosalyn, and Ric disappeared." After a pause, he went on. "Marini and Craig later erased any sign that the accelerator had been used so we wouldn't suspect anything, or maybe the blackout did that by itself, I don't know. What I do know is that Marini kept a secret copy of Ric's experiments as well as his own. Not even Eagle knew about them. The specialists used drugs to interrogate us, but Carter confirmed that no drug can make you confess something you're trying to hide if the questions asked are not specific enough. They never found out about those files. Sergio hid them, probably because he began to suspect that what had happened was related to Ric's experiments, although maybe he wasn't really sure until Colin died. He was the first one of us to find out, which proves he was paying extra-close attention. And remember how nervous he was on the Eagle base, demanding protection?"

"That bastard," Jacqueline said. Her chest and bare stomach heaved in fury. "That *bas*-tard ..."

"I'm not trying to excuse him," Blanes murmured after a pregnant pause. "But I suspect that what Sergio went through was worse than what we've had to suffer, because he thought he knew how it all started."

"Don't you *dare* feel sorry for him," Jacqueline's voice was hard, icy. "Don't even try it, David."

The physicist turned to her, eyes narrowed.

"If Zig Zag is the result of human error, Jacqueline, then we all deserve a little compassion. Regardless, Sergio kept those files on a USB flash disk that he hid at his house in Milan. Carter has been suspicious of him for three years. He sent several pros to search his apartment, but they never turned anything up. And he didn't dare go back again. That would have risked Eagle catching on. But yesterday, when he learned that Marini had been murdered, he took advantage of the situation by combing the place with a team of his own men. He found the flash disk in a false-bottomed box Marini had from one of his magic tricks, and sent the files to Reinhard. I had to come to Madrid to prepare for this meeting, since that was how we'd arranged it. Silberg is the only one who's seen the files, and he spent all night and day going through them. He's got the findings of his study with him now. That's why it's so important that we speak with him."

"But Harrison knows," Elisa pointed out.

"We had to tell him so that he wouldn't get suspicious. In fact, Carter told him himself, but he blamed Marini, saying he'd gotten scared and sent us the files on his own. Silberg knows Harrison is going to confiscate them, but Carter can get them back."

"And then what?"

"Then we'll run. Carter has an escape plan. First, we'll go to Zurich, and from there to wherever he says. We'll stay underground until we ... we find a way to solve the Zig Zag problem."

Elisa pursed her lips. *Yes, it is a problem. Look at us. Look at what we've done to ourselves, what Jacqueline and I have become: scared little rats shaking in our boots and dolling ourselves up so that the "problem" will let us live one more night.* She couldn't help but think that Blanes, Silberg, and Carter might have been just as scared or more so, but there was no way they'd gone through half the shit that she and Jacqueline had to deal with every damn day.

She sat up straight in her chair and spoke with the conviction she always had after making a firm decision.

"No, David. We can't run away, and you know it. We have to *go back*." Their reaction was that of a table of stuffed dolls that suddenly sprang to life. Heads bobbed, bodies jerked, arms waved. "To New Nelson," she added. "This is our only chance. If Ric started all this from there, then that's the only place we're going to be able to 'solve the Zig Zag problem,' as you put it."

"Go back to the island?" Blanes frowned.

"No!" Jacqueline Clissot had been whispering the syllable for some time, slowly increasing in volume until it became a scream. Then she stood. Jacqueline was already a tall woman, and those black heels made her even taller. Her heavily made-up eyes flashed painfully in the dimly lit room. "I will never go back to that island. Never! Don't even talk about it."

"Well, then, what do you suggest?" Elisa implored.

"Hiding! Running away and hiding."

"And in the meantime, we just let Zig Zag pick his next victim?"

"There is nothing that could make me go back there, Elisa. Nothing and no one." Beneath her mane of wild hair and white makeup, Jacqueline looked threatening. "That place is where I turned into what I am now! That's where ... where *he* came into my life! I will never go back. Not even if *he* wants me to ..."

She brusquely stopped, as if she'd just realized what she said.

"Jacqueline ...," Blanes said soothingly.

"I'm not a person!" With a horrifying expression on her face, the paleontologist began pulling her hair as though she wanted to rip it out. "This isn't life! I'm not alive! I'm sick! Contaminated! And that's where I got contaminated! There's nothing that can make me go back there. Nothing!" She raised her hands like claws, as if to defend herself against some physical attack. Her pants hung low on her hips, provocatively low. It was both a sensual and a depressing picture.

Hearing her scream, rage rose like steam in Elisa's head. She stood and faced Jacqueline.

"You know something, Jacqueline? I'm sick and tired of hearing you talk like you're the only one suffering here! You think you've had a hard time over the past ten years? Join the club. You used to have a profession, a husband and child? Well let me tell you what I had: my youth, my dreams, my future, my whole life ahead of me ... You lost your self-respect? I lost my stability, my sanity ... I still live on that damn island every single night." Her eyes were brimming with tears. "Even now, even tonight, with everything I know, something inside me feels guilty for not being at home, in my room, dressed like a slut, waiting for him, waiting to obey his disgusting orders, scared sick when I feel him approach and disgusted with myself for not being able to fight him off. I swear I want to get off that island forever, Jacqueline. But if we don't go back there, we'll never be able to leave. Don't you see?" she asked. And then, without warning, she nastily shrieked, *"Can't you fucking see that, Jacqueline?"*

"Jacqueline, Elisa," Blanes whispered. "We shouldn't ..."

His attempt at reconciliation was aborted when the door opened.

"He got Silberg. Hunted him down."

Moments later, when she thought about it rationally, it occurred to her that Carter couldn't have expressed it better. *Zig Zag is hunting us. We're his prey.*

"It was midflight. One of my men just called. It must have happened in a matter of seconds, because the pilots had already spoken to the escorts and everything was fine ... When they landed, the escort realized the cabin lights were out and went to have a look with flashlights. The guards were on the floor, floating in a sea of blood, totally out of their minds, and Silberg was ripped to shreds and strewn all over the seats. My contact didn't see it, but he heard them say it looked like a slaughterhouse."

"My God. Reinhard ..." Blanes sunk lifelessly into his chair.

Jacqueline's scream broke the silence. It was a thin, little voice, like that of a little girl. Elisa hugged her tight and whispered whatever words of consolation she could muster. She felt Víctor's comforting hand on her shoulder and thought that never had such simple physical contact made her feel closer to anyone as it did at that moment. People who have never known true fear don't know what a hug can mean, even when offered in love.

"The good news is that Silberg sent the documents to the safe address I gave him in case of emergency." Carter paced the room, picking up little things on the shelves in the room and putting them back down again. He hadn't stopped fidgeting since he walked into the room. "Before we go, I'll stick them on a USB so we'll have them at our disposal." He stopped and looked at them. "I don't know about you, but I'd be thinking about getting out of here. There will be time enough to cry later on."

"What's the plan?" Blanes asked bleakly.

"It's almost three. We'll have to wait for Harrison to leave the airport. My contact will let me know when he does. He'll take two or three hours to get back here. They'll have to seal the plane first, then put it in a military hangar and leave. He doesn't want anyone at a public airport getting wind of this."

"What's the point of waiting for him to leave?"

"Because, Professor, *we're* going to the airport," Carter replied sarcastically. "We'll be on a commercial jet, and I'm sure you wouldn't want the old man to see us at the boarding gate. Besides, I'll have to connect the hidden cameras for a while so he sees you and doesn't get suspicious. When he takes off, so will we. There are a few men outside who aren't on our side, but it shouldn't be too hard to lock them in a room and take their cell phones. That will buy us a little time. We'll take the seven o'clock Lufthansa flight to Zurich. I have friends there who can hide us someplace safe. And from there, we'll figure out our next step."

Elisa was still hugging Jacqueline. Suddenly, she spoke, quietly but firmly.

"Jacqueline, we're going to get rid of him. We're going to screw that … that son of a bitch for once and for all. And New Nelson's the only place we can do it ... OK?" Clissot looked at her, nodded. Elisa nodded to Blanes, too. He seemed hesitant, but he said, "Carter, what sort of shape is New Nelson in?"

"The station? A lot better shape than Eagle wants you to think. The warehouse explosion hardly damaged the equipment at all, and the accelerator has been repaired. They've maintained the instruments and have kept them in decent shape for the past few years."

"Do you think we could hide there?"

Carter stared at him.

"I thought you wanted to stay as far as possible from that haunted house, Professor. Have you come up with some way to fix this mess?"

"Maybe," Blanes replied.

"Well, I don't see any problem. We can go to Zurich first and from there to the island."

"Is it under surveillance?"

"You better believe it. Four coast guards armed to the teeth and a nuclear submarine, all at the coordinator's behest."

"And who's the coordinator?"

For what might have been the first time, Carter smiled.

SHIT *happens.* That's the only infallible popular wisdom there is. You don't have to be a great scientist to prove it. You're feeling fine until suddenly one day, out of the blue, you collapse like a house of cards; you plan something with painstaking detail, but you can't possibly cover every imaginable contingency; you predict what's going to happen over the next four hours, but five minutes later you're totally disproved.

Shit happens.

Harrison had thirty years of experience under his belt, and yet he could still be taken by surprise, downright shocked. Even horrified. Despite everything he'd seen over the course of his career, he knew that certain things were milestones. Markers. Events that divided everything into a before and an after. "It's like snow falling up," his father used to say. That was his expression. "Snow falling up." Something that changes you forever.

Like the inside of that Northwind.

That's what he was thinking, sheathed in his overcoat, hidden in his armor-plated Mercedes, as they sped back to Blanes's house. *Some things leave a mark.*

"There's no answer, sir."

His right-hand man was beside him. Harrison looked at him out of the corner of his eye. He was a young guy, with a neat black mustache and blue eyes; a doting father, devoted to his job, an Anglo-Saxon through and through. The kind of man you can say anything to, order to do anything, and know that he'll never question your decisions or ask uncomfortable questions. That was exactly why he had to keep him.... *pure,* if that was the right word. Yes, that might be it. Pure. Virginal. Isolated from the worst. Harrison was smart enough to know that you can let your mind go crazy, but you must never let your hands do the same.

"Should I try again, sir?"

"How many times have you called?"

"Three. It's very odd, sir. And there's still no picture on the screen, just interference."

That was why he hadn't let him get on that plane. It was the right decision. *May a red velvet curtain hide those things from you forever, kid. May you never see snow fall up.*

Of the three agents who had boarded the Northwind with him, two were taken to a hospital, as had the pilots and guards. The third was more or less OK, though he was heavily sedated. Harrison had coped, just like he had with Marini's remains in Milan. He had experience. He was a regular when it came to all things sick and horrifying.

"Call Max."

"I did. He's not answering either."

Dawn was just beginning to break. You could see the light coming over the treetops. It was going to be a beautiful March in the Madrid sierra, though Harrison couldn't care less. He was exhausted after the hours of stress at the airport, but he didn't have time to take a break. Not until he decided what to do with the remaining scientists, with those monsters (Professor Robledo included) who were responsible for horrors like the one he'd just seen inside that Northwind.

A van as dark and swift as his thoughts sped by in the other direction.

"We've got coverage now, sir. I'm trying all the channels, but ..."

Harrison blinked. He was running out of ideas, but with the few he had left he strung together a conclusion. *Neither Carter nor Max are picking up.*

Shit happens.

The scientists knew things that they shouldn't. They had found out, for example, how Marini, Craig, and Valente had collaborated on experiments Eagle wanted to carry out. Carter explained that Marini, having panicked about what was happening, had confessed everything to Blanes in a private conversation in Zurich. Harrison had proof of that conversation.

Carter had given it to him.

Paul Carter. An irreproachable guy, a born warrior, a brick wall of a man, and smart, too. Ex-military turned mercenary: the best kind possible. Harrison had known him for over ten years and thought he knew everything he needed to in order to say he trusted him 99 percent. Carter had fought (or trained the kids who fought) in the Sudan, Afghanistan, and Haiti, and was always available to someone who could pay him for his services. Eagle, on Harrison's own recommendation, had bought him (paying his weight in gold) to coordinate the military side of Project Zig Zag. He had only one rule, as far as Harrison knew. Just one code that he lived by: his safety, and that of his men. That lent him a certain ...

His safety, and that of his men.

Harrison fidgeted on the comfortable leather seat.

"I don't know what to make of it, sir. Max said he'd stay at the house with Carter and ..."

A lightbulb clicked on in his brain. *That van.*

"Dave," he said through the intercom, speaking to the driver without changing the tone of his voice. "Dave, turn around."

"Excuse me?"

"Turn around. We're going back to the airport."

BRAIN *drain.* Wasn't that the term they used to explain the sad state of science in countries like Spain? Víctor tried to distract himself with word games. *Three scientists are going down the brain drain, like taxpayers' money. They're fleeing like fleas. To be hidden in Switzerland, like dirty money; to hide from the authorities and save their hides.* And there he was with the rest of them at Madrid's Barajas International Airport, Terminal One, waiting for Carter to get their boarding passes with fake passports at the Lufthansa counter. He hadn't even been able to say good-bye to his family, though he'd managed to phone Teresa (the department secretary) to tell her that he and Elisa had come down with the same virus and would be out for a few days. He'd taken delight in that lie.

It was almost six thirty, but you couldn't see daylight in that part of the terminal. Just early birds (both men and women) coming and going, carrying leather briefcases and standing in line. The only thing Víctor had in common with them was that he was tired. He'd been up all night listening to creepy, horrific stories about an invisible, sadistic assassin that everyone was desperate to get away from. He was terrified and tired, in equal parts. On the plane, no doubt, fatigue would overcome fear and he'd get some sleep. But for now he felt like he was on a caffeine drip.

"Harrison probably knows what's happened by now," Elisa said. Looking at her, Víctor again thought that not even the most exhausting night either of them had ever had could decrease her beauty. *What a gorgeous woman.* Her long, jet-black hair drove him wild; it framed her intelligent face beautifully. He felt lucky to be with her. The smiles she flashed him, and simply being by her side, made up for everything. It was cold at the airport, or maybe that was just the excuse he used to put his arm around her. *Misery loves company.* That was another saying. A cliché. Like brain drain. But cliché or not, Elisa did seem comforted by that arm around her shoulders.

"He might," Blanes admitted. "But the Zurich plane takes off in less than an hour, and Carter's sure Harrison has no idea where we're going."

"Can we trust him?" she asked, eyeing his broad back as he leaned over the ticket counter.

"He wants to get out of here as bad as we do, Elisa."

Carter came back, fanning out their boarding passes like a blackjack dealer. Víctor was glad he was so cool under pressure, such a natural leader. He didn't need to say anything to get them moving, following him like little lambs, Jacqueline's heels clicking away.

"Do you think Harrison knows by now?" Blanes asked, looking around.

"It's possible." Carter shrugged. "But I know him, and I've tried to second-guess him. Right about now, he'll be at the house, confused, shouting orders and wondering what happened. I left him a few false trails. By the time he figures it all out, our plane will be in the air."

HARRISON stepped into Barajas International Airport's Terminal One, speaking on his cell phone. He'd acted fast. Much faster—he was guessing—than Carter could ever have imagined. He hadn't *lucked* into the position as Eagle's head of security because he was interested in science projects.

"You're right, sir," the voice on the other end of the line said.

"He just checked in five passengers on the seven o'clock Lufthansa flight to Zurich, using fake passports. They recognized him at the counter. E-mailing them his photo was a great idea. He's probably on his way to the gate right now."

Harrison nodded silently and hung up. He knew Paul Carter well. He might be a traitor, but he was the same old mercenary using the same old tactics. *You're going to have a big surprise, Paul.* He glanced at his watch, striding quickly toward the gate with his right-hand man. Six forty-five.

"Have you spoken to Blázquez?" he asked without slowing.

"They're going to delay the flight, sir. The Spanish police have been alerted, too. We'll get them at passenger control."

Harrison congratulated himself, not for the first time, about the state of international panic the world had been living in for over a decade now. Everyone was so afraid of terrorists that orders to do things like delay a flight or detain five suspects in a foreign country where he had no jurisdiction were obeyed in the blink of an eye. Fear was quite useful, even in Europe.

A woman pushing a luggage carrier got in his way. Harrison almost crashed into her and cursed under his breath. His man pushed her aside without stopping. At the same time, Harrison heard the announcement over the loudspeaker, first in Spanish and then in English: "Lufthansa announces that the departure of its Zurich flight will be delayed due to mechanical problems."

They had them now.

"We repeat, the departure of the Lufthansa flight to Zurich ..."

BLANES paled visibly as they rushed to the security line.

"Carter did you hear that? The flight's been delayed."

There were six passengers putting their luggage onto the conveyor belt. Beyond them, a group of uniformed men seemed to be having some sort of confab. Not a single passenger was making it through without a thorough search.

"Flights are often delayed, Professor. Don't get all worked up about it," Carter replied. He passed one of the lines and headed for the next one, his head twisting and turning, straining from side to side on his wide neck, attempting to see something.

Blanes and Elisa exchanged looks.

"Have you seen all those cops, Carter?" Blanes insisted nervously.

Rather than reply, Carter kept walking. He passed the last passenger in line and didn't stop there, either. Then he turned toward the exit. The scientists trailed behind, baffled.

"Where are we going?" Blanes asked.

A black minivan awaited them just outside. The man who was driving hopped out. Carter took his place behind the wheel and turned the key of the ignition.

"Get in, let's go!" he shouted.

Only after they were all settled into the back and the car had taken off did he explain.

"You didn't really think we were going to Zurich on a commercial flight, traveling on tickets bought right at the airport, did you?" He backed up and then accelerated. "I know Harrison. I'm one step ahead of him. I was pretty sure he'd send my description to the authorities ... though it's true he moved faster than I expected. Let's just hope he takes the bait and buys the Zurich story for as long as possible."

Elisa glanced at Víctor and Jacqueline in the backseat; they looked as disconcerted as she felt. If Carter were telling the truth, he was the best ally they could possibly have.

"So we're not going to Zurich?" Blanes asked.

"Of course not. I never even considered it."

"Why didn't you tell us?"

Carter pretended not to hear. After maneuvering skillfully between two vehicles and then getting on the freeway, he finally replied.

"If you're going to depend on me from here on out, Professor, you'd better learn one thing: the truth is something you never *tell;* it's something you *do.* The only thing you tell are lies."

Elisa wondered if, at that moment, he was telling the truth.

"THEY'RE gone."

That was all he could think, his sole conclusion. His colleague had planned it all very carefully. Maybe he'd never even intended to go to Switzerland. Maybe he had private transport, maybe they'd gone to another airport.

For a moment, he couldn't breathe. He was hyperventilating so intensely that without a word, he had to get up and leave the room where the head of Barajas International Airport was briefing him. He walked out into the hall. His man followed.

"They're gone," Harrison repeated once he got his breath back. "Carter's on their side."

He knew why, now, too. *He's trying to save his own skin. He knows this is the most dangerous thing he's ever had to face in his life, and he wants the scientists to help him survive.*

He took a deep breath. Suddenly, the prospects weren't looking so good.

Zig Zag might be the enemy. The Enemy, with a capital E, the most fearful thing of all. But now he knew that Carter was another kind of enemy. And even though the two weren't comparable, his old colleague was no trifling adversary.

From that moment on, he'd have to be exceedingly careful of Paul Carter.

EIGHT

The Return

I know well what I am fleeing from
but not what I am in search of.

MICHEL DE MONTAIGNE

28

BENEATH the rapidly setting sun, the island looked like a tiny rip in a sheet of wavy blue fabric. The helicopter circled over twice before beginning its descent.

Up until that minute, the idea of a strip of jungle floating in a tropical ocean had seemed more like an ad for a travel agency than a reality to Víctor. The kind of place you never go because it's so fake, just bait to lure in more customers. But when he saw New Nelson resting in the middle of the Indian Ocean, surrounded by rings of various shades of green, covered with palm fronds that looked like flowers (from above), white sands and coral reefs like huge necklaces in the sea, he had to admit he'd been wrong. Places like that really *did* exist.

And if the island were real, he reasoned—petrified—then everything he'd heard up until then took on a new verisimilitude.

"It looks like heaven on earth," he murmured.

Elisa, scrunched in beside him by the helicopter window, stared down, riveted.

"Well, it's hell," she said.

Víctor doubted it. Despite everything he'd heard, he couldn't believe that New Nelson could be worse than the airport in Sanaa, Yemen, where they'd spent the last eighteen hours waiting for Carter to tie up all the loose ends and get them to the island.

He hadn't been able to shower or change clothes, his bones ached from having slept on uncomfortable benches at the airport, and he'd had almost nothing to eat or drink besides potato chips, chocolate, and bottled water. And that after the highly distressing flight on the light aircraft they'd taken from Torrejón, Madrid's military air base, made all the more enjoyable by Carter's sarcastic comments.

"You call yourselves scientists, right? You know the expression 'in theory,' I presume. Well, 'in theory' you're going back to the place you left ten years ago, but don't blame me if that doesn't turn out to be the case."

"We never left" was Jacqueline Clissot's taciturn rejoinder. Unlike Elisa, Jacqueline had brought some clothes with her. She'd changed in Sanaa and now wore a baseball cap over her straight hair, a white summer blouse, and a denim miniskirt. At that moment, she looked out the other window, next to Blanes, but she turned her head away when the island came into view.

Víctor didn't care what they said. Regardless of whatever might be there waiting for them, at least it was the final stage of that maddening journey. He'd have time to take a shower, maybe even shave. He had his doubts about the possibility of finding any clean clothes there, but just maybe...

The helicopter jerked violently again. After lurching once more—the Arabic pilot assured them that it was the wind, but Víctor was inclined to think it was more a case of his piloting skills—they regained balance and descended toward what looked to be a landing pad made of sand. To the right was what appeared to be the ruins of a building and a pile of twisted metal.

"That's what's left of the garrison and the warehouse," Elisa said.

Víctor saw her shiver and put his arm around her.

From the air, the station looked a little like a bent fork. The tines were formed by three gray barracks with sloping roofs that were all connected at the northern end, and the handle was stumpy and round. He imagined that was where SUSAN, the electron accelerator, was stored. There were long, circular antennae on the roof above it, stretching their metallic skeletons up into the sky. The whole thing was enclosed by a huge, square, barbed-wire fence.

Víctor was one of the last ones out of the chopper. He followed Elisa to the steps—both of them bent double to avoid banging their heads on the roof (he was practically kissing her behind)—and jumped to the ground, feeling off-kilter from the flight, the sound of the chopper blades, and the sand. He stepped away from the helicopter coughing, and, when he took a breath, his lungs filled with several centimeters of island air. It wasn't as humid as he thought.

"There's a storm south of here, in the Chagos," Carter shouted from the helicopter. He had no trouble making himself heard over the noise of the rotors.

"Is that bad?" Víctor called, raising his voice.

Carter stared back at him as if he were a larva.

"It's good. It's dry weather that worries me, and that's what you normally get this time of year. As long as there are storms, no one will come close. Here, take this."

He held out a box with one hand. Víctor needed two to even lift it, and still he had a hard time not dropping the thing. He felt like a soldier transporting supplies. In fact, it was provisions that Carter had gotten in Sanaa: canned goods and pasta, several sizes of batteries for the flashlights and radios, munitions, and bottled water. The water was vitally important since the warehouse tank had been destroyed and Carter didn't know if they'd installed another one. Elisa, Blanes, and Jacqueline wandered over and got the rest of their baggage.

Víctor was lurching and staggering like a drunkard. The box was extraordinarily heavy. He saw Elisa and Jacqueline pass him, Elisa carrying two boxes (no doubt significantly lighter than his, but still, *two*). He felt pathetic and useless, and it made him remember how much he'd hated PE at school, and how humiliated he always felt when girls were stronger than him. Somehow the idea that a woman—especially one as attractive as Elisa or Jacqueline—had to be weaker than him was something still ingrained in the recesses of his mind. It was silly, he knew, but he couldn't get it out of his head.

As he struggled to make it to the barracks with his burden, he heard Carter behind him, shouting good-bye to the pilot. As head of security on New Nelson, he'd had no problem getting the coast guards to look the other way. And as he'd explained, there was very little chance of Eagle getting wind of their presence on the island, since the guardsmen were trustworthy. But he'd warned them that the helicopter would take off immediately. He didn't want to risk the chance of a military plane spotting them on a routine flyover. They had to be all alone. And as if to emphasize that fact, he heard the chopper's rotors begin to turn faster and looked up just in time to see it whir up into the air, sending flashes of the fading sunlight shooting out from the revolving blades before it faded into the distance. *All alone in paradise,* he thought.

Maybe that thought flustered him, because suddenly the box slipped from his hands. He managed to save it before it crashed to the ground, but one corner of it banged down on his foot. The searing pain smashed any more thoughts of paradise.

Luckily, no one had seen. They were all clustered together outside the door to the third barracks, probably waiting for Carter to let them in.

"Need some help?" Carter asked, passing him.

"No thanks, I'm fine ..."

Red as a beet and totally out of breath, Víctor limped off across the sand once more, his legs spread wide. Carter had already caught up to the others and brandished a bolt cutter as big as his arms. The noise of it cutting through the chain on the door was like a shot being fired.

"The house was empty, and no one came to sweep," he said, as if it were a song lyric, stopping to kick aside some debris with his boot.

It was 6:50 in the evening, island time, on Friday, March 13, 2015.

Friday the thirteenth. Víctor wondered if that would bring bad luck.

"IT looks so tiny now," Elisa said.

She stood in the doorway, sweeping the flashlight beam across what had been her bedroom on the island.

He started to think it might be hell after all.

He'd never seen a more depressing place in his life. The sheet-metal walls and floor were hot as an oven that had just baked several loaves of bread. Everything looked utterly dismal, there was no ventilation, and it stank to high heaven. Oh, and, of course, the barracks were significantly smaller than Elisa had made them out to be: a pathetic dining room, a pathetic kitchen, and totally barren rooms. The bedroom was nothing but naked walls, the bathroom barely had even the most basic features, and, of course, it was all covered in a thick layer of dust. Nothing resembling the dreamy facilities that Cheryl Ross had welcomed Elisa to ten years earlier. Elisa's eyes brimmed with tears and she smiled, surprised. She'd been sure she would feel no nostalgia whatsoever. Maybe she was just exhausted from the trip.

Víctor was slightly more impressed with the screening room, though it, too, was puny and stiflingly hot. Nevertheless, staring at the black screen, he couldn't help but tremble. Could they really have seen Jerusalem during Christ's lifetime on that monitor?

The control room, however, was the place that left him dumb-founded.

A cement-walled chamber almost a hundred feet wide and 120 feet long, it was the biggest, coolest room at the station. There were still no lights (Carter had gone to check out the generators), but Víctor could make out, through the dusky light coming through the windows, the shiny backside of SUSAN, and he was spellbound. He was a physicist, and nothing he'd seen or heard in his entire life could possibly compare with that piece of equipment. He felt like a hunter who, having heard stories of amazing kills, was finally seeing the gun that had fired the shots and could no longer doubt the rest.

Then, startled, he jumped. The fluorescent lights flickered on above him and everyone blinked. Víctor looked at the others as if for the first time, and suddenly realized he was going to live with these people. But he didn't mind, especially not about Elisa and Jacqueline. Blanes wasn't bad company, either. It was only Carter, who just then appeared through a small door to the right of the accelerator, who had no place in his world.

"Well, you'll have power so you can play with your computers and heat up food." He'd taken off his jacket and some random gray chest hairs peeked out over the top of his shirt. His biceps bulged, too large for his sleeves. "The problem is that there's no water. And we can't use the air-conditioning if we want anything else to work. I don't trust the backup generator, and the other one is still busted. And that means it's going to be hot," he added, smiling. There was not a drop of sweat on him, though, and Víctor realized that the rest of them were drenched from head to toe. Listening to him talk, he never knew if Carter was mocking them or if he actually wanted to help them. *Maybe both,* he decided.

"There's another reason to save electricity, too," Blanes said. "Up until now we've always done the opposite: avoid the darkness at all costs. But it's obvious that Zig Zag *consumes* all the energy he can find. Lights, appliances, computers that are on ... that's all food to him."

"And you want him to starve," said Carter.

"I don't know how much it'll help. He uses varying amounts of electricity. In Silberg's plane, for example, all he had to do was burn out the cabin lights. But I think it's best not to give him too much to choose from."

"That can be arranged. We'll disconnect the overall power supply and use only computers and the microwave to heat up food. We've got more than enough flashlights."

"Well, let's get going." Blanes turned to the others. "I'd like us all to work together. We can use this room as our base. There are enough tables and it's plenty big. We'll split up the tasks. Elisa, Víctor: we need to find the speed at which the attacks occur. Why does Zig Zag act over several continuous days and then 'rest' for a few years? Is it related to the amount of energy consumed? Is there a concrete pattern? Carter will give you detailed reports on the murders. I'll work with Reinhard's conclusions and Marini's files. Jacqueline, you can help me sort through the files ..."

While they were all nodding, something happened.

They were tired, or maybe it happened too fast for anyone to react. One second, Carter was on Blanes's right, rubbing his hands together, and the next he'd jumped to the computer chair and was stamping the ground beneath the table. Then he puffed out his chest and looked at them all like a ticket taker interrupting the first-class passengers' conversation.

"Well, Professor, looks like even bad students have their uses. At least they can clean the erasers after class." With dramatic flourish, he bent down and picked up a squashed snake. "I'm guessing his family is close by. It might not look like it, but we *are* in the jungle and little creatures often come inside in search of food."

"It's not poisonous," said Jacqueline, unflustered, taking it from him. "Looks like a simple green swamp snake."

"Still disgusting, though, isn't it?" Carter snatched it back, walked over to a metal trash can and dropped the coiled snake in, its guts spilling out. "Evidently, we need more than brains here. We need a little brawn, too. And that reminds me, I need some help, too. Someone to deal with our provisions, cooking, organizing, taking turns on guard duty, maybe cleaning a little ... You know, all of life's unpleasant details."

"I'll do it," said Víctor immediately, glancing at Elisa. "You can take care of the calculations yourself." She saw Carter smile, as though he found Víctor's offer amusing.

"Good," said Blanes. "Let's get moving. How much time do you think we have, Carter?"

"You mean before Eagle sends in the cavalry? Two, three days, tops, and that's presuming they buy the story I told in Yemen."

"That's not long."

"Well, that's the optimistic view, Professor." Carter replied. "Harrison's smart as a fox, and I seriously doubt he'll buy it."

THE good thing about people who are sad all the time is that when things take a turn for the worse, they seem to brighten a little. As though realizing they had nothing to complain about to begin with. And that's exactly what happened to Víctor. He couldn't say he was *happy,* exactly, but he did feel sort of exalted, like he had a renewed zest for life. His days of aeroponic plants and reading philosophy were long gone. This was a savage world he was living in, one that made new demands on him by the minute. And he liked feeling useful. He'd always felt that no skill is worth much if it doesn't help others, and now was the time to put that belief into practice. All afternoon he opened boxes, swept, and cleaned, following Carter's orders. He was exhausted, true, but he'd discovered that fatigue could be addictive, like a drug.

At one point, Carter asked him if he could cook using a microwave.

"I can make stew," he replied.

Carter stared.

"So make it."

It was clear that the ex-soldier was taking advantage of him, but he obeyed without grumbling. After all, how satisfying was staying home alone working all the time? Now he could actually help other people just by carrying out simple tasks.

He opened several cans, a bottle of oil, and some vinegar, and did what he could, taking advantage of the scarce natural light coming in through the window to create, if not a masterpiece, at least something that might qualify as a decent home-cooked meal. He'd taken off his sweater and shirt and worked bare chested. The air was so dense and heavy with sweat that he thought he might gag, but that just made his mission all the more real. He was a miner making dinner for his exhausted companions, a cabin boy sweeping down the deck.

Amazing circumstances were cropping up all over the place. At one point, Elisa actually walked into the kitchen with her jeans *in her hands*. All she was wearing was a spaghetti-strap top and a tiny pair of panties, and she was sweating profusely. She'd put her thick black hair up into a ponytail.

"Víctor, do we have anything I could use to cut these? Some shears or something? I'm sweating like a pig."

"I think I've got just the thing."

Carter had brought a huge box of tools that lay open in the next room. Víctor selected the steel cutters. It was a marvelous, spontaneous moment between them. He could never have dreamed of a situation like that occurring to him, especially with Elisa. She even smiled; they joked.

"Higher, no, higher, cut them here," she pointed.

"Wow, these are going to be real minipants. Even as short shorts, they'll be short ..."

"I don't care. Jacqueline doesn't have anything to lend me, and I'm boiling."

He thought of his previous life, when he used to feel lucky if he got to have coffee with her in Alighieri's clinical surroundings. And now here they were practically naked (him from the waist up, and her in panties), deciding how short to cut her shorts. He was still scared (and she clearly was, too), but there was something in their fear that made him feel he could handle anything, pleasant or unpleasant. Fear was liberating.

By the time dinner was ready, it was dark and the heat was less stifling. A breeze, almost strong enough to qualify as wind, blew in through the dining room's puny window. Víctor could see clumps of darkness swaying in the night, out past the barbed-wire fence. He put a paper tablecloth down, set places for each of them, and placed a portable lamp in the center of the table like a chandelier. He even tried to serve with flourish, though it didn't really work. Dinner was hurried and silent. No one spoke at all, and Elisa, Jacqueline, and Blanes rushed back to the control room to work some more as soon as they finished eating.

Víctor cleared the table and turned on the transmitter in his jeans pocket. Of all the sounds coming through, he could pick out Elisa's breath. He thought of breath like a fingerprint, and there was hers, the unmistakable pant of her alto voice. He could also make out the scratches of her pencil on paper.

The transmitters had been Blanes's idea, and Carter's stony face soured when he heard it, as if to say, "Professor, leave the practicalities to me," but in the end he'd agreed (not without objecting) to get two-way radios and give them to everyone.

"They're not going to do any good, genius. Silberg was ripped to shreds right in front of the bodyguards on the plane, remember? And Stevenson got it on a micro barge smaller than this room, in front of five men who didn't see or hear a thing."

"I know," Blanes admitted, "but I still think we should be in constant contact. It's just more reassuring, OK?"

That's why Víctor's ears buzzed and crackled with Jacqueline, Elisa, and Blanes's voices—and probably with his own noises, he thought, taking care to be quiet when he cleared the table (he'd have to wash the dishes later using tubs of seawater that Carter had brought up from the beach). Just then, Carter called him.

"Take a flashlight, go down to the pantry, and see what's on the top shelves, in case there's anything we can use. You're taller than me, and we don't have a ladder."

Víctor asked him to repeat himself. Ever since they'd arrived on the island, Carter had showed zero interest in speaking Span-

ish, and although Víctor's English was pretty decent, sometimes
that man seemed to speak gobbledygook. Finally deciphering the
message, he complied submissively, grabbing a flashlight and
heading next door to the dark room. To the open trapdoor.

The gaping black hole.

He shined the light on the opening, saw the ladder leading
down, and had a sudden realization. *This is where he killed the
older woman. What was her name? Cheryl Ross ...*

He looked up. Carter was still in the kitchen dealing with
something. He looked back at the trapdoor. *What's wrong? Is
making stew all you're good for?* He took a deep breath and started down the ladder. Elisa's cough came through the transmitter
in his pocket, distinguishable above the interference. Would she
have heard Carter's order? Would she know what he was doing
right then?

When the pantry roof swallowed him up, he shone the flashlight around. He saw metal shelves crowded with items. The dirt
floor showed no signs of what he'd expected (and feared), though
he examined it carefully. It was cool down there, even a little chilly
compared with the sticky heat of the kitchen.

Víctor saw a gray metallic door at the back, its frame all
boarded up.

He recalled Elisa telling him that everything had happened in
that back room.

Behind that door.

He shuddered. After climbing down the final rungs of the
ladder, he decided it was best just to concentrate on the task at
hand.

Starting with the shelf on the right, Víctor stood up on his tip-
toes and swept the flashlight beam across the top shelf. He saw
two boxes of what looked like crackers and rusty metal cans of
something that was obviously not food. It reminded him of a riddle he'd solved in which a Chinese man points to a *rusty* nail to
say "lusty." *Metal* would be "metar." A hushed conversation came

over the transmitter, muffled by static. Blanes and Elisa were talking about something related to UT (universal time) computations and energy periods. The vibrato on Elisa's voice made his groin tingle.

"Christ, turn that shit off." Suddenly, Carter's boots were behind him, coming down the ladder. "It's bullshit, no matter what our resident genius says."

This time Víctor didn't obey. He didn't even reply. He just kept searching the top shelf until he found some more boxes.

Suddenly, there was a hand on his crotch. A huge hand. He jumped a mile, but not before Carter's thick, stubby fingers had jammed themselves down into Víctor's tight jeans pocket and turned off the transmitter.

"Whoa! What are you *doing?*" he shrieked.

"Relax, Father, you're not my type." Carter flashed a smile in the darkness. "I told you, those transmitters are worthless pieces of shit, and I don't like being eavesdropped on."

Víctor swallowed his anger and went back to his task.

"Please don't call me 'Father.' I'm a physics professor."

"Oh, I thought you studied theology or religion or something."

"What makes you say that?"

"I heard you say something to the Frenchy at the airport in Yemen last night. And I've seen you pray a couple of times, too."

Víctor was surprised at Carter's subtle powers of observation; this was a new side to the man. It was true he'd spoken to Jacqueline about his readings, and he had prayed several times during the trip (he'd never been so motivated in all his life!), but always discreetly, barely even mouthing the Our Father. He didn't think anyone had noticed.

"I'm Catholic," he said. He reached out to lean on one of the boxes and peered over to see what was in it. More cans. He pulled one out. Beans.

"All the same to me, scientist or priest." Carter had begun taking boxes down from the shelves on the left. "Both the scum of the earth, as far as I'm concerned: one invents weapons and the other blesses them."

"And soldiers fire them," Víctor replied pointedly, despite the fact that he really didn't want to start a fight. He checked the expiration date on the can of beans and saw that they were four years too late. Dropping it back in the box, he shone the light onto the next one. Cardboard packages. He stuck his hand in and tried to pull one out.

"Tell me, then," Carter said, behind him. "What does God mean to you?"

"God?"

"Yeah. What does God mean, to you?"

"Hope," he said, after thinking about it for a little while. "And to you?"

"Depends on the day."

The package was stuck. Víctor rattled the box violently. A quick, black shadow darted out inches from his hand and scurried up the wall.

"Oh my God! *Dios mío!*" Víctor yelped in Spanish, jumping back instinctively.

"Now that's *definitely* not God," Carter replied, adding, "*No es Dios*" in Spanish for dramatic effect as he shone his light on the ceiling. "That's a cockroach. Big, yes, but no need to exaggerate ..."

"Big? It's enormous!" Víctor felt sick. He could feel the stew churning in his stomach.

"That's a tropical roach, no artificial colors or preservatives. I've been in places where seeing one of those was enough to make your mouth water. Where seeing a roach crawl by was like scoping a deer."

"I don't think I want to visit those places."

The ex-soldier snorted.

"Well, this *is* one of those places, Father. If you want, I'll take the boards off that door and show you."

Víctor turned to the door and then back to Carter. In the flashlight's glow, the door and Carter's steely eyes were the same color.

"I can't say it's the worst thing I've ever seen, after Craig, Petrova, and Marini. But I can say that what I saw behind that door was the worst thing I'd ever seen up until that moment. And I've seen a lot of things, believe me." Carter's breath was visible, just barely, in the cold of the pantry. The flashlight made his eyes flicker. It was as though he was on fire inside. "Good soldiers, like Stevenson and Bergetti, people who think on their feet, who've been through a lot, they went nuts after seeing what was down here. And Harrison, Eagle's man who's after us right now, even he lost his marbles. He's seen more victims than anyone else, and he's completely deranged. He has panic attacks, crises, shit like that. And Harrison is not exactly a sensitive guy."

Víctor's Adam's apple bobbed in a useless attempt to swallow. Carter's voice trailed off a little, as though he were no longer addressing Víctor but speaking to the darkness surrounding him.

"I'm going to tell you something. Thousands of miles from here, my wife and daughter live in a house in Cape Town. They're black. I have a gorgeous, gorgeous black daughter. She's ten years old and has beautiful curly hair and the biggest eyes you've ever seen. Her smile is so sweet I could stare at her all day; I'm besotted. My wife's name is Kamaria. Means 'like the moon' in Swahili. She's tall and stunning and dark as ebony, with a perfect, firm body. I'm so in love with her sometimes I think I'll lose my mind. And for two years, not a night has gone by that I don't dream of locking her up in this pantry and tearing her to pieces. Doing exactly what *he* did to Cheryl Ross. I can't help it. He appears, orders me to do it, and I obey. I rip my own daughter's eyeballs out and eat them."

He fell silent, breathing deeply. Then he turned back to Víctor, calm and indifferent.

"I'm scared, Father. Like a little boy who's afraid of the dark. Ever since all this started, I scream if a friend startles me. I'm scared shitless if I have to spend the night alone. I've never been so scared in my whole life. And I know that if your God exists, then this *thing* is the opposite of God. The Antihope. The Antigod. The Antichrist. Isn't that what you call it?"

"Yes."

Carter stared at him.

"Don't worry, though. He's after us, not you. If your friends don't find a way out of this soon, he'll kill us all, but he won't kill you. You'll just lose your mind." Suddenly, he was scornful. "So stop being such a sissy about the fucking cockroaches and get back to opening boxes."

Then he turned on his heel and left.

HE woke up with a start. He was at home. He and Ric Valente were cutting up girls' pants. Everything else (the island, the murders) had been a bad dream, thank goodness. The unconscious works in mysterious ways, he thought.

"Look at this," Ric was saying. He'd invented a machine that shredded pants at top speed.

But that wasn't right. He was on the floor, his bare back pressed against a cold metal wall. He recognized the station's narrow galley kitchen. Daylight streamed in through the window. But that wasn't what woke him up.

"Víctor?" The two-way radio on the shelf was talking to him. "Are you there, Víctor? Could you get Carter and come to the screening room?"

"Did you find something?" he asked, struggling to stand up.

"Just come as fast as you can," Blanes replied.

If the tone of his voice was anything to go by, he was terrified.

29

"THE image on the left is from a video; the one on the right is of a time string from the recent past, about twenty minutes ago. We opened it using the video. Look at the shadow behind it ..."

Blanes went up to the screen and scrolled his index finger down the image on the right, to demonstrate. The photos were very similar. They showed a brown laboratory rat with whiskers around its snout and little pink claws. But the one on the right had a slightly sepia tone and a dark halo, as if it had been superimposed several times.

There were other differences, too.

"The eyes on the second one ...," Elisa murmured.

"We'll get to that," Blanes cut her off. "Now, look at this." He walked across the room again and projected another image. "This is a copy of the Unbroken Glass. Notice anything?"

Everyone leaned forward. Even Carter, who stood in the doorway, came in for a closer look.

"There's a shadow around the glass ... like the rat ...," Jacqueline ventured.

"Exactly. We thought it was just a blurry image, but it's actually the split."

"What's that?" asked Elisa.

"Marini explains it all in his files. He discovered it and never let me know ..." Blanes was obviously nervous, almost in a state of anguish. Elisa had never seen him like this before. As he spoke, he flicked between images on the screen, rapidly clicking through them with the mouse. "It seems that when we obtained the Unbroken Glass, something strange happened. He saw the *same* glass twenty minutes, three hours, and nineteen hours after the experiment. It just kept reappearing before him: on a bus, in bed, out on the street ... Only he could see it. When he tried to pick it up, it would disappear. He thought he was hallucinating, so he didn't say anything about it. But he started experimenting on his own and quickly learned that the images obtained from recent time strings had that effect on objects. Then he tried living creatures: rats, at first. He'd film them and open time strings from the recent past. From then on, the same rat would appear every certain time, just like with the glass: at home, in the car, wherever he was ... and only to him. The rats didn't *do* anything, they just appeared. But the lights in the surrounding sixteen inches or so would go out. Marini was sure that the rat was using that energy to appear. He called the appearances splits. He deduced they were the direct consequence of joining the past with the present."

The rats on the screen switched to cats and dogs.

"He started practicing on bigger animals and noticed other properties. Although there might be several animals in an image, only one would split, and not always the same one. He thought it was random. He could predict which one it would be by the shadows around the open time string image, which seemed to be how it began. He also discovered that if the animal died, there was no split. So you could never have a dead animal and also have the *same* animal be alive, even if they were from different time strings. Once armed with that information, he recruited Craig. They did some more tests and concluded that the splits were real, but that they only appeared in the space-time of whoever had done the testing."

"How is that possible?" Víctor asked. "I mean, how can any object or living being be in two different places simultaneously?"

"Well, keep in mind that each time string is unique, and so is everything they contain within them, including objects and living beings. Reinhard had an interesting way of explaining it. He said that every fraction of a second, we are someone new. The idea that we're always the same is an illusion created by the brain to keep us from losing our minds. Maybe schizophrenics just pick up on the different beings that we all are throughout time. But when you isolate a time string from the recent past, the unique objects and beings inside it are also isolated from the passing of time and ... they keep living for the corresponding period."

Carter snorted loudly and changed position, leaning one hand against the doorframe.

"If you don't understand, just ask, Carter," Blanes said.

"I'd have to start by asking if we even speak the same language," Carter sneered. "Nothing you've said has made any sense to me. It's all a bunch of mumbo jumbo."

"Just a minute," Elisa interrupted. The colors on the screen were reflected onto her bare legs as she sat straddling her chair. "Go back a second, put that last image back up ... No, not that one, one more, the enlargement of the rat's wound ... That one."

The sepia photo took up the whole screen, showing a deep gash on the rodent's nose and another cut on its haunches. But they were clean cuts, with no blood.

"Does that remind you of anything, Jacqueline? That mutilation?" Elisa could tell that the paleontologist had already caught on.

"The Jerusalem Woman ..."

"And the dinosaur feet. Nadja pointed it out to me ..."

"Notice, too, that you can't see several of the dogs' or cats' pupils," Blanes pointed out. "You were going to say that before, weren't you, Elisa?"

White eyes. Elisa caught her breath.

"What does that mean?" Víctor asked.

"Marini and Craig figured it out. It actually occurs on parts other than the face and extremities, too. Wait." He flicked back to the Unbroken Glass and enlarged the image. "Look at the right side. There are tiny particles of glass missing ... even ... Look, can you see those minute holes in the center? They aren't bubbles; there are actually tiny pieces missing. Our brains only tend to perceive what we could call the most anthropomorphic defects: on faces, fingers ... But *all* of the objects from the past, including the earth, the clouds, they are all mutilated ... The explanation is mind blowing ... and very simple, really."

"Planck time," Elisa murmured; it had suddenly hit her.

"Exactly. We thought of these images as photographs, or recordings. We *knew* that they weren't, but unconsciously we made ourselves believe it. But these are open time strings. Each string corresponds to a Planck time, the shortest possible interval of reality, so brief that light can hardly travel through it. Matter is made of atoms: nuclei of protons and neutrons with electrons spinning around them, but in such a short space of time that the electrons haven't had time to fill the object completely, no matter how solid it is. There are gaps, holes. Our faces, our bodies, a table, even a mountain would all look incomplete, mutilated. But we only realized it when we saw the Jerusalem Woman."

"Are you saying that during that time we *have* no face?" Carter asked.

"We might or might not, but most likely we don't have *all* of it. Imagine a frying pan with a few drops of oil in it. If you tilt it around enough, eventually the oil will cover the whole bottom of the pan, but that takes time. In a Planck time, it's more likely that there are still places the electrons haven't been able to reach: our eyes, part of our face or head, an extremity, viscera. On such a tiny scale of time and space, we're constantly changing, and not just in appearance. You can't even send a thought from one neuron to another during one Planck time. It's just too fleeting. So, again, what I'm saying is that we are actually *other beings* in each time string. A whole different person. There are as many different beings in us as there are time strings that have transpired since we were born."

"I can't get my head around that," Jacqueline murmured.

"Professor, you know what?" Carter scratched his head, smiling. "I was one of those kids at school who always wanted results. I never bothered with the fluff, the process, I just wanted the answer. Your documentary is fascinating and everything, but what I want to know is, who's been taking us out one by one for the past ten years? Who makes us all have nightmares every damn night, and how can we butcher him?"

"We'll get to that in a second," Blanes replied, opening another file. "Marini and Craig had worked with animals and objects, but never humans. That was too risky: who would ever volunteer to be split? And that's when they thought of Ric Valente."

The next image, totally unexpected, made Elisa's stomach lurch. On the screen, surrounded by numbers, sat Ric Valente, in front of a computer. Elisa recognized the setting immediately.

"Ric started filming himself at night, in the control room, and he used those images to study *his own* splits. He proved that human beings appeared in different time periods; it was an area twelve or fifteen feet in diameter. Ric told Marini that those apparitions really affected him."

She remembered the afternoon she'd come upon him on the beach, utterly engrossed in God's knows what. Could he have been watching one of his own splits? When he saw her, was *that* the cause of their argument, when she thought it was about his not having turned in his results yet?

"One night in September, something else happened. Ric was exhausted, and he fell asleep while the camera was filming. When he woke up, he continued the experiment and opened a time string from ten minutes earlier, when he'd been asleep. A totally different kind of split was produced." Blanes's voice was more anxious now. He showed several slides full of equations. "The first difference was that it appeared almost immediately after the experiment, much faster than Ric was expecting. The area affected was far greater, too: the whole control room lost power. But that wasn't all. It actually *sucked Ric into the time string*. For that brief period of time, the room became a dark world with strange holes in the walls and floor ..."

"Holes?" Jacqueline asked.

"Yes, produced by the electron movement," Elisa answered, "like those supposed cuts on the face." Her chest was tight with anguish. Now she understood the meaning of the hole in her wall during that awful "dream."

"'Lags in the matter' is what Marini called them," Blanes said. "From the perspective of an observer who's actually *inside* a time string, the world looks incomplete. There are certain 'defects' that get filled when enough time has passed to situate all of the particles in their corresponding places, though other holes will open ..."

"So Ric would have seen these holes, these 'lags in the matter,' in his own body," Víctor said.

"No, he didn't see himself that way. His *split,* yes, but not himself. For him, it was just being naked in a world that came to a halt."

Like me, in my dream, Elisa thought.

"Naked?" Jacqueline asked.

"He couldn't perceive his clothes, jewelry, or anything else he wore. Just his body. Everything else was on the outside. The split brought only *him* into the time string."

Elisa turned to Blanes.

"Ric isn't the only one who's had that experience."

She felt all eyes turn to her. Alarmed, her cheeks burning in the dark, she added, "Nadja and I had it, too. And Rosalyn ..."

"I knew about Rosalyn," Blanes confessed. "She told Valente. Her split occurred the same night as his, and she was inside the time string, too. Of course, Rosalyn thought it was just an incredibly vivid dream, but Ric noticed that the lights in her bathroom had burned out and realized what had really happened."

Elisa stared at the equations on the screen without taking anything in. The mysterious jigsaw puzzling her all these years was starting to piece together. *That's what the man with no face was, the white eyes.* She recalled that she and Nadja had both thought it was Ric. What about everything else? How real was that attack she thought she'd suffered? She decided not to bring it up; it just wasn't something she could talk about. But then Blanes said something else.

"Rosalyn told Ric she'd dreamed that his double *attacked* her. He wasn't sure whether she was just exaggerating to make him feel guilty since he'd stopped showing any interest in her, but it worried him. What could have caused that difference? Before, the splits had hardly even moved, just floated like ghosts. He told Marini about it, and they put their heads together. They took long walks by the lake to discuss things in private–" "Sometimes they talked at the garrison," Carter broke in. "They knew none of you would sneak up on them there."

"Finally, Marini thought he found the explanation. The split, in this case, had come from one of the multiple 'personalities' that Ric had *while he was asleep.* So, in fact his *unconscious* was what split then. Sleep is a much more violent activity than we tend to think. Reinhard Silberg thought that the idea that we 'rest' while we're asleep might be an illusion produced by the passage of time. If seen isolated at every interval, our sleeping bodies are much more active than our waking ones: we move our eyes, hallucinate, become sexually excited ... Sergio deduced that either sleep or the unconscious produced a split of the most intimate, brutal part of ourselves."

"So ... that's what Zig Zag is," Jacqueline murmured. "A split produced from Ric's unconscious ..."

Blanes shook his head.

"No. Zig Zag appeared later, not until the night of October 1. That was an even more powerful kind of split. It can't be the same thing that Rosalyn, Elisa, and Nadja saw, because it used such a small amount of energy, and Zig Zag, in contrast, burned out both generators when he appeared. And he's been visiting the present for ten years now, at erratic intervals. That never happened in any of the other cases. We don't even really know if Ric produced him, though all indications would point to that. Valente kept a detailed diary, which Marini got hold of. In it, he wrote that even though Marini had asked him to stop testing with anyone who was asleep, due to the apparent risk, he planned to keep doing it on his own. He was very excited at the prospect. He wanted to find out more about those aggressive splits. They were something that *he'd* discovered. He said that for the first time in history, there was proof of how closely intertwined particle physics and Freudian psychology were. As much as I'd like to, I can't judge him too harshly on that. His last entry is from September 29, and in it he claims that on the night of Saturday, October 1, when the storm was at its most fierce, he was going to produce another split using a new image."

Jacqueline asked the question on everyone's lips.

"What image?"

Blanes closed down a few files and opened others.

"In his last entry, he wrote that he was thinking of using these ..."

He projected several blurry enlargements. Elisa and Jacqueline jumped out of their chairs at almost the exact same time.

"Holy fuck," Carter said.

The photos were all very similar. Each one showed a room with a bed and a sleeping figure. Elisa recognized herself immediately, as well as Nadja. The pictures had somehow been taken from the ceiling. It was them, in their bedrooms on New Nelson, ten years ago.

"The lights in our bedrooms had hidden cameras with infrared," Blanes explained. "Ric had live images of all of us at his disposal every night. Even you, Carter."

"Eagle wanted to spy on us," Carter said, nodding. "They were paranoid about the Impact."

It was all falling into place. Elisa now understood that when

Ric mentioned her solitary pleasures during their argument, he hadn't just been showing off. He really *had* seen her. He could see all of them.

"But which one of the damn pictures did he actually *use?*" Jacqueline almost shouted. More than asking Blanes, she seemed to direct her question at the screen.

"We don't know, Jacqueline. Ric carried out the experiment alone; he didn't even tell Marini about it."

"But...there must be...some documentation...a recording...," spluttered Carter, suddenly nervous. "There were hidden cameras in the control room, too ...," he added. But Blanes just shook his head.

"All records from that night were deleted when Zig Zag produced the blackout. He used all the energy around him and erased everything in the circuits. Ric might even have used another image of himself, though I doubt it. I think he tried one of these. He could have used anyone. But who knows *which* one?" He clicked through them again in reverse order.

"It couldn't have been just *any* of them ..." Elisa could hardly speak. "It couldn't have been Nadja, Marini, Craig, Ross, Silberg, or any of the soldiers."

"You're right. They're all dead, and you can't produce a split of anything dead. So that only leaves"—in that half-lit room, Blanes looked at them each in turn—"Elisa, Jacqueline, Carter, and me. And Ric, who's disappeared."

"But that means ..." Jacqueline had grown pale.

Blanes nodded gravely.

"Zig Zag is one of us."

THE female soldier's name was Previn, or at least that's what the nameplate on her uniform said. She had blond hair and blue eyes and, despite being plump, was attractive. Her most attractive quality, though, was that she kept her mouth shut. Lieutenant Borsello, on the other hand, the man in charge of the Tactics Division at the Imnia base in the Aegean, sat ensconced behind his desk and ran his mouth nonstop. They had one thing in common, though: they both pretended not to see Jurgens. The female soldier did not even glance in his direction, and the lieutenant did even better. He winked furtively at Jurgens and then turned quickly back to Harrison as if to say that he was a man who'd seen it all.

Harrison saw that he was pretending Jurgens's presence didn't unsettle him.

"It's a pleasure to have you here, sir," Borsello said. "I'm at your disposal, although I'm not sure if I understand exactly what it is you want."

"What I *want*..." Harrison seemed to toy with the word. "What I *want* is very simple, lieutenant: four angels, sixteen men, anti-contamination suits, and all the necessary equipment."

"To head out when?"

"Tonight. Within eight hours."

Borsello cocked an eyebrow. He still had that See-How-Nice-I-Am-to-Civilians look on his face, but Harrison saw that the knotted brow was in fact a categorical "no."

"I'm very sorry to say that's impossible. There's a typhoon north of the Chagos right now and it's headed straight for New Nelson. Angels are small choppers and there's over a fifty percent chance that..."

"Hydroplanes, then."

Borsello smiled empathetically.

"They wouldn't be able to land, sir. In a couple of hours, the waves around the island will be thirty feet high. It's totally out of the question. We're a modest outfit here on Imnia. Thirty men in my section. We'll have to wait until tomorrow."

Harrison looked at Previn, the woman. He returned Borsello's smiles and courtesies, but he looked at the man's subordinate. One thing he couldn't stand, one thing nothing could make him put up with, was the cratered moon, that pockmarked obstacle that was Borsello's ugly face.

"We can have a team ready first thing. Maybe even by dawn, if..."

"Can I have a word with you privately, Lieutenant?" Harrison interrupted.

Raised eyebrows, a contained effort to be polite, not to seem taken off guard. And not to look at Jurgens. But, finally, Borsello motioned and Previn vanished, closing the door behind her.

"What exactly do you want, Mr. Harrison?"

With that witch gone, Harrison felt more at ease. He closed his eyes and envisioned possible responses. *I want to kill the wasp buzzing in my ear. I could say that.* When he opened them, Borsello was still there, and, luckily, so was Jurgens. He gave a hint of a smile, like a gracious gentleman.

"I want to go to the island tonight, Lieutenant. And to take some of your men. If I could do this on my own, believe me, I wouldn't be troubling you right now."

"I understand. And I'm fully aware that I am to follow your instructions. Those are my orders, and they come from above. But I'm afraid that doesn't mean I can do something insane. I can't send angels into a typhoon. And,... if you'll allow me to speak freely ..." Harrison nodded. "According to our reports, the individuals you're looking for are on their way to Brazil. The Brazilian authorities have already been alerted. So I don't really understand your rush to get to New Nelson."

Harrison nodded again, as if Borsello had just revealed some absolute truth. It *was* true that all evidence seemed to indicate that Carter and the scientists had gone to Egypt after a stopover in Sanaa. His agents had interrogated a professional forger in Cairo who'd made them passports; Carter had demanded several entry visas for Brazil. That was their only solid clue.

And that exactly was why Harrison wasn't buying it. He knew Paul Carter well, and if he'd left a trail behind, then he *wasn't* on it.

Plus, he had another, more subtle piece of information: military satellites had detected an unidentified chopper flying over the Indian Ocean the day before. That didn't add up to much, because it hadn't gone to New Nelson, but Harrison had realized that the men in charge of reporting visits to the island were Carter's men.

He was sure *that* was the right path. He'd told Jurgens that morning, when they were flying to Imnia. "They're on the island. They went back." He even thought he knew why. *They've discovered how to kill off Zig Zag.*

But he had to act with the same diabolical cunning as his one-time partner. If he showed up on the island in daylight, the watchmen would alert Carter, and the same thing would happen if he ordered the coast guard to be moved or interrogated. It had to be a surprise attack; he had to make use of the fact that there would be no guards on duty during the storm. That was the only way he could catch them. The very idea of it made him tingle with excitement. And yet, what would he gain by telling this idiot his plan?

After all, he already had an unbeatable ally: Jurgens was on his side.

"It's true that we do have a lead about Brazil," he admitted. "It's a possibility, Lieutenant. But I want to discard the possibility of New Nelson before I follow that lead."

"And I want to help you, sir, but ..."

"You have direct orders from Tactics."

"I have orders to follow your instructions, but I repeat, I decide how and when to risk the lives of my men. This is a business, not an army."

"Your men will obey me, Lieutenant. They have direct orders, too."

"As long as I'm here, *my* men, sir, will obey *me*."

Harrison looked away, as if he'd lost all interest in the conversation. Instead, he glanced out at the calm, blue and yellow day outside, above the ocean, beyond the hermetically sealed window of Borsello's office. He almost wanted to cry, thinking that once, a long time before he'd started on Project Zig Zag, before his eyes and mind had come into such close contact with sheer horror, landscapes like that had moved him.

"Lieutenant," he said after a long pause, still gazing out the window. "Do you know the hierarchy of the angels?" Without waiting for a reply, he began listing them. "Seraphim, cherubim, thrones, dominions ... I'll take charge. I belong to a higher order, a superior hierarchy, infinitely superior to yours. I have seen far greater horrors, and I deserve respect."

"What do you mean by 'I'll take charge'?" Borsello asked, frowning.

Harrison stopped looking out the window and looked at Jurgens. Then Borsello did something surprising: he straightened up in his chair and stiffened, as if a high-ranking officer had just walked into the room. From the orifice between his eyebrows, a claret-colored drop emerged and slid down the bridge of his nose. The gun and silencer slipped back into Jurgens's jacket as quickly as they'd slipped out.

"That's what I mean, Lieutenant," Harrison said.

30

THEY'D moved into the dining room. In the gray morning light, the outlines of people and objects blended together. Carter sipped his coffee.

"Isn't there an easier explanation?" he asked. "Some lunatic, a sadist, a professional assassin, a terrorist organization ... something ... I don't know, something more *realistic,* for Christ's sake." He must have noticed the looks everyone was giving him, because he raised his hands in submission. "Just a question."

"Carter, *this* is the most realistic explanation," Blanes replied. "Reality is physics. And you know as well as I do that there's no other explanation." He counted off on his fingers one by one as he spoke, listing the evidence. "First, the speed and the silence: Ross was killed in less than two hours, Nadja in a matter of minutes, and Reinhard in a couple of *seconds.* Second, the unbelievable variety of places: in a pantry, on a barge, an apartment, a plane in midflight ... It's obvious that changing spaces is no problem because he *doesn't move through space.* Third, the mummification of the bodies showed that the amount of time that had passed was different for the victims than it was for all the objects around them. Finally, the degree of shock caused by seeing the scene of the crime, even in people accustomed to dead bodies. And why? Because of the Impact. Both Zig Zag's crimes and the images of the past produce Impact. Marini and Ric suffered from it when they saw the splits. All of that points to *one of us* being Zig Zag. That was what poor Reinhard realized."

"So what you're saying is, one of us might *be him* and not even know it?"

"Elisa, Jacqueline, you, or me," Blanes confirmed. "Or Ric. One of the people on the island ten years ago. One of the survivors. Unless it was Reinhard, it which case Zig Zag would now be dead. But I doubt that."

Jacqueline sat doubled over, elbows on her thighs, staring off into space as if she weren't hearing a thing. But suddenly she blinked and spoke up.

"If Ric's split wasn't that violent, then why is Zig Zag so savage?"

Blanes looked at her grimly.

"That's the key question. The only answer I can think of is the one Reinhard came up with: one of us is not what he or she seems."

"What?"

"All of our dreams … all the things we don't want to do but are impulses that take over …" Blanes was marking his words with emphatic gestures. "Zig Zag is *always* influencing us, even if we can't see him. He's in our subconscious; he makes us think, dream, and do certain things. That had never happened before with any of the other splits. Reinhard thought it had to come from a sick mind, an abnormal mind. That thought horrified him. Because the split was produced while the person was asleep, Zig Zag has taken on incredible strength. You once used the word 'contamination,' Jacqueline. Do you remember? That's a very apt way to describe it. We're all contaminated by the unconscious of that sleeping mind."

"So what you're saying is that one of us is *fooling* the rest?" she asked incredulously.

"What I'm saying is that we're talking about a very disturbed individual."

No one said a word. All eyes turned to look at Carter, though Elisa wasn't entirely sure why.

"If it's a disturbed mind, it must be a physicist," Carter said.

"Or an ex-soldier," Blanes replied, staring back at him. "Someone with so much trauma in their life that they're living a constant nightmare..."

Carter's shoulders shook as though he was laughing, but his lips didn't move. Then he turned, walked into the kitchen, and poured himself another cup of reheated coffee.

"So why does he show no sign of life for years and then suddenly reappear?" Jacqueline inquired.

"That expression 'for years,' makes no sense from Zig Zag's perspective," Blanes stated. "For Zig Zag, everything happens in the blink of an eye, and those periods are what he uses to travel through time, like any other split. For him, we're still in the station, on our way to the control room with the alarm going off. In his time string, in his world, we're all still trapped in that *exact* moment. That's why we can't see him, even though he affects us so profoundly. In fact, I'm sure he's picking us off in a specific order. Do you remember who the first person to arrive in the control room was, besides Ric? It was Rosalyn. And she was the first one to die. And after her? Who got there next?"

"Cheryl Ross," Elisa whispered. "She told me so herself."

"And she was the second one killed."

"Méndez was the first of my men to arrive," Carter said. "He was on guard duty and ... Oh, Christ. He was the third victim! What in the ...

They all glanced at each other uneasily. Jacqueline seemed extremely anxious.

"I was after Reinhard," she whimpered, and then turned to Elisa. "What about you?"

"Wait, there's a mistake somewhere," Elisa said. "Nadja and I arrived together, and Reinhard was already there, but Nadja was killed *before* him..." She stopped suddenly. *No. Nadja told me that she'd gotten up earlier. She was the one who discovered that Ric wasn't in bed.* She corrected herself. "No, that's right. He's picking us off in the same order that we woke up and went out into the hall."

For a second, they avoided each other's eyes, lost in private thoughts. Elisa was ashamed at the relief she felt on realizing that both Jacqueline and Blanes had arrived before her.

"Hold on, everybody." Carter held up a stumpy hand. The color had drained from his face, but his voice had regained its authoritative tone. "If this theory of yours is correct, Professor, then what would happen when he ... or should I say '*it*' ... kills itself?"

"If he kills his alter ego, they'll both die," Blanes responded.

"And if something *else* kills his alter ego ...

"Zig Zag will die."

Carter nodded, as if that were all he needed to know.

"So all we have to do is figure out *which one of us* it is, and kill him or her—regardless of who it is—before Zig Zag takes his next victim. It's obvious that he's not going to kill himself: if he hasn't done it yet, then it seems that whether by coincidence or by design he's leaving himself for last. So we have to do it ourselves." Carter paused and then looked at them defiantly and repeated, "Regardless of who it is. Am I right?"

Was that the solution? Elisa thought it sounded horrific, and yet it was perfectly straightforward, even fitting.

A new uneasiness settled in among them now. Even Víctor, who'd been quiet up until them, was drawn into the conversation.

"It's a man ..." Jacqueline's voice echoed like a stone cast onto the floor. "I know it. It's a man." She looked up at Carter and Blanes, her dark eyes flashing.

"Are you trying to say that women are not perverted, Professor?" Carter asked.

"I'm saying that I *know it's a man!*" she shrieked. "And so does Elisa!" She turned to her. "You feel it, too. Go on, tell them!"

Before she had a chance to answer, Carter said, "Let's say you're right. It's a man. What are we supposed to do? There are still two possibilities. You want us to play chicken, me and the professor? Should we slit each other's throats just to be safe, so you can live in peace?"

"Three," Víctor said very quietly, creating another silence. "Three possibilities. Don't forget about Ric."

Elisa knew he was right. They couldn't discard Valente until they had some proof that he was dead. And, in fact, judging by the kind of "contamination" that she and Jacqueline were feeling, he seemed to be the most likely candidate.

"If we could only figure out which image he used that night," Blanes lamented.

For a second, the memory of Ric Valente overwhelmed Elisa, dragging her back off into an awful world. It was as if those ten years had never passed. She saw his face, his perpetual smile; she heard his mocking tone and humiliating comments. In fact, wasn't he just mocking all of them right now? In a flash, she realized what had to be done.

"I know. There's a way. Of course! There is one way—"

"No!"

Blanes had understood what she meant; that much was clear by how loud he'd shouted.

"David, it's our only chance! Carter's right! We have to figure out which one of us is Zig Zag before he kills again!"

"Elisa, don't ask me to do that."

"I'm not asking *you!*" She was proving she could shout, too. "It's a proposal. It's not up to *you* to make this decision, David!"

He gave her a dreadful look. And the silence that followed was broken only by Carter's cynical, drained voice.

"Forget Zig Zag. If you *really* want to see violence, just lock a couple scientists up in the same room." He took a few steps and stood between them. He lit a cigarette (Víctor hadn't realized he even smoked) and took long drags, seeming more intent on inhaling smoke than expelling words. "Would you two brilliant minds, geniuses of the physics world, explain what you're arguing about?"

"Risks: creating another Zig Zag!" Blanes shouted in Elisa's direction, paying no attention to Carter whatsoever. "Benefits: none!"

"Even if that's true, what else can we do?" She turned to Carter and spoke more calmly. "We know that Ric used both the accelerator and the computers in the control room that night. What I'm proposing is that we film the control room for a few seconds and then go back and open the corresponding time strings to see what he did, and what happened next, including Rosalyn's murder. We know *exactly* when it all happened, because of the blackout. We can open two or three time strings from just before that moment. That might let us see what Ric was doing, or which image he used to create Zig Zag."

"And then we'd know who it is." Carter scratched his beard and looked at Blanes. "Sounds like a well-reasoned plan to me."

"You're forgetting one tiny detail," Blanes said, facing Carter. "The whole reason Zig Zag appeared to begin with is because Ric opened a time string from the *recent past!* You want that to happen again? Two Zig Zags?"

"But you yourself explained it," Elisa objected. "The subject has to be unconscious for the split to be dangerous. And, personally, I don't think Ric was *asleep* while he was using the accelerator that night, do you?" She watched Blanes intently and then spoke again, softening her voice. "Look at it this way. What other option do we have? We can't defend ourselves. Zig Zag is going to keep hunting us down until he kills himself, if he ever does."

"We could try to figure out how to keep him from being able to suck up any energy—" "For how long, David? If we managed to stop him now, how long would he take to come back next time?" She appealed to the rest of the group. "I've been calculating the intervals between attacks and the amount of energy consumed. The period between attacks has been halved. The first one was one hundred and ninety million seconds after Méndez's death, and the second was ninety-four million five hundred thousand seconds after Nadja's death. That's about half. At that rate, Zig Zag has another forty-eight hours before going into hibernation for what will probably be less than a year. He's already killed four people in forty-eight hours. He could get another two or three today or tomorrow and finish the rest of us off in less than six months." She eyed Blanes. "We're damned, David, no matter what we do. Our days are numbered. I just want to be in control of how I die."

"I'm with her," Carter said.

Elisa searched for Jacqueline's glance. She stood right beside her but seemed far off, distant. Something in her posture or her expression made her fade away.

"I can't take it anymore ...," she whispered, her voice hoarse. "I just want to do away with ... that ... monster. I'm with Elisa."

"I'm not going to offer an opinion," Víctor said quickly when Elisa turned to him. "You're the ones who have to decide. I just want to ask one question. Once you find out who it is, are you *absolutely sure* you'll be able to kill whoever it turns out to be in cold blood?"

"With my bare hands," Jacqueline spat. "And if it's me, it'll be even easier."

"Relax, Father." Carter slapped Víctor's shoulder. "I've killed people for a lot less than this. I'll take care of it. I've blown people away for coughing with their mouths open."

"But the person the split came from isn't to blame," Víctor continued, unfazed. "Ric should never have carried out that experiment without permission, but even if it's him, he doesn't deserve to die."

Their only blame lies in being asleep. Elisa was with Víctor on this, but she didn't want to tackle this particular issue right then.

"Regardless, we need to know who it is." She turned to Blanes. "David, that leaves you. Are you with us?"

"No!" he cried, storming out of the room, repeating, "I am *not* with you! I am *not* with you!" in an anguished voice.

For a second, no one reacted. And then Carter spoke slowly, darkly.

"He's a little too concerned with making sure this experiment isn't carried out, don't you think?"

ELISA decided to follow him, reaching the hall in time to see him turn toward the corridor leading to the first barracks. Instantly, she knew where he was headed. He turned left, passed the lab doors, and opened the one that led to his old office. That was one of the areas worst hit by the explosion, and now it was little more than a dark, empty mausoleum. The wind moaned through the cracks in the buttressed walls. The only thing left was a small table.

Blanes rested his fists on it.

Suddenly, she felt like she was interrupting one of his Bach recitals to show him the results of her calculations. When he found mistakes, he used to say, "Now go correct that damn error once and for all!"

"David," she said softly.

He didn't respond. He was just standing there in the dark, hanging his head.

Elisa felt calmer now, though it wasn't easy. The heat and the tension were both unbearable. Despite the fact that all she wore was a tank top and a pair of shorts, her back, armpits, and forehead were drenched in sweat. She really needed to get some sleep. Even just a few minutes, but she had to close her eyes. Nevertheless, she knew (first thing she told herself) that if she wanted to live, she'd have to stay awake, and (second thing) above all, she had to remain calm.

That's why she decided to be totally up front.

"You lied to us, David."

He turned and stared at her.

"You said only the people who carried out the experiments saw splits. Marini got the images of the rats and dogs, but you *both* did the Unbroken Glass. You saw the glass's split, too, didn't you? That's why you don't want us to do this now."

He gazed at her in the darkness.

She could picture what he was seeing: her hourglass figure, backlit, leaning in the doorway, her black hair up in a ponytail, cropped T-shirt short enough to show her stomach, cutoffs rubbing against her thighs.

"Elisa Robledo," he whispered. "The smartest, most beautiful student ... and the most arrogant little fucker."

"You never gave a shit about any of those things."

They were weighing each other up with their glances. And then, simultaneously, they smiled. But David went on to say the most macabre thing she could imagine.

"There's another Zig Zag victim that you don't know about. The one that I killed." His fists rested on the table. He stared down at them intensely, gazing at something only he could see. The whole time he spoke, he never looked up at Elisa. "Did you know that when I was eight years old, I saw my little brother electrocuted? We were in the dining room, my mother, my brother and I. And ... I remember this really well ... my mother disappeared for a minute and my brother, who'd been playing with a ball, started playing with the tangle of cords behind the TV without my realizing. I was reading a book, I still remember the title: *The Marvels of Science*. And at one point, I looked up and saw my little brother all stiff, his hair sticking out like a porcupine's. He was making this guttural sound. From the waist down, he looked like a water balloon; he was urinating and defecating on himself. I threw myself onto him, half crazed. I'd read somewhere that you shouldn't touch someone who was being electrocuted, but at the time I didn't care. I ran to him and pushed him hard, like we were fighting. Just then the fuses blew, and that was what saved me. But in my memory, I have the impression that I somehow ... touched electricity. It's a very strange memory, and I know it's not *real,* per se, but I can't get it out of my head. I touched electricity, and I touched death. And death, the death I felt, was not a calm force, it wasn't something that descended gently and put an end to things. It was taut and hard and it buzzed like a powerful machine. Death was a charred metal monster ... When I opened my eyes, my mother was hugging me. I don't remember my brother after that. I erased the vision of his body from my memory. And that was when I decided to become a physicist. I guess I wanted to learn everything I could about the enemy ..."

He stopped and finally looked up at her. Then, in a broken voice, he went on.

"A couple of days ago, I lived through another terrible moment. The worst one since my brother's death. But that time, I *regretted* having become a physicist. That was on Tuesday. Reinhard called me around lunchtime, after having taken a look at Sergio's documents, and he told me what he thought was happening. I had to go to Madrid to prepare for our meeting, but first ... first I wanted to see Albert Grossmann, my mentor. I *had* to see him. I think I once told you that he was against the whole idea of Project Zig Zag. He helped me discover equations for the sequoia theory, but when he began to suspect the possible consequences of entanglement, he quit, leaving it to Sergio and me. He said he didn't want to commit a sin. Maybe that was because he was old. I was young, and I was glad he'd said that. That's the biggest difference between old people and young ones: the elderly are horrified by sin, and the young are attracted to it. Anyway, that Tuesday after Reinhard told me everything Marini had done, I aged. Overnight. And I needed to go tell Grossmann. Maybe I wanted to be absolved." He paused. Elisa listened, rapt, her head leaning against the doorframe. "He was in a private hospital in Zurich. He knew he was dying, and he'd accepted it. His cancer was very advanced; he had pulmonary and osteal metastases. He was in and out of the hospital every other week. I got them to let me in, even though it wasn't visiting hours. And he lay there, listening to me in agony. I could see death descending over him the way night descends over the horizon. He was terrified when I told him that the murders (which he didn't know about) were connected to Zig Zag's existence. He wouldn't even let me finish. He called me a bastard. 'You tried to see what's forbidden! God forbade us, and you did it anyway! You are to blame, and Zig Zag is your punishment!' He kept repeating it, shouting as loud as he could, coughing, as he lay there on his deathbed. 'Zig Zag is your punishment!' He was already dead, he just didn't know it."

Blanes panted, as though rather than tell a story he'd run five miles. He drummed his fingers on the dusty table like it was a keyboard.

"A nurse came in and kicked me out. When I got to Madrid the next day, I found out he'd died that night. In a way, Zig Zag used me to kill him."

"No, David, you didn't—"

"You're right," he interrupted her, struggling to speak. "I did see the glass's splits. Sergio and I studied them, and we knew the risks of quantum entanglement. I refused to continue, and thought I'd convinced Sergio to quit, too. We swore we'd never tell. But he kept experimenting in secret. Years later, I started to sense what was happening, but I didn't say a word. Not to Grossmann, or to anyone else. Everyone around me was dying, and I ... I didn't say a word!"

Suddenly, he burst into tears.

They were awkward, racking sobs, as if crying were something he had no idea how to do. Elisa went to him and held him. She thought of Blanes's mother, holding her oldest son as tight as she could, touching him to make sure that at least *he* was alive, that at least *he* had not been touched by the powerful machine.

"You didn't know ...," she cooed softly, stroking his sweaty neck. "You couldn't be sure, David. None of this is your fault."

"Elisa ... My God, what have I done? ... What have *we* done? ... What has the entire scientific community done?"

"Get it right, or get it wrong: that's all we can do." Elisa held him as she spoke. "We're going to try again, David. And this time we're going to get it right. Please, let me try ..."

Blanes seemed to have calmed down a little. But when he pulled away and looked into her eyes, she could see sheer terror there.

"I'm as scared of getting it right as I am of getting it wrong," he said.

"THAT'S it," Jacqueline announced from her seat.

"Whatever the professor wants," Carter said, watching the screen; Elisa was at the computer. "Right smack on her ass."

Elisa turned back to the tiny camera hooked up to the control room computer. It was on a tripod behind her, aimed at the keyboard. She nodded, approving of the position. If Ric had used the accelerator that night, she guessed he'd done it from there. Plus, from that position it would also record the door to the generator room, where Rosalyn had died.

She'd spent all afternoon preparing. She convinced Blanes to let her do it alone (she'd had to convince Víctor, too): it was less risky for the group that way, she said, because if there were splits, she'd be the only one to see them. She didn't want any help, even with her calculations, claiming it would just slow her down. But she did have to learn how to operate the equipment. Though Blanes didn't know everything about SUSAN, he knew enough to teach her to turn the particle beams on and off. Víctor helped out by checking the computers. Elisa didn't know much about the programs on them, but the software was pretty outdated and that worked in her favor. The image profilers were more complicated, but she'd only use them if she had to. She wanted to see the images just as they were.

By the time the really strong winds picked up, it was after

six o'clock; you could hear the gales howling, even from the control room.

"That storm might cause problems," Blanes said uneasily.

"That's the least of my worries." *It started with a storm, it can end with a storm.* Elisa tried to think of it as a good sign.

Jacqueline approached her. She'd pulled her thick hair back into a rubber band, and the ends were drooping down like a plant in need of water.

"What will you do ... when you get the images? We *all* need to see them."

Elisa had no trouble picking up her stress on the word "all." But, of course, Jacqueline was right. *If I see Zig Zag, they should, too. Otherwise, they'll never believe me.*

"I'll record them and make copies. I'll need some media."

"So sorry," Carter quipped. "I *completely* forgot to pick up any CDs at the supermarket in Yemen."

"There must be a CD around somewhere," Elisa said.

Carter lit a cigarette and affected a smooth, radio announcer's voice. "They'd thought of *everything* ... except the CDs." He chuckled huskily.

"Maybe there's one in Silberg's lab," Blanes said.

"I'll go see," Víctor offered. He walked out of the room, avoiding the tangle of coaxial cables coiled up on the floor like dead snakes.

"It's all going to be OK," Elisa said.

It was a lie, of course, but they all knew that. She thought they might just think of it as a defective truth.

CARTER pulled the metal door shut.

Like a tombstone seen from inside the grave.

She was all alone now. All she could hear was the moaning wind. It was like being in a hermetic diving bell several fathoms under the sea. An immense, boundless fear gnawed away at her.

She looked at the blinking control lights, the flashing computers, and tried to concentrate on her calculations.

She knew the exact time that had to be explored. The clocks on the computers had stopped on the night of October 1, 2005, at exactly 4:10:12. In round numbers, that worked out to three hundred million seconds ago. She stopped a moment to reflect on how much her life had changed over those three hundred million seconds.

Elisa was sure that she'd calculated the exact energy required to open two or three strings from just before that time. The camera behind her was filming, and she'd send its footage to the accelerator to make it collide with the calculated energy. Then she'd recapture the new beam using the open time strings and upload it onto the computer for viewing. *And then, we'll just have to see,* she thought.

We'll just have to see.

She checked over equations again and again, scanning the columns of numbers and Greek letters, trying to ensure there were no errors. *Now go correct that damn error!* What had Blanes said in class that day? *Physics equations are the key to our happiness, our fears, our lives, and our deaths.* She was convinced she had the right solution.

The yellow lines indicated that the accelerator had reached the configuration levels it needed. In the growing darkness of the control room, those lines seemed to bisect Elisa's sweat-drenched face and her half-naked body, her tank top now tied just beneath her breasts. Unfathomably, it was getting hotter. Carter said it was due to the low-pressure system and the storm. The wind in the palm trees sounded like a swarm of locusts. It hadn't started raining yet, but she could hear the sea roar.

The numbers all added up: 100 percent. She heard a familiar buzzing. The initial process had finished. The accelerator was now preparing to receive the image and send it into gyration at something approaching the speed of light.

Feverishly, she began to key in the data for the amount of energy calculated.

This just might work. This just might identify Zig Zag.

But what would she do if it did? What would she do if she found out Zig Zag was a split that had come from David, or Carter, or Jacqueline ... or herself? Hadn't Blanes been right when he said that getting it right would be as bad as getting it wrong? What were they going to do?

She pushed those nagging doubts aside and focused on the screen.

31

BLANES removed the batteries from the transmitter.

"Take the batteries out of everything you've got on you: cell phones, PDAs, all of it. Carter, have you checked the flashlights and the kitchen sockets?"

"I unplugged all the appliances. And this is the only flashlight that still has batteries in it."

Carter darted back and forth with flashlight in his right hand, his left one extended like a beggar, his palm full of round, flat coinlike batteries. He approached Víctor, who held up his wrist and smiled.

"Mine's a windup."

"What? Come on ..." Carter looked him up and down in the flashlight beam. "Here we are in 2015 and you don't even have a computer watch?"

"I *have* one, I just don't use it. This works fine. It's an Omega classic. Used to be my grandfather's. I like mechanical watches."

"You're full of surprises, Father."

"Víctor, did you check the labs?" Blanes asked.

"There were two laptops in Silberg's. I took the batteries out."

"Good. I told Elisa to disconnect the accelerator and unplug the computers she's not using," Blanes said, cupping his hands for the batteries Jacqueline was handing him. "We should stash all this someplace."

"Leave it on the console." Carter had gone to the back of the room, leaving them in darkness.

"David …" It was Jacqueline's quivering voice. She'd sat down on the floor. "Do you think he'll make his next move … soon?"

"Well, the nights are riskier because the lights are on. But we really don't know when he'll attack, Jacqueline."

Carter came back and found a spot on the floor, too. The four of them took up less than half the space in the screening room. They were all crowded together by the screen, as though sharing a small tent. Blanes sat in a chair backed up against the screen, Carter and Jacqueline were on the floor, and Víctor sat in another chair opposite Blanes. It was pitch black, except for the yellow beam of Carter's flashlight, and hot as a sauna.

At one point, Carter sat his flashlight down and took two black objects from his pants pocket. Víctor thought they looked like pieces of a faucet.

"I suppose I'm allowed to use this," he said, screwing the pieces together.

"Won't do you any good," Blanes warned, "but as long as there are no batteries, go ahead."

Carter set the gun in his lap. Víctor realized that the ex-soldier was staring at his pistol with a degree of passion he'd never shown the others. Suddenly, he picked up the flashlight and tossed it. It was so unexpected that rather than trying to catch it, Víctor tried to move out of the way, and it hit him on the arm. He heard Carter laugh as he bent to pick it up. *Idiot,* Víctor thought.

"That means it's your turn, Father. Thanks to your windup watch, you win the prize: first shift on guard duty. Call me at three if I fall asleep. I'll be on second shift the rest of the night."

"Elisa will have news before then," Blanes said.

They sat in silence for a long time, their shadows like the

mouths of a tunnel projected onto the wall in the flashlight's gleam. Víctor was sure what he was hearing was the rain. There were no windows in the screening room (despite its drawbacks, it was the only place where they could all stretch out comfortably), but he could hear what sounded like interference, the crackling of a TV that wasn't tuned in. And the wind, howling over the background noise. And closer, within the gloom of those four walls, the sounds of labored breathing. Sobbing. Víctor realized Jacqueline had buried her head in her hands.

"He can't attack now, Jacqueline, not this time …," Blanes soothed, trying to convey confidence. "We're on an island. There's nothing for miles around: the only energy he's got are the batteries in that flashlight, and Elisa's computer. It won't be tonight."

The paleontologist looked up. Víctor no longer thought she was a beautiful woman. She was a wounded, quivering wreck.

"I'm next," she said in an almost inaudible voice. Víctor heard her, though. "I know it …"

No one tried to console her. Blanes sighed and leaned back against the screen.

"How does he do it?" Carter asked, stretching. He placed his hands on the wall, behind his neck, and his elbows out to the side. Chest hairs peeked out from his T-shirt. "How does he kill us?"

"As soon as we're sucked into his time string, we're his," Blanes explained. "In such a short space of time, as I explained, if we're inside a time string, we aren't 'whole,' we're not 'solid.' So our bodies and everything around us are unstable. We're like a jigsaw puzzle of atoms. All Zig Zag has to do is take the pieces out one by one, or move them around, or destroy them. He can do that at will, the same way he makes use of the energy in the lights. Clothes and everything else outside the time string and its current just disappear. There's nothing to protect us; there are no weapons we can use to fight back. Inside the time string, we're as naked and defenseless as newborn babes."

Carter sat stock-still, as though he'd stopped breathing.

"How long does it last?" He took a cigarette from his pants pocket. "The pain. How long do you think it lasts?"

"No one's come back to tell us." Blanes shrugged. "The only version we have is Ric's. He said it felt like he was in there for hours, but his split didn't have anything even *approaching* the force of Zig Zag."

"Craig and Nadja survived for months," Jacqueline whispered, hugging her legs to her like she was cold. "That's what the autopsies tell us ... Months or years, suffering intense pain."

"But we don't know what happens to the consciousness, Jacqueline," Blanes added quickly. "Their perception of time might be entirely different. Subjective and objective time. Remember, there are differences. It could all be incredibly fast from a consciousness perspective—"

"No," Jacqueline replied. "I don't think so."

Carter hunted in his pockets for something, maybe a lighter or a box of matches. He still had the unlit cigarette between his lips. But then he gave up, took it from his mouth, and stared down at it as he spoke.

"I've seen a lot of torture in my time. Been on both sides of it, too. In 1993, I worked in Rwanda training Hutu paramilitary groups in Murehe. When the war kicked off, they accused me of being a traitor and I was tortured. One of the chiefs told me they'd be nice and slow about it: start with my feet and work their way up to my head. First, they ripped off my toenails with sharpened sticks." He smiled. "I've never felt anything as painful in my whole fucking life. I cried, I pissed in my pants it hurt so bad, but the worst thing was knowing that they'd just begun. Those were just my feet, two dired-out crusty things on the very bottom of my body ... I thought I'd never make it. Thought I'd lose my mind before they got to my waist. But after two days, another group I'd trained took the village, killed the men holding me, and let me go. That was when I realized that there's a limit to what a human being can tolerate. At the military academy where I did my training, they used to say, "If the pain is enduring, you can bear it. If it's unbearable, it will kill you and it won't last." He let out one of his weary, sarcastic chortles. "Knowing that was supposed to help us through tough times. But this ..."

"Would you *shut up,* please?" Jacqueline desperately covered her ears and buried her head once more.

Carter glanced over at her for a second, but then kept talking in a quiet, gravelly voice, aiming his unlit cigarette at them as if it were a piece of bent chalk.

"I know exactly what I'm going to do when your colleague comes back with that image. I'm going to slaughter the bastard like a sick dog, whoever it is. Here and now. And if it's me ..." He stopped, as if considering a startling possibility. "If it's me, you'll have the pleasure of watching me blow my brains out."

THE tiny UH1Z cockpit lurched like an old bus on a dirt road. Imprisoned by the modern, ergonomic seat, complete with tightly crisscrossed seat belt, Harrison's head was the only part of his body moving, but it jerked and jiggled in every direction his vertebra would allow. Sitting opposite him, their knees touching, was Previn, the woman soldier, her eyes fixed on the ceiling. Harrison noticed that beneath her helmet, her pretty blue eyes were dilated. The others didn't look much better. Only Jurgens, in the back, sat unflappable.

But Jurgens was the other face of death, so he wasn't a fair standard.

Outside, it was as if the wrath of hell had been unleashed. Or maybe it was heaven; who could tell? The four angels flew recklessly against an almost horizontal rain pounding straight into the front windscreens. A hundred and fifty feet below them, a colossal monster rose up with the force of a thousand tons of water arched into a wave. Luckily, they couldn't make out the sea's maelstrom in the dark. But when he looked out the side window long enough, Harrison could see millions of foam torches atop miles of choppy velvet, like a capriciously decorated Roman palace during the carnival orgies.

He wondered if Previn blamed him somehow. He very much doubted she could reproach him for that idiot Borsello's death. At Eagle, they'd applauded the news.

The order came at noon, five minutes after Borsello had been shot between the eyes. It came from somewhere up north. It was always the same: the north gave the orders and the south obeyed. Like the head and body: everything went top to bottom, Harrison thought. The brain gave the orders, the hand carried them out.

The "head" had deemed Borsello's death admissible. Harrison had done the right thing, Borsello had been inept, the situation was imperative, and Sergeant Frank Mercier would stand in for him. Mercier was a young guy, and he was sitting beside Previn, across from Harrison. He was scared, too. His fear was legible in the bobbing of his Adam's apple. But they were good soldiers. They'd been trained in SERE: survival, evasion, resistance, and escape. They knew everything there was to know about their weapons and equipment; they'd received supplementary training in securing and isolating regions. And they could do more than defend themselves: they had XM39 assault rifles with high-explosive bullets and Ruger MP15 automatic rifles. They were all strong as bulls, with glassy eyes and shiny skin. They looked more like machines than human beings. Previn was the only woman, but she wasn't out of sync with the group. He was happy to have them by his side and didn't want them to think badly of him. With Jurgens and those soldiers, he had nothing to fear.

Except the storm.

After the last jolt, he decided to react.

He looked at the pilots. They were like giant ants, with those black, egg-shaped helmets shining around the edges in the instrument panel's glow. There was no way he could take off his seat belt and get up there, of course. But he bent the arm of the mike attached to his helmet, pulling it down toward his mouth, and pushed a button.

"Is this the storm?" he asked.

"This is just the beginning, sir," one of the pilots responded. "These winds haven't even reached sixty-five miles an hour yet."

"It's not a hurricane, though," said the other pilot into his right ear.

"Or if it is, it hasn't been named."

"Will the chopper make it through this?"

"I guess so" came into his left ear, spoken with remarkable indifference.

Harrison knew that the angel was a tough, sophisticated piece of military machinery designed to withstand all kinds of atmospheric conditions. The blades even self-adjusted depending on the force of the winds. Right then, for example, they weren't rotating in the typical crisscross pattern, but instead looked like two diamonds. Still, the very idea of an accident made him anxious—not because he feared death, but because he couldn't stand the thought of not attaining his goal.

"When do you think we'll get there?" He felt sweat coursing down his neck and back, beneath his helmet and life jacket.

"If all goes well, we should be in sight of the island in an hour."

He left the frequency open. The voices buzzed in his ear like a lunatic's hallucinations. *Angel One to Angel Two, over…*

THEY'D fallen asleep, or at least that's what it looked like.

He didn't want to shine the flashlight at them to check for fear of waking them, though that seemed unlikely. It was obvious everyone was absolutely exhausted. And looking at them one by one, he was sure they were fast asleep. Jacqueline was neither peaceful nor silent. Her breasts quivered under her shirt with each breath, and she was making a sort of guttural moaning sound. Carter looked like he was awake, but his lips were pursed into a small, round, black hole resembling the barrel of a gun. Blanes snored.

It was ten to twelve and Elisa hadn't come back yet.

Almost time.

His heart pounded. He wondered if the others could hear it beating, if it would wake them. But he couldn't stop it.

In slow motion, he placed the big flashlight on the ground, took the small one, and turned it on. Baptism by fire, so to speak.

He turned the big flashlight off. Waited. Nothing happened. They were still out.

The glow from the little flashlight was tiny, like the dying embers of a campfire, but it would be enough to keep them from getting scared if anyone woke up unexpectedly.

He left the flashlight on the floor, by the other one, and took off his shoes, making sure to keep an eye on Carter. That man was terrifying. He was one of those violent types who lived in a parallel universe as out of place in Víctor's life of aeroponic plants, math, and theology as a donkey at Princeton. He knew the ex-soldier wouldn't think twice about hurting him to protect himself.

Still, neither Carter nor the Devil himself was going to stop him from doing what he wanted.

He got up and tiptoed to the door, which he'd purposely left open. After padding out into the dark hallway, he took the matches from his pocket. Hours earlier, when Carter had been searching for them to light his cigarette, he was afraid he'd be caught. Luckily, Carter hadn't realized who'd taken them.

Holding up the flickering flame up before him, he turned right and made it to the first barracks' hallway. From there, he could hear not only the rain hammering down but the gale-force winds, too. Víctor cupped his hand around the flame, thinking it might blow out.

The darkness was nerve-racking. He was terrified. In theory, Zig Zag (if that monster actually existed, and he still wasn't sure that he did) wasn't a direct threat to him, but the others had instilled him with a bloodcurdling fear. And the riotous storm, the darkness, and those cold metal walls didn't exactly do much to calm him down.

The match was burning his fingers. He blew it out and threw it on the floor.

For a second, before he struck another one, he couldn't see a thing.

Fear, in large part, is nothing but imagination: Víctor had read that over and over. If you didn't let your imagination run wild, darkness and noises had no power over you.

He dropped the match. No way was he bending down to try to find it. He pulled another one from the book.

In any case, he was almost there. After striking the third one, he could make out the door, a few feet to his right.

"**WHERE** did Víctor go?"

"I don't know," Jacqueline replied. "And I don't care, either." She turned over to try to go back to sleep. Unconsciousness was the only way to keep her fear at bay.

"We can't carry the weight of this ourselves, Jacqueline. Víctor is a big help. If he weren't here, we'd be as lost as a sailboat, with no wind and no sea."

Jacqueline, who had closed her eyes, sat up and looked at Blanes. He was still in the same chair, his head leaning against the screen, his green shirt stained with sweat, legs stretched out and crossed in his baggy jeans. His friendly, open face—stubbly gray beard, pockmarked cheeks, and big nose—was turned toward her affectionately.

"What did you just say?"

"That we shouldn't let Víctor go. He's our only help."

"No ... I mean ... You said something about the wind and a boat."

Blanes frowned.

"It was just a turn of phrase. Why?"

"It reminded me of a poem Michel wrote when he was twelve. He read it to me over the phone and I loved it. I encouraged him to keep writing. I miss him so much ..." Jacqueline fought back her tears. "*The wind and the sea have gone. Only the old boat remains* ... He's fifteen now, and he's still writing ..." She rubbed her arms and looked around, suddenly uneasy. "Did you hear something?"

"No," soothed Blanes.

The room's darkness was overwhelming. Jacqueline was sure it was bigger than the space it occupied.

"I'm next." She was half whining and half pouting, like a naughty girl who's been punished. "And I know exactly what he's going to do to me. He tells me every night. I thought about killing myself so many times, and I would, if he'd let me. But he won't. He likes me to keep waiting for him, day after day. And in exchange, he gives me pleasure and terror, in equal doses. He tosses them to me the way you toss a dog a bone, and I gnaw on them both ... Do you know what I told my husband when I decided to leave him? 'I'm still young and I want to live my own life, do what I want to do, follow my heart.'" She shook her head, flustered, and smiled. "Those weren't my words. He said them for me."

Blanes nodded.

"I abandoned my husband and child ... I *abandoned* little Michel ... I had to; *he* wanted me to be alone. *He* comes to me at night and makes me crawl on the floor and throw myself at his feet. *He* made me dye my hair black, he makes me wear all this makeup, and dress like a ... Do you know why my hair is this color?" She ran a hand through her copper tresses and smiled. "Sometimes, I rebel. It's hard, but I do it. I've done too much for *him* already, don't you think? Left my whole life behind: my job, my husband ... Michel, my only son. You have no idea how hateful *he* is, the horrible things he says about my son. Living alone, at least I can ... I can take all that hatred myself ..."

"I understand," Blanes replied. "But some part of you actually *likes* this situation, Jacqueline." He held a hand up like a stop sign to prevent her reply. "Just a small part. It's subconscious. He contaminates your subconscious. It's like a deep well: you drop the bucket down and lots of stuff comes back up with the water. Dead bugs. Everything inside you, everything there ever was, that he's dredged up and brought to the surface. Deep down, you know there's pleasure there, too ..."

Blanes's face was transforming as he spoke. His eyes seemed to have no pupils. They were like puss-filled, oozing abscesses beneath his brows.

And that was when she woke up.

She must have fallen asleep, or maybe it was a disconnect. She remembered everything about it; it was awful. Blanes's face, changing right before her eyes ... Thankfully, it was just a nightmare.

Jacqueline looked around and realized that something was very wrong.

THE image ended. Víctor shut down the file and uploaded another one.

He didn't know if he wanted to see it or not. Suddenly, he didn't. Even if it were really him (how many poor devils did they crucify back then before they got the Lord?). No, not in the infinitesimal shiver of a Planck time, the tyranny of evanescent atoms. He didn't want to see the Son of God rotting, devoured by a moment so infinitesimally short that it didn't even have room for the Father. Eternity, Infinite Duration, the Beatific and Mystical Rose: they were God's time. What was this ... this Infinite Brevity? What should he call it? Instantaneity?

Any space of time so short that the Mystical Rose was just a stem surely belonged to the Devil. A flash of lightning, a glimmer, the blink of an eye, or even the *idea* of blinking were all infinitely longer. Víctor thought of something awful. In that millionth-of-a-second cosmos, Good did not exist, because Good took longer than Evil.

He'd found them by chance in one of Silberg's filing cabinets earlier that afternoon, when he was looking for blank CDs. Several compact discs labeled "diffs."

Immediately he recalled Elisa's story. They had to be the "diffusions" Nadja had told her that Silberg saved, the unsuccessful experiments, when they opened time strings with erroneous energy calculations and everything had come out blurry or indistinct. How could they still be there? Maybe Eagle thought that was the safest place to store them. Or maybe they were totally unusable. Regardless, he was sure he wouldn't be able to see much, but the name that had come up when he popped the CD in—"crucif," followed by a number—was just too tempting, too persuasive for him to be able to give up that once-in-a-lifetime opportunity.

There were a couple of laptops in Silberg's lab with fully charged batteries. Víctor guessed that the computer technicians who came to the island used them to inspect the CDs. Even though Blanes had told them to remove all the batteries from everything, Víctor had made sure to leave one of the laptops operational. In order not to ruin their plans, he'd done a quick calculation: the flashlight he'd left behind needed less energy than the one he'd taken. So the energy being used now equated—more or less—to what the big flashlight used. And if, despite his safety measures, it was still wrong of him to be doing this, then he didn't care. He'd take full responsibility. He had to see some of those images. Just a *few*. And nothing in the world was going to stop him.

He'd been trembling when he opened the first one. But it was a pale, rose-colored universe, a surreal delirium. The next nine looked like 1970s cartoons drawn by someone on acid. The eleventh, though, took his breath away.

A landscape. A mountain. A cross.

All of a sudden, the cross turned into a post with no crossbeam.

He swallowed hard. Those morphological changes had to be because of the Planck times. The cross, in such tiny spaces, was not a cross. He couldn't see any human figure.

The image lasted only five seconds. Víctor saved it and opened the next one.

It was very blurry. A hill seemed to be ablaze. He closed it and opened the next. A foreshortened version of the cross. Or maybe it was another one, because now he made out another cross on the . hilltop and the edge of another one off to the right. Three.

And figures standing around them. Shapes, decapitated shadows.

A cold sweat drenched his back. The image was incredibly fuzzy, but he could still make out shapes on the crosses.

Víctor took off his glasses and drew his face all the way up to the screen until he could make out all the details. The image jumped, and one of the crosses disappeared almost entirely. In its place there was a stain, floating in space, an oval shape hanging from the wood like a wasp's nest on a joist.

Is that you, Lord? Is it you? His eyes welled up with tears. He held his fingers out to the screen, as if to touch the hazy silhouette.

He was so intent on the image that he didn't hear the door open behind him. The creak of the hinges was drowned out by the pounding storm.

FOR a second, she thought she was still dreaming.

The screen Blanes was leaning against was *perforated*. There was a clean, round hole, the size of a soccer ball. The light shining through it must have come from the control room, on *the other side* of the wall.

What was most disturbing, though, was Blanes.

The right side of his face had a deep, elliptical gouge, as big as his brow, eye socket, and cheekbone. Beneath it she could see (perfectly visible in the glow coming through the screen) dense, reddish masses. Jacqueline thought she could identify them: frontal sinuses, narrow nasal septum, trigeminal and facial nerve cords, the bumpy wall of his brain … It was like an anatomical hologram.

The wind and the sea have gone.

An immeasurable silence had descended. The darkness was different, too. More compact, more solid, somehow. There were no flashlights, no light at all aside from what filtered through that hole.

They've gone: only the old boat remains.

She stood up and realized that she was not, in fact, dreaming. It was all too real. She was herself, and her bare feet were touching the floor, though she didn't feel the cold of the...

Something made her look down: she saw the tops of her breasts, her nipples. She touched her body. She wasn't wearing anything, no clothes, no jewelry. She had nothing on, no cover.

The wind and the sea have gone. They've gone. They've gone.

She turned to Carter, but she couldn't see him. Víctor was gone, too. The only one left was Blanes, paralyzed and perforated, and her.

Just the two of them, and the darkness.

LIMP as a rag doll, Víctor flew through the air and crashed down where the Hand sent him. He banged against the open drawer where the diffusions had been and felt an incredibly sharp pain behind his knees. When he landed, it raised a cloud of dust that made him cough. The Hand grabbed him by the hair and he was lifted up into the bright, starry sky, clear and pure as airborne snow. The slap across his face made his left ear ring and grumble like a rickety engine. He tried to grab something for support and scratched the metal wall behind him. His glasses were gone, but he could make out—right in front of him—an eye so black it looked opaque; it had no iris. So black that it stood out against the second-rate darkness of the room. He heard the mechanism click.

"Listen, you stupid priest ..." Carter's voice, hissing like a blowtorch, seemed to come from the eye. "I'm pointing a carbon-fiber 98S at you, and I've got thirty 5.5-millimeter bullets in the clip. One shot from this distance and you'll be blown clear into next week, got it?" Víctor whined and whimpered, blind without his glasses. "Let me warn you: *I'm not myself.* Something's happening to me. I know it, I can tell. Since we came back to this fucking island, I've become someone else, someone even *worse* than who I was. Right now, I'd be only too glad to blow your brains out, wipe them off me with a rag, and go have breakfast." *Do it,* Víctor thought, though he couldn't say a word, and Carter wouldn't let him try. "If you *ever* take off while you're on guard without telling me, if you turn on any fucking machine without my permission, I swear I'll kill you. That's not a threat; it's just the way it is. I might even kill you if you don't, but you'll have to let me be the judge of that. Don't give me any easy excuses, Father. Got it?"

Víctor nodded. Carter handed him his glasses and shoved him toward the door.

And that's when it all happened.

MORE than feel it, she sensed it.

It wasn't an image, a sound, or a smell. Nothing material, nothing you could perceive with any of your senses. But she knew Zig Zag was there, at the back of the room, the same way she'd have known if a nameless man in a crowd loved only her.

The wind and the sea have gone. Only the abyss remains.

"God ... Oh, dear God, please! Help me! Carter! David! Please, help me!..."

Terror has a point of no return. In that instant, Jacqueline crossed it.

She curled up into a ball against the screen next to Blanes's petrified body, hands over her breasts, and screamed. Again and again. Screamed like she'd never screamed in her whole life, holding nothing back, thinking nothing except that she'd lose her mind. She howled, she bellowed like a dying animal, until her throat nearly split open, until she thought her head would explode and her lungs would fill with blood, until she knew she was insane, or dead, or at least anesthetized.

Suddenly, something emerged from the back of the room. It was a shadow, and as it moved it seemed to drag the room's darkness with it. Jacqueline turned and looked.

She stopped shouting when she saw the eyes.

At the very same instant, she managed to give her body one final, definitive command. She got up and ran to the door as though abandoning a sinking ship.

They've gone. They've gone. They've gone. They've gone. They've gone.

She'd never make it, she thought. She'd never be able to escape. *He* would catch her (he was fast, too fast). But the last remaining shred of her sanity told her she was doing the right thing.

What any living thing in her place would have done after seeing those eyes.

THE image had been processed. The computer asked her if she wanted to upload it. Trying to contain her anxiety, Elisa hit ENTER.

After one flickering instant, the screen blinked and turned a pale pink, showing what looked like a blurry photograph of the control room. She had no trouble identifying the shiny accelerator in the background and the two computers in the foreground. Something had changed, though with such poor definition she took a second to realize what it was. There was another light source; a flashlight by the computer on the right was shining. In its glow, she could see a smudge seated in the same place she was.

She couldn't breathe. Something in her mind cracked and a torrent of memories came pouring out. Ten years later, she was seeing him again. The poor quality of the image left a lot to her imagination. She reconstructed his bony back and big, pointy head. Everything was jagged because of the Planck time; she needed better resolution to be able to make out who it really was.

Ric Valente stared at the computer screen, with no clue that ten years later *she'd* be watching *him* on the same screen. He was alone, and thought he would be forever.

Once she'd recovered from the shock, Elisa hunched over the screen almost the same as Valente, both surveying the past, peeking into history's keyhole, spying like indiscreet butlers.

What's he looking at? What is he doing?

The lights on the control panel where Ric sat told her that he, too, had just opened several time strings and was contemplating the results. The camera angle let her see the screen Ric was looking at, but his silhouette blocked the images on it. *I wouldn't be able to make anything out even if he moved,* she thought. *I need the profiles.*

Something about that image intrigued her. What was it? Why did she suddenly feel so ill at ease?

The more she looked at it, the more sure she was that something wasn't right. There was something hidden, or maybe it was obvious, like those games in which you have to find ten differences between two pictures. She tried to concentrate.

When the image skipped to another time string, she jumped. Now Ric had moved to the left, but everything was still very fuzzily outlined and, as she'd suspected, she couldn't even hazard a guess as to what he'd been looking at, despite an unblocked view of Ric's screen. It was just a big sepia blur. *That must be Zig Zag, but I need to profile it and zoom in.* There was someone else beside Ric now. Though she could see only part of the face and body, she recognized Rosalyn Reiter. That must have been when poor Rosalyn snuck up on him. He was probably trying to explain what he was doing there. That string was from an infinitesimal fraction of time, two seconds before the blackout. It was less than a millisecond long, at 4:10:10. Rosalyn was nowhere near the generator. How had she managed to get inside the generator room and be electrocuted in less than two seconds? It had all happened during the attack, and she was starting to see how it could have come about.

But there was still some tiny detail she couldn't put her finger on that made her uneasy. What was it?

That was the last time string. Before she forgot, she typed in a command string and began profiling, programming the computer to keep working after it had been shut down.

Suddenly, something struck her. Neither Ric nor Rosalyn had shadows. She knew that Rosalyn was dead and therefore she couldn't have split. But what about Ric? Did that mean he was dead, too?

As she sat there, pondering the possibility, she felt another, more intense anxiety.

Turning her head, she looked back at the camera.

The control room was dark. The pinkish phosphorescence on the screen cast the only light, and its glow went no more than six feet. Following Blanes' instructions, she'd disconnected the accelerator an hour ago and unplugged the other computers and components. Her watch battery was sitting on the table (though she knew from the computer screen that it was almost midnight). Outside, the storm still raged. She felt its fury through the walls, and water crashed ceaselessly against the windows.

She couldn't see anything strange. Just shadows. But Elisa felt increasingly apprehensive.

Over the past ten years, she'd grown used to that feeling; it had marked her, as though each night she survived branded her skin with a red-hot poker.

She was sure of it. *He* was in there.

She felt him so close, so near her body, that for a split second she actually reproached herself for not being prepared to receive him. Fear sat like a rock in her chest. She stood, stumbled, and felt her hair stand on end.

And then it was over. She thought she could hear shouting—Carter's voice—and footsteps running through the barracks, but there was no one in the control room.

When she turned her head, she saw her friend standing before her, behind the computer, illuminated in its glow. Her naked body looked rubbery, sticky, like an unfinished sculpture, just a clump of shapeless, ordinary clay. The only distinguishable feature was her mouth, which was huge, black, and dislocated. Elisa's whole hand would have fit between those jaws, even with her fingers spread wide. She had no idea how she even recognized her.

And then Jacqueline Clissot began to disintegrate before her eyes.

32

THE pain was unbearable. She woke, and moaned. She'd been lay-
ing facedown on dust-covered box springs with no mattress, and
the hard wires had left grooves on her face. She couldn't remember where she was or what she was doing there, and staring up at
faces without features and shiny eyes didn't help. A pair of hands
yanked her up mercilessly. She asked to go to the bathroom, but
only when she spoke in English did they stop tugging her in one
direction and start shoving her the opposite way. After a brief, unpleasant visit to the toilet (no paper, no water), she felt able to at
least walk on her own. But the hands (masked soldiers, she could
see them now) grabbed her by the arms once more.

HARRISON had never liked islands.

A lot of mistakes had been made on those lumps of land, geo-
logical glitches just sitting there waiting for man's exploitation.
Those lonely gardens, hidden from the eyes of the gods, were ideal
for breaking rules, transgressing norms, and offending creation.
Eve was the first to blame. But now it was time to pay for that ancient crime. Eve, Jacqueline Clissot: it didn't really make a difference. The serpent had turned into a dragon.

It was almost nine in the morning on Sunday, March 15, and a heavy sheet of rain still fell on the damn island. The palm trees lining the beach quivered like feather dusters held by an up-tight servant. The heat and humidity got into Harrison's nose, and one of the first orders he'd given had been to turn on the air-conditioning. He'd catch cold, of course, because his clothes were still drenched from their landing eight hours earlier, but that was the least of his worries.

Staring out at that setting, hands in his pockets, thinking about islands, sins, and dead Eves, Harrison said, "The two men who went into the screening room had to be sedated. They're tough soldiers, they've seen it all ... So why is *this* so out of the ordinary, Professor?" He turned to Blanes, who sat at the dusty table. His head still bowed, he hadn't touched the water Harrison had brought him. "It's more than a mutilated corpse, isn't it? More than dried blood on the walls and ceiling ..."

"It's the Impact," Blanes said in the blank, empty voice he'd used to respond to all of the previous questions. "Zig Zag's crimes are like images from the past. They produce Impact."

For a second, all Harrison did was nod.

"I see." He left his post by the window and paced the dining room again. "And that ... can ... transform people?"

"What do you mean?"

"Well ..." Harrison moved only those muscles absolutely re-quired to engage his voice. His face was like a powdered mask. "Can it make people do, or think, strange things?

"I suppose so. In some way, Zig Zag's conscience contaminates all of us, because it becomes intertwined with our present ..."

Contaminates us. Harrison didn't want to look at Elisa sitting there, panting like a wild animal, her sweaty shirt plastered to her torso, shorts cut off almost at the crotch, tan skin glistening with an oily slick of perspiration, jet-black hair tangled.

He didn't want to look at her, because he didn't want to lose control. It was very simple. If he looked at her too long, or long enough, he'd do something. Anything. And he didn't want to do anything. At least not yet. He had to be prudent. As long as the professor was still useful to him, he'd keep his cool.

"Let's go over the story again, Professor." He rubbed his eyes. "From the top. You were alone in the screening room ..."

"I'd fallen asleep, but the sparks woke me up. They were shooting out of all of the plugs and sockets: the console, the light switches ... And it was happening in the labs, too ..."

"Did you see it in the kitchen?" Harrison leaned out the door and made a face at the burned smell. "The insulation is singed, and the cords are completely scorched. How could that have happened?"

"Zig Zag did it. This is something new. He must have ... learned how to even suck energy even from components that aren't plugged in."

Harrison stroked his chin as he gazed at the scientist. He needed a shave. A nice shower to bring him back from the dead. A long sleep in a decent bed. But he wasn't going to get any of that.

"Go on, Professor."

The wasp. The main thing is to kill that wasp buzzing in your thoughts.

"I could see by the light of the sparks ... I don't know how I even knew that *thing* was Jacqueline ... I vomited. And then I began to shout."

The dining-room door opened, interrupting them. Víctor walked in, escorted by a soldier. He was as dirty as everyone else, bare-chested, with his shirt tied around his waist. His face was swollen with lack of sleep and the two or three smacks Carter had dealt him. Just the sight of him made Harrison slightly nauseous: his sickly pallor, lack of chest hair, old-fashioned glasses ... Everything about him made Harrison think of maggots, or gangly tadpoles. And to top it all off, he'd pissed in his pants when he walked into the screening room. You could see the wet spot spread down his inner pant leg. Harrison smiled, determined to put up with Mr. Maggot.

"Have a nice rest, Professor?" Lopera nodded as he took a seat. Harrison noted that the woman looked at him with concern. How could she be *friends* with that pathetic idiot? *Maybe she should be there when he's killed. Maybe the slut should watch him die.* He filed that idea away to discuss with Jurgens later and concentrated on Blanes for the time being. "Where were we? So ... you saw Clissot's remains, and then what happened?"

"It went dark. But I knew he'd struck again." He stopped, and stressed his next words. "And then I saw him."

"Who?"

"Ric Valente."

The monotonous sound of rainfall accentuated the silence.

"How did you recognize him, if it was dark?"

"I saw him," Blanes repeated. "It was like he glowed. He was standing in front of me in the screening room, covered in blood. He ran out the door before Carter and Professor Lopera got back."

"Did you see him, too?" Harrison said in Víctor's general direction.

"No ..." Víctor was groggy. "But I don't think I could have really focused on anything at the time ..."

"What about you, Professor?" he asked, not looking at Elisa. "You were still in the control room, weren't you? You'd fainted. Did you see Valente?"

She didn't even look up.

Harrison was afraid. Not because he thought she might do something to him, but because of all the things he wanted to do to her. All the things he *would* do to her, in good time. Contemplating the body he would play so many unknown games with alarmed him. After a pause, he took a breath and expelled it in the form of words.

"You don't know. No reply ... Fine. Be that as it may, my men will find him. He can't get off the island, no matter where he is." He turned back to his new best friend, Blanes. "Do you think Valente is Zig Zag?"

"I'm sure of it."

"So where has he been all these years?"

"I don't know. I'd have to look into that."

"I'd like to know, Professor. Know how he did it, he or his 'double' or 'splinter' or whatever you call it ... how he managed to kill off so many of you. I want to know his secret. Got it? When I was a kid, one of my teachers used to answer my questions by saying, 'Don't look for the cause; the effect is good enough,' But now the 'effect' is in the next room and it's a little hard to figure out." Though he was smiling, Harrison winced like he was in pain. "It's an 'effect' that gives you goose bumps. You wonder what Mr. Valente must have been thinking, to be able to do all that to another human being ... I need some sort of report. After all, this project is as much ours as it is yours."

"And I'll need some time and some peace and quiet to be able to look into all this," Blanes replied.

"You'll get it."

Elisa stared at Blanes, dumbfounded. She opened her mouth for almost the first time since the seemingly endless interrogation had begun.

"Are you insane? *¿Estás loco?*" she asked in Spanish. "You're going to *help* them?"

Harrison butted in before he could respond.

"*¿Estás loco?*" he imitated with a mediocre accent and fake humorous tone. "We're all 'loco,' Professor. All of us."

He leaned over her. Now he could look at her, and he fully intended to enjoy it: she was so beautiful, so sexy—despite smelling like sweat and filth and being totally disheveled—it gave him the chills. He improvised a little speech to take full advantage of the seconds he stared at her, putting on a stern fatherly voice as if speaking to his favorite, spoiled daughter.

"But *some* people's insanity revolves around making sure others can rest easy at night. We live in a dangerous world, a world where terrorists strike without showing their faces: surprise attacks, like Zig Zag. We can't let ... what happened tonight be used by the wrong people—"

"You're not the *right* people," Elisa spat harshly, holding his gaze.

Harrison froze midsentence, his mouth hanging open. Then, almost sweetly, he added, "That may be, but there are some a lot worse than me."

"Possibly, but they're under your command."

"Elisa ...," Blanes cut in.

"Oh, don't worry." Harrison was acting like an adult intent on proving a child's words would never hurt him. "The professor and I have had a ... special ... relationship for years now ... We're well acquainted." He moved away and closed his eyes. For a second, the sound of the rain on the window made him think of spilled blood. He spread his arms. "I imagine you're all tired and hungry. You can have something to eat now and then rest, if you like. My men will comb the island inch by inch. We'll find Valente, if he's here ... if he's findable." He snickered. Then he looked at Blanes like a salesman eyeing up a very select customer. "If you give us a report on everything that's happened, Professor, we'll overlook all your other mistakes. I know why you came back here, and why you ran away. I understand ... Eagle Group won't press charges. In fact, you won't even be arrested. Try to relax, take a little walk ... if you feel like it, in this weather. Tomorrow, a scientific delegation will arrive, and once you give them your findings we'll all be able to go home."

"What about Carter?" Blanes asked before Harrison left.

"I'm afraid things won't go quite so smoothly for him." The Eagle Group badge on Harrison's rain-soaked, brushed-cotton jacket glistened. "But his final destiny is out of my hands. Mr. Carter will be charged, among other things, with having been paid for services not rendered."

"He was just trying to protect himself ... and us."

"I'll try to balance the scales when he goes to trial, Professor, but that's all I can promise you."

Harrison gave a quick nod and the two soldiers followed him out. When the door closed, Elisa brushed the hair from her face and glared at Blanes.

"You're going to give them a *report?*" she exploded. "Don't you see what they're *doing?* They're going to turn Zig Zag into the weapon of the century! Soldiers killing enemies from another time and all that!" She got up and banged her fists on the table. "Is that all Jacqueline's death is good for? A fucking *report?*"

"Calm down, Elisa." Blanes seemed genuinely taken aback by her rage.

"That son of a bitch is tickled pink thinking about the damn report he's going to hand over to the scientific delegation tomorrow! Disgusting pervert! Sicko. And that sick fucker is who you're going to *help?*" She fell back into her chair, crying, and buried her face in her hands.

"I think you're exaggerating, Elisa." He got up and went into the kitchen. "They want answers, of course, but they do have a right, you know."

Elisa's crying tapered off. Suddenly she was too tired, even for that.

"You're acting like Eagle is a group of paid assassins," Blanes called from the kitchen. "Don't blow everything all out of proportion." He paused and then added, in a different tone, "Harrison's right. The sockets are burned and the power cords are totally stripped; it's unbelievable. Anyone want cookies or mineral water?" He walked back in with a plastic bottle and a paper napkin and stood at the window as he munched.

"I have *no* intention of collaborating with those scumbags, David," Elisa said curtly. "You do whatever you want, but I'm not going to say a word." She snatched a cookie and scarfed it down in two bites. God, she was starving. Then she took another one, and another. She swallowed big chunks, almost without chewing.

Then she looked down and saw the napkin Blanes had just placed on the table. He'd scribbled on it, in all caps: MIGHT BE BUGGED. EXIT 1 X 1. MEET IN OLD GARRISON.

IT was still raining, though less intensely. But she felt so sticky and disgusting, all covered in sweat and grime, that she appreciated the clean shower. Taking off her shoes and socks, Elisa wandered down the sand like someone who'd just decided to go for a lonely stroll. She glanced around and saw no sign of Harrison or his men. Then she froze.

A few feet away, the chair sat on the sand.

She recognized it immediately. Black leather seat, metal legs on wheels. On the right side of the chair back, a long, oval slash ran almost halfway across the backrest. Two of the four legs were missing and one of the armrests was encrusted with metal shavings, shimmering like jewels. That chair would have collapsed, if it were just an ordinary chair.

But it was no ordinary chair. The rain had not soaked it, didn't even splash it. No drops of water ricocheted off its surface, though they didn't seem to float through it like a hologram, either. The raindrops were like silver needles shooting down from the heavens: they plunged into the seat and disappeared, only to reappear beneath it and sink into the sand.

Elisa stared, fascinated. She'd seen this chair for the first time when Harrison had been grilling them; it was wound around his legs like a silent cat. He'd walked right through it, the way the rain passed through it now. She'd noticed that one of the soldiers was fidgeting with his computer watch during its entire appearance; no doubt it had stopped keeping time.

She counted to five, and then it disappeared. Elisa wished she had the time (and desire) to study splits. They were one of the most incredible findings in the history of science. She could almost sympathize with Marini, Craig, and Ric, though it was too late to forgive them.

When the chair disappeared, she turned and went through the barbed-wire fence.

She shivered, thinking that Zig Zag wasn't much different from that chair: a sporadic apparition, the result of the algebraic sum of two different times. But Zig Zag had willpower. And his *will* was to torture and kill them. There were three victims left (four, if you counted Ric), and then his will would be done, unless they stopped him first. They had to do something. Fast.

All that was left of the old garrison and warehouse were a couple of charred, blackened walls piled with rubble. Some seemed to have collapsed recently, no doubt in the monsoon winds. Most of the old metal and debris had been blown to the north end, leaving an empty space in the middle packed with hard ground—maybe due to the heat of the explosion—though shrubs had already sprung up in several spots.

She decided to wait by the walls. She left her shoes on the ground, untied the knot in her T-shirt, and ran her fingers through her hair. More than clean it, the rain had clumped it together. She tilted her head back to let the rainwater wash down her face. The downpour was dying off and the sun had started to burn through the sky's thinnest clouds.

Blanes showed up a second later. They spoke very little, as if they'd just bumped into each other coincidentally. Five minutes went by, and then Víctor appeared. Elisa felt awful when she saw the state he was in: pale, slovenly, unshaven, his curly hair all clumped and matted. Still, he gave her a feeble smile.

Blanes looked around. She did the same. To the north, beyond the station, were palm trees, a gray sea, and a vast expanse of sand; to the south, four military helicopters on the landing pad, at the edge of the jungle. There didn't seem to be anyone around, though she could hear the sounds of birds and human voices in the distance. Soldiers.

"We're safe here," Blanes said.

They exchanged glances, and suddenly Elisa couldn't take it

anymore. She threw herself into his arms and held his stout body, grateful to feel his hands on her back.

They both cried, though very differently from how they'd wept up until then, with no noise, no tears. When she thought of her dead friend, Elisa clung to one obsessive thought. *Jacqueline, poor thing, it was quick, wasn't it? Yes, it must have been, there wasn't enough energy to* ... But she realized that who they were really feeling sorry for was themselves: they were lost, broken by the anguish of inevitable condemnation.

She saw Víctor draw near, visibly shaken, and drew him into her embrace, resting her chin on his bony, rain-soaked shoulder.

"I'm so sorry," he whimpered. "Please forgive me ... I'm the one who ..."

"No, Víctor," Blanes touched his cheek. "You didn't do anything wrong. The laptop had nothing to do with it. He used *potential* energy, and he took it from everything. This is the first time he's done that. There was no way to defend ourselves against that."

When Elisa could tell that Víctor had started to relax, she pulled away and kissed him on the forehead. She wanted to kiss, to hug, to love. She wanted to be loved, and consoled, and comforted. But for now, she'd have to postpone those desires and concentrate on the task at hand. After Jacqueline, she'd sworn she would get rid of Zig Zag, even if it cost her her life. Eliminate him. Disconnect him. Kill him. Annihilate him. Snuff him out. Fuck him up. She wasn't sure what expression to use: maybe all of them.

"What happened in the control room, Elisa?" Blanes asked, anxious.

She recounted everything she hadn't wanted to say in front of Harrison, including the disconnect she'd had when she saw Jacqueline disintegrate.

"I left the image profiling," she added. "If they haven't touched anything, it should be done by now."

"Any splits?"

"The computer chair. I saw it twice. But Ric and Rosalyn didn't appear."

"That's odd ..."

Blanes tugged on his beard. Then he started speaking in a tone very different from the one he'd put on for his interrogation. Now he sounded choked and spoke quickly, almost panting.

"OK, I'll tell you what I think. First, Elisa's right, of course. Once we hand over that report, we'll be no good to them anymore. In fact, now that we know where Zig Zag came from, we're actually dangerous witnesses. No doubt they'll want to bump us off, but even if they don't, I'm not going to hand Zig Zag over on a plat-ter so they can turn him into a twenty-first-century Hiroshima. I think we're all agreed on that." Elisa and Víctor nodded. "But we have to play it safe. We can't lay all our cards on the table; we need at least one ace up our sleeve. And that's why we have to really know what happened and find out who Zig Zag is."

"But we *already* know; it's Ric," Víctor began, but Blanes waved him away.

"I lied. I wanted to throw them off the track, get them to orga-nize a big search to distract them. I didn't really see Valente or anyone else in the screening room."

Elisa had already suspected as much, though she still couldn't help but feel disappointed.

"So we don't know any more than we did before," she said.

"I think I know something more," he replied. "I think I know why Zig Zag is murdering us."

"What?"

"We had it all wrong."

BLANES'S eyes were shining. She knew that look: the scientist who, for a split second, finds himself on the brink of truth.

"It came to me after I saw Jacqueline's remains. When the sol-diers took me into the dining room and I was able to calm down enough to reason, I thought about what I'd seen in that room ... what Zig Zag had done to Jacqueline. Why such cruelty? He doesn't just kill us; there's a level of mercilessness that goes beyond all limits, it's totally incomprehensible. Why? Until now we'd talked about a disturbed person, thought Zig Zag was some kind of psychopath hidden among us ... a 'devil,' as Jacqueline said. But I wondered if there could be some scientific explanation for that totally unwarranted savagery, that superhuman brutality. I considered every angle, and this is what I came up with. It might sound strange, but I think it's the most likely explanation."

He knelt down and used the sand like a chalkboard. Elisa and Víctor crouched down beside him.

"Just suppose that, when the split was first produced, the person in question was in a state of rage. Imagine he or she was hitting someone. Or not even that: just some sort of intense, aggressive emotion, maybe directed against a woman. If that were the case, then when the split first appeared the emotion couldn't be changed, couldn't even be *tempered.* There wouldn't be enough time. In a Planck time, not one single neuron could send any information to another. Everything would stay the same, totally unmodified. If the person were experiencing violent urges, or the desire to abuse or humiliate, then that's exactly how the split remains, frozen in that desire."

"Still," Víctor objected, "the person would have to be pretty disturbed ..."

"Not necessarily, Víctor. That's where we went wrong. Ask yourself this: what is our idea of goodness based on? What makes us say that a person is 'good'? Anyone might think terrible thoughts for a moment, even if they repent a second later. But repenting takes *time,* even if it's only a millisecond. Zig Zag never got that chance. He lives in *one single* time string, a minute fraction of time, isolated from the course of events. If the split had been produced a second later, maybe Zig Zag would have been an angel instead of a demon."

"Zig Zag is a monster, David," Víctor murmured.

"Yes, he is. The worst kind: a run-of-the-mill human being frozen in time at a random moment."

"That's absurd!" Víctor laughed, agitated. "I'm sorry, but you're wrong. Totally wrong about that!"

"I find it pretty hard to believe, too." Blanes's idea upset Elisa. "I understand what you're saying, but I just can't believe it. All that torture, the pain he inflicts on his victims ... the obscene 'contamination' of his presence ... those ... sickening nightmares ..."

Blanes stared fixedly at Elisa.

"Everyone has those desires for brief, isolated intervals of time, Elisa."

She stopped to think. She couldn't conceive of Zig Zag that way. Her whole body rebelled at the idea of her torturer, her merciless executioner—that *thing* she'd dreamed about for years and was scared to even contemplate—could be anything other than Absolute Evil. But she couldn't find fault with Blanes's reasoning.

"No, no, no ..." Víctor refused to accept it. The light rain, falling more gently now, studded his glasses with tiny dots. "If what you're saying is true, then what becomes of ethics, what about good and evil, all of that? You're saying it's all just our conscience in some state of *evolution?* You're saying that our morals are random, that they bear no relation to personal decision, to strength of character?" Víctor's voice grew louder and louder. Elisa tensed up, afraid the soldiers would hear them, but there didn't seem to be anyone around. "This is absurd! So in your judgment, any man, the most moral of men ever ... even ... even *Jesus Christ,* could be a monster for an isolated period of time?! Do you even *realize* the implications of what you're saying? So anyone could have done ... what I saw in the screening room! Anyone. What I saw ... what you and I both saw that he did to that poor woman ..." His lips had curled into an expression of horror and disgust. He took off his glasses and ran his hands across his face. "I know you're a genius," he said, more calmly now, "but you're a *physicist.* Good and evil have nothing to do with *time,* David. They are stamped onto our hearts and souls. We all have urges, desires, temptations. Some people control them and others lapse: that is the key to religious belief–"

Blanes cut him off. "Víctor, what I'm trying to say is, it could be *anyone.* It could be *me.* I didn't think that before. Deep down, I always thought I could count myself out because I know what I'm like inside, or at least I think I do. But now I think that no one can count themselves out. We have to include all of humanity in this draw."

"Still," Elisa interrupted, "we have to find out who it is. If it wasn't Jacqueline, then he's got twenty-four hours to strike again."

"True. Stopping Zig Zag is our top priority," Blanes agreed. "We need that profiled image."

"We could go now," she suggested.

"I'm not sure this is the best time ..."

"Yes, now," Víctor insisted. "While they were taking me to the barracks, I saw that there were only two soldiers in Silberg's lab and they were both asleep, and then one more on guard duty outside the room where they're holding Carter." He turned to Elisa. "If you go in through the first barracks, you could get to the control room without being seen."

"I'll try," Elisa said. "The image must be clean by now."

"I'll go with you," Víctor offered.

They looked at Blanes, who nodded.

"OK, I'll keep watch from the kitchen in case Harrison and his men come back. We have to act fast. As soon as we know who Zig Zag is, we'll destroy everything so Eagle never finds out what happened."

She knew what he meant. *We'll destroy everything, including whichever one of us is Zig Zag.*

They said good-bye right there, and Blanes gave her an impulsive hug. Then he pulled back to look at her as he spoke.

"Zig Zag is just a simple error, Elisa. I'm sure of it. An erroneous equation, not some malignant being." Suddenly, she smiled.

His voice reminded her of the professor she'd so admired. *Now go and correct that damn error once and for all.*

STOPPING *Zig Zag is our top priority.* Harrison couldn't agree more with Blanes about that. But he was wrong when he said Zig Zag wasn't some malignant being.

Of course he was. Harrison just knew. The most evil being ever to set foot on the earth. The Devil himself. The only real, true Devil.

He struggled to get up—the years were starting to take their toll—slipped the earpiece back into his jacket, and told Jurgens to collapse the antenna on the directional mike they'd been using to listen in on the conversation from over by the palm trees, three hundred feet away. His idea—sending the soldiers out to comb the island and sticking close by with the mike himself—had paid off.

"We're at a disadvantage in the sense that they're the ones who have all the information," he said, gazing at the lovely shape off in the distance that was Elisa. Her clothes were so scant that, from where he stood, she almost looked naked. "But that also works to our advantage. They're all geniuses, and that means they're ignorant. I knew Blanes was lying so he could meet up with the others alone. But his little lie is quite useful to us. Better to have the army looking the other way, I think. We don't want any witnesses, now, do we? After all, we have no orders to terminate them yet. But we're going to do it anyway. That will be our little secret, Jurgens. We're going to expurgate, to purify ... All right?"

Jurgens seemed to agree. Harrison turned to look at him. When they landed on New Nelson, he'd ordered him to hide on the beach and await the right moment, the moment when he could use his extraordinary abilities.

And that moment had arrived.

"You're going to go into the barracks. Take the long way around so Blanes doesn't see you, and kill Carter and Blanes. Then we'll wait for the others to get what they're looking for, and when they do, kill Lopera while Robledo looks on. Make sure she's watching; I want her to see it. Then lock her into one of the rooms and we'll interrogate her. We need that report. We have all day to make her talk, until the delegation arrives. This could get very interesting. First thing tomorrow, there won't be a single scientist left."

As Jurgens headed off, leisurely, to carry out his orders, Harrison sighed deeply and stared out to sea, watching the clouds break up and the sun make a feeble attempt at shining. For the first time in a while, he felt happy.

With Jurgens by his side, he had no fears. Not even Zig Zag scared him.

NINE

Zig Zag

My God, what have we done?

ROBERT A. LEWIS,
COPILOT OF THE *ENOLA GAY*,
AFTER DROPPING THE ATOMIC BOMB
ON HIROSHIMA

33

ONE hundred and sixty seconds.

He was lying down, his face up. Every once in a while he opened his eyes to see more light filtering in through the filthy window; the rain was finally letting up. He estimated that it was about ten in the morning, though he couldn't be sure since his computer watch had no battery. He'd taken it out the night before, trusting the damn scientist who'd assured him that they'd avoid an attack that way.

Idiot.

They'd locked him into a room in the third barracks, under the watchful eye of one soldier. He could just see the edge of his helmet through the peephole in the door. He felt as good as possible, given the circumstances: he'd been "greeted" on arrest (his nose and mouth were still bleeding). He was detained in the screening room by two young soldiers even more surprised than he was; all the scientists had done was scream their heads off. He'd surrendered immediately, of course.

And now Paul Carter wondered about his future.

He wasn't feeling overly hopeful: he knew Harrison would kill him sooner or later. At least he had that to be grateful for. Otherwise, Zig Zag would do it. The question wasn't *if,* but how and when.

He thought he should devise a plan, because although he thought he could withstand whatever it was Harrison had in line for him, he wasn't so sure he could say the same about Zig Zag.

Over the course of his life, Carter thought he'd seen just about everything one human being could do to another, and he knew people did more evil things than most people could even imagine. But Zig Zag surpassed all limits, all experience, everything.

He hadn't lied to Harrison. It was true that he really knew almost nothing about Zig Zag. No matter how much he'd heard Blanes talk about splits and energy levels, it was all Greek to him; only the scientists understood what they, after all, had created. He was even telling the truth when he said that he'd betrayed Eagle out of fear: anyone who thought guys like him never felt fear—even terror—was just wrong.

And since he'd walked into the screening room no more than *five minutes* after he'd left it (in search of that idiot priest) and seen what had happened in that short space of time, his fear had become uncontrollable panic.

Call it what you like: panic, the Impact, or scared-fucking-shitless.

He'd seen it all in the dim glow of the matches that the stupid priest had pinched: the chairs and screen destroyed; blood all over the walls and floor as if there'd been an explosion; the woman's face—or half of her head, or whatever it was—lying there on the floor at his feet; chunks of her body all over the place. He knew that wasn't the work of a lunatic, a crime that had taken place in five minutes. It was the methodical, deliberate work of a creature with no ability to reason. He was tempted to believe in the forces of evil and demons.

And as if that weren't enough, the scientists were sure—they'd "proved" it with their convoluted theories—that the damn thing might even have come from *him.* That made him fear not only for his own life, but for Kamaria and Saida, his wife and daughter, too. Who knew what might happen to them if he survived?

No, the only solution would be to die–soon. Or try to get away. Escape Zig Zag and Harrison, if it was possible to escape both of them, if–and this thought made his blood run cold–they were in fact two different threats.

Because the fact of the matter was, he was increasingly convinced that Harrison had lost his mind.

And Zig Zag was the one who'd made him lose it.

104 *seconds.*

He felt uneasy, but he wasn't sure why.

It had stopped raining and the sun came out, painting the day, peeking through the clouds and casting its first rays, as always, on the sea. Light loved the sea. Blanes loved both of them. That phenomenal spectacle, the world of waves and particles that was both sound and color, beings and objects, was suddenly before him, teasing, "Look at me, David Blanes. Look how simple my secret is."

No, it wasn't simple, and he knew it. It was a complex, profound enigma, maybe even too intricate for the human brain to comprehend. That secret spanned everything, from the most grandiose to the tiniest details: Orion, black holes, and quasars, but also the intimacy of atoms, subatomic strings, and (why not?) the reason his little brother, his mentor Albert Grossmann, and his friends Silberg, Craig, Jacqueline, Sergio, and so many others had died. The answer took it all on: if the aim of physics were to discover everything there was to know about reality (and that's what *he* thought the aim was), then things like Zig Zag, his brother's death, and the dying breaths of Grossmann, Reinhard, and Jacqueline had to figure into the equation, too. It was all part of the Great Riddle that human beings from Democritus to Einstein had been desperate to solve.

The wise old man stands pondering at the window. That misleading image made him smile bitterly, recalling that in the solitude of his home in Zurich, he used to mull things over while gazing out a closed window. Marini had once told him that it was indicative of the fact that he lived inside his own brain. Maybe he was right, but now things were different. Now he was doing it solely to keep an eye on the entrance outside and make sure that Elisa and Víctor were unhindered in their attempt to decode the computer image.

For now, things seemed to be going well, but his uneasiness didn't diminish.

That sense of apprehension was unlike any he'd ever experienced. Maybe it was due to the possibility that Elisa would come back and tell him that he was Zig Zag. No, he'd already decided that if that were the case, he'd remove himself from the picture. He was sure it was due to something else, some detail he'd overlooked, some tiny variable he hadn't taken into consideration ...

Tiny, and yet vital.

He searched his memory, trying desperately to figure out what it was. Grossmann used to call their goals "pieces of cheese." Memory, he claimed, was like a laboratory rat stuck in a maze, and sometimes you could only find forgotten information by using faculties other than intelligence and knowledge. "Sniff it out, the way a rat finds the piece of cheese."

Sniff it out.

The kitchen was a small room, and the smell of burned wires was still thick in the air. When Zig Zag had attacked poor Jacqueline, he'd scorched all the plugs. He'd seen it himself while he was writing that message to Elisa and Víctor on the napkin.

He looked away from the window and stared at the power cords.

Yes, that was it.

Zig Zag had extracted energy not only from components that weren't being used, but *from things that didn't even use electricity.* He and Carter had disconnected every source of power around, but Zig Zag had sucked energy up the way a pump sucks the air from a bottle. That was the first time he'd done that, as far as Blanes knew. It was like using energy from a flashlight with no batteries.

His mind raced as frantically as an Olympic skier, down a slope of computations. If he'd learned to obtain energy from unplugged appliances, then ...

Four helicopters. Two generators. Rifles, pistols. Radios. Transmitters. Telephones. Computers. Military paraphernalia.

Good God.

He broke out in a cold sweat. If he were right, this was a death trap. The entire island was a trap. Zig Zag could obtain energy from almost anything, so what would stop him? He was making more and more frequent appearances, and the area he was able to exploit was growing larger and larger. It might be miles by now, and that would require even more energy. Where would he get it from?

Bodies. Living beings. Every single person is a battery. We produce energy. Zig Zag can use it whenever his area grows and he becomes weak. And that means...

It meant that the next attack could come anytime. It didn't matter if Zig Zag was Elisa, Carter, or him—the rest of them would all die, too. Suddenly, that mathematical possibility seemed incredibly real. If he were right, not only the four of them, but everyone on New Nelson, was in danger. He had to warn Elisa, but he'd also have to tell Harrison. He'd have to...

"Professor." A booming, unfamiliar voice.

He turned and saw death in the face of the man aiming a gun at him. It was a pistol with a silencer. *No, not now. I have to know, first ...*

"Listen!" he cried, raising his hands. "Listen, you have to ..."

Blanes was glad to be shot in the chest. It let him think for a split second longer. He forgot about pain, and fear; he closed his eyes and saw—in the utmost depths of blackness—his brother. He went to him, knowing that his lips would enlighten him by answering Life's Great Question.

100 *seconds.*

"That's decent enough resolution," Elisa said, loading the first image.

Víctor stood behind her, leaning over her shoulder, staring at the screen. They could each hear their breathing in tandem: a tense, panting duo. On the screen before them appeared a clear outline of Ric at the computer, disfigured by the Planck time.

"My God," Víctor murmured behind her.

The objects surrounding him were clearly defined, too. And that tiny detail—the thing she couldn't put her finger on earlier, the thing that had bothered her so much—now irked her more than ever.

Suddenly, she thought she knew what it was.

"The controls …" She pointed to the screen. "Look at that row of lights. On our console, they're not lit up. See?" She pointed to a series of little rectangles on the keyboard. "That was what I noticed before. Looks like Ric did something he hadn't done on other occasions: he used a satellite transmission."

"From New Nelson? Why?"

"No clue."

It was absurd. Why complicate matters by using a telemetric image to open time strings from the recent past when he had a dozen live video streams to choose from? There was only one possible explanation.

The image he wanted wasn't from New Nelson.

But, what else could it be?

For a second, she was paralyzed by fear. The possibilities were endless, if the image could come from any place and any time in the recent past. And that meant that whoever had given rise to Zig Zag could be anywhere on the planet.

On-screen, the image jumped to the next open time string: Ric and Rosalyn, standing on the left. What he'd been looking at was now clear and well defined. Elisa zoomed in and centered on Ric's screen. She held her breath while it focused in and the new image appeared on the screen.

The most earth-shattering one imaginable.

94 *seconds.*

He heard a noise and opened his eyes. The helmet of the soldier on duty had disappeared from the peephole. When he stood up, the door opened and the barrel of a smoking gun with silencer was aimed at his head. He saw the boots of the fallen soldier in the hallway and raised his hands, eyeing the man with the gun.

"Do you know who I am? Look at me, Carter."

The hollow, perverted voice worried him far more than the weapon trained on him. For almost the first time in his life, Paul Carter had no idea what to say.

"Don't you recognize me?" the voice asked. "It's Jurgens."

He swallowed. *Jurgens?* Frantically, he put two and two together and thought he knew what was going on. Comprehension did nothing to quell his fear, though at least he could react now. He tried to keep his cool and speak calmly. *Don't make him jumpy, whatever you do.*

"Listen, put that thing down and let me talk to you."

"I'm your grim reaper, Carter."

"Listen. 'Jurgens' is a code word …" Carter was trying not to rush, to make sure he pronounced everything carefully, enunciated every word clearly. "My God, don't you remember? 'Jurgens' is the code word we used at Eagle to say that a situation had to be resolved by any means necessary. It's not a *person*, Harrison, it's a *code word!*"

But the sickening expression on Harrison's face let him know that the man was not listening. *This isn't Harrison; this is something Zig Zag created.*

"Can't you see? Can't you see who I am?" Harrison grunted, using that unnatural voice. "Look at me, Carter! Look at me!"

And then he fired.

54 *seconds.*

Víctor was babbling behind her.

"It must be an image from the past. There are ... signs ... aren't there? The time strings have opened, right?"

It was a rustic, outdoor setting, but it was clearly not New Nelson. What appeared to be a small creek ran down the right side of the screen, and toward the top, on some boulders, under a tree (but not covered by it), were three small, white silhouettes, with a larger, dark one at the bottom. Despite the irregularities due to the Planck time, Elisa could tell that the large one was a stocky man, standing by the creek. He held something she couldn't quite make out in his hand (a hat? a cap?), and beside him on the grass was a long pole and some kind of basket that made her think it was fishing gear.

The other three figures were of a different size and build. She zoomed in on them and enlarged the image by 30 percent.

Judging by the long, black hair on one of them, it was probably a girl. She and one of the other figures both appeared in the same uniform sepia hues, which might have indicated that they were naked. The other figure was clothed, though it looked like it wore only a T-shirt and shorts. She couldn't be sure, though. Besides, it wasn't his clothing but his posture that intrigued her. The figure seemed to have fallen onto the rocks. His feet were higher than his head, as if the picture had been taken as he fell. And the position of the other figure's hands seemed to indicate that ... All of a sudden, Elisa understood.

"One of the boys pushed the other ... This must be some event from Ric's childhood."

Her mind was like a whirlwind. Suddenly, things were starting to add up, to fit in with the Ric Valente she knew. *Marini was wrong. He thought Ric had risked it all, used himself, but really he never dared. Ric was ambitious, but he was a coward, too. He was afraid to use videos of people who were asleep because of the splits, so he chose another path: one from his very own past that he probably thought of as innocent, trivial. But what was it? He had always kept a detailed diary, ever since childhood. He told me so himself. That's how he knew exactly where and when...*

"From Ric's childhood?" Víctor mouthed hoarsely, barely audible.

His change in tone made Elisa glance away from the screen for a second and look at him instead. Víctor had grown deathly pale and looked drained. His dirty glasses reflected the computer screen, so she couldn't see his eyes.

Suddenly, she recalled a conversation they'd once had. *Didn't Víctor once tell me, years ago, that ... the fight over that English girl he was in love with ... Ric pushed him and ...*

She looked back at the screen and noticed something else: the image of the boy who'd fallen on the rocks was less well defined. There seemed to be shadows around him.

Shadows.

Her mouth ran dry, and her temples were pounding. Her pupils dilated.

She turned slowly, but Víctor was no longer there: he'd backed up against the wall and stood there trembling. He wore the expression of a man who has suddenly learned that there's no such thing as life after death.

"Kill me, Elisa," he sobbed. "I'm begging you ... I ... I can't do it myself. Kill me. Please ..."

"No ..."

Víctor stopped begging and shouted, in a mixture of terror and determination, "Elisa! Do it before he *comes back* ..."

She just kept shaking her head, not saying a word, just shaking her head.

The door burst open.

At first, Elisa didn't recognize Harrison: he had blood on his hands and clothes, and his face was red, crazed, his eyes bulging out of their sockets.

"Look at him ..." He was aiming the gun at Víctor but speaking to her, frothing at the mouth. "I want you to watch him die, slut ..."

"No!" Elisa cried, while another voice inside her screamed, desperately, *Shoot him! Shoot him!*

Her cry was drowned out by the sudden buzzing of machines all around her. The floor shook as if an earthquake had struck. The computer began sparking and a burned, bitter stench filled the air.

After a few seconds frozen in shock, Harrison fired.

And everything came to a halt.

0.01 *seconds.*

It was like being deaf. And yet she screamed, and she heard herself. And she felt the chair against her buttocks, and touched the table and keyboard.

Víctor and Harrison were still frozen in the same position, one awaiting the bullet and the other aiming the gun, but their figures had changed: a vertical gash ran down the length of Víctor's cheek and his stomach was a red hole through which she could see his spinal column; Harrison had lost part of one arm and his facial features.

And between them, almost in the middle, lay a dead bug. Elisa stared at it in horror. *The bullet. My God. It didn't hit him in time.*

She jumped back and pushed the chair without managing to move it. When she pressed the computer keys, none of them moved, as if they were just symmetrical bumps carved into stone. She noticed something different about herself, too. She was completely naked.

Her face was drenched in sweat.

She knew where she was. And she knew who was there with her.

It was still the control room, but there were certain differences. It looked like it had been decorated by a surrealist. The wall to her right was full of strange, oblong holes, and she could see the beach through them. That's where the only light was coming from. Everything else was darkness.

She felt something else, too. She couldn't have said how, because she couldn't see him, but somehow she *felt* him.

Zig Zag. The hunter.

Her mind, overrun with panic, seemed to disintegrate. Rational thoughts floated to the surface and remained coherent and observant; the rest sunk into the depths of helplessness, into the memory of her fears and fantasies of the last several years.

She rushed to the wall as she stared through the gap in that odd mix of horror and marvel. *I can think, feel, move. It's me, but I'm not really here, I'm someplace else.* She remembered that a few days ago—or a thousand years ago, there was no telling—she'd spoken to her students at Alighieri about the possibility of different dimensions being interconnected *(I put a coin on the overheard).* And now here she was, stuck in the most inconceivable example imaginable.

She touched the wall. It was solid. No way out there. But one of the openings was wide and almost at floor level. She stuck her hand through it and felt nothing.

For a second she wavered. The idea of escaping through one of those openings, somehow, made her slightly nauseous, like the idea of walking through the earth.

Then she noticed the hole in the generator room. It was a huge, elliptical hole in the door. She realized that Rosalyn had managed to run through it trying to escape Zig Zag, and that's how she'd ended up touching the generator, receiving that shock after Zig Zag attacked her. If Rosalyn had gone through one of those openings, she could try it, too.

No matter what, she wasn't just going to sit there waiting for him to attack.

She heaved one leg over, then the other, trying not to rest her weight on the opening's edge, though it was totally smooth. And then she was outside.

Elisa couldn't hear the sea, or the wind, or even her own footsteps. She couldn't feel the warmth of the sun on her skin, though she was nude. *Eve in paradise.* It was like walking though a film set: virtual nature. But the sunlight hit her retinas as always. It must have something to do with the theory of relativity, which stated that the speed of light was one of the absolute constants of the physical universe. Even in a time string, light still traveled, unchanging.

There was a huge hole in her path, a ditch with polyhedral walls, the ground packed into it in neat layers. She looked down, skirting it.

And then she stopped.

In that enormous chasm, thirty feet away, lay a motionless figure.

She recognized him immediately. Forgetting everything, including her own panic, Elisa crouched down at the crater's rim. She could see his head, his pointy face smashed into the earth, fossilized, porous, like a tree root. A milky-white tube imprisoned in the dark earth. *He's been on the island this whole time. He fell through a hole in the matter, trying to escape Zig Zag that night.* But he was dead, or he certainly looked to be. She hoped, for his own sake, that he was.

He wasn't Zig Zag.

Ric Valente stared up at her from the abyss, his eye sockets empty.

In a flash, a vile sense of dread made her turn her head.

Zig Zag was behind her.

Just seeing him staggered her. All those years of terror, nightmares, that nest of vipers that had continued to grow in her subconscious ... it all split wide open inside her, the contents spilling over, almost drowning her.

There was only one thing that kept her from losing her mind at that instant: the lacerating pain in her left thigh. She writhed on the ground, shrieking like a little girl, and saw five symmetrical, parallel gashes on her midthigh. They weren't bleeding at all. Her blood hadn't had time to flow, but the cuts were deep.

Zig Zag hadn't even needed to touch her. She realized immediately that he was in total control of the situation. Nothing hindered him. He could destroy her at will. And the torment she felt now made her wonder what it would be like, to die at the hands of that creature.

Elisa stood, stumbled, and fell, reaching her hands out for support, and then stood again. She ran without looking back, limping. She intuited that this was what he wanted. *He wants me to keep running.* Even the idea that maybe Zig Zag *didn't* want to catch her was horrifying.

She rushed through the gate and kept on toward the beach, her feet leaving no prints in the sand, skillfully dodging holes in the matter beneath her. The thought of falling into one and getting caught (where? how far down would she plunge before the atoms could return and plug the hole again?) filled her with panic.

When she got to the beach, her jaw dropped.

It was like seeing God.

The sea had frozen. Its time had stopped just as a wave came crashing to shore. Now it formed a green brick trench crowned with snowy peaks and filled with endless caverns. Another wave had been frozen as the tide pulled it back out the sea.

Where to now? She stopped and steeled herself up to turn around.

No sign of Zig Zag.

Still, she kept going. She stepped tentatively onto the wave and found no discernible difference between it and the sand. She climbed, avoiding a hole in the matter, and reached the curved crest where it swelled. Touching the foam that came up to her chest, she had to snatch her hand back quickly; it hurt. She felt pricks on her palm and a sharp pain on the soles of her feet. The atoms, clustered and crammed into spaces smaller than they were in solid matter, must be what made the water feel like broken glass. In Zig Zag's universe, the sea could cut her and bleed her to death.

The wave wasn't that high, but trying to scale it would be like rolling naked in a patch of brambles. Besides, where would that take her? The horizon was a mass of enormous gorges and deep pits. One looked as big as the island itself, and there were black bodies suspended in midair above it (what *were* they? dolphins? sharks?) that must have been desiccated as they swam. The bumpy surface of the ocean extended all around, full of frozen swells and crests that would slice through her like razors.

Panting, she backed down onto the shore and found that the sand was not safe, either. It didn't shape and mold to her feet but stayed totally stiff, like a sheet of corrugated metal. The narrow dunes felt like blades. Up in the sky, the clouds sat like motionless smoke rings and scattered clusters, and the emerald edge of the jungle looked like origami gone wrong. She realized what was happening. *The time string has extended its area. But that takes a lot more energy, so it should incapacitate Zig Zag.*

Elisa didn't know where to go, or if she should even bother trying. She fell to her knees on the hard, metal sand, whimpering in pain from her thigh. She waited. Was she waiting for *him?* Or was there a way to get free, or at least to ensure that her demise was as short as possible?

She realized what the only possibility was, but the idea of hoping for it sickened her.

Curled up on the sand, she tried frantically to think. *The area has become so big that he'll need more energy to keep going. He could draw it from human beings.* She felt a glimmer of hope. *When he's used up all the energy, he'll have to stop, even if it's only for an instant, and then the bullet ...*

She couldn't bring herself to hope for that, not saving her own life at the expense of . . .

And yet, even as she thought it, she *was* hoping for it.

Then she looked up and saw it was too late. It was her turn now.

Zig Zag was ambling lightly. He didn't seem to be walking but floating, propelled by some imperceptible wind. Elisa stared at him with the fascination that anything that causes death brings.

She wondered if he were aware, if he felt anything, had emotions, or was capable of rationality. And realized suddenly that he was not. She didn't even think he got pleasure by satisfying his desire to destroy; maybe it wasn't even *desire,* per se, that urged him on, maybe it was nothing like desire. Gazing at him, Elisa was sure that Zig Zag was beyond the distinction between living being and inanimate object. He wasn't an object, but he certainly was no living creature, either. Even in motion, he seemed like an illusion. She decided that he wasn't even closing in on her, wasn't even moving. That was what it *looked* like, but Zig Zag was really already there with her, in front of her, the two of them immobilized in that time string. And as far as volition went, he possessed it only to the degree that a magnet placed by an iron does. That wasn't really volition; it wasn't free will or determination; that was a physical phenomenon.

And everything else was just fury.

Pure fury, no before and no after, no development or evolution, something more intense than any human being had ever experienced. There was no will or awareness behind it; that was just what Zig Zag *was.* His appearance and his essence were one and the same.

Elisa had never seen anything like it, never *imagined* anything like it, except in her nightmares, where evil and fear took shape and came to life. *Mr. White Eyes.* No wonder Jacqueline had called him the Devil. She was incapable of defining, comprehending, or tolerating the almost symbolic air of perversion, the hatred and insanity that emanated from every inch of him, the inhuman cruelty that oozed from his whole being. *David was right: he's trapped in a pure sentiment. It destroys, and that's all it does. That's all it can do.*

As for his sickening physical appearance, Elisa knew that it was just a result of the same phenomenon that had created those chasms in the sea and the "leprosy" on the Jerusalem Woman's face. Displaced matter made him look mutilated, tore off his facial features, turned his pupils into gaping white sockets, amputated a forearm and part of his torso as if he'd been chewed up and spit out by a predator. His position—arms and legs askew, slightly bent—was no doubt the one he'd landed in when Ric pushed him onto the rocks.

As she watched him—and despite feeling she'd lose her mind if she didn't *stop* watching him—she realized something else, too.

She thought of Víctor. How terribly he'd suffered when he came upon the girl he thought he was in love with (his childhood sweetheart) in his best friend's arms; all the awful things that must have crossed his little boy's mind in just fractions of a second, as his brain sank into unconsciousness. Rage, desire, vengeance, sadism, jealousy, impotence. The world crashing down around him for the first time. *Ric wanted to draw from some "innocent" event from the past, but this was what he'd come up with.*

She realized that stripped of all that horror, Zig Zag would be reduced to what he really was, what he had been and what he would have been, if time had not confined him to that one sickening, isolated instant. Now, looking at him up close, she could see his true nature beneath the substantial layers of paralyzed rage.

Zig Zag was an eleven-year-old boy.

.0005 *seconds*

Víctor ran down the riverbed that summer morning in Ollero. Ric and Kelly had disappeared, but he thought he knew where he'd find them: on that mound of rocks, in a place he and Ric called the Refuge. They'd talked about building a fort there.

Suddenly, he stopped.

Where was he running to? What had he just been doing? He vaguely recalled being with Elisa, looking at something. He also recalled Kelly Graham's black hair, and how much she and Elisa looked alike in his mind. And how he'd felt when he found Ric and Kelly, naked, under the pine tree, right where *he* and Ric had planned to build their fort. And what he felt when he saw her, kneeling before him, *touching* him (he knew what she was doing: he'd seen it in Ric's magazines), and when Ric said to him, *What's wrong? Don't want to play, Vicky? Don't want her to do it to you, Vicky?* Ric's look. And, worse, Kelly's. Kelly Graham's look, those catlike eyes.

All girls, every single one without fail, look like that.

Those same lips that had so often smiled at him now wrapped around Ric's member. That deserved every insult he could think of and more. Insults (he discovered then) were like a vice. You screamed and shouted yourself hoarse, you cried, you wanted to destroy the world, and that just egged you on, made you want to keep insulting even more. Oh, if the whole world were a girl's body, or Ric's crotch! If rage could last forever! You'd scream until the screaming drained those smiles and those glances, shout forever, until the end of your last day on earth, your mouth open wide, teeth bared . . .

But he wasn't in Ollero and he wasn't running anywhere. He was in a big, stuffy, hot room. Where was he? Hell? And why was he (*him* of all people) in that awful place? *It's not fair.*

He was blinded by rage. He wanted to explain to whoever had put him there how unfair it was. True, he'd overstepped the mark. For a fraction of a second, or maybe a little longer—but not long enough to change nature—he'd wished, he'd wanted with every fiber of his being, *to eat them alive, screw them, cut off their heads, and fuck their neck holes, as Ric used to say, especially her, her more than him, because she'd betrayed him, it was despicable, she was despicable, and so beautiful, so much like those waxed models in Ric's magazines, who wore black lingerie and knelt before men like little doggies.*

But, come on, that was over twenty years ago, and all it had led to was a big bump on the head, a few hours passed out in the hospital, a scar on his scalp, some worry for his parents, and a happy ending. Ric hadn't left his side the whole time he was there, and when he woke up, Ric had even *cried,* and begged for forgiveness. And as for Kelly, he'd forgotten all about her. It was just kid's stuff. How old were they? Eleven … twelve? *It's not fair …* Life is all wrong if things like that could become, with *the passage of time* (was that the expression?) such wells of evil. Where was the justice, if nature couldn't forgive? He'd forgiven Kelly, and every other girl in the world. He'd forgiven all women. So there was a little trauma. He'd learned to live with it years ago. He lived alone, and despite his feelings for Elisa, and how he yearned for her, he didn't dare let another woman into his heart. He and Ric had drifted apart. What else did he have to do to atone for his guilt? Did God really think each and every word and thought ever said or considered during a few seconds of rage was that important?

And in a flash, he realized what the answer was. Yes.

A pebble tossed into still water makes waves. Wasn't that the root of Original Sin, the first mistake, the Only Mistake? An error made a long time ago, a stain from the beginning that muddies the waters of paradise and drags innocent people down with it. He suspected that very few people had realized that. He was privileged. God was showing him how his mistakes had rippled and transformed the face of the earth.

Really, far from being in hell, he was in heaven. He'd have to go through purgatory first and get shot in the forehead, but that was going to happen very, very soon: he could see the bullet approaching. And only his death, Víctor realized, could stop it all. The key was to die before Blanes, Elisa, and Carter. *Die.*

Suddenly, he was overcome with joy. This was a dream come true, and it was his most cherished, intimate dream. Giving his life to save Elisa's.

That was it.

What other heaven could he hope for?

Ric pushed him and he smiled, fell onto the rocks, felt the blow—and then came peace.

0 *seconds.*

The light was blinding. She turned away from the sun, blinking. *I'm alive.*

She saw clouds like the smoke of distant fires, the crashing sea, the ground beneath her, her T-shirt covering her. The sharp pain in her thigh became more intense and she noticed a warm liquid seeping through the wound. She was bleeding. She'd die soon. But all of those feelings were proof enough for now that she was still alive. *I'm alive.*

Elisa welcomed the blood.

EPILOGUE

IT was neither foggy nor dark.

But in their minds, everything was different.

They were surrounded by utter devastation. The barracks were a tangle of metal, glass, wood, and plastic, including SUSAN, whose metal frame was so dented and mangled that it looked like an oversized child had tired of playing and smashed her on the ground repeatedly in a tantrum. Outside, it looked like a bomb had gone off; the helicopters were completely wrecked. And though nothing looked too burned, everything smelled like smoke, everything was broken and unusable, as though an enemy army had passed through and laid waste to everything in sight. Luckily, some of the soldiers' provisions were still OK. Mostly cans, and they had no can opener, but there was a way to puncture them and get the lids off. One serious problem was what to do about liquids: they found only two bottles of drinking water. But that afternoon the skies opened up and unleashed an almighty shower, allowing them to collect several buckets of rainwater. They washed, and then decided not to go off anywhere to sleep. Neither of them wanted to admit it, but they were afraid to split up.

When night fell, it was hard to do anything. They had no electricity, no functioning batteries, and at first they didn't want to start a fire. So they sat outside by the wall of the third barracks and tried fruitlessly to get some rest.

Once their most basic needs were met, she asked about the dead bodies. They'd found several, both in and outside the station. Harrison and the soldiers could only be identified by their clothes: they were just flat, fabric silhouettes laid out on the ground. But she wanted to know what they'd do with the rest of the bodies. Víctor, Blanes, the soldier from the hallway—and there were Jacqueline's remains to consider, too.

They both agreed they should bury everyone, but disagreed about *when* it should be done. He wanted to wait (they were absolutely exhausted, was his excuse, and someone would come for all of them the next day); she didn't. That was their first argument. Not a big one, but it sank them into silence.

Later he asked, "How's the wound?" He sounded contrite.

She looked at the bandage he'd cobbled together. Her thigh still hurt dreadfully, but she wasn't about to whine. She was sure she'd have scars that lasted the rest of her life, no matter how long—or short—"the rest of her life" was.

"Fine," she said, despite the agony, changing positions. "Yours?"

"Oh, just a scratch." He patted the bandage wrapped around his temples.

For a second, neither of them spoke. Instead, they stared off to sea and into the night. It had stopped raining and the air felt cool and clean.

"I still don't understand how ... how that *thing* didn't get us, too," Carter said softly.

She glanced over at him. Carter looked just like he had that morning, when he turned up with a rifle and the same look of fear on his face that she had on hers, or maybe more. But now she almost laughed, recalling his drawn, pale expression lit by a sun that had hardly moved, one eye closed, the other staring through the rifle's sight, as he hollered and asked her what the hell had just happened.

Good question.

She couldn't explain it to him then (she was bleeding, she felt weak); all she could do was say she thought it was all over.

Carter explained that Harrison missed when he shot him and hadn't even realized it. He'd just laid there motionless on the floor, and when Harrison left he tried to get up. "And then everything seemed to come crashing down. I smelled that burning, acrid smell and went into the control room and saw your friend. He'd been shot, and the old man was just a pile of ashes on the floor. Outside, I found more soldiers who looked vaporized, too. And that's when I went out to the beach and found you."

Elisa thought she could try to give him an explanation now.

"He *could* have killed us," she said. "In fact, he was going to. He extracted the energy he needed from all the machinery and attacked me. I was the next in line, or maybe it was David, but he was already dead, so he came for me. But he was forced to stop to suck more energy from living bodies. It didn't affect you, because you were his *next* victim after me in the time string. The strange thing is that it didn't affect Víctor, either. Maybe we were wrong when we said that the split could kill itself. Regardless, when the attack stopped for that split second, the bullet hit Víctor and he was killed."

"And that *thing* died with him," Carter nodded. "I get it."

Elisa looked up at the black sky and felt a weight pressing down on her. She knew she had no chance of getting rid of it, at least not all the way, but she could try.

"Listen," she said. "You're right. I'm exhausted. But I'm going to bury them now. You don't have to help me."

"I'm not planning to," Carter replied.

Still, he stood when she did. But she realized that she was in worse shape than she thought. Her wound was killing her. So she agreed to put off the funerals for a day and they both sank back down onto the sand.

They'd have to wait until the following day. And meanwhile, she'd pray she was wrong.

Because as the night wore on, she became increasingly convinced that there was no way for them to survive.

"**DO** you know what time it is?"

"No. My watch has no battery and the others all stopped at ten thirty-one. I told you that already. It's probably four in the morning. Can't you sleep?" Elisa made no reply. After a brief pause, he added, "When I was a kid, I learned to tell time by the sun. But you need a clear sky for that ..." He raised an arm toward the clouds, which glowed weakly. "Impossible like this ..."

She stole a glance at him out of the corner of her eye. Sitting on the sand, his back against the barracks wall in the dead of night, Carter almost looked like a ghost, though she knew there was nothing illusory about the way he'd polished off their provisions.

"What's wrong?" he asked suddenly.

"What do you mean?"

"Look, believe me, at times people are a lot easier to read than the sky. You're worried about something. And it's not your dead friends. What's up?"

She pondered her response.

"I was thinking about how we're going to get out of here. Nothing works, no radios, no transmitters ... We have almost no provisions. That's what I'm worried about. What's so funny?"

"We're not shipwrecked on some desert island." Carter shook his head and gave another deep, gravelly laugh. "I told you, Harrison was expecting the scientific delegation first thing tomorrow morning. Besides which, at the base they're probably wondering why he and his team haven't responded to any calls. Trust me: they'll be here for us by dawn. If not earlier."

Tomorrow. Earlier. Elisa stretched out the leg that didn't hurt. The gusts of wind coming in off the sea were starting to feel cold, but nothing in the world could make her go inside and spend the rest of the night in the barracks. If anything, she'd go find something to put on over her sweater or ask Carter to build a fire. But the cold wasn't what was bothering her.

"I know you don't trust me," Carter said, after a sullen silence. "I don't blame you. If it helps, I don't trust you, either. You think I'm a brute with no brains, but you geniuses, to me ... well, you're totally full of shit, if you don't mind my saying so. And considering all that has happened here, that's a pretty tame version. So I think it's better if we confess all our little secrets and get everything out in the open, don't you? Both of us. I know you suspect something."

She looked into Carter's eyes and saw his pupils flash in the dark night. She could hear breathing, but it was her own, as though Carter was holding his until she'd spoken.

"Be honest," he prodded. "You think ... you think that *thing* isn't dead ..."

"No. It's dead." Elisa looked away, up at the sky and the black sea. "Zig Zag was Víctor's split, and Víctor is dead. I have no doubt about that."

"Well, then?"

She took a deep breath and closed her eyes. *Come on. After all, you have to tell someone.*

"I just don't know for sure what might have ... happened," she whimpered.

"Happened ... to what?"

"To everything." She did her best not to cry.

"What are you talking about?"

"Zig Zag managed to extend the area of his time string an incredible distance: the island, the sea, the sky ... I don't know if that entanglement had any effect on the present ... None of our watches work, we're in total isolation here ... We have no way of knowing if anything *outside* has changed. Do you see what I'm getting at?"

"Wait a second ..." Carter shifted his weight, scooting closer to her. "Are you saying that we're living in some other world ... or a different time, or something?" Elisa said nothing. Her eyes were still closed. "Use your common sense, for God's sake. Look at me. Have I changed? I'm no older, no younger. Isn't that enough?"

For a second, their silence was like the darkness: it filled everything, every shape, every space, every corner; it was all over their faces.

"I'm a physicist," Elisa said, finally. "The laws of physics are all I know. And the universe abides by those laws, not common sense or intuition. My common sense and intuition tell me that I'm on New Nelson, in the year 2015, sitting here with you, and that only twelve or thirteen hours have gone by since Zig Zag's attack. But the problem is that ..." She paused and drew another breath. "If things have changed, then the laws of physics might have changed, too. And that means I might no longer understand them. And I need to, because they are the only truth."

After a long silence, she heard Carter's voice, sounding distant.

"So you think all this around us now is ... is *not real?* You think *I am not real,* that I'm going to just disappear? I'm some dream you're having?"

Elisa didn't respond. She didn't know what to say. Out of the blue, the ex-soldier got up and walked around the corner, behind the barracks. A few moments later he returned, silently, and threw something on the sand in front of her. She looked to see what it was: a windup watch.

"It stopped," Carter said. "This was your friend's watch, and I remember he told me it was mechanical ... But it stopped at ten-oh-one. Maybe he banged it when he fell ... Shit ..." He walked up to Elisa and spoke right into her ear, his voice a violent whisper. "How do you want me to prove it to you? How can I prove my reality to you, *Professor?* I can think of a few things that might work ... a few things that might not leave you with any doubts. What do you say? Huh?"

What she heard next petrified her.

Sobbing.

She froze, as Carter wept. Listening to him was awful. She knew he must have thought so, too. He surrendered to his tears like a drink he wanted to finish in one gulp. She watched him move off down the sand, a burly shape outlined in the moolinght.

"I hate you," he murmured between sobs. And then he began to scream. "I hate you! I hate all of you! Fucking *scientists!* I want to *live!* Leave me alone!"

As she watched him wander off down the beach, Elisa finally closed her eyes and fell into a deep sleep, as if she'd fainted.

THE noise that awoke her came from the fence. She saw Carter heading toward the beach, carrying something. Day had broken and it was cold, but she had a blanket over her. The ex-soldier, it seemed, was trying to be nice, and Elisa felt terrible recalling his tears the night before.

She pulled off the blanket and got up, but almost screamed when the pain in her thigh made it clear that it had woken, too, and was planning to stay with her as long as necessary. She had no idea how the wound was going to look today; probably worse. But Elisa didn't want to look. A sudden dizzy spell forced her to lean against the wall for support. She was starving, her hunger violent and uncontainable.

Urged on by this new clarity, she lurched toward the barracks. The sun was a dot on the horizon and the clouds had drifted south-ward, revealing a bright blue sky. But it still must have been very early.

In the barracks, she found some opened backpacks. Evidently, Carter had been hungry, too. She found cookies and chocolate, and devoured them frantically. Then she found a canteen with some water in it. After drinking her fill, she limped out to the beach.

The sea was calm and gentle, different shades of blue showing through in the sunlight. With the ocean as a giant backdrop, Carter was scurrying around like an ant. He'd built two fires and was on his third. They were all in a row on the shore. Elisa walked over and watched him work.

"I'm sorry about last night," he said, finally, not looking up at her, focusing on his task.

"Forget it." Elisa replied. "Thanks for the blanket. What are you doing?"

"Just taking precautions. I'm pretty sure they know where to find us, but there's no harm in giving them a little extra help, don't you think? Would you mind standing in front of me to block the wind? It's hard to get these matches lit ..."

"They should have been here by now," she said, scanning the horizon.

"That depends on a lot of factors. They'll be here; don't worry."

The branches took light. Carter watched them for a second, and then stood and joined her on the shore.

She stared out to sea, hypnotized by the ceaseless rhythm of the waves that came ashore and pulled out, leaving behind a layer of foam that sparkled like jewels, waiting to be covered by the next wave. She remembered what the sea had looked like when it was paralyzed—those sharp waves of glass and hard, wiry foam—and she shivered; it was horrible, and sickening. She wondered what Carter would have thought if he'd seen it.

"Still think this is all just a dream, Professor?" Carter asked. He'd unwrapped a candy bar and stuffed it into his mouth. "Well, you think what you like. I'm no scientist, but I know this is 2015, and that today is Monday, March 16, and that they'll be coming for us any time now. You and your privileged little brain can think whatever you want. But that's what I know."

Elisa kept staring out at the horizon. She recalled the words of one of her physics professors: "Science is the only thing that knows, the only thing to give a verdict. Without it, we'd still think that the sun rotated around us and the earth sat still."

"You want to bet?" Carter asked. "I know I'll win. You speak from the head, and I speak from the heart. Up until now, we've been doing things your way, and look where that got us." He nodded over toward the barracks. "So you've seen what wonders your marvelous brain is capable of. Don't you think it's time to trust your heart, Professor?"

Elisa made no reply.

Science is the only thing that knows.

Carter laughed quietly, but she didn't look over at him.

She was searching the sky, as still and empty as if frozen in time.

ACKNOWLEDGMENTS

MANY people helped guide me through the maddening maze of modern physics. Professor Beatriz Gato-Rivera, at the CSIC Institute of Mathematics and Fundamental Physics, answered questions about everything from university experiments and studies to the most complex issues in theoretical physics, and did so with both patience and kindness. I am tremendously grateful to her. Likewise, I owe Professor Jaime Julve, of the same institute, a debt of gratitude for the warm afternoon we spent together, chatting about all things divine and human. Many thanks to Professor Miguel Ángel Rodríguez in the Theoretical Physics Department of Madrid's Complutense University, for having found time for me in his busy schedule at the always hectic end of the term. Other professors at Spanish universities preferred to remain anonymous but were equally patient and enthusiastic, even reading through my manuscript and making important revisions; I thank each and every one of them wholeheartedly. Obviously, any errors or flights of fancy, as well as the unforgiving opinions of some characters about physics and physicists, are not in any way connected to my excellent informers, though in my defense I will also add that it was never my intention to write a scholarly work on string theory nor to express my own opinions; this is a work of fiction.

For readers who may be interested in finding out more about

the mysterious reality that contemporary physics has opened up for us, mentioning the books on my nightstand might be of use; almost all of them are available in Spanish, published by Crítica in its Drakontos collection. Brian Greene's *The Elegant Universe* is an excellent introduction to string theory. Stephen Hawking's *A Brief History of Time* and *The Universe in a Nutshell* are extraordinary, as are Paul Davies's *About Time* and Gerard 't Hooft's *Understanding Elementary Particles by Gauge Theories.* I must also add Emilio Chuvieco Salinero's *Teledetección ambiental* (not available in English) to this list for having helped me understand satellite image transmission. I also recommend Paul A. Tipler and Gene P. Mosca's *Physics for Scientists and Engineers,* which refreshed my memory about many things I'd forgotten since medical school (where we also studied a little physics), and *Quantum Questions,* edited by Ken Wilber, which is a fascinating collection of texts that are not exactly about physics (some are even mystic), but were written by physicists. And I wanted to save for last a really wonderful book called *The God Particle,* by Leon Lederman (with Dick Teresi). It not only taught me about experimental physics and those enigmatic monsters known as accelerators, but also tickled me pink (parts of the book are laugh-out-loud funny, like a great comic novel) and made me realize that anything, no matter how dry it might seem, can be fascinating if it's told—or written—in the right way. Congratulations, and thanks, to Professor Lederman.

I would also like to thank the amazing people at the Carmen Balcells Agency, without whom this book would never have been published, the editors at Random House Mondadori in Spain, and my loyal readers who are always, always, one the other side of the page. Finally, I couldn't do anything without the encouragement and enthusiasm that my wife and children show me every single day, or that insatiable reader of good novels who is my father.

J. C. S.
Madrid, August 2005